FROM DUST, A FLAME

ALSO BY REBECCA PODOS

FROM DUST, A FLAME

REBECCA PODOS

BALZER + BRAY

An Imprint of HarperCollinsPublishers

Balzer + Bray is an imprint of HarperCollins Publishers.

From Dust, a Flame
Copyright © 2022 by Rebecca Podos
www.epicreads.com

ISBN 978-0-06-269906-0

Typography by Sarah Nichole Kaufman
21 22 23 24 25   SB   10 9 8 7 6 5 4 3 2 1

First Edition

For Bubbe and Papa, may their memories be a blessing.

And for the folks at Throwing Sheyd,
teaching better living through demonology.

Your blood is what builds you and you can't know the depth of this.

—Kristian Macaron

Loew Family Tree

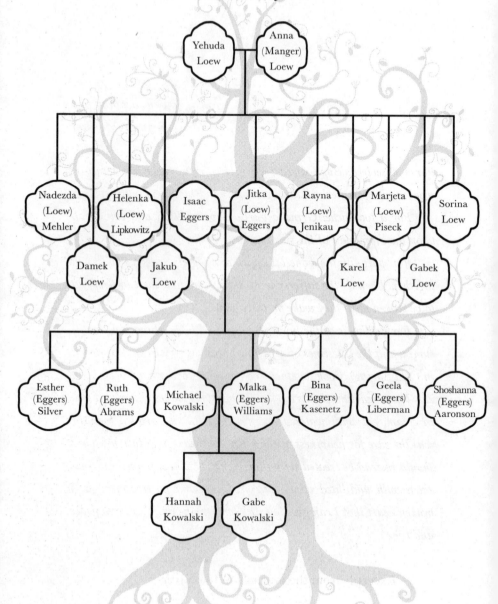

For a nosebleed: Burn sliced beets and saffron. Soak two scraps of wool in vinegar, then roll through the ashes. Place them in the nostrils.

For a toothache: Grind a garlic clove with oil and salt. Place upon the thumbnail of the side that causes pain.

For pain in the bones: Lentils and aged wine, eaten mixed together. Then let the sufferer wrap themselves in a sheet to sleep, not to be woken until they wake on their own.

For weakness of the lungs: Bring sliced beets, sliced leek, lentils, cumin, and the intestines of a firstborn animal (try Benny's Butchery in Cold Spring). Cook together and eat with good, strong beer.

For a heart that beats too fast: Bring three loaves of barley soaked in cream, eat with watered-down wine. (Ravina argued that this was the cure for heaviness of the heart, not heart palpitations, which should instead be treated with three loaves of wheat soaked in honey, eaten with undiluted wine. But me, I've found no treatment for a broken heart that I can give but my own open heart. That, and grace, and time.)

—Excerpts from the journals of Ida Silver

ONE

IF I HAD to pick a birthday to live inside of forever, I think it'd be the one in St. Helena.

We were staying in a rental cottage, the latest stop along a trail of borrowed houses that had been winding its way across the country for years. Before St. Helena, there was the timber-frame cabin in the frozen Minnesota woods. Before that, a historic house in Maine with its windows painted shut and sawdust that trickled down from the ceilings at strange hours. Of all the places we'd lived by the time I turned ten, my big brother, Gabe, and I loved the cottage best. It had wild beach roses in the front yard, bricks painted a pale blue Mom called duck's egg, and the whole Pacific beyond the back gate.

The morning of my tenth birthday, my mom and Gabe and I went down to the water just as sunrise scratched the dark sky pink. We didn't leave it until sunset. We ate french fries from the local snack shack for breakfast, lunch, and dinner. I remember how they tasted, salty as the ocean, crunchy with sand. I spent the whole day in nothing but a one-piece bathing suit—it wasn't until the next summer that I started wearing a T-shirt over my suit to cover what I wanted but didn't have, and what I had but didn't want. Over and over, I hurled my scrawny body into the waves, trusting Gabe to carry me back to shore if the water didn't. I could have spent eternity on that shore. There's nothing I would change about that birthday, except maybe the fact that I knew, even then, that I wouldn't have another like it. I hadn't spent two birthdays in the same town since I was a toddler.

In fact, today's is my very first.

I would *not* choose to live in the Gutter Ballroom—the one and only combination karaoke lounge, bowling alley, arcade, and sports bar in Jamaica Plain—for all eternity. Just for the record.

Mom, Gabe, and I wait for our appetizers at a high-top table while a man screams the Limp Bizkit version of "Faith" onstage. Someone in the lanes bowls a strike, and neon-pink lights strobe overhead in tribute.

"Isn't this place wild?" Mom asks, gazing around in wonder as though we're trapped inside of an art installation. "I can't believe we haven't eaten here yet."

I'd have been happy with fries at the harbor, but I nod. "It's cool."

Gabe grins at my half-hearted declaration. "So when do we take to the stage?"

"Excuse me?"

"Our karaoke duet. How about I take Tegan, and you take Sara?"

"How about you take both?"

"Don't threaten me with a good time. Just 'cause *you* refuse to have any fun in public—"

"Inaccurate and unfair," I shoot back. I don't think serving as store-brand Fred Durst's follow-up act or rolling my ball into a neighboring lane should count as fun. The public part . . . maybe that is fair. Last year, I made the grave mistake of wearing my ragged laundry-day bra to school when the washing machine on our apartment hall broke down. Melly Lawrence (who I beat out for vice president of the debate club, easily) caught a peek in the locker room and asked in a voice as sweet as candy corn if it was *vintage.* Who's to say Melly isn't here tonight, skulking behind the neon planter in the corner? The smallest mistake can haunt a girl forever.

I wouldn't bet against Gabe going solo—we're talking about the kid who came out by belting "I Am What I Am" from *La Cage aux Folles* in his eighth grade talent show—so I stop this train of thought before it crashes on the track. "It's time for presents, right? Presents for me?"

"Yes!" he cheers, easily distracted. He pulls the gift bag I've been eyeing from beneath the table and pushes it toward me. "Happy birthday eve, Banana!"

Technically, I won't turn seventeen until midnight (or 4:14 a.m., however you keep track), but my brother's high school graduation is tomorrow afternoon. When I think about the ceremony and what it means—that this fall, my fifteen-months-older brother is headed to college all the way across the country in Oakland, California—I don't feel much like celebrating.

Gabe is practically bouncing in his seat, though, so I dig through glittery tissue paper to find a half dozen paperbacks I specifically requested, *Her Body and Other Parties* topping the stack. "This is perfect," I tell him honestly, hugging the books to me.

"There'll be more later. That's just your, like, *corporeal* present."

"Is this assigned summer reading?" Mom peers over at the pile, tucking a stray slip of blond hair back into her low sloppy bun. Typically found in jeans, Birkenstock clogs, and a men's button-down, she's dressed tonight the way she clearly thinks one attires themselves for a karaoke bowling bar . . . which means jeans, Birkenstock clogs, and a men's Phoenix Suns jersey from two states back.

"It's not assigned . . . exactly." I then explain my master plan: how these are books my English teacher at Winthrop Academy, the super-competitive college-prep school that brought us to Boston nearly two years ago, referenced in class this year when she complained about the titles she hadn't been allowed to put on the syllabus. I'm going to read them all this summer, then bring them up in conversation with her when I see her this fall, cementing myself in her brain as a standout student. The kind worth writing a college recommendation letter for even though she's swamped with requests from girls she's known since seventh grade.

"Don't you already have a perfect grade in English?"

"Yeah, but only a 3.87 overall, because of Cul—"

"Oh, God." Mom grimaces as the strike lights flash through the bar area again. "We're not talking about Culinary Arts tonight, are we?"

What happened was this. My take-home final last week was to prepare an ambitious dish, the kind we didn't have time to execute in class. I spent most of the evening and night baking one cheese soufflé after another—this one too runny, this one dry, all of them collapsed like dying stars. Our small kitchen grew hotter and hotter, my cheeks flushed with effort and shame. In the end, I turned in a ramekin of inedible garbage, and this morning I spent a solid hour hyperventilating over what the final would do to my grade in the class before it came through the portal: B-minus. The first time I'd gotten anything below an A since middle school, and that had been in PE.

"I'm just trying to cheer you up," Mom says, reaching for the bar menu, though she rarely drinks when the three of us go out. "It's nothing to be upset about on your birthday."

I clear my throat and straighten my spine. "Actually, there's this course through Winthrop's summer program. Food and Nutrition? Less baking, more memorization. Stuff I'm good at. I talked to my college counselor, and if I take it, I can drop this semester's grade from my GPA altogether. And there's an AP French class on the same days that would earn me a college-level language credit if I nailed the exam. My counselor says it'll look good on applications if I complete it before I'm even a senior." Plus it will keep me distracted as my countdown to

Gabe's departure nears zero, but I'm not gonna admit that.

Mom peers at me disbelievingly over the top of the menu. "So you're planning to spend your whole vacation in school?"

"Not the whole summer. They don't start till July. And my counselor says—"

"Okay, okay." She holds a hand up in defeat. "No power on earth could stand against you and the college counselor. Do I just need to sign a form?"

Across the table, Gabe tenses, knowing what's coming.

I clap my hands between my knees to keep from fidgeting. "It costs a little money, is the thing. I guess summer courses aren't covered by my scholarship."

Waving to summon the waiter, Mom asks, "How much is a little?"

"Just four hundred. Per class. But if you think about it, it'll save money when I go to college, since that's one credit down. So it's basically an investment in my future—"

"Oh, Hannah . . . honey, I don't have a lot of freelance work right now, and I lost that extra diner shift when Amber came back from Ohio. We just don't have money to spend frivolously."

This stops me cold. "How is my future frivolous?"

"Of course it's not. But hundreds of dollars because of one meaningless grade, one failed soufflé in your whole lifetime? I promise you, it's not the end of the world. It won't even matter by tomorrow."

Mom and I never fight. Though we've both been snappish today—me since checking the portal, and her because who knows why—we're not locked in some epic, endless mother-daughter battle. We don't usually argue about my grades or my clothes. There are no slammed doors between us.

We're just not . . . close. Not the way she and Gabe are close. By complete coincidence, they look alike, his honey-blond hair enough of a match to Mom's wheat blond that no one ever guesses he was adopted at birth. Even his upturned amber eyes pair well with her gold-flecked hazel. They're both artists—Mom is a freelance graphic and website designer, alongside her rotating minimum-wage day jobs, and Gabe is your archetypal theater kid. They have the same habit of throwing themselves passionately into a project one moment, only to lose interest in it the next, trailing half-painted canvases and half-written one-acts and half-hearted romances across the country.

Meanwhile, I'm the blue-eyed, dark-haired, heavily freck-led sheep. I don't have their knack for making friends easily and immediately in every new place, bringing them home like burrs on a dog, shaking them off once we move on. That's never mattered to me, though, because I have Gabe. It's always been just the three of us—Dad died when I was a baby, leaving us with very nice and very distant grandparents in his native Canada, and if Mom's got any family, they might live at the top of Mount Everest or the bottom of the Mariana Trench, for all that we know. But really, it's been the two of us. My brother has always been there for me. Like when I was nine and had wheezing fits so bad, the doctor diagnosed me with allergy-induced asthma brought on by the high pollen levels of Richmond, Virginia, and he inked fangs in black Sharpie on my pink plastic actuator, which he nicknamed Vlad the Inhaler to make it funny instead of scary. He understands me without even trying. Which has always dulled the stinging feeling that Mom has never tried all that hard.

And I have my grades, meaningless and otherwise. Maybe I'm not charming or effortlessly talented like the rest of my small family, but every perfect grade brings me closer to the future I want, the *life* I want. And as I spend my birthday in this ridiculous themed bar/restaurant destined to become another distant memory of another borrowed city the moment Mom gets the urge to uproot us, I think: *It doesn't look like this.*

I dig my fingers into the spines of my books to stop from slapping the menu out of Mom's hands so she'll look at me. "You can't tell me what I shouldn't be upset about. It's gonna matter to *me* tomorrow, whatever *you* think about it."

Now she does look up. "Then you need to grow up, Hannah, and learn to leave the trivial things behind you."

As we stare each other down, Gabe clicks on beside us like the beam of a flashlight in the dark. "Sooo, subject change? I'm thinking of ordering the surf and turf—"

"Sorry, you two." Mom drops her gaze to knuckle her forehead. "I'm sorry, I shouldn't have . . . I don't think I'm much fun right now. Maybe it would be better if I let you both enjoy the night? I'm . . . not feeling like myself." She does look a little pale, I guess, though it's hard to tell by the pink neon strobing light of yet another strike. "You two should stay. Order whatever you want for dessert, and I'll meet you back at the apartment. Okay?" Without waiting for us to protest, Mom rises to kiss my cheek and Gabe's forehead, leaving him her credit card. Then she's gone.

My brother blinks after her for a second, bewildered as I am, then rallies. "So what do you think?" he asks brightly, picking up the cocktail menu Mom dropped. "A bottle of Dom '98 for the table?"

I can't keep from voicing the fear that's struck me. "You don't think she's getting ready to move again, do you? Like, she's booked an Airstream in Florida and is just trying to figure out how to tell us?" Mom always seems moodiest right before a move—you'd think she'd be happy, since it's always her choice to go.

"No way," my brother says. "She promised, right?"

It's true. Mom promised me when I was accepted as a scholarship student and transferred to Winthrop that we'd stay put until I graduated. And she never breaks a promise. She's fanatic about them; that's probably why I can count every promise Mom's ever made on one hand. I should be more grateful, more gracious—as long as we're here, in Boston and at my dream school, aren't I getting exactly what I wanted? Hasn't my biggest wish been granted?

"I guess. But—"

"Or maybe we should skip the Dom," he says over me. "After all, we have to save room for your noncorporeal present."

"Right after this?" I'm already grinning despite myself.

Of course he's got something planned; it's tradition, one of the very few we've got. The Williams family doesn't follow any religion. We've never been inside a church or synagogue or mosque. Binge-watching holiday rom-coms indiscriminately and flying up to Ontario to stay with Poppy and Grammy Kowalski for a week every August is as deep as we get into ritual. They're what Mom calls twice-a-year Catholics, and if Dad believed in anything, he didn't have time to teach us before his accident. But *we* believe in the magic of birthdays, as Mom taught us to, and observe them religiously. So twice a year, Gabe and I stay up until dawn the way most kids do on Christmas. We always have.

And though our summer vacation only started last week, the countdown's already begun. To our last Netflix marathon, and our last lazy day sunbathing in Griggs Park. Our last order of drunken noodles at the Thai Tiger, and our last time trying to buy tequila snow cones at the harbor with his unconvincing fake ID. We won't be together for Gabe's nineteenth birthday next April. Who knows whether he'll even come home next summer? He might find a real boyfriend out west, one worth keeping. He could fall in love with the rich son of a film financier who'll charter a yacht to cruise them around Fiji for the season. Or, more likely, he'll spend his school break working at Starbucks with other Hollywood hopefuls, supplementing his financial aid, living on lattes and dreams all the way across the country.

Then it'll be just Mom and me.

"What about dessert?" I ask, trying not to sink when Gabe's working so hard to keep me afloat. "Do we need to skip *that* to save room?"

"Nah." He fans himself with Mom's card. "Let's get three."

That's exactly what we do.

After, we skip the T and walk the mile back to our apartment. We pass whole families on bicycles, and hipsters spilling out of specialty ice cream shops and pubs alike. The evening has that early-summer sparkle, the clouds aflame and the breeze warm on my forehead as it ruffles my pixie cut. It's no St. Helena, but Jamaica Plain feels more like home than most places.

For now, anyway.

Our apartment's completely dark when we reach it, which I try not to take personally. Heading for my room to drop off my new books, I stop short when I reach the living room, Gabe dancing in behind me.

"When did you do this?" I ask, stunned.

"After work. Before I met you guys at the restaurant."

I'm staring at the kind of fort my brother and I made when we were kids. A bedsheet draped between the tops of chairs he's dragged from the kitchenette to the family room, and cushions pried from the couch to prop up as walls. He's even detangled the fairy lights from our balcony railing, stringing them up beneath the sheet, and he turns them on as I kneel down to peek inside. On top of the quilt that makes up the floor, there are rainbow-colored noisemakers, a package of popcorn waiting to be microwaved, and his open laptop. Also, a six-pack of the canned sangrias he sometimes buys from the corner bodega where he works—the college guy who works the same shift he does has a crush on him, but won't let him buy anything stronger.

"I love it. What are we watching?"

"It's your birthday, Banana. You pick the genre, put on your pajamas, and I'll start the popcorn. It's gonna be the all-night birthday binge-watch to rule them all."

Hours later, as the clock ticks over to midnight, I stretch my stiffened legs inside the blanket fort. One knee sends an unopened sangria can tumbling. There really isn't much room in here, and the air is too warm with our recycled breaths. The drooping fairy lights illuminate spilled popcorn kernels, crushed noisemakers, and Gabe: curled up on the quilt floor, face loose with sleep.

I nudge my socked foot into his side. I can't even hear the movie over the truck-stuck-in-gravel sound of him, though that's not why I'm doing it—I don't care all that much about the movie. I'd only picked horror to make him happy. It's that neither of us was supposed to sleep tonight. Driving my heel into his ribs with more force, I cry, "You're missing it!"

Gabe only flops over onto his right side, face pressed into the green brocade cushion walls. Mumbling, he burrows deeper into the blankets, then snores on.

Defeated, I turn back to the screen just in time to watch a unicorn spear a teenage boy through the chest, apple-red blood spiraling down its iridescent horn. I close the laptop, cutting off the death moans. There's really no point in watching alone.

I reach over to click off the fairy lights, and it takes a moment for my eyes to adjust, thrust suddenly into darkness. Then I see it: a blacker shadow in the living room just outside the entrance to our fort.

My heart freezes.

The shadow heaves a great sigh and slurs, "Bon anniversaire, Hannah Banana."

I sag with relief. "Sorry, Mom. Did the movie wake you up?"

"Never slept. I was waiting—I just wanted to talk to you." For some reason, Mom sounds relieved too, and a little unsteady. When I crawl out of the fort, I see her more clearly in the faint glow of the streetlamps through the window. Elbow-length braids unraveling, a robe slipping from her shoulder, she holds a crystal champagne flute in one loosely curled fist. In her other hand, she grasps a bottle of bourbon by the neck, like a little girl dragging her Barbie around by its hair.

I blink at the sight. Mom calls herself a "social drinker" who'll happily down a glass or three of merlot among friends. But I've never known her to drink alone.

She crosses to the couch, perching perilously on the arm, and waves me over. I settle beside her on the bare frame, uncomfortable without its cushions. To my surprise, Mom hugs me as tight as she ever has, then hands me her glass by its delicate stem.

"Seriously?"

Her laughter is quiet but wild. "Trust me, we deserve to celebrate."

I smile as if I understand what's happening, then take one sip from the flute and gag—bourbon is worse than sangria.

"Thanks for waiting up just to say happy birthday," I cough out.

"I also wanted to say I'm sorry. About tonight."

"It's okay, Mom. It was nice. The cheesecake was good. And the Baked Alaska. And the lava cake." I shouldn't push this. But emboldened by the disgusting drink and her apology, I suggest, "If you're still looking for a birthday present, you know, there's that class—"

"Speaking of presents," she interrupts with a wry smile, just a little sloppy. From the pocket of her robe, Mom pulls a palm-sized box, which she could've just given me at the restaurant.

Clamping the flute between my knees, I slip a finger beneath the paper.

When I lift off the lid inside, a silver pendant sits on a cushion of foam. It's shaped like an open hand, but also a sort of flower—the three middle fingers straight like a stamen, the thumb and pinky shorter, like curled petals. Small turquoise stones set in the palm form a rough almond-shaped eye. At the tip of each finger, a tiny engraved star—the same one that decorates the local synagogues.

"I know it's not really your style. It . . . wasn't mine, either, when I was your age."

"Is this Jewish?"

Mom lifts the bottle of bourbon, sipping straight from it before plucking the hand from the box. "A hamsa. It was from a friend of your grandmother's—one of my childhood treasures. We need to get it polished. It's been sitting in a drawer for a long time. I can take it to the place on Washington Street." She stares at the pendant, entranced.

"Wait, it was from . . . Grammy's friend?"

Mom laughs. "No, I meant *my* mother's, of course. Someone who meant a lot to me growing up."

"I . . . oh."

I'm afraid that anything I say will buckle this fragile bridge between us, so I only stare at her in silence. We've never met our grandmother on Mom's side, never met any of her relatives. Mom rarely talks about the people or place she comes from, or anything that happened to her before Dad, for that matter. I've never even seen a picture of her as a kid, though we've seen plenty of Dad—we got a whole box of photos from Poppy and Grammy, and hear the same stories about his childhood on the shoreline of Lake Huron every time we visit. Sometimes, it feels like I know more about the father I can't remember than I do about Mom.

Gabe and I tried to investigate when we were younger, mostly for the thrill of putting on our raincoats and pretending to be detectives. But it was pointless. As surnames go, Williams—the maiden name Mom reclaimed when she gave up Kowalski after Dad's death—is everywhere. Our Google searching was foiled almost as soon as it started, especially with no hard information to go on, not even a home state. All we have is a small collection of useless facts. Like once, while Gabe and I eavesdropped on her playing "two truths and a lie" with friends (and after her second glass of social wine), she let slip that she was born in a black farmhouse besieged on all sides by wildflowers. That's just how she described it—as if she'd spent her childhood there at war with the earth itself. Like battalions of flowers broke themselves against the gutters, pressed their seed heads to the windows, bruised their petals trying to squeeze beneath the doors.

Since she definitely does *not* have a tramp stamp of a Picasso face, we knew the bit about the farmhouse and the flowers must be true.

Another sip of bourbon, and Mom shivers—whether from the taste of it or to shake herself free of some spell, I don't know. She drops the hamsa into my palm and says, "It's a very long story. But we'll talk. I guess it's about time we did."

She runs cool fingertips through my pixie cut, then plucks the near-empty flute from where it's still clamped between my legs and leaves me alone again.

Though sleep seemed as if it would be impossible after that, it isn't. I dream about places I've never seen—wildflower fields and woods, a towering palace and a dark, fast-moving river—and wake early Saturday morning on the blanket floor of the fort with stale breath and an emotional hangover. The midnight visit from Mom feels at first like part of my dreams, but when I uncurl my fist, I find the pendant, its eye stamped into my skin.

I turn it this way and that, inspecting it again in the dim morning light of our fort. It's half the size of my thumb, and every detail—the eye, the stars, even the unreadable words etched across the back of the hand, maybe the jeweler's signature—is exquisite. When I roll over to show Gabe, he's no longer beside me. He must've woken up early this morning and gone to his own bed, hoping for an hour or two of sleep before his big graduation day.

We never abandon our birthdays early.

Swallowing the storm in my throat, I crawl out into the living room and go to the hallway bathroom to wash up. The charm I set carefully in a paper cup in the dispenser to keep it safe while I scour the night from my breath. I reach for my toothbrush, look up—and freeze with it halfway to my mouth.

Blinking into the mirror, I watch as a girl with cinnamon-colored freckles, impossible golden eyes, and horizontal, knife-slit pupils blinks back.

TWO

AFTER A LONG, frozen moment staring into what are apparently my own snakelike eyes in the mirror, I run.

Past Mom's room and down the hall, I throw open Gabe's door. My brother's still asleep when I hurl myself onto his bed. Pulling off his plaid comforter, I shove at him until, grunting, he rolls over.

Gabe cracks one eye, then shoots upright, shouting, "Holy fuck!" He presses his fist against his heart, as if to slow its beating. "Christ on a cracker, Hannah, *why?*"

He thinks it's a prank.

"They're not contacts!" I shriek. "They're my fucking eyes!" My own heart is a bird—it's flown right out of my chest and is thrashing its way up my throat. I lock my teeth to keep it from escaping, and to stop myself from screaming again as Gabe stares up at me in horror.

Getting control of himself, he rubs a hand through his blond hair. "Okay. It's gonna be okay. Let's just . . . let's go show Mom."

But Mom already stands in the doorway, drawn by our

shouting. She's staring at me too, horror-struck. "Oh, Hannah," she whispers, barely loud enough for me to hear. "I thought . . . I . . ."

While she stands frozen, Gabe has already leaped from his bed, snatching up the dress shirt he's laid out for graduation this morning. "We have to go to the doctor, right?" He slips into his Vans and grabs his wallet from yesterday's chinos before tossing them aside, ready to rush me to the clinic in his button-up and boxers. "Get your shoes, Hannah."

"Wait," Mom whispers, stopping us both. She clutches the doorframe so tightly, the wood creaks beneath her bloodless fingers. "Just . . . stop and let me think."

"Mom—" Gabe protests, practically quivering in space.

"D-doctor Rubin's office is closed today. We'd have to . . . to go to the hospital—"

"Okay, fine, the hospital, whatever! Let's go!"

"Wait," it's my turn to say. Dr. Rubin's is a small practice, just him and a receptionist and a nurse on staff, and only a few blocks away. All I can imagine in this moment is the trip to BWFH, the closest hospital to us—a teaching hospital, where we went to get Gabe's wisdom teeth pulled last year. Getting on the T, sitting in the emergency room, the folks on the train and the patients and the nurses and the med students, all staring at me, all shocked and disgusted. "I . . . I don't want to go to the hospital. I *feel* fine. I can see fine. I can wait until Monday. And our insurance sucks, right?" I know Mom's still paying off Gabe's teeth. "Plus, you can't miss your graduation."

Gabe assures me that he absolutely fucking *can* miss his graduation. But after an hour of reasoning and yelling and pleading, roughly in that order, he leaves, still insisting on skipping the parties afterward. Better than him sitting on my bed all day, at least, waiting for my eyeballs to fall out of my head. With a last, haunted glance back at me, Mom floats out the door after my brother.

Good thing I've never relied on her to solve my problems.

I spend most of my seventeenth birthday alone in my bedroom, at my computer desk, taking advantage of the quiet to do some deep research—just me, a fresh Excel spreadsheet into which I start to compile possible causes and symptoms and treatments, and every relevant Google search I can think of. And I find plenty of scientific reasons why a person's eyes might change colors spontaneously, rare though it is. A virus, for instance. There's a doctor who, months after recovering from Ebola, woke to find himself with pale-green eyes instead of blue. I passed a night with my head in the toilet back in February, nauseated and chilled, but I'm pretty sure that was a case of undercooked chicken tacos.

It could be pigmentary glaucoma. Or a head injury, which has been known to cause keyhole or peanut-shaped pupils, though I doubt the tennis ball that beamed me in gym class last week would qualify. A congenital defect seems unlikely to all of a sudden show up at seventeen. One website claims that eating large amounts of honey or salmon or olive oil can make one's irises lighter and brighter, but from the site design,

I have my doubts as to its scientific validity. It's hard to trust a resource written in Comic Sans. Besides, I hate fish that isn't tucked inside a sushi roll, and I'm pretty sure the plastic bear of honey that sits in our pantry turned to sweet cement long ago.

My very specific search for "human with snake eyes" turns up even less helpful nonanswers. Advertisements for Halloween contact lenses, and articles on a legendary Viking warrior named Sigurd Snake-in-the-Eye. There's a page about therianthropy, the fantastical ability of human beings to shapeshift into animals, that sends me down a research hole. Fun (actually terrible) fact: in Ethiopia, Jews have long been believed to be wizards and witches, capable of transforming into hyenas to rob graves at midnight. I remember the hamsa, still in the hallway bathroom, then scroll past illustrations of wolfmen, werecats, and the Navajo yee naaldlooshii.

In the end, I open a new tab and search for a pair of dark sunglasses instead.

Mom will take me to Dr. Rubin the moment his office opens on Monday morning, and I'm sure he'll solve the problem. Medicated eyedrops, some kind of laser surgery at the very worst.

I'm pressing purchase on a pair of extra-dark-lensed glasses with a prepaid Visa that came from Poppy and Grammy— I spend extra for express shipping—just as Gabe bursts back into the apartment. Mom makes us dinner in silence, never meeting my strange eyes, then retreats to her bedroom. It's Gabe who stays with me. We tuck ourselves back inside my birthday fort, still assembled, forgotten in the chaos of the day.

"What if they don't change back?" I can't stop myself from asking.

"We'll get you color contacts," he says lightly, rolling over on his side. "Or we'll get me some. Who's even gonna care about your boring yellow eyes when I've got spiderweb eyeballs?"

It turns out, I don't need them. My eyes are back to blue when I wake up Sunday morning.

But I hardly notice. Because now, a wolf's vicious, curved ivory canines sprout from my gums, scraping my lips when I scream at the sight of my reflection in my phone's camera. Gabe bolts upright beside me, nearly toppling the fort, but I run for my bedroom, grabbing my quilt from my bed as I pass, and crawl into my closet. I don't come out, and I won't let my family in. Instead, I tuck myself into the shadows to hide behind the garment bag full of my Winthrop uniforms, pressed and put away for the summer.

Mom sits on the floor just outside the folding doors. "Hannah, please. I know you're scared. But . . . but you're not alone." After all of her frozen panic yesterday morning, she's at least trying to sound calm and in control.

"What—" I grunt around the fangs, wincing as they saw against my skin.

"I . . . I don't know what's happening, but . . . I think I know somebody who can help."

"Doctor?"

She hesitates. "A specialist. Someone who heals."

If she means to drag me to a megatent in Idaho to pay some faith healer with his own local TV show to put his hands on me, I swear, I'll go for her jugular. But I don't know how to tell Mom all this—like, physically, without grating my human lips raw—so I simply ask, "Where?"

Another long pause, and then, "Just let me handle this, okay, honey? This . . . whatever is happening to you, I promise you, we'll figure it out. But I need you to stay here. To stay safe, with Gabe. Just, will you do that? Hannah, promise me you'll let me fix this?"

I work my jaw awkwardly to get out, "I can't . . . stay like this." I really can't, whatever *this* is. I need to get back to normal, back to my life. I'm supposed to be starting college applications—I'd put it in my planner for Monday, once we were past the graduation festivities. I'm supposed to be talking Mom into shelling out for summer school classes that might give me the slightest edge over my Winthrop friends with money and family connections. Because I'm not my brother; I can't get by on bottomless charm and talent like Gabe can. He could do anything, become anything, with just a drop of effort. I'm half sure he picked the California College of the Arts by throwing a sticky frog at a wall map. He might eventually use the same method to pick his major. It doesn't matter. He'll be great at whatever he settles on. He has an ear for language, a flair for theater, and a steady hand at art. I've got none of that. I don't even really have a head for math, my best subject in school. I have to study weeks before a test. I don't think I've ever seen Gabe study a moment for anything.

All I've got going for me is determination and a jumbo pack of flash cards. It takes me so much work to accomplish what Gabe simply flings himself into, then floats away from triumphantly. I know that, and I'm not bitter. These are cold, clean facts.

I take all the right classes, read the right books, sit with the right kids, find a way to afford the right makeup and clothes and laptop bags to fit in, or at least, good dupes. I'm in the crowd competing for class valedictorian next year, with a good shot at the ivies, or Northwestern or Duke. Harvard, Columbia, Cornell . . . and Duke . . . all have solid undergrad credentials, and top master's programs in health policy and management. From there, I will graduate and snag a job as a medical and health services manager at a prestigious hospital. According to a pamphlet I picked up at Winthrop's career center, median pay is just about six figures, with higher than average demand. A stable, safe future, which requires zero competency with a scalpel. No blood on my shoes at the end of the day. Ideal for detail-oriented, highly organized, leadership-qualities-out-the-eyeballs me.

Nobody can help loving my brother, but I don't need anyone to love me like that. I just need to be good enough that they can't help but sit up and notice me.

It's almost funny. Mom was never neglectful—we always

knew we'd have food, and clothes, and a roof over our heads, even if we were never sure where that roof would be by the end of the month. It's just . . . sometimes, it feels like no student-of-the-month award or A++ essay or glowing teacher's recommendation could make Mom pay me her full attention.

Well, I've got it now.

"Listen, Hannah," she says, pulling me back to the present. "I'm going to fix this. Okay? I'll go back and make it right. I've . . . I've made mistakes, I know. So many of them. But everything I've done . . . I only ever wanted to keep you safe. I'm *going* to keep you safe." She slides my closet door open just enough to reach inside and feel for my hand.

I get the strange feeling she isn't even talking to me, but I give in and let the certainty in her words lift me off the closet floor.

Gabe isn't so easily comforted.

"Mom, this is crazy. Mom!" he protests, sliding his body between our mother with her small suitcase, and the front door. "Just stop for a minute and talk to us, okay?"

"I won't be gone long. A week at most."

"You're really leaving us, like right now, and you can't even tell us where or why? Hannah needs to go to the hospital, clearly. She needs *you*."

With my blanket wrapped around me up to my nose, I hover in the entryway, watching them both, relieved to let Gabe speak for me.

"Hannah needs help, and this *is* me helping," she insists. "If this doesn't work, then we'll go to the doctor as soon as I get back. It might not even be a week—a few days, I hope, depending. Just watch out for your sister. Take care of her while I'm gone, okay?" Mom shoves the loose strands of her hastily clipped-up hair away from her face. With no makeup on and swimming inside her crookedly buttoned shirt, she looks younger than her age. Young, and afraid. "And . . . don't let anybody in. Not even if you think you know them."

"We won't," I mumble through fangs and fabric, just as Gabe asks, "Why?"

"Because I'm your mother, Gabriel, and I said so, and that's final." Her words are rimed with ice, so that even my six-foot-one brother seems to shrink from the chill.

It's my turn to freeze as Mom wraps her arms around my blanket-encased form. "We have a lot to talk about when I get back," she murmurs into my hair, "about me. About *you*. There's so much you don't know, and that's my fault, too. You don't even know my name . . ." She stops, a quiet sob in her voice.

"What does *that* mean?"

Mom holds me tighter. "Trust me, Hannah. I'll tell you everything as soon as I can. Just wait for me, and I'll make this right. I promise."

There's a moment when I want to cling to her and beg her not to leave. I never told Mom, but I used to have these nightmares that I'd wake up and find all of our belongings boxed up, our borrowed keys left on the kitchen counter, and her and my brother gone already.

But Gabe's not going anywhere. And Mom . . . she'll be back in a few days.

I force myself to meet her eyes. I've never really known her, and I see that clearly now—not any better than she knows me. But my heart does loosen a little with her promise. Mom wouldn't make one she couldn't keep. This condition, whatever it is, is a problem, obviously, but it doesn't have to be a disaster. With school out for Gabe and me, there's nowhere we have to be. My Winthrop friends will understand a few days of unanswered texts—they probably won't even notice me sliding out of the group chat. Afterward, my little family can just pretend that none of this ever happened.

And that everything I've been working toward since I can remember matters at all.

THREE

THE DAYS STRETCH into one week, then two. Every morning, another change—fur and claws and bones that don't belong. Once, most frightening, I wake with gills and feel as if I'm trying to breathe on top of a mountain. Like years ago when Mom took us hiking up Wheeler Peak in New Mexico, and I got altitude sickness, and the air felt impossibly shallow in my lungs.

Gabe suggests daily that we should go to a doctor. And daily, I agree.

But we never do.

At first, I open the spreadsheet I started that first morning and use the endless hours at home to dive into research, my old friend and comfort. Mom wouldn't answer my questions, but the answers have to be out there, don't they? Modern science has explained almost everything that once seemed unknowable. Except I can't find anything, not even a sketchy website in Comic Sans, that can tell us what's happening to me. No combination of search words that can solve the puzzle. Nothing on message boards obsessed with medical anomalies. Nothing even in supernatural lore or surrealist fiction that approximates what's happening to me—it's not as simple as turning into a wolf or a cockroach, even if I woke with pincers instead of fingers one day . . .

As I'm sifting through fairy tales, I stumble across a site on Jewish folklore. I stay, remembering the tidbit on the therianthropy page. There's a section on spells and hexes, and the Pulsa Denura does sound pretty epic, but the article soon devolves (or evolves) into a debate over the distinction between a prayer and a spell, a ritual and a superstition, a Hasid and a sorcerer, a healer and a witch. Which is interesting, but not immediately helpful. In desperation, I find a Craigslist ad for clearing curses under local services (*Have you experienced unexplained bad luck?* Dr. Morris Swack asks. *Do strange things happen to you that you can't account for? Do you do everything right and it still doesn't work out?*), but even if I were desperate enough, it's not like I have 8,716 Swedish krona on me.

All the while, I don't leave the apartment.

We live on delivery from our favorite restaurants, which Gabe orders and goes downstairs to retrieve, instead of listing our apartment number. He abandons his friends for what should've been the beginning of their last two months together before they all leave for college, and keeps me company in the pillow fort we never took down. It's grown gradually more dilapidated, though Gabe shakes the crumbs out of the quilt over the balcony every few days, and I refluff the cushions. Some days, we hardly leave it. We watch Netflix and fall asleep with cold pizza in our laps. Some nights we try staying up, wondering whether I'll change if I never fall asleep. But it isn't like the werewolf movies Gabe used to love, where bones break and reform, agonizingly, with every full moon. I always fall asleep before sunrise, if only for a few minutes, even the nights I try my hardest to stay awake. Gabe too. And I never feel it happen.

Two weeks become three, and we still don't hear from Mom. I start to wonder, despite her promise and Gabe's reassurances, whether we will. Maybe something happened to her—a carjacking, or a crash on a dark country road while attempting to "go back and make it right," whatever she meant by that.

"Maybe she found that Airstream in Florida after all," I suggest to Gabe one evening over our delivery burrito bowls, his clunky noise-canceling headphones secured over my feathered, owl-like ears to muffle the sound of my own voice, and his.

"Mom wouldn't—"

"I'm joking," I mutter. "Mostly."

"You're just worrying. You don't really believe she'd ditch us," he challenges.

"Why not?" The softest, most pathetic part of my heart pulses painfully. "Mom's spent our whole lives running around the country, right? She never wanted to stay in Boston in the first place. Maybe once she was gone, she just . . . decided to keep going."

Gabe shakes his head—his previously short, combed-back haircut is starting to grow out and flop across his forehead, just like mine. "She loves us, Hannah. She loves you."

"So then where is she?"

My brother shrugs and shovels guac and black beans into his mouth, which I recognize as him parachuting out of this conversation before it can spiral beyond his control.

The morning I wake up with green-gold scales scattered across my body—a patch here, a stripe there—Gabe announces he's going out, vowing to bring home something stronger than canned sangria. He's gone for hours, long enough for me to finish the half of the breakfast pizza I was saving for him, long enough after that to start to panic. Huddling in the fort, I sink into certainty that he isn't coming back either. That he's on a bus to Grammy and Poppy's house in Ontario, or fuck it, to San Francisco, off to start his new life a month early.

The worst thought of all: maybe Gabe heard from Mom, and wherever they are, they're together.

But my brother comes home in the early evening. His left forearm is wrapped in plastic, and there's a thick layer of ointment blurring what lies beneath.

"Sorry, sorry, wasn't as easy as I thought it'd be to find a tattoo place taking walk-ins today," he explains. Then he peels off the wrap and rinses his arm clean, showing me the green-gold scales inked permanently into his skin from wrist to elbow.

Relieved and guilt-torn and struck with love for my big brother, I start to cry.

"Get dressed, Banana," he says firmly. "We're going out."

I pull on long sleeves and jeans despite the steamy heat of

the July night. He chooses the loudest T-shirt he owns, electric purple with bright-blue lightning bolts across it, and leaves his fresh ink unwrapped and glistening. Then we strike out for drunken noodles at the Thai Tiger, just across the street. I walk with my head down, terrified that somebody will see me.

But I soon realize that what's always been a little true is even more so now. Nobody casts a second glance at the small girl beside Gabe in dark sunglasses and oversize, drab clothing. He pulls all eyes, like a black hole dragging every bit of light toward himself.

A few days later, when I wake with a forked tongue, my brother goes into the bathroom and bleaches his hair even blonder, then dyes it a shade of turquoise called Voodoo Blue. In the fourth week, he goes back to the tattoo parlor for a vertical labret piercing—a silver ball nestled in the center of his bottom lip. He finds the most obnoxious prints he can in local thrift stores, all with the same goal: on the rare occasion when I agree to leave the apartment, we know it'll be him that everyone's staring at.

I'm starting to think we'll go on like this until we max out Mom's credit card, Gabe changing his body while I try to shrink mine, canceling dental appointments and making excuses to get out of our trip to Grammy and Poppy's in August. I've given up completely on the idea of the Food and Nutrition and French IV classes, which started weeks ago when June turned into July—no perfect GPA or early college credits for me. And Gabe's already mentioned deferring college to stay in Boston, without actually saying aloud that we might well still be trapped in this apartment come fall.

That's when the envelope arrives, addressed to me.

Gabe brings it up with the mail on one of the days he's remembered to check our box. There's no return address, and no clear sign that it's from Mom. Our address, along with my name, is printed in strange handwriting, smaller and neater than hers, with the lowercase *i*'s in *Jamaica Plain* capped by hollow circles instead of dots. There's no whiff of the Masters Hand Soap she uses after painting or any messy work. I swear, the spearmint scent lingers on everything she touches. There isn't even a letter of explanation inside. Just a slip of thick cream-colored paper from a Temple Beth El, in someplace called Fox Hollow, New York.

My quick search turns up a small town in the Hudson Valley, population: 4,800. Primary attractions: its many historic houses, a quaint downtown shopping area, and a thick, twisting tributary of the Hudson nicknamed the Hollow.

We return to the paper, which reads:

Jitka Eggers passed away on July 19 in Fox Hollow, NY, at the age of 98. She was the beloved wife of the late Isaac Eggers for 59 years. Born in Prague on February 4, 1922, she was the daughter of Yehuda and Anna (Manger) Loew. Jitka was the sole survivor of the Holocaust in her family, fleeing by train at the age of 16 in 1939 as part of Kindertransport, a mission that rescued thousands of children from Nazi-occupied Europe during World War II. Among the lost were her sisters, Helenka Lipkowitz, Nadezda Mehler, Rayna Jenikau, Marjeta Piseck, and Sorina Loew; and her brothers, Damek Loew, Jakub Loew, Karel Loew, and Gabek Loew. She immigrated from England to Brooklyn, NY, in 1942, and was married to Isaac the year after. They soon moved to Fox Hollow, where she had lived since.

Jitka was a devoted stay-at-home mother to Esther Silver, Ruth Abrams, Bina Kasenetz, Geela Liberman, and Shoshanna Aaronson, all still of Fox Hollow, and of Malka Kowalski. She was the cherished grandmother and great-grandmother to many, and an active member of Temple Beth El. Graveside services will be held on Wednesday, July 21, at 10 a.m., at Sons of Jacob Cemetery, 50 Birch Road, Fox Hollow. Shiva will be held after the funeral and until Tuesday, July 27, from 3 to 6 p.m. at 4 Woodland Lane, Fox Hollow, the home Jitka shared with Esther and Bernard Silver. Memorial contributions may be sent to Beth El Synagogue at 178 Orchard Street, Fox Hollow.

May her memory be a blessing.

July 21—that was yesterday.

"Did Mom ever say anything?" Gabe asks, after a long moment. "About any of this?"

I shake my head. "I mean, she mentioned her mother when she gave me the hamsa, but she never told me places, or names . . ."

You don't even know my name.

34

We've found our family and the grandmother we never knew to miss, only three days too late.

Though Mom had dropped the revelation that our family was Jewish the night before my birthday, I hadn't paid it too much attention in the past six weeks, except in passing during research; my daily transformations sort of stole the show. Now, I read up on shiva, the traditional Jewish period of mourning when the family and community of the deceased assemble to grieve together.

It's clear enough that Mom didn't send the envelope. She wouldn't have reached out like this, without any explanation or warning after weeks and weeks of nothing. Hell, she would've addressed the letter to Gabe instead of me. And she obviously had no hand in the death notice, or it would've listed her as Malka Williams instead of Kowalski. Still, somebody from her hometown—someone close enough to Mom to know about me—wanted to make sure we were aware of Jitka Eggers's death.

Gabe tries Mom's phone for the millionth time, and as always, it goes straight to her full voice mail. My texts, too, go unanswered, and as usual, her freelancer email for her graphic design job returns only a one-sentence out-of-office message that she'll be traveling for the summer.

"What do you think? There's an address here for . . . Esther and Bernard," he reads aloud. "Esther is Mom's sister, right? Bet we could find her phone number. Should we, like, call her?"

"And say what? Her mother just died, and we don't know if she sent us the notice. Maybe it was another sister. Or a niece or nephew, I don't know."

What I do know is that no matter who contacted us, the whole family will be in Fox Hollow, New York, to mourn according to the rules of shiva. Everyone with a connection to my mother's past and possible knowledge of what's happening to me, gathered in one place.

It feels like a lead.

It almost feels like hope.

FOUR

GABE AND I stand side by side in front of the farmhouse and look over the land that—to hear Mom tell it—tried so hard to swallow her whole.

"It's . . . not what I expected," he says.

The house *is* black. And sure enough, instead of a neatly tended lawn, it sits in the middle of a meadow, surrounded by wildflowers that polka-dot the rustling, waist-high grass with color. Yellow black-eyed Susans, spiky purple prairie thistle, bright-red bee balm, and others I can't name. They cover a plot of land carved out from the surrounding woods, sliced by the long driveway that winds from the road and through the trees behind us. The flowers whisper against one another when the breeze blows. Past the black house, there's a weather-beaten barn with boarded-over doors, and more trees beyond that. All of that's as I'd pictured.

But I'd imagined the house to be small and mean-looking. A little two-bedroom buried somewhere out in the flyover states, with a water-damaged porch and a swaybacked roof. The kind of dilapidated structure you'd find at the top of a pretentious

New Yorker article about the decline of rural America. Though Fox Hollow sits in the forests of the Hudson Valley instead of the middle of the country, Mom's hometown is rural enough. But the house . . . it's as big as our whole apartment complex in Boston. Three stories high, with a single dormer window set in the pitched, blue slate roof. Its many shutters pop against the shingle siding, painted a pale, sweet lilac. The front door of the same color is propped open, screen banging lightly against the frame when the hot July wind blows.

So no. It's not what I expected, either.

A lace curtain lifts behind one of the first-floor windows, then drops back. I wonder whether we look like Hansel and Gretel, stumbling upon the witch's house in its beautiful but cursed clearing in the woods. Or perhaps we're the witches ourselves, invading from the big city beyond the fairy-tale forest.

Gabe shoves his aviators up into his hair, which is looking extra wild. His sides are freshly shaved, and the long top is still a bright teal. What will Mom think of his transformation? When she left us, he was his honey-haired, virgin-skinned, jeans-and-Henley self. Now, between his hair, the opalescent tattoo winding up his left arm, his ridiculous shirt, and the lip stud, nobody would glance away from Gabe long enough to notice me.

Seized with a sudden anxiety, I reach up to pat the slouchy knit beanie pinned low over my forehead, despite the heat— still in place.

The screen door swings wide then, and a woman steps onto the porch. Her face is pale above her high-necked, below-the-knee black dress, her stocky legs encased in tights. I don't recognize Mom in the woman's features, but her dress is torn below the collarbone on the left side, a narrow slice of skin showing through. I remember from my research on the train ride, and then the shorter bus ride, that it's a Jewish tradition of grief. Only a child, a parent, a spouse, or a sibling of the dead will tear their clothes, and since our grandmother was ninety-eight when she died, she must be one of our aunts.

"Shalom aleichem," she calls tentatively. "Are you kids here to sit shiva?"

"We're, um, Gabe and Hannah?" My brother says it like a question. "Your sister, Malka? She's . . . she's our mom."

By the way her thick, dark eyebrows knit together, and her hand flutters dramatically to her cheek, and the bewilderment in her voice when she says, "You're *Malka's* children?" I figure she isn't our mystery contact in Fox Hollow.

Gabe reaches the same conclusion. "You haven't talked to her lately, I guess."

"My sister hasn't spoken to any of us," the woman says— our aunt, confirmed—her face moon-pale now, and just as cold. "We haven't heard from her in seventeen years. Haven't seen her in thirty or more. Honestly, we didn't think Malka knew about Mama. We don't have her number, couldn't find her any-where, didn't know where she lived, or if she was even alive herself."

Despite the summer air, I'm suddenly shivering.

"I'm—I'm sorry," Gabe stutters. "We didn't . . . we thought somebody had—"

"She was supposed to call and tell you we were coming," I cut in. I'm as thrown as Gabe by this information, but if Mom isn't here, I don't think this is the time or place to reveal all to the woman who only just learned about our existence. "I guess she didn't. She's forgetful." As if it's *so* our mom to forget to phone her family following the death of her own mother.

"That right?" our aunt asks, uncertainty written across her features. "How did you all hear about Mama?"

I shrug helplessly. "She didn't say. We thought maybe somebody in town told her." Not a lie.

She shakes her head. "If they did, I don't know about it."

Gabe shoots me a glance. Pressing my lips together to keep them from trembling, I give the slightest shake of my head, trying not to panic. It's not as if I'd convinced myself that Mom would be waiting to greet us on the front lawn with a magical cure. Or that she was ever here at all. But I had hoped . . .

Our aunt's eyebrows don't unhitch. "We never even knew Malka had a daughter. Last we talked, she'd married a man we'd never met and adopted a little boy. That was you, I guess," she says, nodding toward Gabe. "We got some baby pictures, a few phone calls with you making noise in the room. And then nothing. We never heard from her again."

My heart sinks to the driveway, settles into the crushed rocks and dust. "Surprise," I say weakly.

"And my sister sent you here? Alone?"

"She . . . she got held up. With work. She said she'd call, or email . . . Maybe her message got lost?"

"That's possible." The woman's face softens. She *wants* to believe us, wants her sister to be out there, trying but failing to reach her, the silence a simple miscommunication. I see the abandoned hope rekindle in her eyes, and know she won't turn us away, even before she says, "If you're Mali's, then I guess that makes me your aunt Esther." She climbs down the front steps and walks toward us, the path from the front door to the driveway so narrow the surrounding flowers snag on her stockings. She eyes Gabe first, predictably. "You look a little different from your old photos," she says dryly, but not meanly. Then her gaze skips to me. "Hannah." She tastes my name for the first time.

I flinch as she reaches for me, but Esther only rests a warm palm beneath my chin, tipping my face up toward the light.

"Shayna punim," she murmurs, searching for her sister, I guess. She peers into my blue eyes, and whether she sees what she expects, I can't tell.

At last, she notices our suitcases, and my overstuffed backpack.

"You don't have any place to stay, do you?" Esther asks. She must see the truth in our matching grimaces.

"We just came straight from the bus station, but we'll get a hotel," Gabe's quick to say.

"I can tell you, there's not much around here. The Stellar Motel a town over might have space, but I wouldn't recommend it. They had carpenter bees, last I heard. Besides, you're family—you'll stay here while we get this figured out. It's a little crowded this week, of course, but we've still got space upstairs."

"No, that's okay. We didn't mean to—"

"We'll stay." I cut him off again. Though his amber eyes (smudged with gray eyeliner like the lead singer in Creatures Such as We, his favorite band; he went all out for this trip) grow round as stoplights, I tell Esther, "We really appreciate it."

"Let's get you settled in, and you can call your mother to tell her you made it safe and sound. Then maybe she and I can speak."

"I'm sure she'll want to."

It's a promise Mom would never have made: one with no hope of being kept.

As Esther turns, Gabe mouths, *What are you doing?*

I try to smile as if I know, even though I'm wondering the exact same thing.

He bites at the barbell under his lip, as has become his habit when he's especially anxious, but he follows me.

We roll our suitcases along after Esther as she climbs the wraparound porch. The boards moan lightly beneath our shoes, and a pair of antique rocking chairs tip forward and back as we pass. On a tray table beside the door sits a porcelain pitcher and serving bowl of water; we're supposed to wash our hands before entering to honor the dead, I learned in my research, but Esther doesn't stop, so neither do we.

It's cold inside the house, a blast of air-conditioning drying the sweat that beads below my beanie. I stifle the urge to wipe a hand across my forehead, wary of knocking it out of place.

Esther leads us down a long hallway, the wood-beamed ceiling dark overhead, pale-green flowered wallpaper pressing in on both sides. All of the heavy doors that line the corridor are shut except for one, and here, Esther does pause. Inside, people gather in a parlor half the size of our entire apartment. Everyone wears simple, somber clothes and sits in quiet pockets of conversation on solid wooden chairs and blush-pink settees. It's an elegant room, nothing out of place except perhaps the gingham bedsheet tacked to the wall above the pale stone fireplace. It must be covering a mirror—another mourning custom, just like the tall candle in a blue jar that burns on the mantel.

A girl around my age stands alone beside it, hands tucked inside the pockets of a black suit jacket she wears over a black shirt and cuffed jeans. The long hair rippling over her shoulders glows watermelon pink in the candlelight. She looks up, and we lock eyes.

"On second thought," Esther murmurs beside my ear, startling me, "let's get you all situated before introductions. That way I can, um, prepare everyone."

We move on. Beyond the parlor, a staircase with an elaborately carved railing leads up. Our aunt rests one hand on a newel post capped by a gleaming horse's head, like a waist-high chess piece. "We've got quite a few folks staying here at the moment—Papa's family from the city, and some of my sisters wanted to stay together a night or two, though they all live in the area. But we can find you beds on the second floor. Hannah, we'll put you in with your cousin Aviva." She must see the flash of horror on my face because she adds, "Unless—maybe you want something a little more private?"

"Private sounds good."

Esther frowns. "It would mean sharing a room with your brother."

"We don't mind," I hurry to say.

She nods and leads on.

The hallway spills out into the kitchen, large and bright, with egg-yolk walls, tiled floors, thick plank countertops, and a back door that must lead to the field behind the house. I take a deep breath of air that smells like every good thing. Baskets and plates and bowls crowd each surface, full of bagels, pastries, hard-boiled eggs, potatoes, various salads and casseroles. Chicken soup with whole bones bobbing inside it simmers in a huge pot on the old but tidy stove.

"Folks have been kind to us," Esther explains. She reaches toward a platter of chopped veggies, but just nudges it back from the counter's edge, taking nothing from the plate.

We pass a kitchen island with a rack of copper-bottomed pots dangling from the ceiling and trail Esther up a steep staircase off the back of the kitchen, each step just a little taller than it should be. Our suitcases thump behind us.

"The third floor is where your mom slept when she was a girl," our aunt huffs, pausing on the landing. Unlike the rest of the house, the staircase is cramped and plain. "Most private place there was, with all us sisters. There isn't even a way up from the second floor. None of us wanted the room; too hot in the summer and freezing in winter. We didn't have air-conditioning back then, of course, or any wiring in the room for lights. And there was definitely something in the walls. Mice, or squirrels. We never found out. But Malka moved right up the moment Mama and Papa let her. It's been updated since she left, though I have to say, it's still not exactly roomy."

We squeeze through a doorway at the top and set our suitcases inside a room with a steeply sloped ceiling. There's a twin bed with a patchwork quilt folded at the foot and a bureau in one corner, and that's about it.

"I'll dig up an air mattress. One of my sisters must have one. I do hate to squeeze you in like this, but it should only be for a night or two. After that, you can take another room, if you'd like. Folks are pretty much clearing out tomorrow night, after Havdalah."

I don't know what that means, but I'm eager to be alone, anxious to breathe again, so for now, I don't ask.

"It's clean up here, at least. I keep up with the house myself, but I—I was away this past week," she stammers, her broad face paling. "One of my girls just had her third, a little boy, and I was staying with her. Just for a few days, to help out. I didn't . . . I wasn't on top of things as much as I should have been."

I don't know what to say to this; not Esther's regrets, or

the revelation that she's a *grandmother*. She must be a lot older than Mom, or else got married much younger.

Anyway, my silence doesn't matter. Gabe speaks for us. "This will be perfect," he says warmly. "We're just grateful you could find a place for us on short notice. Or, like, no notice. And we're really sorry about your mom."

Why didn't I think to say that?

"Thank you." Her hand drifts up to the tear in her dress as her eyes glisten. "Only wish Mama could've seen you both, before." She clears her throat. "Anyhow, we won't be sitting shiva after sundown, or tomorrow, on account of Shabbat. You'll meet the family tonight. There's a bathroom back down the stairs, first door off the kitchen, if you want to wash up." Her eyes dart to Gabe before she manages to look away. "Or if you want to change for dinner." Then she leaves us alone.

Gabe nudges the door shut behind her with his foot. "I believe that shade was meant for me."

I cut my eyes toward his shirt, where flamingos sipping cocktails from hollowed-out pineapples dance across the fabric. "Black would've made a better first impression."

But we both know why he chose to make this exact impression. He shrugs carelessly, flinging himself down on the bed with a squeal of rusty springs. "Why bother? Once they see my Instagram, they'll know I'm going to hell anyway."

"Technically, Jews don't believe in hell." I tug at the top drawer of the bureau, warped with time. It takes some work before it jerks open, and I'm rewarded with a puff of sawdust and a few mothballs rolling idly inside. I muscle it back into place. "I read about it on the bus. So you'll be fine. You could even be buried in a Jewish cemetery if you wanted to be Jewish. Not all, but some."

Gabe presses a hand to his chest, gasping melodramatically. "Because *gay?*"

"Because tattooed and pierced."

"Oh." He lifts his left forearm overhead to inspect his skin, the green and gold scales that wind upward. Looking at them, I feel this great pang of love and guilt, like always.

He drops his arm to the stiff mattress with a *whumpf*. "She hasn't been here, Banana," he says, unable to joke his way around the truth any longer. "Why are *we?*"

My stomach plunges. "We said we'd—"

"I mean, why are we *still* here? You heard Esther. She hasn't seen or talked to Mom. Nobody has."

"We don't know that for sure. Just . . . that Esther doesn't think anyone has."

"We should have called first."

"We have to try," I insist.

In the end, it was my choice to come. I booked the train and bus tickets. Gabe had doubts all along, but I wanted the future I'd planned on—valedictorian, then a top college, then the perfect career—and I wanted my life. Out of everything I'd lost since my birthday, most of all, I missed lying out on a beach towel in Griggs Park just beyond the reach of the weeping willows' shade, wearing little more than a bathing suit. Back when my body was just a body, even if I had complaints about it, and not a trap that springs over and over again.

"It's not like I'm giving up," Gabe protests. "But look . . . these people might be your family, but are you really ready to trust them?" His gaze drifts toward my hat, which he must've been wondering about all day.

I take a deep breath and carefully pull loose the bobby pins keeping it secured. As best I can, I run a hand through my sweat-damp black hair, sloppily grown out of its pixie cut over the last six weeks into a finger-length shag. Though Gabe tries to keep a straight face, I can't blame him when his eyebrows tick upward at the horns that sprout from beneath.

"Badass," he whispers.

I want to cover them immediately, but there's no point pretending to be normal around my brother. There when I woke up this morning, the small, slate-colored horns coil backward like a ram's. At least they could be covered up for a trip like this. My disfigurements aren't always so easy to hide.

There are two small windows in the attic bedroom—one that faces the driveway and the road beyond, which must be the dormer window, and one that looks out over the barn in back of the house, its mossy roof at eye level, the wildflowers brushing up against the gray boards. I try to imagine Mom standing here when she was my age, with this same view. I can't picture it.

"So no one here has seen her. That doesn't mean she wasn't in Fox Hollow," I insist. "She said she was going 'back.' Where else could she have meant? Where else did we stay long enough to get to know anybody? And it's not exactly a coincidence that somebody here contacted us. There has to be something here, or someone, that can help us find her."

"Maybe we should call Poppy and Grammy," he suggests, not for the first or even the fiftieth time. They still have no idea that anything's amiss. They only really talk to Mom to coordinate our visits to Canada, which won't come up till next month, and the tickets have been booked for ages. Gabe and I Skype with them every few months in between, but our conversations don't last long. Mostly, Poppy and I trash-talk *Detective after Dark*, this soapy TV show about a crime-solving vampire we both secretly love. That and Dad's DNA are about all we have in common.

"We're not telling them."

"They can help—"

"They *can't*. They'd just try and make us come to Ontario, or worse, come and get us. Mom said she knew somebody who could help me, the specialist, and if there's any chance she's been in this town, then they might be, too. They might even have sent us the death notice. We can ask questions, do research."

"Okay, fine . . . But why do we have to stay in this house, with all of these people?"

It's true that after spending six weeks in self-imposed quarantine, the last place I want to be is one where everybody might *see* me. But I remind him, "Whoever sent it wanted us to come to Fox Hollow. And if it wasn't Esther or her family, then we need to find out who. Maybe they'll reach out to us, once they know we're here—it's a small town, right? News travels. But they can't do that if we're stuck in a bee-infested motel twenty miles away."

And the truth is this: if we go home—if we ask for a ride back to the tiny local bus station, travel the forty minutes to Hudson and catch the next train to Boston, retreat into our small, safe apartment to watch cartoons night and day . . . then what? What if we never find out what happened to Mom? And whatever is happening to me can't be cured? What if Gabe throws away his future to work at the corner bodega for the rest of his life? It'll just be us—the beloved high school star who wasted his talent, and the monstrous little sister he was told to take care of, like a pet gremlin. There's no way I'm letting that happen to either of us.

"You're sure?" my brother asks.

"I'm sure."

I tear my gaze away from the barn, from the high-up windows all glassless and black. Instead, I stare into the bright wildflowers until my eyes water, forcing myself to hope.

THERE'S A BOY outside the barn.

Malka watches him, leaning halfway out her window. To catch a breeze, she tells herself, and not for a better view. It's unbearably hot in her attic bedroom every summer, like sleeping inside an oven, more so since it always smells of the kitchen below. Herring, challah, onions . . . everything her mother creates drifts upward, for good or for ill.

At least it's private. The house isn't as crowded as it once was, even with Geela home for the summer from Stern College for Women in the city, where she stays with Papa's cousin during the semester (though she still takes the train to Fox Hollow each weekend). Now that Esther, Ruth, and Bina are married and have moved into their own houses nearby, there are empty bedrooms for her to pick from downstairs. Still, Malka prefers it up here, where it's quiet.

At least, it is when Shoshanna and Geela aren't bursting through her bedroom door, trailing family gossip and small jealousies. As the youngest, Malka's always been everybody's obedient, sympathetic ear. She carries the weight of their complaints the way she carries Papa's expectations and Mama's protectiveness, as stifling at times as the summer heat. Papa makes the rules—supposedly—but it's Mama's fear that guides his heavy hand. It's Mama who always sends him to bring her home in the middle of the few sleepovers she's been allowed to attend, having woken in terror over the well-being of her youngest. It's Mama who insisted her bicycle be given away when she sprained her wrist in a roadside tumble, and Mama who refused to allow her daughters to sign up for driver's ed. It's Mama who says no to class trips out of state. Mama who burst into tears when Malka brought home a book of colleges across the country, prompting Papa to offer, as an alternative to living at home and commuting, that she could stay with his cousin in Brooklyn like Geela does during the semester. Like Shosh will when she joins their sister at Stern this fall.

Once Shosh leaves the house, then Malka will bear her parents' rules and love all alone.

Footsteps pound up the staircase from the kitchen, reminding her how unalone she is right now. She spins away from the window just as Shoshanna barges in without knocking. "Mali, did you see him?"

Malka holds her palms out as her sister barrels straight into her, knocking them both back onto her bed. "Who?" she asks, and if Shosh weren't so flushed and breathless, she'd hear in it that Malka already knows who she's talking about.

"The guy who came about Papa's ad in the *Plainsman*. He's tall. And cute." Shosh grins conspiratorially. At nineteen, and with Malka's eighteenth birthday only a few months away, Shoshanna is her closest sister in age. "And he'll be here all summer."

"Like—" Malka's own breath hitches. "Like, he's *staying* here? With us?"

"As if!" Her sister giggles. "Not unless he wants to sleep in the hayloft."

Of course he wouldn't be living with them. Her parents have strict rules about everything, including boys. Neither she nor her sisters are allowed boyfriends while living at home, and have not been allowed to visit boys' houses since fifth grade, not even their school friends. They're allowed to hang out with boys in public only within the town limits, if her parents know the boy and his family well—preferably through Beth El—and if Papa drives them to and from Fox Hollow's one diner, or the Pineapple, the town's small theater. They are only allowed dates at the Pineapple if one of their sisters accompanies them. Their mother says it's not her daughters who she doesn't trust; it's the world she doesn't trust to have a care for what's most precious to her. As if Malka and her sisters are nothing but treasured jewels Mama fears to lose.

And Papa? He's happy to enforce the rules, and remind them of the pain they'll cause their mother, who has already suffered so much in this life, should they protest.

So of course, a strange boy won't be staying in their house, sharing their bathrooms, crossing paths with them in the night . . .

"But," Shosh says cheerfully, "he'll be around all the time. He's going to be helping Papa pull out those dead oaks, the ones the gypsy moths get to." Their father's been wanting to cut those down before one of them drops onto the barn roof and takes it down. Though Mama would probably welcome the barn's destruction. It came with the land when Papa bought it, and is one of the many things the girls are forbidden from. A deathtrap, she calls it, riddled with opportunities for tetanus, perched forever on the verge of collapse.

"Where did he come from?"

"I don't know. Geela says he's new in town—she answered the door when he knocked, and heard Papa talking to him. He doesn't have family in Fox Hollow. But he's Jewish. And *cute*."

Malka hadn't gotten a good look, half hidden as he was by the flowers. Mostly she saw broad shoulders and the brim of a baseball cap. She'll have to take Shosh at her word. "Is he staying for Shabbat?"

"He has to go see about an apartment—he doesn't have a place to live yet, but Papa said there's one for rent over Frager's—but he'll be back soon after, and he's staying for dinner. If we hurry, you can see him before he leaves! Come *on*," Shosh pleads, tugging her arm. Her perfectly round face practically glows with anticipation. And is that . . . Yes, her sister is wearing lip gloss. She also smells of an unfamiliar perfume. Probably rubbed it on from a sample in some magazine the moment she heard a boy was coming to dinner. "Mali, let's *go*."

Used to following her sisters' commands, Malka twines her long, blond hair into a braid, fingers trembling with the excitement of something, *anything*, new. Still, she giggles along with Shosh as her sister tugs her by the wrist from her room, down the attic staircase, and through the kitchen, where she just catches a glimpse of her mother before they're out the back door and sneaking through the field. The boy is behind the barn when they edge around it, inspecting the oak trees alongside Papa—all but one, the tallest of them, are leafless, dead or dying.

With hushed squeals, the sisters sink down to the earth, jostling the wildflowers. They link elbows and lie flat beside the old building under the beating sun. At last, Malka gets a better look at the boy. His face is still shadowed by the brim of the baseball cap and turned away, but she sees the dark curls spiraling out from beneath it, and the lean biceps that strain his cuffed T-shirt. She eyes the dusty brown cords that ride low on his hips, and the strong, tanned fingers he skims across the flower tops as he listens to Papa.

Cute or not, the boy could be a jerk, or deadly boring, she reminds herself. But the truth is this: Malka's whole life is a tightly controlled loop between farmhouse, school, and synagogue. Her parents' overprotectiveness has nothing to do with their religion, or at least, not in the usual way. Her family isn't even the most observant at Beth El, a conservative temple. It's more complicated than that.

None of her grown sisters have strayed far; Esther still lives in Fox Hollow, and Ruth and Bina are practically neighbors in nearby Warborough. All lived at home while attending college close by, or until they married their childhood sweetheart, like

Esther and Bernie. It's expected that Malka will do the same, though she won't apply to college until the fall, when she'll be a senior at the small high school where Papa teaches history. If she wants to go farther than Ruth and Bina, she'll join Shosh and Geela at Stern. This is all but decided. Just as it's all but decided that she will pick a nice boy from her hometown, or one from the city who Papa's cousin and his wife can vouch for. She will pick a safe, sensible career . . . or rather, a job, one she can give up when it's time to raise the children, the way Mama did. And she will bring those children to her parents' house for Shabbat dinner each week, as her sisters do with their husbands and young children. They say it's to be with family, but Malka knows it's to see Mama, who never learned to drive herself and hardly likes to leave their property, and who would surely sink into unending sadness without the comfort of her daughters around her, as Papa often reminds them.

Of course, Malka doesn't want that for Mama. But while she's only seventeen, her greatest fear is that her life will never, ever change. That she'll be buried here, maybe right out in these damned flowers. That she won't even make it as far as the trees, or within sight of the river.

So the fact that the boy has no roots here makes him fascinating. Whether he's cute is almost beside the point.

Her parents will be watching him whenever he's around. Watching their daughters, too, for their own good.

Still, Malka has hope.

FIVE

WHEN IT'S TIME for dinner, I repin my hat so securely that my scalp hurts, which at least distracts me from my stomachache. I'm dreading the evening, don't even want to go downstairs. I'd much rather slide beneath the dusty plaid quilt and come out only after midnight, when everybody's long gone or asleep. Then I could explore without being seen, like a bat in the dark.

But I'm the one who insisted we come, and insisted we stay. While the thought of all that attention makes my skin crawl, we'll have to face everyone eventually. Better to do it when it's only the horns I have to hide. Who knows what I'll wake up with tomorrow?

Esther knocks on the attic door half an hour before sunset. She pauses at the sight of me, with my winter clothes in July, and at Gabe in a kelly-green-and-white checked bowling shirt and khakis—one of his more low-key outfits. Bewildered by what she probably thinks is city fashion, she withholds comment and simply asks, "Did you get ahold of your mom?"

Gabe nods, his jaw tight. "She's really sorry about the mistake."

"Mm," is all Esther says.

As we enter the dining room, large and dazzling in the prismed light of the crystal chandelier overhead, Gabe murmurs just loud enough for me to hear above the chatter, "Fuck me. We have insta-family."

The Eggerses are gathered around a table as long as the room and so crammed with chairs that a ghost couldn't slip between them. In each chair sits a stranger, only not. Because I see pieces of me and Mom all over. There's my black hair, and my mother's wheat gold. Her hazel eyes, my small but wide-ribbed frame, my freckles on a middle-aged woman and a preteen boy. I don't see the pink-haired girl in the suit jacket from this afternoon; she must be among the five percent of Fox Hollow's population that isn't related to us.

Gabe throws his arm around me to squeeze my shoulder, and as always, I feel braver beside him.

We try to keep track of everyone's names while Esther introduces them. "There're your aunts—that's Shoshanna, Geela, Ruth, and Bina. And their husbands, your uncles, Aaron, Jacob, Eli, Dan. Bernie, my husband, is over in the corner by the plant. Then we've got your cousins . . . There's a load of those as you can see, can barely remember them all myself." Polite laughter circles the dining room at that. "The littlest ones are mine and Ruth's grandchildren, so they'd be your . . . what, second cousins? First cousins once removed? Who knows, but there they are." She waves at the three lap-bound babies. "And these," she announces as if everyone weren't aware already, "are

Malka's children, Gabriel and Hannah Kowalski."

"It's actually Williams," Gabe corrects her. "Our last name."

"Oh," Esther says. "I didn't know."

Ever since reading Jitka's obituary, I've kicked myself for never considering the possibility that Mom wasn't using her real maiden name, that Williams was a fake. Then again, who would've guessed something like that about their own mother?

Aunt Esther continues, clearing her throat through the awkward silence. "If you two want to take a seat, we've got the candles to light." She points us toward our chairs, wedged between Bernie-by-the-corner-plant and the preteen boy with the freckled nose and cheeks. He gapes at my brother's fluffed-up blue hair and guyliner in total awe.

I stare downward, childishly pretending that nobody can see me if I don't look at them, which gives me a chance to inspect the table. Every plate and cup on the lace tablecloth is bone colored and gold rimmed, and so thin I feel like it might split down the center if I spear my salad too enthusiastically. I'd always wondered whether Mom's unwillingness to talk about her past meant she'd left some awful situation behind, like a childhood spent in terrible poverty.

Apparently not.

Esther takes the empty seat at the head of the table, right in front of a big bay window that frames her in purple twilight. Drawing a long match from its box, she lights a pair of thick white candles in a polished silver candlestick, elaborately filigreed. She waves her hands between the flames and her face three times, as if gathering the light to herself, then covers her eyes and says the blessing in a breathless tumble of consonants strung together by choked *cha*s. When she uncovers her eyes again, the whole family choruses, "Shabbat shalom!" around us. Then they turn to kiss and hug the person beside them; I end up in Uncle Bernie's brief, brusque embrace.

After that, it's a blur of blessings. Over the ceremonial handwashing, over the wine, and over the challah, the braided, golden-brown bread I've bought from the kosher delis at Coolidge Corner just because we like the taste. We pass two loaves around the table, ripping pieces off to eat with a sprinkle of salt, which reminds me that I haven't had anything since Boston. Suddenly, my stomach is a yawning pit.

This signals the end of the serious rituals, luckily, and the beginning of dinner. Bowls and plates are passed around so the relatives stationed near the smaller pots of chicken noodle soup and bowls of salad can dish it out. Then the chatter begins again, immediately turning to us.

"Tell us," Aunt Shoshanna commands between bites. "What do you two know about your grandmother?"

Gabe raises his linen napkin to his lips, where only I can see him spit a small bone from the soup into its cloth folds. "Not much. The obituary said she was born in Prague?"

"Pah, and that's how you found out? From her obituary?" Aunt Ruth asks, aghast. "Malka never told you?"

I want to defend Mom, but from what? The truth?

"Such a shonda," Bina, the aunt with the slight build like mine, mutters bitterly.

Gabe's top teeth strum his piercing.

"Please," Aunt Esther cuts in. "Shabbat is for peace." She turns to us, her voice deliberately soft. "Mama lost everybody during the war. They were living in Prague when the Nazis occupied Czechoslovakia. Maybe you know the history already, though you don't know ours. Her father, your great-grandfather, was an important man in the community—they say his ancestors were rabbis—and a very talented artist. But it would've hit their family like the rest: Bit by bit, bad news after bad news. Thrown out of public pools, then put under curfew. The children kicked out of school one month, then banned from parts of Prague they'd been in and out of their whole lives. It got worse and worse, horror by horror, but Mama's family was trapped. Everybody was. Pushed out of their fine homes and apartments. They would have had to wear the yellow Star of David at all times. Across the country, Nazis were destroying synagogues and cemeteries. As they took the Jews out of Prague, Mama's family was put on a train to Theresienstadt. Some of them died there, others were sent on to Auschwitz and Majdanek. Eight brothers and sisters, her parents and grandparents, everyone she loved . . . all gone. Only Mama made it out before the war. She found her way to America when she was only a little older than you, Hannah."

There's a weight inside of me, solid and spiked, like a pit inside a peach.

"We didn't know any of that," Gabe says faintly.

"Mama never liked to talk about it. In fact, she never told us. We only know what happened in Prague from history, and the facts of her family's deaths. We found out through a genealogical website, thanks to your aunt Ruth. Mama always carried her grief with her, but she didn't want that for us, and she wouldn't want that for you two. So I don't tell you this to make you sad. But you deserve to know where and who you came from. Jitka Eggers was a brave, brave woman."

"How did she die?" I surprise myself by asking.

"Her heart," Aunt Geela near-whispers. "It was a heart attack. She'd been perfectly healthy the Shabbat before, for a ninety-eight-year-old woman. I—" She presses a shaking fist to her lips.

"Geela found her out in the field behind the house, almost to the trees," Esther finishes, while Geela's husband pulls her close. "You know, Bernie and I came to live with Mama after Papa passed, more than twenty years ago, alav ha-shalom. We'd offered for her to live with us at the time, of course, but she wouldn't think of leaving this house, and we all hated to imagine her out here in the woods, alone. She was in her mid-seventies by then. So we moved in, raised the youngest of our daughters and sons here, and saw them all leave again. Bernie splits his time between home and the city for work, but I'm always here to help . . . except that, as I said, Leah had just had the baby." She nods toward a young but tired-looking woman with a newborn in her arms. "I was staying with her in town.

Just for two weeks. We tried to get Mama to come to town too, stay with one of my sisters, where things were a bit quieter. When she refused—said that she was starting something, a new art project, and she wanted peace and quiet—I was happy. Mama hadn't painted in so long. We made sure we all took turns coming out to visit her and spend some time, at least once or twice a day. She had no real health problems," Esther says urgently. "She was always strong for her age, and still so sharp. Of course we worried, we always worried, but . . ."

Ruth picks up the story when it seems Esther can't go on. "They told us she hadn't eaten or drunk anything in days. There was plenty of food in the house, and we were always offering to take her into town for lunch. She made excuses. She said she was busy with her project. We just . . . we never imagined what was happening."

"I'm sorry," I say to Geela, to everyone, horrified.

"We never even found the painting," Geela murmurs.

Shoshanna shakes her head and smiles. "We miss Mama, of course we do. And we'll always wonder why. But you know, I don't think she would've guessed, during the war, that she would go at the age of ninety-eight, on the land where she'd married her husband and raised her daughters, in a field of flowers."

"To Mama," Aunt Bina says suddenly, too loud in the quiet room, lifting her wine glass. "L'chaim."

"L'chaim!" the aunts and uncles and cousins cheer, raising their glasses to sip, so we do the same.

Not for the first time in the last six weeks—not for the hundredth time—anger at Mom flash-heats my blood. She claimed that everything she'd done was to keep me safe. But from what? From this place and these people who've taken us in? What was she so afraid of that she kept us away?

I'D SET MY alarm for five so I could rise and groom before the rest of the house, but I wake before it even goes off, with an aching back and a few lingering images from dreams. A castle on a hill over a frozen river, with cloud-piercing spires. Busy cobblestone streets. Ice-glazed roofs, bright red and green and bronze against a silver winter sky. At first, I wonder if that's what woke me.

But no, the air mattress is to blame. It's completely deflated, leaving nothing between me and the hardwood floor but a wrinkled puddle of rubber. Probably sat in Esther and Bernie's basement for years, unused, before he was made to dig it up for us. I lie there, listening to the AC whir up from the vents and feeling just a bit salty with Gabe, even though I was the one who told him he could have the attic's only bed (knowing my brother would be too much of a gentleman to refuse). My beanie's come loose in the night—I slept in it in case a relative were to chaotically pop into the attic unannounced—and I slide my fingers through my hair to work any persistent bobby pins free from the short tangles before tugging it on again. Still sleep-fogged, it takes a moment before the obvious hits me, but then my whole body clenches like a fist.

Of course, the horns are gone.

Heart leaden with dread, I force myself to sit up, a stripe of pain lighting down my spine. Stupid mattress. Except as I reach behind me to knead my muscles, I cry out—not from the agony in my back, but in my fingers. Gabe jerks upright in the bed behind me, fumbling for the wall switch, and I blink in the light before examining my hand. Wicking the blood away with my T-shirt hem, I find a half dozen cuts, shallow and small but throbbing, as though I've pressed my fingers down on a bed of nails.

"Oh, fuck . . . ," Gabe mutters.

"Is it really bad?" I ask, fresh blood beading up, a tremor in my hands and in my voice.

"No, it's . . . we can cover it. It's not that bad, Banana. You're okay." He flies to his suitcase and pulls out the plastic first aid kit we took from beneath our kitchen sink and stripped of anything useless—latex gloves and ointments and thermometers—and restocked with whatever we might need. He pulls out packets of antiseptic wipes, cloth compresses, a box of Band-Aids and adhesive cloth tape, piling them at my feet, then kneels on the flattened mattress behind me. Carefully, he pulls the fabric of my T-shirt from my back, and I yelp, the sensation like dragging a brush through knotted hair.

"Arms up," he says softly, and as gingerly as possible, peels my shirt over my shoulders, leaving me in my sports bra. I examine the black fabric of the tee, stippled straight down the back with dozens of holes just big enough to see the skin of my palm through. I clutch it to my stomach, letting it soak the blood from my fingertips, while Gabe fumbles with one of the packages. "Okay, I'm just gonna—"

"I want to see," I say, though I very much don't.

I feel him pause, then rise. He goes back to the bed for his phone and takes a picture while I try to keep from shaking. Not with pain; my hand has settled into a dull throb, and it only feels like there's light pressure against my spine. But a single thought plays over and over, as always, like a song you can't shake until it drives you crazy:

My body isn't my body. My body isn't my body. My body isn't my—

"Here," Gabe says, holding his screen up for me to see.

Dorsal fin. My brain supplies the words, an unconscious thought. It's mottled and wicked looking, just like the webbed needle-spines that run down a stonefish's back. The finger-length spines start just below the nape of my neck. No wonder I tore my shirt—and my skin—to shreds.

"We'll put the cloth compresses over it, tape the spines down," Gabe assures me. "They seem flexible. As long as they don't shift, they shouldn't tear much. Wear a sweatshirt, and don't let anyone pat you on the back, I guess. We'll check it throughout the day. Nobody will know."

He's right. The spines are somewhat collapsible, and once they're padded and taped as flat as possible, I reach back to feel the rise of them beneath the cloth. Under bulky clothes and a hood pulled tight around my neck, you won't be able to tell. I can hide this, at least for the day. Shiva ends after next Tuesday, which means we have four days, counting this one—four days to find answers, to find someone who might tell us where Mom is, before the house clears out. Esther will demand to speak with our mother, and there won't be any excuses left. But I'll be lucky to make it that long without discovery. One morning, I'll wake up with something worse, I know it, like fur bristling across my skin. Gabe and I have no plan for that, beyond me faking an illness and hiding beneath my covers. I just hope it doesn't happen before our long-lost family gets to know us well enough not to call the Centers for Disease Control on me.

Or an exorcist.

Quickly and quietly, I grab clothes and my backpack with my toiletry case inside (holding it by the loop, since I can't wear it) and tiptoe down the steep staircase to wash up in the bathroom off the kitchen. The world outside of the small, square window is just softening to purple, the moon a pale stamp on the sky. The mirror over the sink is covered, too, which is fine by me. Trying to keep the Band-Aids on my fingers dry, I splash water on my face and finger-comb my hair with my undamaged hand. I'm in a hurry to get back to Gabe and the safety of the attic.

But when I pass back through the kitchen, it isn't empty any longer.

A woman in a floor-sweeping bathrobe stands with her back to me, hands braced on the rim of the huge farmhouse sink, head bowed.

As I rock back in surprise, the checkered sage-and-white tile groans beneath my weight, giving me away. The woman snaps around: Aunt Shoshanna. Black curls frame her face, perfectly round and pale, like a bread roll before baking. "Good morning, Hannah."

I tuck my bandaged fingers inside the billowing sleeves of the one hoodie Gabe packed: pumpkin orange, with sharks swimming across it. "I didn't know you were staying here."

"Just for the night. None of us are shomer Shabbat except Esther, but we all thought we'd walk to synagogue with her. We'd walk every Saturday growing up. It's not even three miles, but Mali—Malka, I mean, your mom—was the baby, so for a while, one of us would carry her a good part of the way." She recalls this with a tilted smile and distant eyes.

"We didn't even know we were Jewish," I confess. "I mean, that you all are Jewish."

"Oh, but you are. Because your mother is. That's how it works."

I'd read about matrilineal descent in traditional Jewish law. It's still strange to think a thing like that could be planted in me at birth, could survive without any tending for seventeen years, without ever seeing the light, and only now burst into bloom. I don't know how I feel about that, so I just nod.

"Of course, Gabe would need to convert, if he were

interested," she says, almost apologetically. "Unless his birth mother was Jewish—do you know?"

"I . . . no."

"It's a matter of Halacha—Jewish law, that is. But know that we consider him Malka's son in every other way."

If the quills along my spine weren't taped down so securely, I think they'd bristle. When somebody tries to assure you of something you've known your entire life, it's hard not to take offense.

"Will you and your brother be joining us?" Shoshanna continues before I can muster a protest.

My heart hammers in my chest, in my ears, in my still-throbbing fingertips at the thought of it: a synagogue full of people staring at us over the tops of their prayer books. Maybe I can hide behind Gabe in a dimly lit Thai restaurant, but in our mother's synagogue? Unlikely. Still . . . we can't pass up the chance to see all of the people who knew Mom growing up, and might have some piece of the puzzle to drop into place. Maybe our mysterious mailer is among them—they sent a notice from the synagogue instead of whatever newspaper might have printed Jitka's obituary, after all. Mom's sisters haven't seen or heard from her in years, but that doesn't mean that nobody has.

"Sure." I smile thinly. "We'd love to."

"Wonderful. Everyone will want to meet you. Word spreads, a town like Fox Hollow, and folks will be curious about Malka's children."

Lifting my shoulders so the oversize hood pools higher around my neck, I ask, "Has nobody around here really heard from Mom in eighteen years? That's what Esther said."

My aunt sags back against the sink. "At first after she left us, we'd still get phone calls, little presents in the mail on our birthdays, postcards from the places she traveled to. Some beach in the Florida Keys one month, Morocco the next."

This story sounds familiar. Mom's always been a wanderer. While I've never seen a childhood photo of her, there are plenty of pictures of her ankle-deep in oceans every shade between navy, turquoise, and gray; drinking a bottle of beer in an out-door bar, all of the signs in Italian; riding a donkey down a narrow cobbled street between white buildings, her honeyed hair tucked into a bandanna. As far as I can tell, the longest Mom's ever lived in one place was with Dad in Colorado. She left Colorado with us right after the accident, and hasn't stopped moving since—that is, until I convinced her to settle us in Boston. It took a detailed spreadsheet mapping out my future, what I could do with a stable high school education at a place as prestigious as Winthrop, where I'd already secretly applied and been awarded a huge scholarship, just to convince her that this thing I wanted so badly *might* be nearly as important as whatever she was searching for from town to town and state to state, but could never seem to find.

"We got pictures when your brother was adopted," Aunt Shoshanna continues. "We thought maybe, now that she had a child . . . now that she remembered what *family* meant . . . she was coming around, coming back to us. We thought she'd come home. But she never did. And before your brother was a year old, we stopped hearing from her altogether. She didn't have a cell phone then, so we'd call the house, and your father would say she'd gone out, even though we could hear Gabriel crying in the background. We sent letters, and she never answered. Then one day, the line was disconnected. And our letters came back undeliverable a few weeks after that, with no forwarding address. One of your uncles even paid for a site where you can find people's addresses, but all we found out was that your father had died. I'm truly so sorry about that, Hannah. We thought we'd hear about it if she—if something ever happened to her, too. But we never knew for sure. It breaks our hearts that Mama passed without knowing that Malka was alright."

"That doesn't mean she didn't love Jitka," I insist, maybe because I want it to be true. I want to believe at least that much of Mom.

"Oh, Hannah—I didn't mean to make you think you had to answer for your mother. She made her own choices, and she had her reasons." The words are generous, but Shoshanna's jaw is tight around them, broadcasting their bitter taste.

"What *were* her reasons? Why did she leave?"

Her forehead puckers. "If she never told you, I'm not sure it's my place."

"But it was so long ago! That's all history. It's not like it's hurting anyone to talk about it."

Shoshanna's laughter has thorns. "History. Right. Okay, I

will say, my sisters always thought I was the boy-crazy one, until your mom up and ran away with the farmhand."

"The farmhand?" I splutter.

"Close enough. He was a boy Papa hired to do some work around the property. We lost a stand of big old oak trees to gypsy moths and a harsh winter, and Papa wanted them taken out before they fell. He probably should've hired a company, but he didn't want trucks and machinery trampling through the meadow, digging up the flowers. It was Mama's favorite place in the whole world. So he posted an ad in the local paper, and this boy answered. He had experience and a strong back. Cute, too. He was around most of the summer—they were big trees, and it was slow work—till our parents found out he and Malka had something going on. They gave him his tools and his last check and sent him on his way, and we all thought that was the end. We figured he'd move right on out of town. But Malka had a bad fight with our parents over it, and stayed home from synagogue one day—"

"What did they say to each other?" I can't stop myself from interrupting.

"Don't know, exactly. Geela and I were upstairs getting ready for services—we could only hear the shouting, not the words. Anyway, when we got home, she was gone. Just a note on the fridge, saying not to come after her. And the boy was gone too, left town with her. Abandoned his room above Frager's. Malka wasn't even a month away from eighteen, and we thought for sure Mama would've called the police, begged them to find her and bring her home, but she did nothing. And Papa followed her lead." Shoshanna's eyes fog over, peering into the past. "After all that trouble and grief, I guess it didn't work out. I can't even remember the boy's name now. It's been too long."

"He—the farmhand, that wasn't my dad, right?" I have to ask.

"No. It wasn't Michael—that's your father's name, isn't it? I remember your mother telling us about him. I remember how happy we were that your mother had found somebody. He sounded like a good man."

This is too much to take in at once, and I'm figuring out my next question when the grandfather clock in the parlor tolls six times.

Shoshanna straightens, shoving herself off from the sink. "I better get upstairs to dress. The men will be up soon." She pats my shoulder as she passes by, and I hope she doesn't feel me flinch. "We'll talk more. Be'ezrát hashém, we've got time." She shuffles out of the kitchen in her bathrobe, leaving me with the ever-more-complicated mystery of my mother.

SEVEN

WHILE GABE AND I get ready in the attic, I share what I learned from our aunt.

"Mom pulled a Princess Bride?" he asks, scrubbing a palm across his faint morning stubble. "Okay, that's interesting and all, but what does it mean? Like, let's say Mom ran off to live happily ever after with the farmhand. What does that have to do with—" He waves a hand at me, this body, this goddamn dorsal fin.

Though I have nothing to hide from my brother, I still shrink at the gesture, my body curling in around the edges. I'm armored up for synagogue in a baggy long-sleeve black crewneck and black jumper dress that brushes the floor. "I don't know. It's something though, right? If we can figure out where she was and who with, maybe we can figure out where she is. It's a lead."

He nods encouragingly, ungelled teal hair tumbling over his forehead. "Definitely. So what do we do with it?"

That, I don't have an answer for just yet.

Once we're ready—Gabe practically funereal in slacks and

a pink short-sleeve satin dress shirt with enormous pearl buttons—we wait with the gathering family in the parlor. I press myself into a corner, half shielded by my brother, while I thumb through a condolence book set out on the side table for shiva visitors to sign. Though I tell myself it's to pass the time, I know I'm looking for a name that I won't find—Malka Williams/Kowalski/Eggers was never here. But I read each entry just in case, stupidly hoping . . . Which is how the name *Ari Leydon* catches my eye. Not the name, actually, but the handwriting. Small and neat, with circles above the lowercase *i*'s.

"Be right back," I mumble to Gabe.

I slip out of the parlor, down the hall, and up the attic stairs, where I start digging through my backpack, into the zippered pocket where I've kept the two clues we have: the hamsa, still in its cardboard box, and the envelope. The one Jitka's obituary came in, with its strange handwriting. Small and neat, with hollow circles above the lowercase *i*'s.

Our family walks in a pack along the forested road. I know from our cab ride yesterday that it'll eventually turn to more closely clustered homes, a fair few with plaques marking their age and historical significance, then to quaint downtown Fox Hollow. We only glimpsed the outskirts from the bus station yesterday, and won't get the chance to see it this morning, since the synagogue's only a block or two from the station. But from where we start walking at Mom's childhood home, it's so rural that we haven't even reached a neighboring driveway before I finish catching Gabe up on my discovery.

"Detective Williams," he says with an approving nod and a quick golf clap, quiet enough that aunts and cousins won't hear. "You're sure the handwriting's the same?"

"Not *sure*, but whoever it is, we should find them, right?"

"Definitely." Then he nearly slaps me in the head as we march through a thick cloud of gnats.

After the hour-long walk through the damp morning heat and patches of bugs wherever the hidden river nearly touches the road, I should be relieved to reach Beth El Synagogue. It's a squat brick building with plain windows, mercifully air conditioned once we pass through the front doors. But even my brother can't protect me from the eyes that seek us out, the weird bananas in the Eggers bunch. I tuck my head down and try to blend, following our family into the . . . I don't even know what it's called, the main room with two rows of pews on either side of the carpeted aisle, small and fairly packed. There's a stage at the front of the room with a wide wooden podium, draped in a velvet thing like a tablecloth. A stained-glass cupboard just beyond it is the fanciest thing in the synagogue. As a Black woman around Mom's age in a suit dress and a striped shawl takes the stage, Gabe and I sit, sandwiched between our aunts and cousins.

I can't pretend I pay close attention to the whole service; I don't exactly speak the language, and it's wildly uncomfortable to sit in the pew for any length of time without leaning against the hard backrest. Mostly, I try to follow along with our family.

I stand when they stand, sit when they sit, face the fancy glass cabinet and the Torah they take out of it (research!) as a man carries it around the room. He moves slowly enough for folks to lean in and press their prayer shawls or prayer books to the fabric cover to kiss. Then it's back to standing, sitting, staring up at the stage, and looking down at the prayer book unopened in my own lap. I think about the fact that Mom must've known these rituals, must've spoken these words, but never taught them to us. She never even gave us the choice to learn.

The only part of the service in English is a sermon the rabbi gives on the Torah reading, which was apparently about loving God and fulfilling the commandments from our hearts, specifically on a holiday called Tu B'Av that happens to fall today.

"Though Tu B'Av is thought of as a minor holiday, like a Jewish Valentine's Day, in rabbinic literature it's a time of comfort and healing after the grief of Tisha B'Av, the saddest of days on our calendar. We don't forget the heartache of the five calamities, or the First Crusade, or the expulsions of the Jews, or the Shoah. But today, we place our faith in love. A love that does not pretend away pain, but grows to encompass it, like a scar around a healing wound. A love that exposes and embraces the best and worst of us. A love that stays.

"We're commanded by the Torah: V'ahavta l're'echa kamocha. You shall love your neighbor as yourself. We're commanded: V'ahavta et Adonai elohecha. You shall love Adonai your God—this is today's Torah reading. And we're commanded: V'ahavtem et ha-ger. You shall love the stranger. If we can figure out how to do that, then we might better love our families, our partners, ourselves. So that is the work of Tu B'Av, to embrace a scarred world and to trust the world with our scars. To choose, in the face of pain, to love and to be loved."

I don't know about all of this. Not just the God parts—I never gave a lot of thought to him . . . her . . . them? About the same attention I paid to Santa Claus, I suppose. Why would I need an omniscient, all-powerful force controlling creation when I learned about biopoiesis in seventh grade? But really, it's the part about trust that turns my stomach.

I trust my brother, and I guess I trust myself—parts of myself, anyway. My hard work, my goals, and my determination that nobody else should ever see how hard I sweat so that the Hannah I am at Winthrop can shine. How can I trust a neighbor, a stranger, a magical sky being with the whole truth when I don't trust myself? Even my mother doesn't know who I am.

After the rabbi's closing announcements, including a mention of Jitka's shiva to resume tomorrow, we all rise for the last time. Esther immediately beckons us out of the Eggers crowd to bring us to see the rabbi, just climbing down from the stage. "Hannah and Gabe," our aunt says, "this is Rabbi Kayla. I thought you might want to say hello, ask any . . . questions."

Since our names are all the information the rabbi needs to give us meaningful nods, she obviously knows who we are already. Her eyes glow bright and warm. "Yehi zichra baruch," she declares, or something like it. "That's something we say to those who are grieving; may her memory be a blessing."

Even Gabe doesn't know how to answer this, and Esther has melted away, leaving us on our own. So I step up. "Thank you. We never . . . we didn't really know Jitka."

Of course, she knows this already. "Esther tells me you've only recently discovered your roots?"

"Very recently."

"I thought you might be wondering what it all means. It's weird, right? Nobody's ever surprised to learn that they're Catholic, or a Buddhist. But with us, these things happen. Judaism is more than religion, you know. More even than ritual and tradition. It's family." The rabbi smiles down at our blank faces. "We are all the children of Abraham, Isaac, and Jacob, and of Sarah, Rachel, Rebecca, and Leah. We are all united by the actions and sacrifices and the covenant of our ancestors. We were all born into the ancient story of our people, which still unfolds today. Know this, and everything else can be learned."

"I'm not, though," Gabe says with a lemon-twist half grin. "Since I'm adopted, I'm not their child, right?"

Aunt Shoshanna said the same this morning—albeit more subtly—but it's a different thing to hear it from Gabe. He's never used his own story as a punch line before, as a weapon.

Rabbi Kayla shrugs. "Judaism being a family also means it's one you can choose. Only you can decide who you are. But this isn't the time for lessons. Come and see me if you have any questions, all right? And try the rugelach at the kiddush—those little rolled pastries. Mimi Shapiro makes them, and they're delicious."

After she walks away, I turn to Gabe, gathering the courage to ask what he meant a moment ago, the small shame of having said nothing to Aunt Shoshanna writhing in my stomach. "Hey. Are you—"

"Ooh, look," he interrupts, pointing to the back of the room. "I spy a member of my tribe."

"According to Rabbi Kayla, they're all our tribe."

"No, not yours, *mine*."

I follow his gaze through the milling congregants to a flash of watermelon hair. The girl from yesterday's shiva stands in one of the back pews, seemingly alone. The crowd clears just long enough for me to get a better look as she turns to leave; today, her hair is piled up into a thick topknot so I can see her undercut, a triangle above the nape of her slim neck, short and dark. I feel a warm shiver down my own bladed spine. "You think?"

"With that shave? Strong odds. I didn't know if I'd find one in the wilds of upstate New York." Gabe reaches into a pew and tugs one of our young cousins toward us—the one who's been gazing worshipfully at my big brother since last night, like he's his new hero. "Who's that?" he asks.

Our cousin blushes beneath his freckles. "That's Ari. Her bubbe used to live next door to ours. Mrs. Silver? Now they're Leydons, though. I think our moms all grew up together."

"Wait. You said her name is Ari Leydon?" I ask.

He nods, and I waste no time skirting the crowd, sticking to the wall so that nobody bumps into me by accident and makes an unfortunate discovery. We spill out into the hallway just as Ari leaves through the synagogue's front exit. When we throw open the doors a moment later into the bright, beating sun, she's crossing the lawn toward the parking lot.

"Hey, girl in red!" Gabe shouts at her back.

She isn't even wearing red, just dark cuffed jeans and a slim navy button-down. But she stops in her tracks anyway.

"I knew it," Gabe mutters, then calls out, "You're Ari Leydon?"

She doesn't answer, but she doesn't move either.

"I'm Gabe, and this is Hannah. Williams?"

Ari turns to face us now, and I see her unobscured and daylit for the first time. Dark brows and steel-blue eyes. High cheekbones and a sharp jawline. No makeup, but gray nail polish that flashes when she shadows her eyes to stare at me. "You look a little like her," she announces in a low voice.

"Like . . . my mom?"

"Like Jitka. When she was young. I've seen pictures. She had your mouth."

Without meaning to, I press a hand to my lips, tracing their shape.

"Our mom is missing," Gabe says, quietly this time, glancing around to make sure none of our aunts or uncles are within earshot. "We haven't seen or heard from her in six weeks. Do you know her?"

She shakes her head. "I don't. But . . . I saw her."

My brother braces his hands on either side of the doorframe so that I'm barred behind his leanly muscled arms. "When?"

"Maybe a month ago? She came to my house to talk to my mom. It's a long story . . . a *weird* story." Ari glances toward the parking lot, then reluctantly, as if someone is forcing her to, turns back to ask, "You guys want a ride home?"

JUST BEFORE SUNDOWN that night, Malka throws open the door at the first knock to find Ida Silver, their neighbor who visits her mother regularly, and her daughter, Rachael. Short, round Mrs. Silver is in her usual colorful layers despite the heat, like a flower in full bloom. A self-described opshprekherke— a Jewish healer who practices with whispered charms, herbal remedies, and rituals—she wears the signs of her trade around her neck and at her wrists. A chai pendant on a red cord, a magic square, a medallion inscribed with the text of the Ana Bekoach. All to protect her from natural disasters, diseases, spells, and evil spirits . . . supposedly. The fox tooth she gave Malka's mother last month, worn dutifully in a silk pouch beneath her nightgown, probably hasn't cured Mama's insomnia so much as prescription pills have. But Mrs. Silver would rather walk down Main Street without a stitch of clothing than go without her charms.

Rachael Silver is her mother's opposite. Stark and cool, with a sharply pointed chin, sharp dyed-black baby bangs against powdered skin, and black platform shoes below her eggplant-purple velvet dress, all capped by a perpetual half frown. She's the bare-branched tree in winter beside Ida's flower, but Malka knows that, on the inside, she's alive and soft and green.

Still, Malka's face must fall at seeing them on the porch instead of the boy, because Mrs. Silver cackles. "You mean you weren't crouched behind the door waiting for this alter cocker?" She pats Malka's cheek with a callused palm that smells of garlic, which she uses in most of her cooking and cures.

After the Silvers come her oldest sister, Esther, twice her age, and her husband and young children. Then Ruth and Bina and their husbands and babies. Then at last, when the parlor is packed and noisier than even in their childhood, he arrives.

And when she runs to answer the door, Malka realizes at once that Shosh was wrong. He's not cute. He's *gorgeous*. The loose curls combed back from his face, falling behind and just below his ears, are rich and dark as potting soil. Pale-blue eyes fringed with dark lashes. A proud nose, a Czech nose, over the dark stubble of a mustache she imagines scratching against her skin. Upturned lips she also imagines pressed against her . . .

"Shabbat Shalom," he greets her, and her cheeks flash-heat as if he's said something dirty. "I'm Siman."

"Shabbat Shalom," she murmurs back.

After Siman has been introduced to the family, and the blessings recited and the meal begun, talk returns to the stranger at the table.

"And how old are you?" Esther asks him, though she keeps

a wary eye on her three youngest sisters. Now that she's a mother to her own children, she seems determined to act as though she's their mother too. Never mind that Mama sits at one head of the table across from Papa, as always.

"Nineteen," he answers.

"Are you in college, then?"

Siman smiles pleasantly, lips curling further. "Not yet, ma'am."

Malka presses her napkin to her own lips, trying not to laugh at Esther's grimace. So she can act like a stern altetshke, but doesn't like to be addressed as one?

"After I graduated high school early, I wanted to travel," he continues. "Get a better look at the world before I go back to textbooks. It's been a whole different kind of education."

Though Malka has a full plate of food in front of her, there's an insatiable feeling like hunger in her belly, and it only grows with every word he speaks.

"And your parents don't mind this?" Mama asks in a strained voice.

"They've got a lot of kids, like you, ma'am. I'm the oldest. They couldn't pay for school anyway, and they're happy to have one fewer of us around." He laughs, loose and carefree. "But I send them postcards wherever I go and call home every month. More when I can find a phone to call from."

"But how can you afford to move around so much?" Bina interrupts, keen-eyed as her father.

"I saved up a little money from working through high

school, but I also teach English lessons while I travel, or take on jobs between trips. Like this one." He nods gratefully at Papa.

The good mood that's buoyed Malka through dinner crumbles a little. Of course, this is just another job, just another stop before he wanders off. To Spain, or Morocco, or any of the million places more exciting than Fox Hollow, New York.

But not until the end of summer, she reminds herself.

Then it's Papa's turn to tell Siman the story of his family, and how the Eggerses came to Fox Hollow.

Like Mama, Papa was born in Czechoslovakia and raised in an Orthodox Jewish family. Unlike Mama's people, Bubbe and Zayde Eggers had the luck and the means to leave before the war. Papa spent his very early childhood on their modest but successful vineyard in the lush countryside of Mělník. His family even kept horses. But when things started to turn bad— worse than usual for Jews, that is—they didn't wait. They sold everything they could as quickly as possible and came to stay with Zayde's brother, already living in New York.

Great-Uncle Bernard lived not in the crowded tenements of the Lower East Side, but in a nice apartment on the Upper West Side, so even Papa and his parents did not have to share a room there. Bernard had built his own small empire in the garment business, opening a fine dress factory with many employees. Zayde Eggers joined him, and both of their fortunes grew. The men pressed Papa to join the business once he finished high school, and then college. But Papa wanted to move away from the city, build himself a nice house in the countryside such as he should've grown up in. To marry a nice girl and fill it with their children. Bernard knew just the shadchanit to find Papa a wife through the old ways, even though it was the late forties by then and plenty of Jewish men were finding wives the way anybody else did. And Papa hardly considered himself Orthodox anymore, striving less to be like his own father and more like his older cousins. They had been born in America, and so spoke perfectly unaccented English, and picked which parts of Halacha they followed for themselves. They wore modern clothes without kippahs, dated girls outside the faith, and played cards for money on Shabbat.

Still, it was mother's dearest wish that he take a good Jewish wife and raise his children in the faith, so it was the shadchanit who found Mama for Papa. She had come to America alone, and without much money ("A modest girl, in character and fortune," the shadchanit put it), but a beauty, and the granddaughter of a rabbi, and also from Czechoslovakia. What more could Papa want? And him, the handsome son of a prosperous businessman, now college educated, with an eye toward family. What more could she want?

Here, a small frown flutters across her mother's face, creases her brow, before she replaces it with a grateful smile. She's old now—already forty-seven when Malka was born, she's older than some of Malka's friends' grandmothers. Mrs. Silver, her true and only friend, is almost two decades younger. But Malka can imagine the girl she was back then, as little as she knows of her mother's story; only that her own parents died in Prague during the war, like everybody else Mama loved. Poor, scared, and grieving, she must have been like a girl in a freezing ocean. When a ship appeared to pull her from the water, she dared not complain about the accommodations on board.

"And so," Papa continues his own story, "we moved outside the city to start our family. I got hired on at the high school, and there was land for sale on the outskirts of town, a natural meadow. Cheap, but good. I saw the river, and the big trees, and the wildflowers that grew every year. I knew Jitka would love it. We never did get horses, but maybe someday we'll fix the barn up, and then who knows? Anything is possible. Like my parents and my uncle, I've made us a good home in America, a good life, b'ezrát hashém."

"But who was here before you?" Siman asks politely.

Papa hesitates, having expected nothing but the usual noises of admiration. "What do you mean?"

Across the table, Mama lifts an eyebrow, and Malka stifles a smile.

"It's just, the barn looks older than the house," the boy explains.

He's right. While the well-placed pine logs have held the structure intact, its shutters hang from their hinges, the windows sit glassless, and the roof sags like the heavy belly of a pregnant dog. It's easy to see why Mama, perpetually afraid for her children, has forbidden them from going near it. And from the woods beyond their property, where they might be lost forever, and from the river, which might suddenly flood its banks on a clear day and sweep them away . . .

"That came with the land," Papa admits. "So did the foundation of this house. There were a few old buildings out here, not much, built a long time ago, before the town incorporated the land. It's all Fox Hollow now. And what do you think of our town so far?"

"Beautiful, sir," Siman says. There's nothing disingenuous in his deep voice, or pale-blue eyes.

But when Papa looks down at his plate, the boy looks to *her*, looks straight into Malka's eyes, and *winks*.

This time, she doesn't even try to hide her smile.

EIGHT

THE TRIP BACK to Jitka's house should only take minutes, though it feels longer from the cab of Ari's orange behemoth of a pickup truck, where we slip in and out of awkward silence. "Your family won't be home for a while," she tells us as we drive through the historic district. "There's a kiddush after services. That's, like, a Shabbat lunch with prayers down in the synagogue rec room. Everyone stays to talk and eat the lox before it's all gone." She raises her voice so Gabe can hear her from the narrow jump seat behind Ari, where he's bouncing up and down.

I'd have thought he'd claim the passenger seat like he always does—his birthright by fifteen months, he insists—but now I see that he wanted to be able to shoot me significant glances and dramatic brow furrows without Ari noticing.

"You're sure they'll stay?" I ask, wincing as my back knocks against the seat. "You weren't going to."

"No, I wasn't," she says, evidently uninterested in explaining.

"Is your house around here?" I try for a new topic as we leave the closely clustered houses behind and pass into the shade of the trees. "Our cousin said your mom grew up with ours."

"They were best friends. Bubbe's house is—was—the next one down the road if we keep driving past Jitka's, but still almost a mile away. Unless you cut through the woods. Now we're downtown. My parents run an antique shop, and we live over that."

"So you've always lived in Fox Hollow?"

"Forever," she confirms. "And I can't wait to leave."

"Why?"

She cuts her eyes toward me. "You ever lived in a super-small town?"

"Sure. Like, seven of them."

She laughs, low and hoarse but not mean—I'm attuned to the laughter of people who've found a fault in you, always ready to correct course. "That's not the same thing. Nothing changes here, and nobody wants it to. Everyone's known you since your baby naming, so they don't see *you* as you grow up. Just the four-year-old in a princess dress who wandered off at the Fox Hollow Memorial Day parade, then had to ride around the town green on the 4-H float while they called out her parents by name through a bullhorn, because of course everyone knew who she was."

"Oof," Gabe contributes from the back.

"Nice that everyone cares about you, though," I push back.

"Sure, they care. That's why they get mad when they think you're trying to change."

I study Ari as inconspicuously as possible—her eyebrows as they pinch together while she talks, her fists as they tighten around the steering wheel until the leather squeaks, the curve of her ear, where half a dozen earrings wink in the sun. At Winthrop, a girl like this would probably sit with the alt kids in the back of study hall, their boots chunky, their piercings as creative as their parents will allow, some band like Creatures Such as We blasting from their one-in-one-out earbuds. Not with my friends, for sure.

Not that I'm sitting with them either, wherever they are.

I guess it's possible to be lonely in a town like this . . . in theory. But you'll never convince me that it's harder to grow up someplace where everyone knows your name, instead of in towns where even your teachers don't remember you, and don't really bother to until you start spending all your weekends studying math flash cards (because math has never come easy) and start turning in 100s on every single multiplication quiz. No way it's that lonely in a place full of people who love you.

Once at the house, we lead Ari into the parlor as if it's ours. It's a different room empty of mourners and Eggerses. Ari sinks awkwardly onto a settee with carved wooden legs, resting her elbows on her knees, hands clasped. I take one of the chairs opposite, and Gabe stands at my side, leaning on the high back behind me so he's perched like a falcon over my shoulder.

"So," he prompts.

"Right. So." She takes a deep breath, twisting her fingers in her lap. "You know that our moms were friends? So were our grandmothers. My zayde was in the army, and he was overseas a lot when Mom was a kid, so your grandfather would come around to check on them. And Jitka was . . . she wasn't well, a lot of the time. So Bubbe spent a lot of time here, helping her with that."

"Like, she was a nurse? Or a therapist?" Gabe asks.

"Bubbe was a healer. At least, *she* said she was; Mom doesn't believe in any of that stuff. She called herself an opshprekherke—I know it's a whole mouthful. They're like, this tradition in Jewish folk medicine. Women who worked in the shtetls of the Pale of Settlement, where Bubbe's family came from . . . my family, I mean. If you were regular-sick, maybe you went to a doctor. But if you thought someone or something had cast an ayin ha'ra on you, an evil eye that was making you sick, you went to an opshprekherke. Like a specialist."

A specialist. Someone who heals.

"Mom came to Fox Hollow to see your bubbe, didn't she?" I realize aloud. "Before she left home, she told me so."

"Well, she was three years too late," Ari says flatly. "What did she want a healer for? She didn't say, exactly."

I keep my face carefully blank. "I don't know. I didn't even think she believed in that stuff . . . Do you?"

"No." Her slate-colored eyes flash. "I mean, everyone has superstitions, right? Bubbe just . . . had a lot of them. For a fever, bury an iron knife beneath a bush. Keep a tooth from a dead fox close while you sleep to cure insomnia. Roll pieces of wool in vinegar and ashes, and stuff it up your nose to stop a bleed." She looks more uncomfortable by the second, one high-top squeaking as she taps it rapidly against the floor. "It was all stuff her mother taught her, and her bubbe before that. Basically, anything could be a symptom of an evil eye if you believe in it, and that's how she'd treat it. But a lot of what she did was pray with people, and meditate, and help them make peace with what couldn't be fixed. Some people, like your grandma . . . they'd been through a lot in their lives. And she helped. It wasn't all crazy."

Because she sounds so defensive, I protest, "I wasn't gonna say it was—"

"Anyway, it doesn't matter what I think. I brought it up because your mom *does* believe in it, apparently."

Then Ari tells her story, which is this:

Nearly a month and a half ago, Mom showed up at the Leydons' downtown apartment, above their family's antique shop. Ari was reading in her dad's office when Mom knocked, but their apartment is small and the walls onion-skin thin, so she heard her mother open the door and say, "You?"

Ari shut her book. Unfolding herself from the chair, she poked her head out of the office and peered down the hallway. She thought she recognized Mom—not who she was, but what she'd come for. She looked just like the people Ari had seen on her bubbe's front stoop when she was a kid, when she'd go to Ida's so she could watch Ari while her parents worked. Men and women from Beth El—which Ida would bring her to, even as her parents never did—came over, sometimes with mild complaints. Pain in the knees, or a toothache the dentist couldn't treat or explain. Some, though, came with a look of long suffering in their tired eyes. Ida never turned them away. She'd have them sit in the living room while she put a glass of milk and a plate of rugelach on the kitchen table for Ari. Though Ari knew she wasn't supposed to interrupt, Ida never closed the kitchen door or forbade her from listening.

Sure enough, the woman at the door then, who looked so much like her bubbe's most desperate visitors, said wearily, "I, um . . . I didn't want to bother you, Rachael, but . . . I'm looking for your mother. I went to her house, but it's . . . has Ida moved?"

For a long moment, Ari's mother didn't answer. "Shoshanna was in the shop yesterday, picking up some books she got rebound, and she didn't tell me you were back. Talked about everything from their kitchen remodeling to their kid's strike against frozen pizza, but never mentioned you, Malka."

Ari knew that name, knew Malka Eggers had been her mom's best friend from childhood, though she never said much about the woman. Malka was a cautionary tale among the older folks in Fox Hollow: the girl who ran away from home and got too lost to find her way back. She shifted forward for a better look, but the floor creaked beneath her feet, giving her away. Both women turned to spot her. Mrs. Leydon gave her a tight smile, said, "Never mind, Ari, go back to your homework!" then tugged Malka by the arm into their TV room.

Understandably curious, Ari crept after them, pausing on the other side of the archway and just out of view to listen.

"You have nerve," her mother said in a low, cold voice. "A lot of nerve, showing up now. My mother was good to you, Malka, and she spent her dying days without knowing where you ended up. None of us ever knew whether you were alive or—"

"She's dead?" Malka interrupted, faint enough that Ari could barely make out her words.

"For three years now."

A long silence, and then, "I'm sorry, Rach. I didn't know. She—she was so young, I hoped—"

"What do you want?" her mother demanded. "Why are you here? How did you even know where to find me?"

"I knew your married name—Shosh told me, years and years ago. I looked you up. I . . . I couldn't find Ida listed." Now, Malka seemed to steel herself. "We need to talk. About . . . about that summer. There's something I need your help with, but . . . see, my sisters can't know that I'm here, so if you could just—"

"No."

"But it's—"

"*No*." The word was a quiet thunderclap, if such a thing were possible; though Ari could barely hear her, the cold finality of the word seemed to rattle the windowpanes. "It's been over thirty years. You don't know me anymore, and you don't get to stroll through town, tear my life apart, and leave again."

Ari knew now that she shouldn't be listening in, but she

couldn't help it. If Ida Silver had been an open door, welcoming any and all who needed her, Rachael Leydon was a window barred by hurricane shutters. Never mean, but closed off, careful. It was as though she was always expecting calamity, in a town where nothing calamitous ever happened.

Was Malka Eggers the storm she'd been preparing for?

"I'm not trying to tear anything apart!" Malka lowered her voice as Mrs. Leydon shushed her sharply. "Believe me or not, I'm trying to make things right."

Ari's mother snorted in response.

"I know I hurt you, leaving you behind," Malka plowed onward. "I wish I could've stayed, explained . . . I wish I could've done things differently. But my mistakes are mine, and I've had to live with the consequences. My daughter shouldn't bear them."

Another moment of silence, and then, "I only heard you had a son. You have a daughter too?"

"I do. Her name is Hannah, and she's just around your daughter's age, it looks like. I had to leave my children behind. I'm here to fix what I've done, for her, and then . . . maybe I can fix us. I just need your help. We're—God, this is so hard to explain, to you of all people—we're in trouble, Rachael. Me, and my kids, and anyone who's—" she hesitated. "We're all in danger, because of me."

"What, are you in trouble with the Mafia or something? I don't think they're much of a presence in Fox Hollow, but if somebody's threatening you, for God's sake, go to the police."

"This isn't police territory. That's what I'm trying to tell you. It's Ida Silver territory."

"Oh, Malka—"

"I swear I didn't want to pull you back into my mess."

"Are you even going to see your family?" her mom demanded suddenly. "While you're sneaking around town, asking me about *my* mother, do you even plan on speaking to yours?"

"I . . . I can't. Mama can't know that I'm here, nobody in my family can, or none of us would be safe. I needed Ida because . . . something happened that day, the day I left. I was at your house, Rach."

"I . . . when? What?"

"Your mom wouldn't have told you, but . . . all right, listen. I gave her something that day. She was supposed to hold on to it for me, and now I need it back. God, this would be so much easier to explain if you believed in—"

"Stop, just stop." Ari's mother sounded so tired all of a sudden. "I obviously don't know what's happened to you in your life. I mean, how could I? All I ever got from you were postcards, a couple of random emails, then *nothing*. For eighteen years, nothing. So you don't know about my life, either. My mother wasn't well when she died, and clearly, neither are you. Those superstitions she was always on about? They became full-blown delusions in the last years of her life. She couldn't live in that house alone anymore, and she insisted on keeping her weird charms and amulets around her at all times in the nursing home. She was terrified of strangers. When a woman from a local charity was visiting the residents in their rooms to read to them, my mother had such a bad paranoid episode, they had to sedate her. It was dementia, plain and painful and simple. And now you show up, and you tell me we're all in danger, and it's *Ida Silver territory* . . . Malka, that's insanity."

"Rachael, please. It's important. Those charms, her things, if I could just look through them to see—"

"I trashed them. Threw them out when she died. I couldn't get rid of them fast enough. And now I'm gonna have to ask you to leave. Again." Her voice was dry as dust. As bones.

"You didn't," Malka whispered.

"What, you can throw away your family and your best friend, but I can't toss out some old costume jewelry?" her mother remarked, as bitter as Ari had ever heard her.

"All right," Malka whispered, defeated. "Just . . . I'm sorry, Rachael. I really am. For a lot of things. For Ida, and for the way I left . . . everybody. I just want you to know, okay?"

Mrs. Leydon said nothing to that, and Ari had just enough time to retreat to the office before Malka was hustled out the door.

Now, Ari reaches to pry a slim, battered leather wallet out of her back pocket. "Two weeks ago, I found this, in a car parked at Bubbe's house." She pulls out a sheet of paper, much folded and unfolded, I'd guess from the worn-thin creases, and holds it out. "I don't know how long it was there. I hadn't been by in a while, and you can't see the property from the road, not through the trees. Nobody would've noticed when she ditched it."

Gabe takes it, reading quickly. "It's a rental car receipt," he announces, "from a company in Hudson, New York—that's where we got off the train, right? Mom too, I guess. It has her name and address. Her signature, too."

"I told Mom, and she called the car company to get it towed, but she told me to forget it, that it would just hurt your family if they found out she'd been in town and left again without seeing them. Mostly, she was mad at me—I'm, um, not supposed to hang around Bubbe's old place. She moved into the nursing home years before she died, but her house never sold. There was termite damage, and funky wiring, and who's looking to buy an old, broken house in the middle of the woods, anyway? Mom didn't even put it on the market, so it's just been sitting. But I go there sometimes.

"Anyway, when Jitka died, and your mom wasn't even at the funeral, I figured something was wrong. Like, really wrong. Mom just says she's run off again, like people ditch their rental cars all the time, but . . . I thought if she had kids back home, they should know."

"So it *was* you who wrote to us." I share a look with Gabe, who mouths *Detective Williams*. "Why didn't you say any of this when you sent the death notice?"

"I tried. But every letter I started, I just sounded . . . like Bubbe." She drags a palm down her face, then shoves it into her hair, forgetting that it's pinned up. "If I sat around waiting to write the perfect letter, I'd never send it at all."

"Why *did* you send it?" Gabe asks.

Ari's foot taps all the faster. "I figured if you'd heard from her, or if she'd come home already, you'd just give her the notice. I thought she deserved to know. Or if you hadn't, and she really was . . . I don't know, missing? You could tell your dad, and he'd deal with it."

"We don't have a dad," my brother says.

"You don't even know us," I say in the same breath.

Clearly torn on which of us to respond to, Ari chooses me. "I know. But Bubbe would have wanted me to help if I could. She's the one who taught me about tikkun olam—that means different things to different, like, denominations of Judaism, but Bubbe said the world was broken in a lot of ways, and it's our job to repair it, however we can, one good deed at a time. She never charged the people she helped, just did it because she believed it was right. She would tell me to do the same. And . . . look, she died three years ago. She wasn't even—she didn't make a lot of sense at the end. I hardly got to see her. Mom thought it was better, like I should hold on to the good memories I have with her. But . . . I figured if Bubbe *was* out there, somewhere, I would want to know. So now you know."

My heart, which has been full up with my own pain and fear for the last six weeks, expands just enough to ache for Ari in the moment.

But while I'm trying to figure out what to say, how to comfort a stranger, she stands abruptly. "Okay, I should go. This is all giving me some really fun flashbacks and everything, but I have a shift at my parents' store at noon. I hope I didn't mess anything up, or make things worse."

"Well, bye," Gabe says.

"You didn't mess things up," I assure her. "Can we . . . can we talk again? Tomorrow, maybe?"

My brother shifts his hand to my shoulder, fingers flexing until I wince beneath them and he loosens his grip.

Already facing the parlor door, Ari hesitates. "I don't know anything more than I told you. But good luck, okay?"

I'm losing her—*we're* losing her—I can feel it. "You know the town," I rush to point out. "You know people who knew our mom. Maybe there's someone who can help us."

"Look, at the risk of sounding like *my* mother, why don't you guys just call the police? Or at least your family—you have like, so many people here. If you've just been on your own for the last month, what have you been doing?"

I try to think of an explanation less pathetic than *we didn't know they existed*, but settle on a slightly less pathetic, "It's . . . kind of complicated. Our family is kind of complicated."

At that, Ari turns back to look at me, wary eyes roaming across my face until I worry that I'm flushing beneath my freckles. "Yeah," she says at last in her softest voice yet. "Families are."

"So . . . can I give you my number, at least?"

Ari sighs, but nods. She makes me repeat it twice, saving it in her phone. At least, I hope she is. "Okay, I've got you." Then she leaves with an awkward finger salute and a faint dimple.

Gabe rounds on me the minute the door closes. "Really, Banana? You're bringing her in, like *in*? Did I miss the part of the story where we formed a detective club that drives around in a van, hotboxing and solving mysteries?"

"We need her," I insist.

"She already told us everything she knows."

If that's true, then we have a few answers, but so many new questions, each more worrying than the last. Did Mom actually think that Ida Silver could help me? I don't need a degree in health policy and management to have figured out this probably isn't some obscure medical condition, but something . . . stranger. Still, a Jewish healer?

What about the rental car? Mom can be forgetful, sure, but she wouldn't just wander into the woods and forget a whole automobile. Could it be she's still in town, lying low? I decide to hope for that outcome, refusing to consider other, darker explanations . . .

And what did she mean by that "my mistakes are mine and Hannah shouldn't have to bear them" speech? She'd said something like it in Fox Hollow; how she'd made mistakes, but done everything to keep me safe. I'd assumed she meant regular, mom-level missteps. Or hey, maybe she'd regretted dragging us around the country for sixteen years. The way she spoke to Rachael Leydon, though, made it sound as if whatever's wrong with me is somehow her fault.

I share my thoughts with Gabe before conceding, "Maybe

Ari thinks she's told us everything she knows. But we needed a lead, and she's it."

"You think we can trust her?" he asks, clearly dubious.

"You don't? I thought you said she was a member of your tribe?"

"Sure, but like, superficially. I'm a chinos gay, not an emo gay. Or, I was."

A text chimes on my phone, saving me from responding to that. I pull it out and see an unknown number and open it to read:

Now you have me

Esther mentioned yesterday that the family was clearing out after Havdalah, and we find out at sundown (always sundown with these . . . our . . . people) that this is a ritual to mark the end of Shabbat. The family gathers in the dining room one more time, and again, Esther leads the blessings. First over wine—everyone older than thirteen gets a shallow glass of it, us included, while our younger cousins get grape juice. Next, over a gorgeous spice box the size and shape of a pomegranate, enameled red. We pass it around the room, and when it reaches me, I cup its weight carefully and take a deep breath of cinnamon and citrus and cloves, and other unidentifiable scents.

Esther says a third blessing over a braided blue and white candle with multiple wicks, so that the miniature sparks flare into one bright flame, and the last, over the wine again. I sip mine tentatively, then slip my glass to Gabe to finish. Our aunt douses the Havdalah candle by pouring the last of her wine into a shallow silver dish and extinguishing its flame in the dregs.

We eat a light meal—bread and fruit and coffee set on platters for everyone to serve themselves. Then everybody leaving for their own homes says goodbye, promising to see us at shiva over the next three days.

That's all we've got before we run out of excuses to stay in Fox Hollow: three days.

With the house empty except for Esther and Bernie, there's no excuse not to move downstairs. I feel a little panicked at the thought of leaving our safe, stuffy nest in the attic, however briefly it belonged to us. But at least the dark oak sleigh bed is more comfortable than my ex air mattress. I crawl onto the floral peach-colored quilt, exhausted. The tape on my back tugs against my skin unpleasantly, spines ripping through and catching on Gabe's hoodie. I manage to squirm out of the sweatshirt, knowing he'll thank me for saving it. I throw on a tank top I don't mind shredding, one I'd never wear on its own, and lie on my stomach on top of the quilt.

The next thing I know, my alarm rings me awake, panting and heart pounding despite hours of inaction. Was I having a nightmare? I lie very still, trying to remember. Buried within the ordinary slush of my dreams like an ice chip hiding in a snowball, there's that castle. Those foreign streets. The frozen river and the red roofs. The images linger, sharp as a memory, the same as last night. I've never dreamed like this before.

Though I'm still sprawled atop the quilt, there's a weight

across my back from shoulder blades to waist, the sensation of something slick and warm and foreign against my skin. Forcing myself to keep calm, I reach back with trembling fingers and feel for the spikes that I know in my quickly sinking heart have vanished.

Instead, I've woken up with wings.

NINE

"GOTH AS HELL," Gabe says, whistling in astonishment.

Swiveling to stare at myself in the hallway bathroom mirror, I'm forced to agree. Not that I'd wish to wake up with wings, period, but couldn't I have sprouted fluffy white dove's wings, or jewel-bright butterfly wings? At least it would've been a pretty mutation. But no. The wings that have burst from my shoulder blades and through my tank top are a burnt-looking brown, stretched between impossibly delicate bones, like a fruit bat's. The skin is so thin that veins show through, spindly and black beneath the bathroom lights. They're flexible enough that when I experiment, pinching one between my fingertips with a deep shudder, I can tug it down and wrap it partly around my torso, where Gabe suggests we harness them with his belt—a faux-western cow-print abomination he retrieves from his suitcase.

We pin the wings to my back around my waist, a pillowcase tucked beneath the leather to prevent injury to the delicate membrane, and I wrestle his hoodie back on. But as soon as I do, it's obvious that this won't work. My body does *not* look right. The sweatshirt protrudes nearly half a foot behind my shoulders, fabric bulging. I can't explain this away, and I definitely can't sit shiva with my bulked-up waist and jutting shoulder blades, not even in the most shadowy corner. I can barely even sit.

There's nothing to do but deploy our only backup plan.

Gabe goes down to tell Esther, already shuffling around downstairs, that I'm bedridden by a migraine. When our aunt comes up to see me and bring me a glass of water and a breakfast plate, I'm strategically propped against the pillows in such a way that the hideous wings are wedged between them, with the quilt pulled up to my chin. The curtains are drawn, the lights off.

Following my brother's very helpful Acting Tips, I wince dramatically as hallway light washes across the room.

"So sorry," Esther stage-whispers, closing the door gently behind her. She all but tiptoes toward the bed, setting the water down on the nightstand with the faintest click. "Gabriel told me you're feeling poorly. What can I do?"

"Not too much," I say in a small voice of long suffering. "I just have to sleep it off. Sometimes it takes a day or so. But I have my pills." I gesture weakly toward Gabe's ADHD medication, sitting on the nightstand as a prop, trusting that our aunt won't examine the label. "I can try to come down to shiva this afternoon," I bluff.

"Nonsense, you rest the whole day if you need," she insists in hushed tones. "You'll have the house to yourself all morning, anyway. Bernie and I are headed over to Leah's in just a few—our daughter with the newborn. We'll be gone through lunch, so feel free to eat anything you can find, if you're hungry, or sleep if you're not. But we'll be back by three, before any visitors come calling, and I'll look in on you then, all right?" Though she doesn't reach out and touch me—we only just met—her concern is like a cool hand on my cheek. I wouldn't have guessed, with Gabe around to take care of me full-time, but I've missed being mothered.

As soon as Esther and Bernie's car rumbles away down the driveway and out of earshot, Gabe slides back into the bedroom. "What now?"

"We call Ari. Obviously."

He eyes me. "And bring her up to your sickbed? Should I blindfold her? Let's just wait out the day."

"What if I wake up with a snout tomorrow? Or hooves?" I toss the blankets off, already scrambling for my phone despite the wings that threaten to tip me backward. "I tell everyone I have walking pneumonia, and we waste another day? Even if we don't run out of diseases, we'll run out of time. I can't just hide in the dark forever." And I can't keep hiding behind Gabe forever, I don't say.

"We can't hide *those*," he reminds me unnecessarily.

"I know."

We decide that Gabe will greet Ari on the porch, preparing her as best he can, warning her not to freak out. He hates this plan, and I feel sick and scared at the thought—my hands shook as I pulled up her number. Perched on the edge of the settee in the parlor and wrapped inside of a throw blanket from my guest bedroom closet, my brother's hoodie abandoned, my breath starts to slip away from me. But I remind myself that what matters is finding Mom. Finding her, and curing me, and going home. Nothing else is important—not this town, not this house, not the disgust I expect to see in Ari Leydon's eyes when she sees *me*. It'll be worth it to have my life back. All of this will fade away like a nightmare come morning, and I'll be happy again.

If some small voice inside of me whispers, *but will you?* I push it away as I hear Ari's truck pull up to the house.

A car door slams.

Footsteps crunch across the gravel, then creak onto the front porch.

Voices murmur, and the front door opens, and my heart is a time bomb behind my ribs, beating toward its destruction. I clasp my hands between my knees to stop them from shaking now. It feels like I'm clinging by my fingertips to a cliff's edge, about to let go.

Then she's standing in the parlor doorway, my brother hovering behind, shooting me a look that says it's not too late for him to stop this, to drag her back out into the sun, away from me. But it *is* too late, because Ari's staring right at me, taking in my obviously strange shape beneath the blanket. She stabs a hand through her bright hair, shower-damp and loose this morning—the tips skim her biceps below her cuffed black T-shirt sleeves. "Someone want to tell me what's going on? Why I'm up at eight on a Sunday, when I told you I don't think I can help you?"

I take a shuddering breath. "You know how you said your bubbe was a healer, and Mom knew it?" I've gone over this little speech hundreds of times in my head in the last half hour. "And how *I* said we didn't know what she wanted from Ida?"

"Yes . . ."

I'm not sure how Gabe prepped her, but some things you have to see to believe. So I stand up.

And I let the blanket fall.

It hits the floor just a second before a gray-faced Ari.

TEN

"YOU COULD'VE CAUGHT her," I hiss at Gabe while cracking ice cubes out of their tray and into a glass in Esther's kitchen.

"*You* could've eased her into your situation a little more gently," Gabe counters, filling the glass with tap water when I shove it at him. "Maybe skipped the dramatic fucking reveal."

I flip him off, even if he's right. "Just stay here, okay? She doesn't need a crowd." Ignoring his bruised expression, I return to the parlor as quickly as possible without spilling the water. Though I'm afraid I'll enter the room to find Ari gone, she's still there, sitting cross-legged on the floor where we left her, head cradled in her hands. "Are you . . . how are you feeling?"

"I'm . . . ," she croaks.

Slowly, I set the glass down in front of her, then scoot backward a few feet. I'm draped in the blanket again, as if that's worth anything, and trying not to feeling bruised myself. But really, why did I hope for anything else? This was a mistake. The kind I *never* make. "Gabe wanted to leave you alone but I—it was my idea. I'm so sorry I called you."

When Ari lifts her head at last to look at me, I find a fire burning in her steel blue eyes that I didn't expect. "You don't have to be," she says, "because I'm not."

I rock back on my heels. "No?"

"Are you kidding?" Ari gathers her hair off her neck with fumbling hands and winds it into a low knot as she speaks. "I thought—I've spent *years* thinking that the best things I remembered about Bubbe, the things she believed and the way she made me believe, were just, like, the seeds of this poison plant that was gonna grow in her and take her away from me someday. All the stories she used to tell me, the people she thought she was helping, the way she talked about the world, it was like . . . like anything was possible."

"She sounds really great," I offer, wondering how I would remember Jitka if I'd ever had the chance to meet her.

"She was. And then she got sick." Ari reaches out for the water and takes a long sip, her slim fingers wrapped tight around the glass. "Everything my mom told yours, about Bubbe near the end? That was all true. I mean, Mom didn't let me around her very much in the last years—she said it was better I didn't see—but I saw enough. She'd lose it when strangers came around; she'd make me and my mom hold charms to prove we were who we said we were. It was a lot. She'd refuse her medications and ask for spinach, beet, or pomegranates. Mom says she was always delusional, that it just, like, manifested as religiousness. I . . . I miss her, all the time, and I didn't want to think of it that way. I didn't want to think of *her* that way, when she was, like, the only person who . . . She let me be who I was, you know? She didn't expect me to wear dresses, or be good at science or the piano, or get invited to girls' birthday parties, or anything. She just loved me." Ari's cheeks are damp, even as she laughs. "But she was right, wasn't she? Everything she was doing, trying to fix a broken world, believing what she did . . . She was right, all along. I mean, do you get that? You're actual fucking *magic*, Hannah!"

I tug the blanket tighter around my misshapen shoulders. "This isn't magic, Ari. It's like . . . a curse." I can't believe I'm saying the word until it's out there, but once it is, I know there's no other.

"It can't be both?"

"I mean, maybe, but I don't want this. I just want to go back to normal. That's why my mom was here—she thought your grandmother could fix me. But she's gone, and we can't find Mom, and I don't know why I thought I could handle this. Like, I keep telling Gabe we can do this, we can figure out what's happening. I want him to believe me. But honestly . . . I have no idea what to do next." Now I can feel my own tears coming, burning in my cheeks and all the way down my throat, because it's the truth. I thought if I was smart enough, brave enough, then maybe . . .

Except I'm not.

I'm a kid, and I've never been as smart as my friends or teachers think. They've barely glimpsed the work it takes me just to tread water at a school like Winthrop. And brave? I've never even had the guts to make my mom talk to me, force her to look me in the face and explain the source of the forever-canyon between us, too afraid that I already know the answer: she's never been content, and I've never been enough to make her feel otherwise.

"Okay, I'm sorry. But hey, now you have me." Swiping her palms across her eyes, Ari Leydon levers herself slowly to her feet and holds out a hand to help me up. "So let's go get your brother."

When I take it, warm and surprisingly strong, I feel something new sprout in my belly. The last person to hold my hand who wasn't Gabe was Atticus, a boy I dated last fall because we mistook our chemistry during a mock trial in civics class for romantic chemistry. We only ever kissed once, mouths closed, right before Christmas vacation, then didn't speak once over the break. We weren't dating by the time school started again. And in the whole three-month-long relationship, my heart never once jumped the way it does when Ari brushes her thumb across my knuckles and hauls me to my feet. She gives my fingers one last squeeze before her hand falls away, then turns to leave the parlor.

Whatever this feeling is, I steal an extra moment to grip it tight and tug it out by the root before it can burst into bloom.

"Here's one thing—okay, one of the things—I don't get," I start once we're gathered around the kitchen table. "I thought 'Ida Silver territory' meant healing—the stuff you talked about. The nosebleeds and the insomnia and all that. But Mom said we were all in danger because of her, right?"

Ari nods. "She sounded really scared."

"So why *would* Mom go to your grandmother instead of the police?"

She shifts in her chair, water glass gripped tight even though she's already drained it. "See, this is part of what I couldn't say in a letter. Bubbe helped people who were sick, but sometimes, they came to her for, um, *protection*."

"From what?" Gabe asks what I'm afraid to.

She reaches up to fiddle with her earrings; today, there's a small silver dagger through her cartilage. "You know how a Catholic might talk to a priest if they thought they were, I don't know, haunted or possessed? Judaism has its own monsters. There's the dybbuk, a dead soul that possesses a living body. Or estries—those are like, female vampires, really scary, but weirdly, you can cancel out their powers by braiding their hair. And shedim—they're sort of, like, demons? But not the way you might think of them. Rav Huna, this famous Talmudist, said 'Everyone among us has a thousand on his left hand and ten thousand on his right hand.' Bubbe used to tell me stories about them. How they feed on smoke produced from burning blood, and they can travel from one end of the universe to the other in an instant, and you can't see them unless they want you to, but they're everywhere, and only God protects us from them."

At this, we're speechless.

Ari flushes, reading our silence. "I'm not saying there are

vampires or whatever in Fox Hollow, or anywhere, or that your mom believes there are. But we can't really rule anything out now, right?"

I wish I could laugh her out of the house, like her mother did mine. When I look up at Gabe, his whole face pleads for me to do just that. He doesn't believe a word of this. Ironic, since it's always been Gabe who has bad dreams after scary movies, however much he loves them. I, on the other hand, reasoned at a young age that a ghost or ax murderer or alien clown showing up the same night I'd seen a movie about them was statistically unlikely. But in the past six weeks, I'd be lying if I said I'd been able to convince myself through cool logic that this is some mutated super flu, or Ebola, or too much sushi. So maybe I'm ready to consider the insane and the impossible. "No, we can't. Which is a problem. We don't know what Mom wanted from Ida. Or why she thought she couldn't see her own family."

"She said it wouldn't be safe," Ari remembers, frowning. "You don't think this has anything to do with what happened to your grandmother . . . right?"

"What do you mean?"

"I don't know. She was obviously afraid of somebody or something. I don't think she was only trying to cure you, but to protect people. Jitka included. And a month later, your mom is . . . somewhere, and Jitka's gone."

My brother shrugs. "She was ninety-eight. She died of a heart attack. It sucks, but it's not exactly suspicious."

"But it wasn't just that. She hadn't eaten or drunk in days, and there was plenty of food at the house." I remember the conversation over Shabbat dinner, uneasiness settling in my chest. "Plus she lied to our aunts."

"When?" Gabe lifts an eyebrow.

"She told them she was starting a painting, that she wanted to be alone to work on it, but they never found one. Sounds secretive to me."

"Actually, she said she was starting an art project," he corrects, "and so what? She decided to watch TV instead."

"She decided to watch TV while casually starving and dehydrating herself?" I shoot back.

"Maybe she died a completely natural death." Ari interrupts our bickering. "Or maybe your mom was afraid for a good reason, and her family was in danger, and your grandmother got caught up in it. Just like you're caught up in it." Her eyes drift toward the blanket draped over my winged shoulders.

I pull the fabric tighter around my throat. "Say all of that is true. Do you think Jitka knew any of this? And if she did, what was she really doing the week she died?"

"I guess you haven't found, like, a forge in the attic, with a big half-built sword lying around?" She asks. "Or a bottle with 'Hannah's mystical cure' written on it in Sharpie?"

"If any of that exists, it wasn't on the tour," Gabe says.

"So maybe we look a little harder," I suggest. "There could be *something* around here, some clue the family would've missed. And Esther and Bernie won't be back for a few more hours. When's the next time we'll have the house to ourselves?"

It's hard to know where to begin when we don't know what we're looking for—maybe a diary, or a letter, or a copy of *Mystical Curses and Cures for Beginners*—but we figure Jitka wouldn't keep anything supernatural or suspicious in plain sight when she lived with her daughter and son-in-law. So we probably don't need to check the kitchen cupboard with the slow cooker, or inside the dryer, or anyplace else Esther or Bernie might stumble upon. The basement seems as good a place as any to start, so we head down the splintered wooden staircase off the front hallway.

At the bottom, Gabe stops short. "How old *is* this house?"

The room isn't just unfinished—it's a hollowed-out pocket of earth. The walls are rough stone, the floor dirt, the ceiling a grid of ancient-looking wooden beams as thick as tree trunks, electrical wires snaking between and below them. A single exposed bulb, hanging by a thin cable, is the only thing to light the room. Even the dank basement below our apartment complex, stuffed with old bicycles and still-sticky highchairs, half its fluorescents burned out in the low ceiling, seems cheerful by comparison.

"I think your grandparents built the house, but it was supposed to have been on an old foundation." Ari shivers a little in the chill and the damp—I feel the tremble through my arm, pressed against hers in the tight stairwell.

"What was here before?"

"Another house. The Hollow overran its banks during the Great Depression. Town was far enough away that it didn't do too much damage there, but there were some old houses out here in the woods on the outskirts, and they got wrecked, then abandoned. My bubbe's house was built later, otherwise it would've been flooded—it's even closer to the river than this place. I guess it was easier to take the original house down and rebuild when your family bought it. This basement, though, was part of whatever house had been here before. Who knows how old it is."

It's a large room, but there are few places to hide anything. Some Home Depot–esque metal shelving against one wall, holding dusty paint cans, a battered toolbox, and spare water-warped two-by-fours from some past home repair. In the minimal light through a tiny window set just below the ceiling, I can see a small door in the far corner beside the boiler, rusted steel set in stone.

Gabe sees it too. "Coal room, I bet."

"What's that?" Ari peers into the gloom with us.

"What it sounds like. There'd probably be a coal chute in the outside wall if we looked. Someone delivers the coal, shovels it into the chute, and it pours down into this little room for you to feed into the furnace. Nobody burns coal anymore, obviously, but some old buildings still have the rooms."

"How the hell do you know all that?" I ask.

"From every horror movie set in an old house, ever."

"Okay, since you're our architectural expert . . ." I jerk my head, motioning him forward to explore. I'm not sticking my face into an old coal room, to be eaten by ghosts or black widow spiders, whichever.

But as he hesitates, Ari pushes past us. Her high-tops track prints across the dull dirt floor. Before I can say anything, she wraps her hands around the door handle. A padlock latch between the wall and the door sticks—there's no lock on it, but it must be rusted shut. She braces her heel against the stone and throws her weight backward. With an ugly squeal and a tumble of loose grit, it gives, breaking off completely. Ari lands in the dirt, but Gabe and I are the ones who scream, clutching at each other.

Ari stands, shaking dust from her hair and brushing it from her black pants. Calmly, she pulls her phone out of a cargo pocket, puts it in flashlight mode, and opens the door to peer cautiously into the gaping hole beyond. "There's nothing. I mean there's a room—maybe five by five—and a bunch of coal dust, and . . . wait, that's the chute, but I can't see into it from here."

And then, unbelievably, she steps inside and disappears.

I don't let go of Gabe while we wait. Vampires and ghosts and demons seemed impossible upstairs in the parlor, but a creepy door in a dank basement is enough to strip away that sunlit logic. From the depths of the room, we hear the clank of iron, and then her voice echoing out: "Nothing in the chute, either!"

When she's emerged and there are no dark corners left to explore, we retreat quickly and gratefully to the first floor. "Where next?" Gabe asks.

We check the bedrooms, now empty of guests' suitcases,

peeking into drawers. Some hold folded linens, but they're mostly empty, as are the closets. In one of the bedroom closets, we find a shoebox in the very back behind hanging coats. It's labeled "tapes," but when I lift the lid, it's full of decades-old Victoria's Secret catalogs with a stranger's name on the mailing label.

"My God," Gabe laughs into our puzzled faces. "We just found somebody's pre-internet, PG-13 porn stash."

"What? No." I pull back my hand. "Mom didn't even have a brother."

He eyes me witheringly.

"Oh. You think one of our aunts—"

"Stole old magazines out of some rando's recycling bin to keep her company at night? Yeah. That's exactly what I think."

"*Oh,*" I say again. My ears must be bloodred. I glance sideways at Ari, who peers into the box with interest. Carefully, I lower the lid. "Probably not magical."

The bedroom that's clearly Esther and Bernie's, we skip— no chance Jitka would hide something there—and soon, the only room left is our grandmother's. I tell myself that we're detectives conducting important on-site research, not snoops, or, worse, ungrateful trespassers who lied to be let inside her house.

The master bedroom is as stately and gorgeous as the rest of the farmhouse. There's a wrought-iron bed, the posts shaped like spindly black trees with branches crossed at the headboard and footboard, crowned by leafy black boughs. A pale-green carpet patterned with pink rosebuds covers much of the floor, complementing the leaf-green bedspread and dusky-pink drapes. Below the window, there's a dark wood desk with a slanted top. A drafting table.

While Mom does most of her design work digitally, she's constantly painting or planning by hand, and she's got a drafting table she's lugged from state to state, from rental to rental, even when we left most everything but our clothes behind. Hers is cheap and battered-looking, the simple metal legs splotched with paint drops and pastel crumbs. Jitka's is much sturdier, with a footrest and slim drawers for storage. I cross to it, dragging my unbandaged fingers across the polished top. They come away clean, no streaks of charcoal or graphite or even dust—this drafting table was well cared for, but it hasn't been used recently, I'd bet. I ease open a drawer no taller than a thick book to examine its contents. Tubes of oil paint are arranged side by side and neatly squeezed from the bottom, like properly rolled toothpaste, instead of the shriveled, spattered tubes my mother jumbles together in a plastic tackle box. The brushes I find are expensive, both bristle and sable, all pristine. Mom burns through hers, the tips carelessly ragged and paint-crusted. It's a little sad, though. I never thought I'd miss Mom's mess, but this is like walking into a chef's kitchen and finding no mixing bowls in the sink, no flour-freckled rolling pins, not an open jar of spices in sight.

It doesn't seem as though Jitka's been painting, unless she took incredible care to clean up the evidence before her unexpected death.

The drawer below it holds a pad of canvas paper, like the kind Mom uses to practice painting techniques. Pages have been torn out, but what's left in the pad is blank. I wonder whether Jitka's art was realistic and illustrative like Gabe's, or moody and abstract like Mom's. Maybe Esther knows where she kept her work. It's not like I have an eye for art, but I want to see some part of Jitka, to know something about the grandmother we never met.

All of a sudden, the warm smell of peony and citrus drifts through the room. I turn to see Gabe by a vanity table with a sheet draped over its mirror, holding a crystal bottle of perfume.

Eyes burning just a little, I catalog it as one thing I now know: Jitka's unfussy, summery scent.

I shake my head. There are no ceremonial daggers with jeweled hilts in the vanity drawer, no potions or written incantations or fantastical research notes in the wardrobe hung with simple, modest dresses. No holy rocket launchers lie in wait for us to discover under the canopy bed. Soon, we're back in the parlor, dustier and sweatier but just as empty-handed.

The grandfather clock says it's only half past ten, and I breathe easier. But time won't do us any good if there's nothing here to find. Maybe she really wasn't mixed up in Mom's strange business. I guess sometimes, death is just death.

I ask the obvious because nobody else has. "What now?"

Ari shoves a strand of watermelon hair that's sprung loose back off her forehead. "There's nowhere else we can look?" She spins slowly in place, as if some clue might be hidden in the poker stand beside the fireplace and we just haven't noticed it yet.

"There's the barn," Gabe offers.

I look to the windows again, but as they face the front of the house, of course the only thing beyond the pollen-flecked glass is flowers.

Ari hesitates. "Bubbe told me it's not safe. Like, structurally. Lots of water damage from the big flood, and it was never renovated or rebuilt. She made me promise never to play around it when I was a kid and she'd bring me along on her visits with Jitka. I don't think anybody goes out there."

Which makes it the perfect hiding place, I think. "It's where she died. They found Jitka between the house and the trees."

"Near the barn, then," she confirms, biting at her full bottom lip in a way that's not un-Gabe-like, but it's a very different look on her.

We make for the kitchen, unbolting the back door that spills us out into the field. We wade into the wildflowers, waist-high in patches, shoving aside the tangled leaves and flower heads. Twilight-blue and purple and white, sunny yellow and blazing orange. The July sun sets every color on fire. Bees flicker between the plants, nearly alighting on Gabe and Ari.

Me, they don't come near.

The barn looms ahead, and Ari was right about it. The doorframe leans to the left, the grayed boards and mossy roof sag to the right. If there ever were panes in the windows up in the loft, the glass is long gone, leaving empty black sockets behind.

Gabe makes his way to the door, crisscrossed by boards and nailed shut. He tugs the rusted iron latch anyway, then tumbles back into the flowers when the whole thing swings open, door and boards and all. Leaning close, I can see that while the old nails are still driven firmly into the doorframe, the holes in the boards have been gouged out enough that they'll still hang on the nail heads, but slip free under the slightest pressure.

Somebody wanted to be able to get in, but to keep people out by maintaining the illusion that it was still shut up tight.

"This is not normal," our architectural expert says under his breath. He steps in front of me just as I start to drift forward into the black of the barn, gallantly and obnoxiously sweeping us behind him. "It might not be safe," he stage-whispers. Though Ari scoffs her protest, and I roll my eyes, I stick close behind my brother, happy enough to let him burst through spiderwebs in my stead.

Inside, the air is hot and heavy, and the darkness is starred by dust motes in rare shafts of light where the sun pierces through a hole in the roof or the boards. The smell of it prickles my nose—the sweet-musty stench of ancient straw underfoot, the musk of wet animal fur and dried-out droppings still clinging to the place, and the sharp, oily stink of machinery. It's all faded, like memories pressed between pages.

As my eyes adjust, shapes blossom out of the darkness. A few empty stalls. A rake and shovel, bloodred with rust, propped against the wall, and the grayed wooden shafts of old farm tools that litter the straw like animal bones in a predator's den. But there's nothing strange or spectacular that I can see.

Ari glances at the loft above us, the floor pinpricked by light from beyond. "Think that would still hold our weight?"

"We can find out." I point toward the far wall, where a ladder glints dully from the shadows. Unlike everything else in the barn, it's not a moldering antique, but a modern aluminum stepladder. Someone must've muscled it in after prying open the doors.

Because I'm the smallest, Ari suggests I climb first, and I agree despite Gabe's protests. He follows close behind, because he's better equipped to catch me and pull me up if the floor collapses. Ari braces the ladder, standing clear of the loft and any falling boards. Or girls.

The top rung is just short of the loft floor, so I brace my palms against the boards—they creak, but not ominously, seeming strong enough to hold—and haul myself up. And, because I'm the first, and since the loft is bright enough with the light through the high windows, I immediately see the long figure in the center of the loft, on a carpet of brown hay. It's shrouded by a gingham bedsheet just like the ones in the house, but identifiable by shape.

There is a dead body in the dust.

THOUGH THEY'VE YET to be together without one of her parents present, Malka dreams of Siman.

They stand in the parlor, bodies pressed close, her hand tucked inside his. The skin of his palm is the warmest she's ever felt, warmer even than Geela's when they were kids and she'd caught a fever so high, Mama put her in a cold bath while Papa called Dr. Markowski in the middle of the night. Mama, too, was in the dream; she sat on the pink silk parlor couch in front of Malka and Siman, her own hands clutched in her hair. Where her always too-thin fingers claw at the curls, they lose all color. Dust—on her mother's palms, her hair, now her cheeks. Like her ancestors in their grief, she claws at her clothes, dark fabric shredding across her breastbone. In her dream-wisdom, Malka knows what her mother knows. That she and Siman are leaving home, leaving Fox Hollow, and not for the city some fifty miles away, or even the coast, but for someplace as far beyond Mama's reach as the loved ones she left behind in Prague, in graves.

When Malka wakes, the still-hovering face of dream-Mama is nearly enough to keep her away from him.

It is very nearly enough.

As he has the summer off from teaching, Papa's around much more often. Any time he catches the girls clustered at the windows, watching Siman go after the dead oaks one at a time with a chainsaw—first he notches the tree on a side that doesn't face the barn, then cuts through all but a hinge, felling it exactly where he wants so that he can strip off the branches and slice up the trunk to transport—Papa barks his annoyance, and they scatter. It's not like he'd forbid his daughters from speaking to Siman, or trekking out to bring him cold water. They're not Orthodox, let alone medieval. But her interest in Siman is . . . private. She handles it the way she did her film in their photography class last year, carefully unspooling it, threading it onto the spiral and sealing it in its developing tank, all in total darkness.

In the third week of summer, Ida Silver drives Malka and Rachael into town and drops them off at the Pineapple The-atre, named for the strange stone architectural flourish on top, like spiked fronds. It only has two screens, since it can only afford to show two movies at a time. A pair of posters out-side advertise the films playing now: *Pretty Woman* and *Back to the Future Part III*. Surely Rachael could get them into *Pretty Woman* just by stomping up to the teenage clerk in her chunky black Oxfords, plaid schoolgirl skirt, and tiny white polo tee, but even if she were willing to break the rules, Malka's not sure she *wants* to see what's in an R-rated romance.

Still, she can't help staring longingly at Julia Roberts, who clutches Richard Gere's tie on the poster, his whole body bowed around hers as if he'd follow wherever she led.

Rachael twists her purple lacquered lips into a sneer. "It's Cinderella in hooker boots. Let's skip this and go to Tunes instead."

"Excuse you, you love Disney," Malka reminds her best friend. There's been many a night when those platform Oxfords come off, the fuzzy toe socks go on, and they lie together on the Silvers' couch, hip-to-hip with tangled legs, to watch the magic castle appear on screen. While Malka's family does come from money, they don't own a television. The Silvers, on the other hand, have two, plus a VHS player. More than half the time, Rachael picks out Disney movies from the tiny rental shelf in Tunes, Fox Hollow's music shop.

"Yeah, the animal shit. *The Fox and the Hound. The Great Mouse Detective. The Rescuers.* I can't stand the princesses. Oh, look, another girl who needs a prince to whisk her away, except this time she lives under the sea instead of in a village. Pass."

"Did you ever even see *The Little Mermaid*? That's not what it's about!" Malka took the Adelman twins to see it last year while she babysat, claiming it was for the seven-year-olds, but really using them as an excuse. "Ariel made a deal with a witch, okay, she's not the brightest starfish in the sea. But it wasn't for a guy. She was obsessed with forks and thimbles and whatever way before Eric came along. She wanted to be human, and live on the land, and she did something about it. Which is more than most people would. Like, Cinderella was brave enough to go to the ball, when it would've been easy to stay home with her mice where she was sad and safe." Malka feels her stomach churn with the shame of self-recognition, but plows on. "So what, the princesses fall in love? They want to change their lives, and they leave everything and everybody behind to do it. I think they get props for that."

"Falling in love doesn't change your life," Rachael mutters bitterly, purposefully missing the point, Malka thinks.

Besides, when has Rachael ever been in love? Malka knows she's secretly soft—this is the same girl who wept when the fox and the hound's friendship ended forever in that forest clearing. But she's never shown any interest in a boy, beyond quirking a penciled eyebrow whenever they gallop past at school in loud packs. She always tells Malka that they don't need boys, screw 'em, she and Malka will move to the city together after high school, to any city, anywhere in the world, and start their new lives, the Eggerses' rules be damned.

"We'll see," is all Malka says in return.

ELEVEN

THE FEAR THAT I'll wipe out Gabe while plummeting earth-
ward is all that keeps my hands clamped to the mossy boards. A
scream sticks in my throat, but the voice in my head is bleating
MOM MOM MOM MOM MOM until it's all I can hear.

I must make a sound, because my brother hurries up the
rungs, wrapping a fist around the hood of my sweatshirt,
ready to haul me back down and away from danger. I slip away,
though, heaving myself up and over onto the floor. Bits of
ancient hay cling to my skin and clothes as I scramble forward,
gulping down as much musty air as I can. Panic stuffs my ears
with cotton and numbs my hands so that I barely feel the splintered wood beneath them.

Behind me, Gabe must've cleared the loft himself, because
he shouts, "Hannah, stop!"

I don't listen. As I decided yesterday, there is no going
back from now on. Hissing his annoyance, Gabe crawls up
beside me.

Ari clangs up the ladder next. "What? What is it?"

Neither of us answers. Though I was the one who rushed

forward, I stand frozen over the figure on the floor, knees locked to stop my legs from shaking. So it's Gabe who bends down and peels back the sheet. Side by side, we look at the body.

I sink to my knees as the future I've started scripting—one in which I scramble down the ladder and out into the sunshine to call 911 even though it must be weeks too late, then wait for the Eggerses to return as I mentally catalog the last truly loving things Mom and I said to each other, which might've been months ago, or years—all of that unwrites itself in an instant.

This isn't our mother.

Whoever it is, aside from being dead, he's perfect. A boy, maybe Gabe's age or a little older. Hair so close-cropped it's a shadow, high cheekbones, and a strong jaw with a tapered chin. The same contrast shows itself in his graceful neck and corded shoulders, just visible above the point to which Gabe had pulled back the sheet. His skin isn't ice blue or pocked with rot, but an earthy gold. There's no whiff of decay; in fact, he smells like nothing. Not a single fly buzzes around the body, though I've seen plenty of them in the barn.

He's so perfect, I reach out to touch him.

I didn't even notice Ari kneeling in the dust to my left until she grabs for my wrist, but it's too late. My fingertip grazes the boy's cheek. Though I'm prepared for the kind of unnerving cold I felt the day I found my childhood pet mouse dead in its shavings, the body doesn't feel like that. It doesn't even feel like skin.

More like clay.

"It's a sculpture," I whisper. I brush my palm across the shorn hair to find it's clay as well, delicately stippled and painted near black, like the eyebrows. The painfully human-looking lips are made of the same mica-flecked clay that shines faintly in a patch of direct sunlight.

"OhthankGod," Gabe exhales in a rush. "But also, what the fuck? Why is it up here? And what's it for?"

"I think . . . okay, don't laugh at me, but . . . ," Ari stammers, "this kind of looks like a—a golem?"

Gabe blinks back at her. "Like . . . an evil hobbit?"

"Not *Gollum*, a golem," she corrects him. "It's . . . you know. The Golem of Prague?"

He turns to me, and I shrug.

"Okay . . . story time, I guess. So, this famous rabbi in the 1500s needs to defend the Jewish ghetto in Prague from pogroms and anti-Semitic turd wagons. And so he builds a golem—it's like a robot, sorta, made out of clay and magic. Something inanimate, but given a soul. Or a . . . breath of life. Supposedly, he gets permission from God himself in his dreams, and wakes up with all of these Kabbalistic formulas in his head. Kabbalism is, like, a philosophy of Jewish mysticism. Bubbe was into it, pretty obviously. The rabbi has to decode these holy formulas and then purify himself so they'll work. He fasts for a few days and prays hard. Then he crafts this . . . being out of river clay, and does the ritual to bring it to life. It works, and the golem protects the ghetto and helps its people. But then something snaps. It gets violent, smashes buildings, pulls up trees, throws boulders at passing pedestrians, all of that."

"Why?" Gabe asks.

"I don't know, exactly. Bubbe said there were a few versions of the legend." She frowns, remembering. "In one, the rabbi forgets to deactivate the golem before Shabbat. In another, it falls in love and gets its big clay heart broken. But in every version I've heard, it goes on a murderous rampage and has to be put down."

"Put down?" I repeat slowly.

"It's how all these stories end. Golems start out as perfect servants and protectors, but sooner or later, something just . . . happens to them. They always turn on their masters. The thing is, they're supposed to be big and strong, like giants, and this . . ."

Gabe casts a dubious gaze down at the clay body. "It looks like us."

Grasping the sheet, Ari lifts it a little farther, reaching to feel beneath. At first, I have no idea what she's doing—I know it's just a sculpture, not alive or anything, but I don't think we need to check it for anatomical correctness. But she pulls back almost at once with a drawstring bag, like a jewelry pouch, clay shavings and straw clinging to the black velvet. It must have been tucked beneath the arm.

Carefully, Ari empties its contents into her lap. A folded sheet of paper slips out, along with a battered-looking little book. A fine-tipped paintbrush and a tiny plastic pot fall to the floor beside them.

Gabe reaches for the brush, the same kind I found in Jitka's drafting table, and the pot. While I pick up the sheet of paper, he screws the lid off and sniffs. "Paint," he announces, then holds up the brush. "Obviously, I guess."

Gingerly, Ari plucks the book out of the hay and holds it out to show me. No bigger than her hand, its leather binding might have been red once, but has weathered and faded to faint petal pink. A thin leather strap, worn shiny with use, holds it shut. She unwinds the strap carefully, though I expect it to dissolve to dust at any moment, and the cover drops open with a distinct crackle. She flips slowly through the pages, rippled and yellow and age-spotted, like skin.

I shift to look closer, but she's already frowning in disappointment. "It's not English."

Sure enough, there are words scrawled in ink, cramped and splotched, and totally incomprehensible. It's not even a Latin alphabet, or any that I recognize.

Ari seems to guess my unasked question. "This is Hebrew, I think—I recognize some of the letters. I think that's ayin, and this looks like kaf, or a sloppy vet. But it's cursive, and obviously not modern. And I only read print Hebrew, and barely understand that."

My heart dips—what good is a book or a diary we can't read?—but rises again when I unfold the sheet of paper. The material, at least, is modern, thick and crisp; canvas paper. It must be from the pad in Jitka's bedroom. And this time, the handwriting dashed across it *is* in English.

"It's a letter." I hear my own voice shake, and work hard to steel myself before I read aloud:

To my Malkala,

I hope you'll never read this. I hope that you'll come home soon, and I'll crumple this letter up and pretend I was never so foolish as to write it. But if you find your way back and I'm not here, and if I'm right about the trouble you're in, then you'll need to know how to protect yourself and the family with the only weapon I can give you.

To teach you to create such a being, the craft and incantations and meditation, would take years together—I know because that's how long it took me to teach myself from my father's parting gift. Perhaps we'll have that chance yet. But to bring it to life requires little. With your sister out of the house, I've been able to perform the rituals, though it's taken so much out of me. Every time I stand, the room swims, and when I'm finished at last I may well be crawling back to the house. I am old, Malkala. Older than I ever dreamed I would be. But there's still time for you, and all you need is your own inheritance, the legacy of your family, the stories I should have told you. Few people remember the old tales anymore, the ones their grandparents and great-grandparents knew for truth, and fewer believe them. But we know them to be true, just as I know this: You are your greatest weapon.

You must paint Truth on the golem's forehead—in case you've forgotten your Hebrew lessons:

אמת

If I've done my work, he'll be yours to command. He will protect you and those you love, where I cannot.

It's getting late, and the light in the loft is fading. It's the fasting, I'm sure, but I've been seeing things. Hearing things, too, from the woods. Beyond the trees.

I wish that I could explain everything to you while holding your hand, so you would know my own story at last. I wish I could see you once more, truly see you, to forgive you and to beg your forgiveness properly. There is so much to be sorry for, and not enough time to say what needs saying—not even if I'm wrong, and am around for years yet. There would never be enough time to make up for what we've lost. How I wish I'd known sooner that the people we love don't belong to us. All we own is our love for them, and that's ours to keep forever.

And here is what matters most: I love you, my little girl, my sheifale. Then and now and forever, I love you, as I know you love me, and as I love your children without knowing them. That will have to be enough.

Maybe it's all there is.

In death or in life, love,
Mama

I feel like the ragged, dusty basement below my grand-mother's beautiful home, my rib cage a rusted iron door. If it were pried open right now, who knows what might tumble out?

"None of this makes sense," Gabe insists through the tremble in his voice. "I don't care if she was the spunky, water-aerobics
type of old person. There's just no way a ninety-eight-year-old
woman is prying boards off a barn door, hauling around lad-
ders, sculpting an entire freaking person."

He has a point. But as I inspect the loft floor, I notice the
thick dust that furs the boards around the golem and the sheet,
displaced by our footprints and, possibly, an extra set leading
from the ladder to the golem—I hadn't stopped to check for
preexisting prints as I was freaking out about the body. There's
no mess besides a few clay shavings, no tools, nothing to suggest it was built recently. "I think this has been here for a while.
Maybe a really long time."

Ari stares at the book in her hands. "Is this real? Is it all
real? It's just . . . Some stories have to be just *stories*, right?" she
insists. As though stories are dead things, clay things, incapable
of harm.

Because I can't possibly answer it, I ignore the question for
now. "What does this mean? Why would Mom need a *weapon*?
And what does that have to do with me?"

But Gabe and Ari don't have any answers either. "One thing
at a time," Gabe says. "Whatever Mom was worried about, it
seems like she told Jitka after all, and Jitka believed her. We've
been dancing around the question of what the hell is happening
to you, but if it's all part of the same deal—if these transformations or whatever aren't anything that can be explained
by science, but something else—well, isn't this our chance to

find out? Either this golem thing is real, or it isn't. We can sit around wondering forever, or we can paint the thing's head like the letter says to. If nothing happens, then at least we'll have an answer, right?"

"Are you kidding me?" I say. "The horror movie aficionado is suggesting we recite mysterious incantations we don't understand over a magical monster?"

"So what, then, we go back to the house and make a spreadsheet, debate the pros and cons until Esther's home and we lose our chance?"

Ari asks the obvious, nodding at the maybe-golem. "And what if something *does* happen?"

Gabe reaches over to tap the letter. "You said they're supposed to protect the people who bring them to life, yeah?" He scratches his stubble, leaving a streak of dust across one cheek. "So whatever's causing . . ." Gabe gestures broadly at me, then spreads his arms like airplane wings. "If it's not just something from Mom's past, but something, I don't know, present? Somebody Jitka thought we needed protection from? I say we go for it."

Ari and I share a look. What am I supposed to say? If we climb down the ladder and pretend we were never here, we're basically admitting that we're scared. And I'm tired of being scared.

I turn back to Gabe and nod.

"Okay," he says. "Okay. Um, maybe you guys should back up a little bit." Then he dips the paintbrush into the ink pot.

I obey, and feel slim fingers thread through mine and cut my eyes sideways to Ari. Her clenched jaw could cut steel.

The faint clatter of the brush against the loft floor lets us know that Gabe has done his job. Now he, too, crawls backward, hay clinging to his pants and stuck through his hair. We crane our necks to see around him, Ari's fingers pressing into my knuckles until they crack.

And nothing happens.

"Okay," she says, grip loosening, fingers fluttering away. "Well, that answers—"

Something shivers through the barn.

It's like bass blasting from a powerful set of speakers, only so low, it's inaudible. It rattles me down to the fingertips, as though I'm made of glass. I worry, for a moment, that it might shake me apart. Beside me, Ari drops to her knees and presses her hands to the floor for balance, while Gabe grinds the heels of his palms into his ears, as if he can hear the sound I can't. I expect the vibrating floor to splinter, expect to look out the shattered windows and watch the flowers flatten themselves against the earth, see the black farmhouse in the distance crack down the center. We're at the epicenter of an earthquake, we must be. It's the only logical explanation.

But logic falls away when the still body before us arches its clay spine, opens its carved jaw, and lets out an animal bellow, as though waking from a nightmare.

TWELVE

IN MY WHOLE life, I've never run so fast as I do now. Ari and I scramble down the ladder, Gabe half falling after us. We brace him by the elbows for the barest second, and then we're all leaping over dead farm equipment, plowing through moldering hay that sends up clouds of dust and gnats. I make straight for the door, but crash into Ari when she stops and stoops down in front of me. I land in a spot of thinly spread hay, rattling my whole spine.

Gazing up, dazed and smarting, I watch Ari pivot, hefting a rusted pitchfork. She points it toward the loft, as if about to launch it javelin style through the ceiling. Even with hay in her hair and knees ashen with dirt, she looks epic, like a sculpture herself.

She's also an idiot. This is clearly an occasion for flight, not fight.

Gabe must've realized we weren't still running behind him because he's back all of a sudden, hauling me to my feet. "Where's Frankenstein?" he asks in an extreme Gabe stage whisper.

I swallow hard around a serious case of dry mouth. "His monster."

"Huh?"

"If you're making a reference, Frankenstein was the doctor, not the monster." I'm pedantic in a crisis.

Ari says, "I think the point is that the doctor *was* the monster—"

"None! Of! This! Is! Helpful!" he interrupts, forgetting to keep his voice down. His lip piercing winks in the low light as he gazes toward the loft above us.

"We can't handle this by ourselves," I insist, looking to Ari. She knows way more about this stuff than we do, and must see that we're in above our heads. The world has split open and shown us its wild heart, and here we stand with an old pitchfork.

But there's that strange, fierce fire in her eyes again, like the northern lights in a dark sky. "Actually, I think we can. Listen."

I try to stifle my panicked breathing. There's nothing coming from above, not even groaning boards, which seems to be Ari's point. "Why isn't it following us?"

"I don't think it can. If that's a golem up there, then it's under your control." She gestures at Gabe with the pitchfork, then lets the tines drift toward the floor as she loosens her fighting stance. "Your ritual, your servant. That's what Bubbe would say."

"But . . . but I don't want a servant," Gabe splutters.

"If only you'd stopped to make a spreadsheet, you might've figured that out," I can't help but snap back.

"Point is, it won't hurt us. It can't. Not if our grandmothers were right."

We listen for another moment, then all as one, creep toward the ladder. Through gestures and whispers, it's decided that Gabe will go first this time. He tucks Ari's pitchfork awkwardly under his arm to climb. I follow, with Ari behind, so this time I'm second in line to breach the loft and have to peer around my brother to see.

The golem is so silent and still, I wonder if maybe we imagined it all—the animal scream, the spasm of its clay bones, the strange vibrations of the earth itself. Except that the body now lies curled on its side in a fetal position, facing us—forearms cradling its tucked head, knees to its chest, bare feet crossed. The sheet that covered it has fallen away, so I can see that where a flesh-and-blood body might heave for breath, ribs rising and falling, it's utterly motionless. So, no literal breath of life, then.

But when Gabe calls out a trembling, "H-hey!" the head lifts.

And the eyes open, human-looking and pitch dark.

"Can . . . um, do you understand us?" he says, enunciating the way he might for a small child.

The creature tucks its head back into its arms.

Ari starts to explain, "Golems can't sp—"

But then, in a voice like the opening of a door that's been

locked for decades, it croaks, "I understand."

Dizzy all over again, I hear my pulse in my ears. Maybe I should find it easier to accept this magic, the way it's apparently shaped and reshaped my body like the tide does the beach, but this . . . this is a whole person. And now, looking down at the body curled tightly on the floor, I feel sorry for it. "Do you have a name?" I ask. My voice is hoarse, but as gentle as I can make it.

Again, the thing lifts its head, but looks to Gabe instead of me. "It is for him to say."

"You're its master," Ari reminds Gabe, a tremble in her words. Maybe she feels like I do—stunned by an inhuman creature's humanness. "It won't have a name unless you give it one."

Gabe drags a hand through his mussed hair. "Yeah, let's, uh, put a pin in that. C-can you move?"

The creature can, with help. My brother sets the pitchfork down reluctantly so we can lever it to its feet. I try not to shudder at the gritty-smooth feel of the golem's lukewarm skin. Gabe grabs the bedsheet and beats the dust from it, then folds and wraps the cloth around the golem's body. As he works, he rambles about the contemporary and extremely queer version of *The Odyssey* his theater department put on for their spring play in his junior year, when he was the lead siren seducing Odysseus at a college toga party, and how his friends stole and filled the prop keg with real beer on closing night. "Like riding a chariot," Gabe laughs nervously as he adjusts the makeshift toga. "You never forget how."

146

Though the golem shows no sign of modesty, Ari and I look elsewhere while my brother works—whether it's a boy like Gabe or not, it is Gabe-shaped. I busy myself with gathering the debris of our little ritual, along with Jitka's letter and the unreadable diary. "What next?" I ask Ari. "What do we *do* with it?"

"I don't know." She eyes the ladder. "I don't think anybody would find it in the barn, but . . ."

"But we can't just leave it behind," I say, finishing her thought. We brought it to life, or something like life. Aren't we responsible for it now? I'm not a mom, obviously, but I know you're not supposed to just abandon someone (something?) you brought to life. "Anyway, half the town will be dropping by here in the next few days, and who knows when Esther and Bernie will leave again. They're gonna notice us loitering out by the condemned barn. We should take it somewhere we can get to easily, without anyone seeing."

"I think I know a place," she says.

It takes all three of us to get the golem down from the loft and across the barn, its steps stiff and wild as a marionette in the hands of a bad puppeteer. Outside we wait, blinking in the fresh air and baking sun, while Gabe slots the boards back onto the nails. Leaning against the warm wood to catch my breath, I tip my head back and drink in the sky. It's the truest blue, powdered by clouds and contrails. I wonder if a plane ever flies low enough to see the Eggers plot of land, multicolored with the dark house at its center, like the seed head inside a flower.

In the shadows of the loft, the golem's skin looked as dull as a regular person's, but in the light, it shines faintly, those tiny flecks of mica sparkling when they catch the sun. The Hebrew word for "truth" is still inked in Gabe's ultrafine print just below its hairline, like a small, strange tattoo. Other than that, it seems more human than ever. The hair that was painted delicately across the clay looks real now, I notice with a start, a close-shorn stubble over its head and brows. And the strong, perfectly made fingers are topped by short, perfect nails. All of which feels impossible. Or magical.

I watch it marvel over its own body and feel another great pang.

Ari explains her plan. "My bubbe's old house—it's close by, and it's safe."

I can tell from the look on Gabe's face that he doesn't want to rely on Ari more than we already have. But what else can we do?

"Sounds good," I say, sweating under my heavy sweatshirt and the weight of my wings. "I guess it's not air conditioned?"

"Nope. But it's not so bad, and I think my parents have a portable fan at the shop. Actually, there's a couple things we could pick up. Nobody would see us. They're at an estate sale an hour away, and the shop is closed on Sundays. And I've been thinking . . . There's so much we don't get, just in your grandmother's letter. I've been wishing Bubbe was here to ask, and I realized: maybe there's a way she *can* tell us."

"Like . . . a séance?" Gabe asks, shifting the weight of the golem's arm across his shoulders as we round the farmhouse.

Ari snorts. "I think she'd reach through the veil and slap me if I tried. Séances are a pretty big no in Judaism. But that diary gave me an idea. Bubbe kept these notebooks, kind of like diaries, though more like her own encyclopedias. She wrote about the people she knew and helped, but also recipes, remedies, prayers, old stories. I looked through them once when I was little. Serious stuff. She insisted on bringing them to Valerie Manor—that was the nursing home in Beacon—along with all her charms. My mom wasn't lying about that—her room was pretty intense. But she *was* lying to your mom when she told her she'd trashed it all."

"Seriously?" My heart jumps.

"She wouldn't give me any of Bubbe's, uh, *superstitious* stuff after she died—she said she didn't want me to remember Bubbe by her delusions—but I kept an eye on the trash when we were packing and bagging her room. So I know Mom didn't throw them out. At least, not that day. What little we didn't get rid of or donate ended up in the shop's storeroom. I know, because Mom once sent me down to get one of her embroidered tablecloths, and I recognized the boxes. I never looked through them because I didn't want to piss Mom off, but I bet that's where the notebooks are. They could have answers. Maybe Bubbe even wrote about your family, since Jitka was her friend."

I feel almost cheerful at the thought of some good old-fashioned primary-source research. "You think?"

"I mean, if I owned a diary, you can bet I'd be writing about you tonight."

Probably Ari means the collective you: that me and Gabe

and the whole thing about bringing a creature from ancient Jewish folklore to life deserves an entry. So I wrestle the blush from my cheeks as we wrestle the golem into Ari's truck. It rides with Gabe in the jump seats, and as we head toward town, my brother is looking supremely uncomfortable—either because of the truck's terrible suspension, which rockets him into the low ceiling as we sail across every pothole, or at being crammed in so close to a supernaturally animated mud creature. Probably both.

As for Ari, she keeps throwing nervous glances in the rearview mirror, though the golem only sits stoically with its hands in its toga'd lap.

We pass the bus station and enter downtown Fox Hollow for the first time. The houses with their historical plaques give way to antique-looking storefronts, sturdy brick, with the doors and windowpanes painted teal and apple red and cotton candy pink. All have scalloped awnings with charming cursive script spelling out the names of the businesses. But there are more than a few For Sale and For Rent signs between them.

"That happens around here," Ari explains when I ask. "We don't get that many tourists, people from the city or from Connecticut looking for a weekend getaway. Everyone goes to Beacon and Rhinebeck and Hudson. Fox Hollow is one of the oldest towns in the state, but there are cuter places, and, you know, most of them have a Starbucks."

We slow outside a store with *Forget-Me-Not* curling across an awning the same pale, purplish blue as its namesake flower.

Ari turns down a private alley that seems way too tight for her beast of a truck, but she threads the needle, and parallel parks in the weedy back parking lot like a pro. "Here's us. Maybe . . . maybe someone should stay in the car with the golem?"

"I'll come in," I announce.

Ari nods and steps out of the truck. As I unbuckle to follow, my brother catches my arm from behind. "I don't like this, Banana," he says. "We don't *know* her."

I knew he was thinking this already, and I shake my head. "We can't use that as a bar, we only know each other in this town."

"Exactly." He cuts his eyes toward the still-silent golem, then back to me. "I don't trust anyone but us."

THIRTEEN

AS SOON AS I step inside Forget-Me-Not, I know Mom would love it. She loves flea markets and vintage stores and "upscale" junk shops. Sometimes she's on the hunt—for old window shutters to turn into jewelry hangers, or a chipped cupcake platter to paint and use as a makeup stand, or a suitcase to fill with soil and plant succulents. Half the time, these projects turn out brilliantly; the other half, they're abandoned unfinished by the building dumpster. But just as often, Mom is looking for inspiration. She wanders the narrow aisles, eyes peeled for something—a retro color combination or unusual pattern—that will break her latest design project wide open. That's how she talks about her art. Like it's a locked chest, seemingly impenetrable, until glanced at from just the right angle so that a weakness appears. A loose hinge, or a crack between the boards, to be bashed in or pried apart.

More and more, this seems like my mother's philosophy for everything. Find something you want, and smash everything around it to pieces—families and hearts and best friends—until it's yours. How else to explain why she fled

Fox Hollow and never looked back, leaving a trail of miserable people behind her?

"Maybe you can find something for the golem to wear while I go through the storeroom," Ari suggests, interrupting my black thoughts. "Something less . . . Greek?"

Most of the clothes scattered throughout the showroom are way beyond retro, more like antiques: a lilac lace nightgown, a deep-green velvet smoking jacket with a checkered lining, a tree of ladies' hats with veils, or plastic fruit, or fake birds perched in a nest of real feathers. I could pick anything; we're not planning a stroll down Main Street, and from what little I know about golems, fashion doesn't seem like a priority for them. Still, it—he?—deserves dignity, so I try to choose well. I strip a dummy of a white short-sleeved knit pullover with navy stripes. It seems like something Gabe would've worn when the drama club did *On the Town*. There's a pair of cuffed olive trousers hanging from a trellis, a soft leather belt strung through the loops. No shoes anywhere, so I hope Gabe packed an extra pair or two.

The price tags attached to the clothes send my heart thumping, but when I bring my haul to the storeroom, Ari looks up from a box full of folded holiday tablecloths and says, "It's just, like, a loan. My parents won't notice till they do inventory, and I'll have everything back by then."

"Definitely. We can switch him over to Gabe's clothes at some point. I hope he likes anime-print blazers and plaid boat shoes." As I unclip the pants from their hanger and carefully fold the outfit, I ask something I've been wondering. "So . . . your parents weren't in synagogue with you yesterday?"

"They're not Jewish."

I must make some noise of surprise because she looks up at me. "I mean, obviously Bubbe was, and I am, and technically Mom is. But she doesn't call herself Jewish. She hasn't been to synagogue since I can remember. Longer than I've been alive, I think."

"You still go, though?"

She shrugs, muscling open the flaps on a new box. "They're my people. It's my place." Then she sits down and shoves the box away with the toe of her high-top: not the one we're look-ing for, clearly. "What about you? Did you like it?"

Taking her cue, I sink down onto the nearest cardboard box, which squashes slightly under my weight. "I don't know. It's weird to think of myself as Jewish," I confess, in a way I couldn't to Shoshanna. "Like, I don't even know that I believe in God. Plus I'd never been inside a synagogue." We switched schools three times between seventh and eighth grade, and I hadn't made new friends fast enough to snag any of the bar or bat mitzvah invites circulating the middle school halls. "Most of what I know about it, I learned on the train ride here. Noth-ing bad has ever happened to me because my grandmother was Jewish, or because my mom used to be Jewish . . . or maybe still is? It's—"

"Complicated," Ari agrees. "I know. But so is Judaism, I think. It's weird to say a religion is about more than God, but that feels true. It's, like, a shared history, and it belongs to me, and it belongs to you too, even if you never knew about it until just now. Because the things that happened to your grandparents, and great-grandparents, they shaped your life, in some way. So you don't have to, I don't know, throw on a yarmulke and dance the hora around the town green to identify that way. It's yours to claim, and nobody can do it for you or take it from you. Just like nobody could tell me that I like girls, or say that I don't. That was mine to decide."

Something deep in my body warms at this. Like a blush, but far below my skin, down in my chest. In my bones.

And I wonder: When was the last time that I decided, well, *anything* about myself? Like, did I choose Atticus as my boyfriend because I wanted to kiss him and hold his lightly sweating hand during study sessions for two months, or because he asked me to the winter formal and the rest of my friends had boyfriends and wanted me to quadruple-date with them, and I didn't want to disappoint them?

"Hey," Ari's voice nudges me from my thoughts. Her forehead is creased with concern, her pierced eyebrow lifted. "Are you okay?"

Whatever shows in my face, I smooth it over, because this is definitely not the time or place to spiral. "I'm fine." And I decide to be, at least until I'm alone and can have my existential crisis in peace and quiet.

So I make myself stand and rip the tape from the box I've been sitting on. I rifle gently through some folded clothes, printed scarves, and soft, bright sweaters. Between the garments, maybe tucked inside for safe packing, is a jewelry box. It doesn't look particularly expensive, covered in pale-gold faux leather that's scuffed black in places, peeling off at one rounded corner. There's a keyhole, but the latch must be broken, because the lid lifts easily. Tumbled together inside on the mint-green satin lining—sort of as if somebody had gathered and stuffed the contents in hurriedly, to be packed away for years—is a strange assortment of trinkets. They look like they belong in a child's treasure box: a round, egg-sized gray stone that rattles lightly when I pick it up, a wooden spool of thick coral yarn, a little pill box which, when I pry it open, holds a handful of sharp, curved canine teeth a little longer than my thumbnail. Not human, at least. There's a sachet like a homemade tea bag, but tied with yarn. It smells faintly green and woody, a little like licorice when I lift it to my nose. A dull, chunky silver necklace that looks like broken costume jewelry—it's missing the clasp. I stir around the odds and ends; none of them seem valuable. But then, none of it belonged to my grandmother.

I call Ari over to show it to her, and she beams. "Her amulets! I *knew* Mom didn't chuck this stuff."

"Do you know what all of it was for?"

She shrugs. "Not everything. If she told me . . . I wish I'd listened better."

It's interesting, for sure, but not what we're after. I move to the next box, and this time when I peel back the tape and lift the flaps, I'm rewarded with a neatly packed stack of notebooks inside. Nothing classy or cloth-bound, just plain spiral note-books, rippled with age. Their covers are tattered around the edges, peeling corners and yellowed paper. But when I hold one of the books up to show Ari, she shouts with delight, sets back the jewelry box, and bounds over to take it from me, cradling it carefully.

"There you are," she says, voice hushed and reverent, as though the book is something holy.

We retrace our route, out of town and back into the woods, eventually passing the mouth of Jitka's driveway, her house hidden behind a screen of trees and deep in the wildflowers. It's a few minutes more before another gap appears in the trees. Ari turns onto a paved driveway, though the blacktop's faded to a mild gray, spiderwebbed with cracks where grass and weeds stab through. The truck rocks as we rumble toward the end, where a pale-pink stone farmhouse waits, one story and just a fraction the size of the Eggerses', the whole front overtaken by dried brown vines and bramble.

"Those were climbing roses," Ari murmurs, pain a prickly bloom behind her words. "Once."

"How much do you come here?" I ask.

"Just a few times since I got my driver's license. But I left some supplies, so we should be sort of comfortable."

The grass swishes around our knees as we climb out. Ari lifts the box of notebooks out of the truck bed, puffing for breath, small biceps straining. It took both of us, sweating and cursing, to haul it out of Forget-Me-Not. "Hey, uh . . . golem!" Gabe says uncertainly. "Can you give her a hand?"

The golem stares at him.

"Can you, um, help her?" He tries again, nodding in Ari's direction.

Wordlessly, the golem, still betoga'd, takes the box, holding it aloft as easily as a carton of eggs.

Ari whistles low, speaking for all of us.

Together, we circle the stone house, summer insects chirping and whirring and droning in its depths. Ari leads us to the back porch, all bowed wood and chipped red paint. One of the windows, its thick frame a flaking red to match, screams in protest as Ari jimmies it upward. It lifts, and though I expect her apocalyptically shredded pants to snag on a nail or splinter, Ari slips gracefully over the sill. Soon, she's standing in the sliding door, beckoning us inside.

Ari was right—the heat isn't so bad in here, thanks to the shade from the trees overhead. We pass through a small kitchen where once-bright-blue cabinets hang loose on their hinges, and a farmhouse sink just like Jitka's is stained with rust, inexplicably clogged with leaves. The wood floorboards, pale and rough, are coated in dust except for a clean track down the center of the room. Clearly, Ari's trod here recently.

Through the creaking door and into a living room bare of real furniture, I'm stunned to find a kind of camp set up. There's an orange plastic Adirondack chair in front of a brick fireplace big enough to lie down inside. A Tupperware bin beside it acts as a side table, with a camping lantern and a pile of books set on top. On the stone hearth is a six-pack of Corona Extra with one can missing from the plastic rings.

"Are *you* squatting here?" Gabe asks, begrudging respect in his voice.

"No. It's just . . . our apartment is small. So is this town. Sometimes it feels like you can't go anywhere to get away from people, and all of them have ideas about you, and they're all watching you. So I come here. There are snacks in the bin if you're hungry. Just the one chair, but I've got a blanket in the back of the truck for winter emergencies."

While Ari heads back the way she came, I give Gabe my shopping bag of clothes and leave the room to pace the kitchen until Ari returns with an old but clean quilt, with the same sweet/musty/earthy old-book smell as the antique shop.

She smiles as she notices me covertly sniffing. "Our whole apartment smells that way. I think it comes up from the floor."

I abandon pretense and take a deep whiff, realizing that Ari smells just as good, and I haven't taken the time to notice until now.

When we figure enough time has passed, we go back in to find the creature dressed. It looks sharp and extra human in the trousers and pullover, still-bare feet aside. Gabe grins and spreads his arms, as if to say, *look on my works, ye mighty*, like he chose the outfit himself. I feel a prickle of irritation with my brother. But it's unfair, and I smother the feeling at once, leaving only mild guilt behind.

Across the room, Ari sets the books and lantern aside and opens the bin, pulling out a bag of potato chips, a package of rice cakes, and a box of pistachio cookies, which get my stomach grumbling—it's past noon by now, and we never did have breakfast. I take the cookies from her as she settles on the hearth beside me. She tosses the chips to Gabe, then asks him, "Is it, uh, hungry?"

The golem shakes its head once. "I do not eat."

"We can't keep saying 'it,'" Gabe protests. "That's, like, dehumanizing, you know?"

Though I could remind Gabe that the golem *isn't* human, I agree; "it" doesn't feel right.

My brother teethes his lip stud in thought and asks, "Are you a boy?"

"I am . . . I."

"*They*, then," Gabe decides.

Ari rubs a hand across her forehead. "I don't get it. It—they're not supposed to be able to do any of this. Speak, look human, none of it." She gestures toward the golem, who, from a slight distance, and wearing a pair of aviators, could pass for an art student. "Golems are big and strong and loyal, and that's all they are," she continues. "They're massive lumps of clay with limbs."

"Well that's just rude," Gabe scoffs. "Ignore her. You look great, kid."

The golem narrows their volcanically dark eyes. Not in anger, I don't think, but as if struggling to see something in the distance.

"Did you just *command* your golem to ignore me?"

Gabe smirks and settles lazily into the Adirondack chair. "A suggestion only. You heard them. They're their own person. Ish."

It's then that I decide to take back the title of group leader—a position I always pick at Winthrop, because I know my strengths, and want the chance to disguise my weaknesses. This is my curse—or whatever—that we're trying to break. It's my body, and *my* life. "All right, enough. We have one objective right now: to read through Ida's notebooks for any information in there about Mom's past, or"—I gesture vaguely in the golem's direction—"about our present circumstances."

I take the book from the top of the stack of journals and flip it open to read aloud: "For headache, bring cypress, willow, fresh myrtle, olive, poplar, sea willow, and cynodon grass. Boil together and pour three hundred cups on one side of the head, then the other. For migraines, slaughter a rooster with a silver dinar, so that the blood flows over the side of the head affected. Then hang in the doorpost of the house, to be touched when entering and exiting." I lower the notebook. "There's a page and a half in here about night blindness."

"Bubbe's work wasn't all ghosts and demons and vampires," Ari says, a little defensive. "It was, like, ninety-five percent night blindness. But it's all in there. Her stories, her memories, her cures, her work as an opshprekherke. You just have to look. And . . . be careful, okay?" She gazes lovingly at the notebooks. "They're important."

Duly warned, we retreat to our corners to read. It's

painfully slow going. If only the notebooks were organized in some way—old-world remedies separated from stories separated from diary entries. But of course that's not the case. Every page must be skimmed, and sometimes a paragraph on toothaches turns into a recounted memory of a customer from a decade earlier, turns into a scribbled list of blessings. There are no dates on the entries to help us search around the time of Mom's flight from Fox Hollow. And it doesn't help that Ida Silver's handwriting is terrible, somehow both pinched and swirling, and I have to squint and spend far too long making sure I don't miss anything.

I haven't even gotten through the first notebook when Gabe announces, "Shit, it's after two. We should get back before Esther and Bernie beat us there."

He's right, and I know it. But how can I go home only to sit in my guest bedroom for the rest of the afternoon and evening, counting the wildflowers in the field and stewing in what-ifs? What if the journals are just a cul-de-sac instead of the road that leads to Mom? What if Ari decides this is all too much, turns the golem over to the local sheriff, and deletes our numbers? What if tomorrow, I wake up *worse*?

Rolling my shoulders, the joints aching with the unfamiliar weight of wings and slick with sweat, I focus on the notebook in my lap. "I think . . . I'm gonna stay. Just for a little longer."

"We can't, Banana, we—"

"*We* won't. I think Ari should drive you back, and—and I should keep working." When Gabe doesn't answer, doesn't move, I dare a glance up.

My brother scrubs a palm over his jaw, studying me from across the room. "So what's the plan? You'll get back into the house how? You're supposed to be bedridden."

"You could cover for me. Keep Esther out, and sneak me in through the kitchen after they go to bed. I did it for you in Spring Valley," I remind him. Spring Valley, Minnesota, was our home for only a few months before Jamaica Plain. We were staying in a one-bedroom cottage on the grounds of a little vineyard; Mom designed their logo and website for pennies and a bottle of merlot, as she said, so she got a good deal on rent. I slept in the tiny bedroom, with Mom on the pullout couch and Gabe on a wooden cot and throw bed beside it. We lived largely off what Mom brought home from the local diner. She worked long hours as a waitress, but that didn't make it any easier to help sneak Gabe out to meet his chem partner after bedtime, then back in again after an evening decidedly not spent comparing ionic and covalent bonds. Not when he slept four feet from Mom, for God's sake.

My brother is not amused. "This is a bad idea, Hannah."

"Don't worry about me so much," I joke weakly. "You're not my mom."

It's the wrong thing to say. I sense this at once, like I sense Ari watching us wordlessly by the heat prickling the back of my neck. And I watch Gabe as he struggles to keep his face blank. "Fine. Stay. The lesser Williams will go sit shiva for you."

I flinch. "What's that supposed to mean?"

"Nothing." Then he slips on a smile like a mask. "I should go."

Ari starts to stand. "I left my keys in the kitchen, let me—"

"Nah, I'll walk. Just down the driveway and to the left, right?"

"It's over a mile by the road," she says.

But he's halfway out the front door already. He throws a peace sign to the golem, saying, "Stay here, okay? Take a nap if you want to . . . if you do that kind of thing." Then he's gone, with a last inscrutable look for me.

We sit in stifling silence for a moment until Ari breaks it with a nervous laugh. "Why don't we take a break, too? We've got hours now."

"Where would we go?" I ask, tugging the strings of Gabe's hoodie tighter around my neck.

Ari grins and winks—*winks*—and I'm as helpless to stop the smile that steals across my face as I am to stop a damned thing about my body.

AS JUNE TURNS to July, the summer heat thickens and boils over like soup on a stove. Fox Hollow has a town pool beside the high school, but it's always overcrowded. Instead, Malka and her sisters walk down to the river to swim. There hasn't been much rain, so the Hollow is low and green and slow moving. They spread their clothes on the thin bank, more naked in their bras and underwear than anyone but their own blood has seen them. They're used to each other's bodies: Shosh's spaghetti-thin limbs, Malka's curves, Geela's wide shoulders and square waist and strong legs. Shosh and Geela lie on their modest summer dresses while Malka wades straight into the water. Even as her skin stings with cold, she sloshes forward down the slope just until it's up to her ribs. It's supposedly thirty-odd feet at its deepest in this stretch of river. The current is mild today, but if she were to pick up her feet and float on her back, who knows how far it could carry her?

There's a noise behind her on the bank—rustling brush, a bird flapping its way out of the bushes. Malka spins around to see Siman among the reeds, his long-lashed eyes flickering with surprise.

She should scream.

Mama would want her to scream. It isn't just boys her mother doesn't trust, but everybody and everything. She doesn't trust the dark. She doesn't trust the woods or the river, and only allows them to swim in the Hollow when the water is low, and because it keeps them close by. She doesn't trust her daughters' friends, or their parents. The world, according to Mama, must be waiting for a chance, a single moment of neglect, a spell of permissiveness, to snatch her children away.

Malka doesn't scream. Instead she lifts her chin, and calls out, "Take a picture, it'll last longer."

Her sisters shoot upright to look. Finding Siman, they shriek (the correct response) and roll to clutch their clothes to their bellies. Unfrozen at last, Siman claps a hand across his eyes as they jump up and scramble into the trees and off toward home, toward safety.

Malka doesn't move.

"I didn't mean . . . I didn't know . . . ," he stammers, still self-blinded.

"What are you doing here?" she speaks over him. It's Sunday, and Mama and Papa drove to the station this morning to take the train down to Brooklyn to visit Papa's cousin. Malka can't believe Papa would let Siman around the house without him.

"I leave my tools here over the weekend, and came back to get my handsaw. Doing a favor for Mr. Frager. The car wasn't in your driveway, so I didn't think anybody was home. And it was hot, and I come down here to cool off when I'm working sometimes, but . . . I swear I didn't know you were here." He's still blushing beneath the blindfold of his hand.

It's cute, his embarrassment, like he's never seen a girl in her underwear. Malka can't believe that's true.

This is what Siman would see, if he let himself: The purple matching bra and panty set she bought with babysitting money, then immediately hid in her backpack and then stuffed under her bed, where it's sat since summer vacation began. Her full breasts and pinched waist and round hips, which Ida Silver calls "zaftig." Climbing out of her car last week, her red hair wild, amulets clanking against her chest and the smell of Spanish chamomile on her breath, Mrs. Silver looked at Malka and laughed, "Such a ripe fruit! What a blessing you are to your mama . . . or is it a curse?"

Wading back to the bank with some regret, she tugs her sundress on over dripping skin. "You can look now."

Slowly, he drops his hand. "I guess I should—"

"I'll walk back with you," she offers quickly, as little as she wants to go back. At least they're alone, something she hasn't managed yet this summer.

He smiles shyly, nodding, and they make their way through the trees together.

"Do you like it here?" Malka asks.

Siman looks up at the woods around them, suntanned face dappled with shadow and light. "It's a pretty town. Quiet. The people are nice."

"I guess so."

"Don't you like it here?"

Malka thinks through her answer as she picks her way over roots and brush. "I do, it's just . . . it's a little small. It's, like, five square miles, and half of that is river and woods."

"I've seen smaller. You know there's a town in Wyoming with a population of three? Only a guy, his wife, and his son live there. It's just a modular home with a convenience store and a few gas pumps."

"I guess we're not that bad then." And really, that's the best answer to the question "what's so bad about Fox Hollow?" *We're not that bad.* It isn't poverty stricken. There's a lower-income neighborhood on the north end—about three streets long—but even then, they're mostly historic homes converted into multifamily housing, a few scallop-shaped shingles missing from the roofs, paint uncurling from the shutters. There are no department stores clamoring to plant their poison roots in town, putting the mom-and-pop bakery and family-owned kids' clothing store and the Pineapple out of business. There are no factory chemicals in the Hollow causing mutated fish and animal die-off. So, knowing her complaint might sound ridiculous, she picks her words carefully. "It's just that I've been in class with the same twenty kids since kindergarten. And everyone at synagogue remembers what I look like in diapers."

He laughs, but Malka could pull her own hair out. She's waited a month to be alone with Siman, and with her one chance, she talks about herself in *diapers?*

To cover, she rushes ahead. "I know I'm lucky to have my

whole family around. My sisters all went to college in eastern New York, and married nice Jewish boys who grew up around here too, and now they all live close enough to come to Shabbat dinner every Friday. I can't even imagine not seeing them every week. I can't imagine my parents not being a room or a floor away all the time. It's just, um . . . Sometimes it's hard, when everyone's always known you."

Siman nods along. "I get that."

"Right," she says, encouraged. "Like they all decided who I was seventeen years ago, and nothing I do will change that now."

"Home is like that. Even when you go away and come back, people pretend you never left and never changed."

"At least you got to leave home, though."

He holds back the whippy limb of a willow for her to pass under. "Can't you?"

She blinks as they leave the trees and cross into the meadow, the wildflowers so colorful in the sunlight, they're almost painful to look at. How can she begin to explain what's keeping her here, that she's grown up knowing it was her job to stay? That her mother's many losses, barely spoken of, can't be made up for, but her children are her comfort, her night-lights in the dark, who can at least stave off the fear and sadness that will never leave her? She can't make him understand before they reach the house, so she doesn't try. "Maybe. Where should I go? Where did you go?"

Siman pats the old barn affectionately as they pass, trailing his hand along the mossy wood. "I went to Europe for a little while, France and Spain mostly. Then I spent two months backpacking the Shikoku pilgrimage in Japan, between the eighty-eight temples. I would sleep in fields if I couldn't find a henro house. I took the Trans-Siberian Railway through some of the Soviet Union. When I was in New Zealand, I hitchhiked from Queenstown out to the Te Anau Glowworm Caves. You take a boat down through the narrow waterways, look up at the cave ceiling, and see thousands and thousands of these tiny blue lights blink around you, like stars." He nudges her elbow gently with his. "You should see it someday."

"Where will you go next?"

"I don't really know." As they reach the back door of her parents' house, he looks at her full-on for the first time since she spotted his shocked face by the river. Obviously, he's recovered. His blue eyes are lighter than the cloudless sky above them, and his cool smile sets off thousands and thousands of little stars inside of her. "I'm not going yet."

FOURTEEN

THE RIVER, WHERE it runs through the woods behind Ida Silver's old house, is maybe fifty feet across, much wider than I'd expected. It's a little shy of the high-water line at the moment, a slice of the sharp slope down to the hazel water exposed, but the Hollow is faster moving than I expected for a river twisting lazily through the woods. After struggling through brush and trying not to trip over half-buried tree roots, I'm sweating worse than ever, but I stay back and pick a spot up the slope with a cluster of wild shrubbery at my back, where I'm hidden from—who? There's nobody in these woods but me and Ari. I tell myself this as I give up and strip off the hoodie, hoping at least to catch the wet breeze on my skin.

By the time I've got the hoodie up and over my wings and look for Ari, I see:

Bare white skin.

Damp pink coils of hair.

Steel-blue eyes flashing back at me.

She might not be naked, but she's left her black T-shirt and pants slung over a branch that hangs over the skinny riverbank, and her racerback bra and boy shorts don't leave much to the imagination. The sight does strange and swooping things to my stomach.

"You coming in?" she calls back to me.

I manage a head shake, then look away just in time to hear the gentle splash of her sliding into the water. I look everywhere but the river—down at the dirt and up at the pieces of bright-blue sky through the branches—until she climbs out and scales the bank right in front of me, carrying her sneakers. The long stretch of her legs below her boy shorts glitters with river water.

Ari drops down to sit beside me, winding her sopping wet hair back into its bun and wrapping a thick hair tie around it. "Do they hurt?" she asks, abruptly but gently.

I roll my shoulders for the hundredth time today. "Not much. And never when it happens, if that's what you mean. I just fall asleep, then wake up changed. That's the curse, we guess."

"So tomorrow?"

"Something new," I confirm.

"That . . . will be interesting," she says, clearly rattled.

"What will you tell your parents? If you're spending time with me—with us, I mean—they won't wonder where you are or what you've been doing?"

"Hardly." She reaches down to brush damp sand from her bare feet. "Summer's their busy season, between tourist traffic and estate sales and flea markets all across the eastern seaboard.

If they're not in the shop, they're traveling to acquire stuff or sell stuff. It's one reason I used to spend so much time with Bubbe. Like, they're off to Pennsylvania tomorrow afternoon and won't be back till Tuesday morning, so I'll be on my own for the night."

"What about your friends?" What possesses me to ask this, I don't know. I regret it immediately.

"My friends aren't around this summer. Nik is in Ohio visiting his mom, and Loren's family has this vacation cottage at Lake George, so they go every weekend. She used to take me. But she just got this boyfriend, and they're pretty serious. And it's fine."

"What about your girlfriend?" What is *wrong* with me? "Sorry, that's not—"

"It's okay," Ari says, shoving her feet into her sneakers. "I'm one of, like, two lesbians at our tiny school, so far as I know? Julia Cook—she's the other one. And I kind of can't stand her. She interrupts in history class to counterteach us about the Napoleonic Era. She gets a ninety-seven on a physics test and wastes five minutes of class time at Mr. Purcell's desk arguing for a ninety-nine, so we all have to stay five minutes late. She thinks Sylvia Plath is *whiny*. I read all these books where queer kids flock together, but I'm not *flocking* with Julia Cook anytime soon. So yeah, that limits my options. I talk to some girls I met online on queer Tumblrs or Twitter, but we don't live anywhere near each other. And my parents might be cool with me staying home alone, but driving to the city by myself, not so much. I'm pretty much stuck in a small, shallow pool until I graduate next year, go somewhere with an actual queer culture, and just . . . with people like me, you know?"

It's taken me this long to realize what should've already occurred to me. I was fooled by her general Ari-ness; how, in the short time I've known her, she's seemed surer of herself than anybody I know, except maybe my brother. Like, I think people carry around this idea of themselves, this image, while their friends have this whole other idea of them, and their teachers another idea entirely, and their dentist, et cetera. But then some people seem so completely the person they mean to be at all times—alone in their beds, in the school cafeteria, in the passenger seat of their best friend's car—that each image matches up perfectly, five-cherries-in-a-slot-machine style. Ari just struck me as one of those people who've hit the self-esteem jackpot.

Except that she's spent the whole day in the company of total strangers, and never once been interrupted by a text, or summoned by a phone call, or excused herself to live whatever life she had going on before us. So maybe I should've guessed that Ari Leydon is as lonely as I am.

I feel a pang of protest and remind myself: I have Gabe.

"What about you?" she asks. "Your friends, a boyfriend? Do they know where you are?"

"No. I mean, there is no boyfriend, and my friends think I'm in Canada?" I laugh a little when she does. "It's not as shitty an excuse as it sounds. My grandparents live in Ontario.

Supposedly, I'm camping in the foothills of the Rockies with no reception."

"Sounds like a great summer. Very restful."

"Mm." I can feel my smile fading. It's been six weeks since I muted our group chat, and who knows if they're even mentioning me anymore.

"Well, anyway." Ari interrupts this bleak thought. "I didn't mean to burn through our research time, it was just so fucking hot in there. And I used to swim with Bubbe when I was little, though she never told my parents. Mom doesn't like me going near the river. She says it's not hygienic. As if there's Guinea worm or dysentery in the Hollow."

Forgetting my own troubles for a second, I cast an anxious glance up and down her drying body.

She laughs. "Don't worry, there isn't. Maybe some leeches. But what are *you* worried about?" It's her turn to study me from head to toe to wingtip. "What's gonna fuck with you?"

Maybe I should feel embarrassed, but I laugh again in return, letting my tightly coiled nerves loosen just a bit. "So you're not freaked out anymore?"

"I'm completely freaked out," she admits, but her smile lingers. Unlike Gabe, she has dimples in both cheeks, and the deep valleys of them do something to my chest.

Or maybe it's being looked at and being forgiven for what I am. Like my rib cage has cracked wider by an inch, my heart gleaming through, and she doesn't hate the sight of it. It is a good feeling. A free feeling.

Sighing, Ari leans back on her elbows, a thoughtless slump that I envy. Every time she moves her body, it's thoughtless, like nobody's ever belonged in their own skin the way she does. "Okay, back to work. So, what do we know?" She ticks the facts off on her fingers. "Your mom makes a mistake; maybe she's talking about taking off with this boy. The farmhand, whoever your aunt was talking about. That seems most likely. But what does that have to do with you? And why would it be 'Ida Silver territory'?"

I shake my head, frustrated. "We wouldn't be here if I knew that."

"Okay, fine." She holds up her hands. "Just trying to talk it through. So put a pin in that. So they run away together. Then what? Where do they go next? Why don't they ever come back?"

I shrug, wincing as the membrane of my wings brush my back. "Mom's been everywhere, from Morocco to Mexico and everyplace in between. But I always thought she traveled alone. I've never seen pictures of her with a guy. And she was single when she met my dad. She'd been working for this traveling rodeo show, doing design stuff for them, some costuming, posters, whatever. The rodeo set up in Denver, where Dad lived back then, and she says it was love at third sight—he was an accountant for some big law firm that helped sponsor the event, so he got to sit in their box all week, and they kept crossing paths. He died before my first birthday, though."

"I'm sorry, Hannah."

"It's okay." And then, so she won't spend the next five minutes awkwardly struggling with whether or not to ask, "It was a car accident. Well, Dad was riding his bike. The other dude was in the car—he was fine, obviously. Fell asleep at the wheel after a night shift. Just a normal death." Well, *that* was an awkward-as-hell way to put it. I stare at the river downstream, tempted to throw myself into the swiftly moving waters.

"That's horrible," Ari says simply, "normal or not."

"Yeah. I guess it is." I don't really like thinking about the life we could've had with two parents, with a home. Who would? "The part that really sucks—well, one of the parts—is I just get the feeling that we would've, like, gotten each other, you know? I mean, he was an accountant. We probably could've compared spreadsheets."

She nods thoughtfully. "I'm really sorry you don't have that. It really, really sucks when nobody sees you."

I clear my throat. "Anyway, whoever that boy was, he definitely wasn't Michael Kowalski."

"Hmm. Well, maybe we could find him. You can find anybody online. And he must know something about that summer."

"Shoshanna couldn't remember his name. Just that he was staying over a place called Frager's? And that they left town together less than a month before Mom turned eighteen, which would've been the end of September in 1990. That was forever ago. You think your mom would remember this guy?"

"Maybe. That's what straight best friends do, right?" She sniffs. "Talk about boys? Except I'm not sure how to start that

177

conversation. 'Hey Mom, remember that ex-friend you despise, who you refused to believe was in trouble? You don't have her ex-boyfriend's Twitter handle, do you?' Maybe . . ." She runs a finger across her bottom lip as she thinks, and I try not to trace its path with my eyes. "Frager's is a bookseller downtown. They've been in Fox Hollow since the twenties, I think. They're as old as the synagogue. Harold Frager, the guy who runs it now, is like three generations deep."

"So he might know?"

"Probably not. That's a long time to keep records, and he would have been a kid then. But even if he doesn't, Harold keeps copies of the *Hollow Star*—that's our little town paper that goes out three times a year, so it's more like a triannual yearbook than a newspaper, I guess. There's an August edition, and the boy would've been in Fox Hollow in August of 1990, at least for some of it. They should have it. They have every edition since Harold's dad started saving them. They store them in this steamer trunk in the coffee nook. Mom says they think of themselves as a mini hometown museum, since we don't have one. What would we even display? That one arrowhead Darcy Keating found by the river, which turned out to be from the seventies, but with the store stamp washed away?"

I consider this. "You really think a farmhand would've been in the paper?"

"It's possible. I once read an article about a family on vacation who stopped at the Pioneer Diner on Maple. They weren't famous or anything, just tourists from New Jersey passing through. The dad said the Reuben sandwich was the best he'd ever eaten, and tipped fifty percent. *That* made the *Star*, so who knows?"

And so we each have our tasks. Gabe is stranded at Jitka's, ducking upstairs regularly enough that Esther doesn't feel the need to check on me, letting strangers clasp his hand while they murmur their condolences for a grandmother he doesn't remember. Ari is off to interrogate Harold Frager at his bookstore. And I stay behind at Ida's to read through her notebooks in the company of the golem, still in the Adirondack chair with their palms on the knees of their trousers, watching the barest breeze stir the tall grass beyond the front windows.

I finish scanning the first notebook and dive into my second, but I've only gotten through a page on the healing properties of Spanish chamomile before I let the book fall shut again. "No chance you can read, is there?" I ask the golem, half joking.

They turn their head toward me, where I'm cross-legged on the floor. "I do not remember."

"Wait, so you do remember *some* things?"

"I believe so," they say carefully, considering. "I know that I have never been, before now. There was nothing, and then there was the barn, and voices, faces . . . His, then yours. But I knew the language of the words he was speaking, and that's something. Even as his words were the beginning of me."

"Who, Gabe?"

"Gabe." They speak my brother's name as if it's a work of

art, too, as if it's a poem. Their fingers drift up to his hand-writing, small and unsmudged across their skin. Then their pitch-dark eyes meet mine. "Do you know what came before that? What I was before Gabe?"

It's my turn to shake my head. "I don't know. We don't know enough about you. But we're working on it. We'll figure it out." I promise them what my brother has promised me so many times. Maybe our grandmother built the golem, but we brought them into our world. Into our impossible mess. Don't we owe them something?

They interrupt my thoughts. "Would you like to see if I can read?"

I cross to their chair and hold the notebook open while their eyes roam the page, thick eyebrows quirked in concentration. As they study the text, I study them, and I can believe this face was sculpted and brought to life by an artist's hands. The soft ridge of their brow, the strong bridge of their nose, the mathematically perfect lips. What's more, I'm astonished to find they no longer look like clay—the micalike glimmer has settled into a faint sheen. If they were a painting in a museum, I would stand in the gallery while the crowds seethed around me, deep in my feelings that human beings really are miraculous works of art.

They shake their improbable head. "This does not make sense to me."

"That's okay. I'll keep going."

While the golem retreats into their own thoughts, or memories, or dreams, I retreat to my place on the floor with renewed determination. And this time, I don't have to read for long. Only a dozen pages into the notebook is an entry, undated like every other, but with just the names I've been looking for.

I sit with my dear friend while a nor'easter beats at her windows. If not for the rain, the house would be quiet. Isaac's shiva ended yesterday, and the last of her girls have gone home. At least, the last of the daughters she'll speak of. It's the strangest thing. When I dared to ask whether Malkala would be coming back to Fox Hollow to mourn, she acted as though her youngest wasn't a real girl, settled down now, as close as a nonstop flight, but as if she were only ever a dream. It troubles me. With her husband's passing, alav ha-shalom, I worry she may retreat further—not into grief, but into the numbness that feels preferable to feeling, tending, and properly treating a wound.

I cannot cure sadness, and wouldn't if I had the gift. Only when we allow ourselves to grieve for what's lost can we heal, and helping to heal is what I do.

So I've made it my task to keep her tethered to the present, even if it means prodding at the past. I've reminded her that someday, she'll want her children and grandchildren to know where she came from, and by extension, where they came from. If we set it down on paper, then it will exist outside of her, and never again will she have to go through the retelling. So, we sit together in her parlor, drinking our tea with a bissel of brandy for courage. I will write my friend's story, and b'ezrát hashém, it will outlive us both.

PRAGUE, 1939

YOU ASK FOR my story, bubeleh, but I don't know when it starts. With the war? With my birth? With the day my táta met my máma, both of them children, peering at each other around their own parents' legs on the street in front of the Altneuschul?

Who can determine, in all of history, the very moment when we each begin?

I'm sure enough of the *where*, at least. Josefov was my home, and our family's home for generations. For centuries. My parents were the first ones in the remembered history of each of their families not born inside of Prague's Jewish Quarter, and then only because of the reconstruction. All those crooked lanes had become crowded with poor Czechs and Jews, immigrants and trade workers whose businesses disappeared when the factories arrived. The Vltava River flooded often, so the basements of the old houses were damp and dark with mold, and the courtyards were plagued with sickness. When the city authorities decided to raze the run-down homes with dynamite and replace the narrow alleyways with planned streets, nobody fussed too much. And after the renewal, many of Prague's Jews moved back, my people included.

Our life there was a good one. We had one of the newer apartments, large enough for all of us. Táta was a very talented sculptor, you know, though he never saw the fame of some of his friends. He attended the Vysoká škola uměleckoprůmyslová, the Academy of Arts, Architecture, and Design, though it was called something different then, and studied as a young man under many artists. Otto Gutfreund, the Jewish sculptor, was a teacher of his, and something of a mentor, before he drowned in the Vltava. Bernard Reder, also Jewish, took an interest when he was living in Prague. I grew up around great men, in and out of Táta's shop, and I couldn't remember a time when I myself didn't know the feeling of clay and softwood beneath my fingertips—Táta preferred to plan with clay, then build his final projects with walnut or boxwood, which could be carved like cheese. My father thought I had great promise, and I thought I might be just like him, and study at the Academy. Then Reder moved to Paris, a few years before the war, and I thought maybe I would do that, too, returning home to Prague after, of course.

Then I saw in the papers that Reder's Paris studio and the work inside of it was destroyed by the Nazis when they came. But he fled, and survived.

Not only were we raised in a home with a healthy love of the arts, but of G-d. Both my parents were religious. Táta in particular had a lineage of scholars and rabbis, my dědeček—his own father—being the most recent one. Supposedly, one of his ancestors was the great rabbi Judah Loew ben Bezalel, who built the golem rumored to rest in the attic of the Altneuschul, our own synagogue. Even his good friends, when I asked around, would laugh and pat my head and say that it was true. But by the time I was a teenager, I'd decided it was only local lore, just like the stories Máma used to tell us. About the beautiful and wise princess Libuše, who long ago stood on a cliff overlooking the Vltava, pointed to the hill over the river, and told her people to build a castle there, prophesying a city whose glory would touch the stars. About Dalibor, a good man who was sentenced to death and imprisoned in a tower of the Prague Castle. He would play his violin while awaiting execution, and the people were moved by his music, and knew he was dead the day he played no longer. And one of her favorites, "The Underwater Palace," about—well, surely you know it, with all of your reading.

I'm wandering from my own story and into others, but is it not impossible to say where one story ends, and another begins?

Where was I?

Máma. The ten of us kept her very busy. Even as a child, I'd have to count on my fingers as I named my older brothers and sisters to keep them straight:

Damek.

Helenka.

Jakub.

Nadezda.

Karel.

Rayna.

Marjeta.

Gabek.

Sorina.

I haven't spoken their names aloud in . . .

You see, I was the youngest, younger than Sorina by three years, a long spread for a family like ours. I wish it hadn't been so. But in March of 1939, when the Nazis infested my city, my homeland, I was the only one of the Loew children who was still, at sixteen, a child.

Táta had forbidden me from leaving the apartment building; we knew they were coming, of course. President Hácha had signed over our country without a fight to stop the Germans from bombing Prague. We'd listened to his words on the radio very early that morning, huddled together in our nightclothes. But I snuck out in the cold to watch them march through the Staroměstské náměstí like some terrible parade.

Yoshua said it felt like the beginning of the end of the world.

He was . . . a boy I knew. From synagogue, from the neighborhood. We lived in the building across the street from his family, the Freunds. A boy I liked, to tell the truth. Oh, he was handsome. I hardly thought he noticed me. But that day, when he saw me headed for the square from his own window, he followed me into the street. So we watched together as the Nazis went past, on foot and motorcycle and bicycle. We left before the trucks and tanks arrived, but of course Táta had already found out, and was furious. I half thought he'd lock me in my room forever, slipping old matzo beneath the door once a day.

That night he came up to speak with me. Sorina and Gabek, the only of my siblings still in the house, had gone to bed, and so too had Máma, but he guessed I'd be awake. My bedroom looked out onto the street, and the small balcony of the Freunds' apartment seemed so close that night, I could nearly touch it. I was very afraid, of course, for myself and my family and my homeland . . . but I was fifteen, and only just realizing how my very heart stammered when I thought of the boy I'd grown up knowing. So I was preoccupied when Táta came into my room, and told me he was sending me away.

I started to cry, to protest, to promise I'd listen from now on, but Táta wasn't punishing me. There were people, he told me—good people—who helped Jewish children escape from the atrocities happening across Europe, bringing them to the relative safety of the United Kingdom. The first such train had left Prague only the day before, and I would be on the very next one. I would leave Czechoslovakia, cross through Belgium to the coast, and travel by boat to England, where I already had a family to take me in—a college friend of Táta's, a painter. Having a sponsor made it that much easier to get me a seat. My parents had been working on this in secret, you see, ever since Hitler had set his sights on our homeland. Because for all that we had some money to our name, where on earth could we all go even if we did manage to escape together? Almost no place was taking in Jewish refugees, you might remember.

This was my way out, Táta said. I would leave within the month, and only I would be going. The Kindertransport only took children under seventeen. Again, I wept, with fear instead of anger. "How could you send me away alone?" I cried. "If you love me, can't we stay together?"

Táta was quiet for the longest moment. And then he told me a new story, or rather, a very old one in a new way. "You remember 'The Underwater Palace'? The tale your máma heard from Babička Setzer? It's the fairy-tale version, the one that we tell in Prague, because it is pleasant, and teaches us that wondrous things are possible, and beautiful things may grow from grief.

"However, this is not the story that I, as a child, was told."

Here, I have gone back and recopied my dear friend's words so that I might add my own. I believe it is important. As Jitka says, it is difficult to tell one story without the other.

"The Underwater Palace" is indeed a tale I've read, and the gist is this: a young girl, the only daughter of a wealthy merchant, has been betrothed to a man she cannot bear to marry. For she had another love, a secret love, who came to her one night a month as she stood on the bank of the river Vltava under a full moon. She would watch the shimmering waters from the dock until a striking young man would row his boat into view, climb ashore, and embrace her in the damp sand. Each time he begged her to leave with him, and she always replied, "Not yet."

This continued until the night before her unhappy wedding, when at last they both grew desperate. Having been sent away once more, the young man rowed away from shore only to stop, stand in the bright moonlight, and shout, "If you truly love me, you will follow me!" Then he dived into the river and disappeared.

The girl's father and fiancé happened upon her in this moment, having gone out to look for her when she did not return home. They watched from too far a distance as she stood on the muddy bank, entranced and heartsick, then dived into the river herself. They shouted for her as her father plunged into the water to pull her out, but it was too late—she had been carried away by the current. Nothing remained but water and moonlight, and her body was never found. Her father, now childless, sank into grief. He was tended to by his sister, a midwife by trade, but wished only to live alone with his memories, and his bitter regret.

One year later, the girl's aunt was summoned in the middle of the night by a servant in elegant dress, who claimed her help was needed. Assuming one of the wealthy wives of Prague was giving birth and required a midwife, she dressed quickly and followed. The servant led her down to the shore of the Vltava where, to her bewilderment, a boat was docked. She climbed in, thinking to be rowed across the water, and closed her eyes for the journey—she had a fear of the river since it had taken her niece. When she opened them again, she was astonished to see a glittering palace, as grand as Prague Castle, and all the shifting blue-green colors of a waterfall. Odd plants wavered in the surrounding gardens, stirred as if by an unending breeze. As she stepped out of the boat onto an algae-green dock, she saw schools of fish in flight above her like birds, and realized that, while she was breathing, she must be beneath the river itself, and not across it.

The servant knocked on the great gates of the palace, and a young man the aunt knew must be a prince answered, dressed all in green with gold adornments. "We have been expecting you," he told her with a handsome smile. "Follow me, if you please." And he led her through ice-blue corridors aglow with pearly light. In a glittering chamber on a polished blue-and-green abalone throne sat none other than her niece—and greatly pregnant, at that!

The aunt felt faint at the sight of her, but agreed at once to stay and help her niece through the birth of her child. In no time, the healthy daughter was born, and both parents were suffused with joy. At last, the girl explained to her aunt that she had not drowned that dreadful night, though she had decided to follow her love to his grave. Instead, she woke in the palace and discovered that her suitor was not merely a young man, but a water demon who ruled the Vltava. It may sound fearsome, but the aunt was wise, and had observed the prince's love for his wife and child. She knew that some shedim do love, and observe the Sabbath, and even keep mitzvot.

In short, shedim can be as complicated as people.

The aunt was overjoyed, and promised to tell the girl's father all that had passed below the water, so that he could set his sorrow aside and be happy for her. But the girl grew pale and shook her head. "No, auntie, you must not!" she insisted. "If the world above knew of us, it could endanger our lives down below. Though I grieve for his grief, it is best that he never be told."

The aunt agreed reluctantly. After showing her to a treasure chamber inside the prince's cathedral to fill her pockets with gold as payment, the servant escorted her back to the boat. She was returned to the surface and the shore, unharmed, and kept the girl's secret (for again, she was a wise woman). Only on her brother's deathbed did she whisper the truth to him, so that he left this world glad in the knowledge that his precious daughter was alive, happy, and in love forever. With that told, I return to Jitka's story.

My táta then recalled his childhood version of "The Underwater Palace," which began as Máma's story did, but had a different ending entirely. In this telling, the aunt returned to the surface and she watched her brother live his life as though half dead, starved and sleepless from grief. She knew that she had made a promise, but surely if her niece could see her father now, she would feel tender toward him, and make just one exception? In truth, the aunt was terrified for her brother, sure that he would soon meet a more final end than his daughter's, and fear makes fools even of the wise. The aunt confessed the entire tale, hoping that her brother could now move on with his own life, knowing his beloved daughter lived still.

But that was not what happened.

Instead of turning to peace, the father's sorrow festered and turned to anger. How could he ever be at peace, knowing his daughter was as close as the Vltava, but forever out of reach? How could he sleep knowing that a demon had her in his clutches? He blamed himself no longer, but in turn blamed her prince—the sheyd who had claimed his only daughter, stolen his most cherished belonging and the only thing that mattered to him in this world. And now, his granddaughter was trapped as well.

In desperation, the father sought the help of the most powerful rabbi in Prague, a holy man with knowledge of the supernatural. He begged the rabbi to help him by slaying the demon, freeing his daughter from her vows. Then, she and the baby could come home.

The rabbi explained that he was only human, and did not have the power to slay the demon, only to trap him, cutting him off from his kingdom and thus his powers. But, he cautioned, all dealings with demons are uncertain, and he could not say what their meddling in the supernatural might affect. And who was to say that, when freed from her promises, she would still return to her father? Children are as unknowable as any creature.

Certain of his daughter's misery, trapped in a strange kingdom, the father insisted.

And so the rabbi waited on the dock under the full moon for the sheyd to row himself to shore. The sheyd had his wife and daughter, and so had little need to leave his kingdom again. And yet, each night he would come to the surface and stand in the damp sand of the Vltava and gaze upon a world that could offer him nothing, for his strange heart was already as full as the moon.

There, the rabbi used the most secret words to command the sheyd into a small chest, trapping the prince like an animal in a dark cage. He wound a silver chain around it, each link engraved with the Seal of Solomon, to trap him there and cut him off from his powers. The demon was bound, and the rabbi took the chest home with him, forever to be his burden and responsibility.

The father waited all night by the dock, and the next day, and the next. Every day until the winter came, and he took ill from the cold, but still he would half crawl to the riverbank, certain his daughter would soon emerge. On his deathbed, he had his sister—then very old herself, and heartsick that she had not been able to save her brother from his grief after all—help him down to the Vltava. And there he died, still waiting to see his daughter one more time.

The poor man never knew that, with the sheyd lost to his kingdom, the palace had collapsed, throwing the daughter and her baby girl from the demon realm into this one, where they drowned at once at the bottom of the deep river.

"This," Táta finished, "is the story my father always told to me. He had his reasons, as you'll learn in time. But tonight, the lesson is this: It's a parent's job to know when to hold tight to their child, and when to let go. We send you away because we love you, Jitkala. Because if we keep you here, you may well drown with your city."

And so with many tears, it was decided. My family would stay in Prague. I would go on alone.

The night before my train left, the family gathered to celebrate Shabbat together. When I think of them, it's always as they were then: Sorina in her best dress and with flour in her hair from the challah she'd helped Máma bake. Damek with his sweet smile. Helenka, with roses in her cheeks as she looped her arm through her husband's. Jakub, his pale-blue eyes and booming laugh as he told us stories from university. Nadezda with her two young children on her hips, tired but determined. Karel, whose singing voice was like a strummed harp. Rayna, lovely and solemn as a Torah scroll. And Marjeta, who was so much older than me she'd been more like an aunt than a sister, and who would take me into Staroměstské náměstí for ice cream when I was little, and gave me her cone when mine spilled to the cobblestones. My grandparents were there too—Babička Loew, and Babička and Dědeček Setzer—and all Máma and Táta's brothers and sisters who could travel to us.

The things they gave me that night, they claimed to be sending with me for safekeeping, to hold on to for a while and bring back after the danger had passed. Nobody spoke aloud what we all feared: that what was happening in other places would happen in Czechoslovakia—the riots, the fires and the vandalism, the harsh laws imposed upon Jews, the murders and the mass arrests. There had been rumors of the camps in Germany for years, and now in Austria, and in Bavaria near our own border. I think it was in all of their hearts that some of us may never see each other again. I was old enough to understand this, at least.

Babička Loew gave me her spice box to tuck into my suitcase, the one shaped like a pomegranate, which you've certainly seen. Babička and Dědeček Setzer, their silver etrog box. Mama gave me our best Sabbath candlesticks, which had been passed down from Babička Setzer and her mother, and so on.

Not until the Shabbat candles burned very low, and my niece and nephew had fallen asleep on the parlor floor, did Táta pull me aside to give me his presents. Which, if I tell it truly, were both gift and curse. First was a small book I had never seen before, very old—I worried it would turn to dust beneath my fingertips. I unwrapped the leather thong that bound it, and though I had expected a prayer book, I found a diary. As Máma's candlesticks had been handed down through her family, he explained, so this had been passed through Táta's. He told me it might have been the rabbi Judah Loew ben Bezalel's, or perhaps his son's, for there were no accounts of daily life or preserved memories within its pages. No, these were instructions.

"For what?" I asked, squinting at its pages. My Hebrew was fluent, of course, but the handwriting was harder to interpret, and it was written in an older and less familiar form, for you know how those letters have changed some throughout the centuries.

"For imbuing a creature with the breath of life, my sheifale," he explained solemnly. "For building the golem."

And so I learned that, in Táta's mind at least, the stories of my childhood were true.

Half unbelieving, I asked, "Why wouldn't you keep this and use it, if you're so sure it's real?"

"What good is clay against tanks?" he asked bitterly, and I will never forget the look on his face, the utter despair. I now believe, in that moment, that he knew the next words out of his mouth to be a sweet lie. But I felt better when he smiled through his beard and said, "Keep it with you, Jitkala. When you come home, we will go down to the banks of the Vltava, gather our supplies, perform the rituals, and find out together whether it's real, eh?"

The second of his gifts was even stranger, if you can believe that, but I don't like to speak of it.

All of these things I carried with me to England, all that I had of my family. And one more treasure besides.

Late that night, after my siblings and aunts and uncles and grandparents had left, and Máma and Táta were comforting each other in their own bedroom, I lay awake in mine. I heard a ping against my windowpane, and then a sharper snick, as if a bird had flown beak-first into the glass in the dead of winter. Of course, when I climbed from my bed and shoved up my window, I saw differently.

Across the street, Yoshua stood on his family's balcony, a fistful of pebbles slipping free to patter the street below.

I have told you that he was handsome, Ida. Truly, he was beautiful. Dark eyes, high cheekbones, and a slim, stubbled chin. Strength and grace, he had. Somehow, he'd grown from a tangle of spindly limbs and sharp angles into an almost-man. I stood gazing at him from across the street, which suddenly felt very far, and realizing that I was a little bit in love with Yoshua Freund.

Without saying a word, he tossed something toward my window—I thought it was another stone, stupidly, and I almost batted it aside, but made myself catch it in the air before it too could fall to the cobblestones. Not a rock, but a napkin wrapped tightly and tied with yarn. When I plucked out the knot, I found a locket in the folds of the cloth. It wasn't very old or precious, nothing like the rest of my presents. I don't think it was an heirloom. A simple gold oval etched with little flowers, one he might have saved up to buy himself. And inside, he'd cut out little pictures of us. I recognized them from our class photos in the school yearbook—he must have torn the pages from the library, which seemed very daring to me, and like proof of his own affection. To me, it was the most wonderful thing in the world.

Maybe he did love me too, at least a little.

But he never got to tell me so. He shut his window before we could be discovered, and I shut mine, and I left early for the train station the next morning.

I never saw him again.

I never saw any of them.

This part of the story, you already know. After the war, I came here—my host family told me not to go back to Prague right away, that little but memories would be left for me. Instead, they helped me find connections and work in America. And it was in America, with the help of Isaac and his parents, that I learned what happened to them all.

Babička Setzer died of an illness not long after I departed, and maybe that was a kindness for her. The rest were sent, like so many of my neighbors and friends, to Terezín—Theresienstadt, they call it here. And if they didn't die there—it wasn't a death camp, not officially, and Hitler claimed it was, in fact, a city he had built *for* the Jews to protect us during the war, can you even imagine? But still, many thousands did die of sickness and starvation, and many, many more were sent on to Auschwitz and Majdanek and Treblinka. That's where the rest of my family died. My grandparents, my aunts and uncles, my parents, my brothers and sisters, and, my G-d, the children . . .

I later learned that Yoshua's mother had gotten him a seat on a Kindertransport train as well, after his father was taken to Terezín. It was scheduled to leave on September 1 of 1939, months after my own rescue. But that was the very day the Nazis invaded Poland, and the war began, and so the train didn't leave. Of the 250 children who would've been on board, only two survived the war, did you know?

Yoshua wasn't one of them.

I keep my family's belongings, at least, in places of honor and safety. As for Yoshua's locket, I couldn't bear to share that with anybody. So when Isaac bought this land and built the house, our home, I walked down toward the river. Not all the way to the banks of the Hollow, since it's known to flood, but into the trees beyond that old barn. I wrapped the locket in scraps of plastic sheeting left over from construction, put it in a tin, and buried it by that oak—the big one, with the branches like a spider's legs.

Maybe someday, I'll take it out again.

Lately, I've also been thinking of Táta's book. The diary.

I've read it through many times, translated as best I can, looking for . . . I'm not certain what. I know Táta did the same, adding his own notes, even. I recognize his writing, and the more modern Hebrew. He had a theory, it seems, that golems go mad because they have no memory, no home, nothing to tie them to anyplace or anybody. That only a word and a breath binds them to life, and while that's enough for the present, no future can be possible without a past.

But I'm not so sure. Sometimes . . . not so often, you know, but sometimes I dream of my childhood, a good dream. Of Máma's voice, and my brothers and sisters at play. Of the shop, and Táta's strong artist's hands, and Yoshua's gentle smile. I'll wake in the middle of the night, and remember where I've been and what I've lost. And then I wish that I were bloodless. I wish I were clay.

I believe the past can drive you mad as anything.

FIFTEEN

I'M SITTING ON the back porch steps when the rumble of
Ari's truck out front announces her return from town. Jitka's
story seemed to eat up all of the air inside the house, and so
I've brought the journal outside, where I'm burning under the
strong sun that glints off the silver hamsa in my hand. I dug it
out of my backpack for inspection. Mom told me it came from a
friend of our grandmother's, and Ida seemed the obvious candi-
date. But I hadn't known they were this close, enough that Jitka
could spill all of her heart's secrets into Ida's hands.

I've never had a friend like that.

I slip the charm into the zippered pocket of my joggers as
Ari comes through the house and out the back door.

"What's up?" she asks.

I try to summarize, but I must do a poor job, because Ari
drops down onto the weathered wood beside me, scoops the
journal from my lap, and starts reading on the page I've book-
marked with a thumb. "Damn," she says when she's finished,
resting her elbows on her knees and cradling her chin. "You
think it's all true?"

I glance back toward the house, and the animated clay being inside of it. "Seems true. Your grandmother never told you any of this?"

"Well, I knew about the Golem of Prague, like I told you, and I knew Judah Loew ben Bezalel built it—them—but I didn't know he was connected to Jitka's family. I didn't even know her maiden name."

"Neither did I, till last Thursday."

We sit in silence for a moment, listening to the chirps of katydids and summer frogs, before I remember Ari's mission. "So, did you find anything at Frager's?"

"Actually, yeah." She tugs her phone out of her shorts to pull up her photos, leaning in and shading the screen so we can look together. "Check this out—August 1990."

It's a picture of a short article in a yellowed paper called the *Hollow Star*, the local one Ari had mentioned. The headline reads "Beth El Celebrates Love on Tu B'Av."

"Tu B'Av—wasn't that yesterday?" I ask, remembering Rabbi Kayla's speech.

"Yup. Holidays move around a little on the Hebrew calendar, because it's lunar. I guess Beth El used to put on a little party for Tu B'Av back then, maybe because the congregation was bigger." She zooms in on a small gallery at the top of the article, the photos faded. Little girls in ruffled dresses with poufed shoulders hold hands and dance in a circle; an elderly man hands his beaming wife a bouquet of flowers; and a much younger couple about our age, seemingly unaware they're being photographed, sits on the lawn with their heads bent close.

Ari flips to the next screenshot—a close-up of the same photo. The boy is good-looking in a sort of timeless way, with soft dark curls and an easy smile and bright eyes. But I quickly skip past him to the girl beside him—my mother, younger than in any photo I've ever seen of her, wearing an open, unfamiliar smile.

"Here." Ari scrolls on to a close-up of the caption: "Malka Eggers and Siman Melkes enjoy the sunshine."

I lean in closer still, forgetting the wings until they knock against her shoulder through the fabric that barely restrains them, and I jerk away again. "That's it! If we have his name, we can find him—"

"Already found him," she cuts in. "I showed this to Harold, and turns out, he did remember. Not Siman, exactly, but the policeman who came to ask his dad questions. I guess they found the body of a drowned boy in the Hudson in the fall of 1990, with a door key in his pants pocket. It had a plastic tag printed with their shop address—Harold recognized it. They thought it might've gotten swept in from one of the tributaries."

"The key?"

"The body." She scrolls to the next picture. "This is a screenshot from an online obituary database."

Quickly, I realize what I'm looking at: a scan of an old death announcement in a newspaper, with a grainy black-and-white picture of a boy. The same boy from the *Star*, only a little younger. They must have used a yearbook photo.

"When . . ."

"October 1990. This obit was from his hometown news-paper."

We both know what that means.

"If this was in 1990 . . . They didn't even get a chance," I say, feeling sorry for my mother for the first time since, well, since I locked myself in my bedroom closet and spent the next six weeks feeling extremely sorry for myself. Mom left everything and everyone behind for him, and at best, they had a month or two together before she lost him, just like she'd lose Dad. Unless . . . "You don't think my mom had—that she had something to do with it?" I stumble over the question, the sheer size of it.

Ari's eyes go wide, and absurdly, all I can think in that moment is how dark her hair must be beneath the pink dye based on the color of her eyelashes, and how her eyes aren't pure steel in the sun, but flecked with tiny spots of ocean blue. I refocus.

"Like, she was a witness, you mean?" Ari says slowly.

"Or a . . . perpetrator," I land on in place of something worse. "All we really know is, they were gone by September, and his body was found in October. And if we're talking about some catastrophic, life-changing mistake that kept her away from Fox Hollow forever . . . What if all this time, she's been running away? Like, she started when she was our age, and never stopped?"

Ari considers this, clearly uneasy. "Let's not assume the worst, okay? Take a breath. For now, let's say that something happened, something really bad, and she got scared, took off, and never came back." She continues, working through the story we told her in Jitka's kitchen: "Years later, she gets married, has kids, loses her husband—by sad but nonmagical means—and immediately, she's running again. This time, with you guys. Didn't your mom say that everything she'd done was to keep you safe?"

"Yeah, I figured she meant it, you know, like how moms do when they're talking about something that makes them uncomfortable. 'I never gave you the sex talk because I was trying to protect you!' That kind of bullshit."

"But your mom came back to the town she's been avoiding for three decades. She went to *my* mom, who apparently hates her guts, for help. And according to the letter we found in the barn, Jitka believed she needed a weapon. A whole ass golem, in fact. It doesn't seem like your mom was just uncomfortable."

This fresh take on my life story is dizzying. In the version I've grown up believing, Mom is a wanderer, an artistic, nomadic soul, and my brother and I, her luggage. It's what I told myself while mutinously packing up my rented rooms for yet another move. It's unsettling, rewriting my whole life with Ari instead of with my big brother. But maybe Gabe and I are too close to the story. So trapped in the details that we can't see the big picture. Because all of this is starting to make a terrible sort of sense. "If that's true—*if*—then what exactly was she running from? Not, like, the cops. Not according to what she told your mom. That's the big question, right? I mean, you don't need a 'weapon' to fight a curse. So if she wasn't just coming back to find a healer, what did she come back to fight?"

"I don't know," Ari says for the millionth time, but then adds, with strength, "We'll figure it out. We'll keep reading. We'll find the answer."

It's the same promise I gave the golem, and I'm no more certain it can be kept than I was when I made it. "What if we don't? The shiva ends after Tuesday. What if time runs out, and Esther sends us home, and Mom's still gone, and I'm still . . ."

Ari's eyes flash to the wings trapped beneath my sweatshirt, and she stretches out tentative fingers.

"Don't," I snap, shooting to my feet.

Only when I see the hurt wash across her face do I realize she wasn't reaching for them, but for me.

I pause for just a second, a pang in my own chest, but then I mumble, "I'm gonna keep reading," turn away, and head inside, leaving Ari behind.

It's better this way, I tell myself. What would be the point of sitting there, letting her take my hand? What's the point of letting Ari look at me like she was? As if . . . she could see every beautiful and monstrous thing about me, and still like the view.

That's just a trick I'm playing on myself. She'd never look at me this way if she knew who I really was—messy and strange and scared and lost and always one slip-up away from failing everything and letting everybody down when it really counts. I can't afford to let that Hannah loose. Because if . . . *when* we find Mom, find a way to undo whatever she did, break the curse, whatever it takes, I have to go back into the world, back to holding the perfect pose until every muscle in my body aches. As long as nobody sees me for who I really am, and comes to the inevitable conclusion that it's not good enough.

So I'll leave this disastrous and true version of me in the wildflowers. I'll leave our family, the way Mom once did. I'll leave this beautiful girl in high-tops with a dagger through her ear before she has any chance to figure me out. And, in the fall, Gabe will leave me, no matter how much he loves me. He'll feel the west coast sun on his face and never look back.

So I ask the question my mother must have considered, over and over again, since October of 1990: What's the point of love when, whether slowly and painfully or suddenly and tragically, everyone loses everyone?

IMPOSSIBLY, THE SUMMER grows hotter.

Malka, Geela, and Shoshanna spend whole days down in the Hollow, though her sisters are too spooked now to strip down to their underwear. They only bunch their skirts around their hips to dangle their feet in the fast-moving, pine-green water, and read paperbacks or magazines on the shady bank while their legs drip dry. But they never do it when Siman is working in the field, and to Malka's disappointment, he never stumbles upon them again. And she doesn't dare go down to the river alone, at a time when Papa or Mama could see she's plainly trying to cross his path.

Still, it seems to her that she and Siman can speak without speaking. With glances and half smiles and subtle shrugs across the table at dinner once a week, or when Mama invites Siman into the kitchen for iced tea during the heat of the day. And when she stands in her bedroom window and stares out at the barn, she knows that he's in there, maybe up in the loft, too far from the window for the sunlight to reach, thinking of her. They hardly say more to each other than "Shabbat Shalom," but whenever they're close, the air between them crackles with every silent wish.

Malka feels it, at least, and hopes and wishes and prays that she isn't imagining things.

On the first Sunday of August, and a day before the actual holiday, Beth El hosts its annual Tu B'Av festival. As far as celebrations of romantic love go, it's never terribly romantic. That's for the best, since half of the Jewish community in Fox Hollow is related to one another, and a large portion of them to Malka.

But it's nice. There are long card tables set up on the lawn, pearl-colored crepe paper twined around the chair legs. At the food station, there are platters of kosher cookies, slices of fruit, and Mrs. Guralnick's dairy-free banana bread, beside a glass dispenser of bright-pink punch. Music plays from a clunky boom box set up on the concrete temple steps, borrowed from one of the congregants along with their apparently endless collection of klezmer tapes.

Malka and Rachael have their own patch of grass beside the synagogue's message board, announcing today's festival and next week's ritual chair committee meeting. "It's hot as balls," Rachael complains, flapping her black mesh skirt with the jagged hem away from her pale shins.

"How would you know?"

Her friend barks with laughter. "Malka Eggers making jokes! Give me a cookie?"

"Give me your drink?"

They trade, Malka sipping warm punch out of a plastic cup while Rachael eats carefully so as not to get powdered sugar on her purple lipstick. She sets the cup on the lawn and tilts her head back, letting the sun blaze orange behind her eyelids.

"What if we snuck away down the street to Tunes, brought back a Stone Roses tape, slipped it in while nobody's looking. *I don't have to sell my soul, he's already in me*," Rachael sings in a wildly overly accented imitation of Ian Brown. "*I don't have to sell my soul, he's already in me. I want to be adored . . .*"

Her friend falls silent, and Malka senses Siman before she even opens her eyes, she swears she does. He settles in the grass on her other side, unburdened by cookies or punch.

"You're not hungry?" she asks, forcing herself to speak normally.

"Maybe I'll get something later." He grins. "I'm happy where I am."

"I didn't know you were coming today."

"Me neither. But I was passing by and saw you, thought I'd stop for . . . this music."

They listen together to the dueling violins, stifling laughter.

"I'm getting out of the sun," Rachael murmurs sourly, startling her—Malka's forgotten about her, and feels momentarily guilty as her best friend's shadow passes over her.

But then there's Siman, and they're sitting so close together, his cargo pants brush her skirt, their elbows knocking as he repositions himself. She hasn't been this close to him since that day by the river, and his pale-blue eyes silvered by sunlight leave her stunned. Together, they watch little girls in long white dresses link hands and circle dance under the guidance of Rabbi Starr, Beth El's first female rabbi. Malka barely notices the reporter taking their photo. When his hand finds hers on the warm green grass, she knows then that each unspoken word between them only waits for breath and the chance to make it real.

"Come to the house tonight?" she asks in a rush, hardly daring to move her lips. "Park far enough down the driveway so no one will see you and walk around to the back door. My parents will be in bed by ten, so I'll wait in the kitchen after that."

He's still watching the dancers, eyes narrowed against the sun, but a wide smile curls across his lips. "I'll be there."

SIXTEEN

FOR THE THIRD night in a row, I dream of the city with the castle sprawled like a giant on the hill above a frozen river. And this time, instead of flashing briefly through it like I would a strange picture sorted into the wrong album, I pause. I stand inside of it. It's not my dream—that is, it shouldn't feel like it is. But it does. I've never been here before, but I recognize the neighborhood. I taste the name on my tongue: *Josefov*. I know its cobbled but clean roads, the jagged silhouette of its tiled rooftops and clock towers and spires against the silver clouds, thick with snow. My breath is brittle in the cold, and maybe that's why passersby around me hurry along, heads together, hats pulled low, shoulders hunched in their winter coats. But it feels like more. Like *fear*, noxious as smoke on the wind.

I weave through the streets and sidewalks between the tall, tight-pressed buildings, following the crowds . . . until a set of hands pull me back into the arched doorway of a store. A Kosher butchery. I can practically taste their chopped corned beef, as though it's a familiar dish. I try to shake the stranger's hands off, until they turn me by the shoulders to look. Then I stop struggling.

Dark waves just curling out from under a fisherman's cap, and equally dark eyes. High cheekbones and a firm jaw with a tapered chin. A long, graceful neck above the high collar of a gray wool coat.

It's a face I know.

"What do you think you're doing, meshuggeneh? It's not safe. We just heard on the radio—*they're* here." He pauses, pretending to spit twice on the butcher shop's steps. "Come home with me, now." Then, laying fever-warm fingers against my cold cheek, he says in a tenderer voice, "Jitka, you don't want to see this."

Despite the instinct to lay my head in his palm and let him lead me somewhere safe, I pull back. "I need to," I say, feeling as though I'm reciting from a script I've memorized, like Gabe in one of his plays. Turning, I burst from the doorway back into the throng. I hear the boy's muttered curse behind me, and sense the heat of him as he follows close.

We pass the Altneuschul, my family's synagogue and the oldest in the city, in Europe, according to my father (no, not *my* father), its gothic roof rising to catch a flare of weak sunlight. I flick my hand out to trail my fingers across its unassuming stone wall before we're swept onward. We move around the border of the cemetery, where gravestones jut from the snow, as crowded and crumbling as they say the homes of Josefov used to be, before the renewal of the ghetto.

Yoshua presses against me (Yoshua, that's the boy . . . how had I forgotten his name? How could I ever forget Yoshua?) so that we won't be separated. We veer left with the mob at the Maiselova synagoga, then onto Pařížská. As we near Staroměstské náměstí, the Old Town Square, I hear sounds in the distance—the hum and rumble and roar of a great crowd, almost as loud as the churn of engines and the grind of tires on stone. "Jitka," Yoshua cautions once more, lips against my ear, tugging at my arm. "We can't be here . . ."

I take his ungloved hand, so much warmer than mine, and tuck my chin into my scarf. "Just for a moment?" I plead through the fabric. "I need to *see.*"

Reluctantly, he lets me pull him onward.

When we emerge into the square, we're blocked by a wall of broad backs in winter coats and caps. Above their heads I see our own mounted policemen, Czechoslovakians, patrolling the sidewalk. Despite their efforts, the crowd won't be moved or quieted. "Pfui!" folks shout, some howling with rage, some hissing, some weeping, but they're not jeering at the Czechs. Beyond them—I see now as people shift to accommodate one of the pacing horses—*they've* arrived.

On motorcycles, bicycles, and in troops wheeling anti-tank guns. Red flags snap in the freezing wind, *their* symbol emblazoned like a squashed, poisonous spider. A soldier on a motorcycle stops with the pace of the parade, and someone from the throng surges forward to batter his helmet, before receding. The soldier turns to the crowd to seek the man out, then seems to reconsider at the sight of our twisted faces, riding on.

It's like a terrible parade, celebrating the end of my country, my home.

"They're headed for Václavské náměstí," a woman beside me cries to her friend, tears streaming through the powder on her pale cheeks.

Wenceslas Square, the center of everything.

"It's like the beginning of the end of the world," Yoshua cries.

I clutch his hand all the tighter as, above us in the gunmetal sky, an enemy plane screams past.

When I open my eyes in the dark, the chunky old alarm clock on the nightstand tells me it isn't four am yet. I start to roll to my back, but the wings stop me; I still have them. I haven't changed yet, so I shouldn't be awake. That's how it works. Every time I fall asleep, I wake up new.

So why is tonight different from all other nights?

Shoulders aching under the sustained weight, wings unfurling, I rise to my knees on the bed. I scrub my wrist across my eyes and try to piece together that wild dream, and the evening that came before it.

I camped at Ida's until Ari had to go—her parents are leaving today for Pennsylvania, and wanted her home for dinner. "More like, they want to feel good that we had dinner together before they left," she explained. I would've stayed until Esther and Bernie went to bed, found my own way back to their place through the woods along the river, but Ari rightly pointed out that perhaps it wasn't the best idea to forge through the forest alone at night, and it didn't occur to me at the time that I could've taken the golem for company, if they would've obeyed me. So she dropped me off at the mouth of the driveway, promising to see us tomorrow, and I made a wide circle around the house, camping out behind the barn until Gabe texted me around nine that the relations were asleep.

He let me in through the back door as planned, and we crept up the stairs to my room. Avoiding the still-strange expression on his face, I told him everything I'd learned yesterday. Jitka's story—our family's story—and how Ari had found out about Siman's death. Our new theory, the one I couldn't quite believe, that Mom hadn't spent her whole life running toward some unnameable happiness, but away from some unknowable fear.

He ran a hand through his fluffed-up teal hair, chewing at the barbell in his lip. "This is . . . a lot of information. But if she *was* scared to stop moving, why would she settle us three hours from her hometown for the last two years? That makes no sense."

I could have shrugged my tired shoulders, left it as yet another unsolved mystery about our mother. But I knew the answer, and my brother deserved to know, too.

"Because I made her." At his uncomprehending look, I told him what I'd never told him before. "When I found out I got the scholarship, I wanted to go to Winthrop and stay there until I graduated. I was never gonna get into the kind of colleges I wanted, hopping from public school to public school every six months, begging for recommendations from teachers who can't remember my name. I needed extracurricular activities, and college-level classes. Nobody was going to want me without them. I needed to be better. So . . . I threatened to live with Poppy and Grammy if she didn't let me." I turned my gaze to the bedsheets so I wouldn't see the pain of my betrayal on his face. "She gave in pretty easily after that. I think she *was* trying to protect me, in a way. She wanted me to stay with her, even if it meant staying in one place. I thought, back then, that she actually wanted me with her. She had the chance to get rid of me, and she didn't take it, and I've spent the last two years trying to show her she didn't make a mistake. Like I was worthy of it. But it was never about *me*. It was practical. A security measure."

"Banana . . ."

"I don't think I would've actually left," I rushed onward. "I wouldn't have gone to Canada."

"It would've been okay," my brother said gently. I looked up to meet his warm amber eyes. "If you had left, it would've been okay. I get it."

"But—" I wrapped my arms around my rib cage to keep whatever was building inside of me from breaking free. "Aren't you mad?"

"You're my sister, but you're, like, yourself, too. You don't owe *anybody* your dreams, Banana." Gabe lay his hand on the bed palm up, the scales inked into his arm seeming to shimmer in the bedside lamp.

I should've taken it.

"Is that why you're going to college in California?" It came out more hostile than I'd meant. He was being a good brother, and I was being shitty sister. Deliberately misunderstanding, blaming him for the same choice I'd threatened to make. Still, I couldn't stop myself. "There are good schools everywhere, and you could do anything you wanted. But you don't even have a major yet. It's not like you're getting your PhD in microbiology, studying some rare bacteria only found on the bathroom floors of LA-area Starbucks. You didn't have to pick a place so far away from me. Unless that *is* your dream."

Gabe's hand on the blanket curled into a loose fist. "If that was true," he said, too calmly, "I wouldn't be here. And I wouldn't have spent my last summer in Boston with my sister, instead of my friends and boyfriend. Ish." His cheek dimpled, inviting me to smile with him, at his expense.

Instead, I snapped, "Go home, then. Ari and I can do it."

Never mind that I'd already snapped at Ari, and the mood in Ida's house had been frosty despite the heat thereafter.

"You don't actually mean that," he said, smile never slipping.

It shouldn't have pissed me off. I *didn't* want my brother to go, not ever. But something came over me in that moment, some mean, feral impulse to tear apart the very thing I relied on before I lost it anyway. "Why not? You think I need you?"

"Okay, Hannah—"

"You think I'm not smart enough to figure this out? Gosh, how *will* I go on without you in the background, making witty little jokes and playing dress-up with your golem?"

At that, he leaped up, speaking stiffly. "You know what, fine. I'm not your mother, right? Unlike her, I'm actually here.

But you want to do this on your own? I'll leave you and your spreadsheets alone."

And then he left. And I was alone.

I wasn't really angry with Gabe. Even in the moment, I knew that. I was furious with Mom. With the mistakes she'd made, for which I was paying, and with whatever dream she'd chosen over her family when her own mother had no choice but to leave and lose the people she loved. I was furious about what had happened to Jitka, too, on a level I'd barely begun to deal with. But Gabe was right: he was here. And the best punching bag is always the one in front of you. Sometimes you just close your eyes and punch, praying it can withstand the blow.

That explains the sharp stone in my chest now. I'm used to waking up and feeling sorry for myself, but this is different. First what I said to Ari, then to Gabe. Like a wolf, I'm snapping at every hand that reaches for mine. Who'll be my next victim—Aunt Esther? The golem?

The golem.

It was their face in my dream, I remember. But they weren't a golem. They were a beautiful, terrified boy named Yoshua.

There's an explanation for this, I tell myself. *You fell asleep with Jitka's story in mind and replayed it in your dreams, casting yourself as the star and the golem as the boy she loved. That day, the square, the terrible parade—it was all the way Ida recorded it. A nightmare, and nothing more.*

Except that I've been dreaming of that same city, its streets and river and rooftops, for three nights now.

Before I can question this further, something out the window snags my eye: a brightness beyond the barn, like a flashlight's beam between the trees.

I press my face against the glass to get a closer look, but it's too far away, the meadow too wide. In fact, if I can see the light all the way from the house, it must be strong. And it's not a single pinprick, but a diffused glow that reminds me of the distant beam of the lighthouse on Little Brewster Island, which I could see from Boston Harbor on a foggy night. Except I don't remember seeing a lighthouse on the banks of the Hollow on any map. Maybe a powerful camping lantern?

I should wake up Gabe. But then there's my pride, and my shame, all mixed into a bitter, roiling brew inside of me. I'm working myself up to swallow it down and knock on my brother's bedroom anyway when it strikes me: Somebody is possibly working their way up from the river, through the trees, headed for the barn. The barn in which my grandmother left a weapon for my mother, hopeful that she was coming back to find it . . .

Once the thought seizes me, I shove my feet into my sneakers and break for the door. Down the hall, with only a prickle of doubt as I pass my brother's borrowed bedroom. Down the stairs and into the kitchen. I fumble with the latch on the back door, tugging at the chain with uncooperative fingers, cursing myself. Then I'm out, streaking through the flowers. It's drizzling steadily, and the air is unexpectedly cool on my flushed skin. The wet grass quickly soaks my shoes and the hem of the joggers I fell asleep in, each knee-high blade jewel-tipped with rainwater in the glow from the barn. I sprint forward, my unrestrained wings whipping behind me for anybody to see. No matter. It's too late to turn back now.

Past the barn, I dive into the trees, heedless of the wings—they'll be gone by morning, so who cares what damage I do? There's only a few dozen yards of woodland between the field and the riverbank. As I push through thin, whippy branches and tangled brush, following the light, I catch sight of something through the trees: a silhouette in the clearing ahead. Small and curved, with long, wind-wild hair.

It's *her*, I know it's her.

I summon the breath to shout, "Mom!"

The woman takes a step forward, hands raised, reaching for me. And I can smell Mom, I swear I can, her spearmint-soap smell and her *mom-ness*, which I know in my blood. Head down, I barrel toward the river as she raises her arms—

Not to embrace me, but straight out in front of her, as if to stop me, to warn me.

Taken aback, I dig my toes into the forest floor to slow myself, catch my sneaker on a root and go sprawling. I plant myself into the damp soil and the low ferns, skin scraping over half-submerged tree bark. When I claw back the hair from my eyes and look up, the silhouette is gone. I crawl forward until I stagger to my feet. My right ankle stings, but not enough to matter, and I stumble toward the riverbank.

The light hovers over a particular spot halfway between

the banks, in the middle of the rushing water, like the source is buried at the bottom. A pearlescent, marbled glow.

There was this tumbleweed of a motel where we once stopped on the highway between homes when I was a kid. Gabe and I climbed a short chain-link fence and snuck into the cement square of a pool house. Everything was switched off except for the lights embedded in the walls below the surface of the water, rippled by our bodies as we slid inside. This was dangerous in retrospect—I was eight, and a weak swimmer, never having had lessons. But I had my then-scrawny big brother with me, and so I felt safe in the wavering teal light, sure that if anything happened, he could save me.

I'm reminded of that night, except that I'm alone out here. There's only the sounds of the river and my own panting—

And the stink of something foul in the air that wasn't there before, blotting out any lingering spearmint. It smells of old, moldering things. Slimy, rotten things. Corrupted things. It's so strong, so *wrong*, that my knees give way, as if some vital hardware has been rattled loose, and I drop to the forest floor.

When I open my eyes, morning birds chorus in the branches above.

Groaning, I lie still on the dew-damp earth for a long moment. Did I pass out or something? Fall and bang my head on a tree root on the way down? Close my eyes and wish myself back asleep?

Peeling myself slowly out of the dirt and the weeds, I notice first that the weight has, very literally, been lifted from my shoulders. My wings are gone. The second thing I notice, as I reach back to examine a strange new sensation at the base of my spine: I have a tail.

I drag my brother back out into the field while the sky is still pink with sunrise. He's sleepy and grumpy and still nursing yesterday's wounds, the ones I inflicted, which I can't blame him for. I stammered a sloppy semi-explanation before pulling him from his bed, but nothing's been fixed.

At least I won't have to fake sick and sneak out today. The tail—a scaled, skinny whip like a lizard's that kinks and curls of its own accord—was easy enough to tuck and belt into my baggy-kneed boyfriend jeans, then disguise with an oversize, army-green corduroy button-up, the hem dangling halfway down my thighs. Another item borrowed from Gabe's closet, it smells like him, his Old Spice and the citrusy face soap he uses and, because he's an eighteen-year-old boy, a little hairspray and sweat.

"Like, I'm not trying to diminish your lived experience or whatever," Gabe hedges, bringing me back to the now, "but last week I had this nightmare that I could have sworn was real, too. I was eating crazy noodles when all of a sudden they turned into, like, a whole takeout carton full of snakes, and tried to slither up my nose, so I had to fight them off with chopsticks—"

"So how did I get outside?" I demand, swatting through a patch of wild sunflowers.

Gabe shrugs. "Sleepwalking?"

But when we reach the riverbank, the truth is clear enough. The damp, gritty soil is stamped with footprints, and not only mine. In addition to my thrifted Keds, there's a set that was definitely made by a barefoot human.

And a set that definitely was not.

They're difficult to make out. One fairly clear print is as long as Gabe's shoe at least, but three-pronged, like a bird's. I stoop to examine another. There are puncture marks at the tips of the toes, like . . .

Like claws.

My brother starts toward the waterline, digging his heels into the sloped bank and peering down, but I grab a fistful of his shirt to stop him. Whatever came out of the river last night, I'm not ready to meet it.

We head back into the woods. I start to turn us toward the house, pausing as the rising sun pierces the leaves of a massive oak tree on the verge of the meadow. It's surrounded by thick stumps sliced off low to the soil, the last survivor of a felled grove. Its branches twist above the rest, splayed and curved like a clawed hand.

Or like a spider's legs.

Remembering this detail from my grandmother's story, I press forward.

"What are you—"

"I just want to see something," I call back.

Gabe follows me and waits while I bend low and circle the wide trunk of the old tree. Kicking aside brush to inspect the base, I spy a pile of smooth gray river stones between the gnarled knuckles of two protruding roots. I kneel and shovel them aside, prodding at the earth below. A few seconds of digging, and I hit something solid: the lid of box, like the tea tins Mom brings home from antique stores to keep scissors and pens and paintbrushes in. It's not buried, exactly, just wedged in a hollow between the roots with dirt hastily scraped over it, so it isn't hard to pry out.

Gabe squats down beside me. "How did you know this was here?"

While I think I did a good job recapping Jitka's story, I guess I forgot some of the details. I catch him up on her confession to Ida, the treasure she hid when she first moved to Fox Hollow, as I work off the lightly rusted lid. There's a fist-sized bundle of plastic sheeting inside. I lift it out and peel the plastic back to find, as promised, a simple gold oval of a locket on a thin chain.

Gabe plucks it out of its nest, unclasping it gently. The little locket falls open on its hinge, and my heart stammers between beats. On the left is a tiny black-and-white photo of a teenage girl. Even if I hadn't known it was Jitka, I'd guess she was a year or two younger than me, and that we could be related. It's not like looking at a picture of myself with a sepia filter or anything, but the resemblance is there. The freckles thick across her nose and cheeks, for instance, blurry but noticeable in the worn photo. They must have been distinctive, just like mine. I'm surprised our family didn't mention it.

Pressed into the right side, there's another face I'd recognize even if I didn't know who it belonged to. Because I've seen these large dark eyes, these high cheekbones, this slim chin.

It's Yoshua's face, and it's the golem's.

"Holy whoa," Gabe murmurs, sweeping a hand back through the wild blue flame of his bed hair.

I think part of me already guessed it, but I'm still too stunned to speak. In the last ten minutes, I've gathered enough evidence to form two extremely fucking impossible-but-possible conclusions:

The dream was real.

So was the nightmare.

SEVENTEEN

I THOUGHT I knew what it meant to be in over my head—I've spent the last two years in Boston feeling like the captain and only passenger of a little dinghy on rough seas, knowing the smallest wave might tip me. But now, the boat has capsized, the hull smashed, and I'm sinking through ice-cold water with nothing to grab hold of.

It's bad enough that curses and clay people are real. But there's something else here, something with claws, something poisonous and putrid and tied to my mother, and we need to tell somebody, so they can tell us what to do.

But who?

I don't know how much Aunt Esther, or anyone in our family, would believe. We could explain everything: *Did you know your mother had a first love in Prague, who she longed for even after she married your dad, so much that she built a golem in his image, which we sort-of-accidentally-on-purpose brought to life to possibly protect your missing estranged sister—oh, yeah, Mom's actually missing—from some three-toed thing that's stalking your property, and also I have a tail?* We could show them the golem, with their beautifully human features and cool skin and lack of pulse. We could, of course, show them my tail . . .

And then what? How much danger would we be putting them in, and what would it get us? Knowing adults, they'd most likely call somebody else for help. A plastic surgeon maybe, or the police. And what could any of them do?

Meanwhile, Mom is still missing, and I'm coming around to the likelihood that it's not by choice. It's been weeks since Ari saw her. She could be hurt, desperate, de—

No. I saw her last night, I know I did. She was warning me to keep back. I *smelled* her. If a monster was really there, then so was she.

I plan to take our discoveries to Ari, but on our way upstairs, we run into Esther and Bernie coming down. "Well, we thought you both were still in bed!" our aunt says, then gives us a second look. "Feeling better today, Hannah?"

I'm fully dressed down to my damp sneakers, tail tucked and hidden, while Gabe's in his pajama T-shirt and basketball shorts—at least I stopped him from going out in his boxers.

"We went for a walk," my brother explains. "You know, Boston is all car horns and cement. It's so nice and quiet here. Makes you want to get up early."

Esther nods, accepting this. "Well, why don't you come on down to breakfast? And then we can spend some time together before shiva, just us."

On the one hand, I want to lie my way out of this. We have so little time, and so much to figure out. We need to get back to Ida's, to keep searching.

On the other, who knows how many opportunities I'll have to get to know my aunt? I wish we could spend this whole time listening to her memories of her mother, relearning the names of her sons and daughters and sisters, memorizing the sound of her voice and the smell of this kitchen and the color of the wildflowers. Instead, we're constantly biding our time until the first opportunity to slip away. And it's true here, too, that time is running out. Whatever happens, we won't be in Fox Hollow much longer.

But we're family, and that means something I've just begun to process.

So, sharing a helpless look with my brother, I return to my room just long enough to text a scrambled summary to Ari, then go down to breakfast. I perch uncomfortably while we eat between bursts of polite conversation, and then we spend the morning with our aunt and uncle. Gabe tells them about our childhoods with his signature flair, turning our many rushed trips between our many temporary homes into a lifetime of adventures. Esther tells us more about her life in Fox Hollow, skipping lightly around the hole our mother must have left in the Eggerses' lives. She brings out a thick old ivory quilted photo album, flipping through pictures of the family we never got to meet. Few photos survived from either side before the war, she tells us, but there are plenty from the later years of Jitka and Isaac's life.

Just as I did in my aunts and cousins, I recognize pieces of them. My grandfather had Mom's strong nose, and my grandmother had my freckles, as I knew already, and my dark hair, trapped between wavy and curly, and Mom's hooded eyes and soft curves. As documented in photos printed and pasted into the album by her children, she aged into a woman with a short, steel-gray cap of hair and a frail frame, the years without Mom and without her husband deeply engraved in her face.

I can't tell whether she looks stern, or sad.

That's how we spend our time until lunch. After, we retreat to our rooms, where I text Ari again, and when visiting hours start at three o'clock, we take our seats in the parlor, waiting for the citizens of Fox Hollow to give us their sympathies. Soon enough, visitors of all ages start to trickle through, wearing sober expressions and clothes as modest as mine. Gabe, hunkered down in one of the chairs instead of beside me on a pink settee, wears a pair of his Before chinos with his subtlest cuffed T-shirt in eggplant purple, though it does have a neon-green pocket the size of a paperback novel. Most folks cast him a second glance as they walk past me.

It's an interesting ritual. No one rings the doorbell, I guess so Esther and Bernie don't have to answer the door. They walk right in and take a seat, waiting for our aunt or the other assorted family members who've gathered to speak to them. They stay briefly, exchanging handshakes or hugs or remembrances of Jitka, then leave with as little ceremony as they came in. Nobody really tries to talk to us, and if we're supposed to approach them, I have no idea what to say. So mostly, I sit quietly until Ari arrives to find us.

My heart gives a *thrump* far beyond relief at the sight of

her: the pink cloud of her hair gathered into space buns that show off her piercings, down to the dagger. She wears a deep-green jumpsuit and, suspiciously, a JanSport. She's closely trailed by a woman who looks as if she wants to be anywhere else, a thin, pale, dark-haired white woman full of angles: sharp elbows and shoulders and collarbone, a small, pointed chin, and a hard line of a mouth that is nothing like Ari's full-lipped smile. Still, something in the way they look at each other tells me this is Ari's mother—maybe a combination of familiarity and undisguised annoyance.

Rachael Leydon, at last.

She peels off from her daughter not long after entering the parlor, pulled into low conversation with another citizen of Fox Hollow, so Ari's alone when she joins us in the corner.

"You brought your mom?" I murmur.

"I know. I didn't want to. But I told her where I was going, and she figured she should sit shiva before they go; Dad's already got the car loaded. Optics, I guess."

That seems ungenerous—Rachael did grow up next door to the Eggerses. If Ida and Mom were close, Rachael probably loved Jitka, too—but hey, I don't know Ari's mother.

With Rachael surrounded by quietly chatty townsfolk, we sneak away to my bedroom to catch Ari up on everything that's changed overnight, including myself. She dumps her backpack on my bed and sits while Gabe paces the room, shooting nervous glances out the window at the woods. I tell her about the dreams I've been having, and how last night's starred the golem—or the boy in whose image they were apparently made—and how we found the prints by the river this morning, and the locket in the box beneath the tree.

Instead of looking skeptical, as Gabe had, a spark of recognition lights her eyes. "No, that makes sense."

"It *does?*" Gabe almost squawks.

"I've been pounding through the journals all morning," she says, unzipping her backpack to pull out one of several she's apparently brought with her. "We already knew we were looking for something supernatural. If whatever is happening to you is a curse, *something* must have cursed you, right? And probably not an angel, or an ibbur, or anything good—"

"An ibbur?" I interrupt.

"Like, a righteous ghost, or spirit. Dybbuks are the baddies, and ibburim are the good version. They possess people, yeah, but only to do something important for which they need a body, like keep a promise or perform a mitzvah. And then they go. Bubbe wrote about a woman who thought she was haunted or possessed by her dead husband. But she wasn't scared—she said it was, like, comforting. He was a decent guy, I guess, and Bubbe talked to the woman, and told her to perform a mitzvah, and that would give him peace and be the end of it.

"So anyway, I thought maybe we were looking for a dybbuk. Maybe even Siman, since we found out that he died. But they don't leave footprints, and definitely not claw marks. Shedim, though . . ." She flips to one of a dozen pages marked with Post-it tabs; I'm reminded of my Winthrop textbooks. "Here, this is a quote she copied down from the Babylonian Talmud. 'Six things were said about demons: three in which they resemble ministering angels, and three in which they resemble human beings. The three in which they resemble ministering angels are that they have wings, they fly from one end of the earth to the other, and they know the future . . . And the three in which they resemble humans are that they eat and drink, reproduce, and die.'" She skips ahead down the page. "And this, too—remember I told you about Rav Huna, when we met? Well, here's a passage from the same Talmud that mentions him: 'If the eye had the power to see the demons, no creature could endure them. Abaye says: They are more numerous than we are and they surround us like the ridge round a field. R. Huna says: Everyone among us has a thousand on his left and ten thousand on his right. Rava says: They are responsible for the crushing in the Kallah lectures, fatigue in the knees, the wearing out of the clothes of the scholars from rubbing against them, and the bruising of the feet. If one wants to discover them, let him take sifted ashes and sprinkle around his bed, and in the morning he will see something like the footprints of a cock.'" Here, she looks up at me.

Footprints, three-pronged and clawed, large as a man's but not a man's. If you ask me, they looked less like a chicken's and more like a dinosaur's prints.

"If one wishes to see them,'" Ari continues reading, "'let him take the afterbirth of a black she-cat which is the offspring of a black she-cat, the firstborn of a firstborn, roast it in fire and grind it to powder, and then let him put some into his eye, and he will see them. Let him also pour it into an iron tube and seal it with an iron signet that they should not steal it from him, and let him also close his mouth, so that he should not come to harm."

Gabe sits down on the floor, dropping his head into his hands. "Demons are real? Demons. *Demons?*"

"Maybe it's all real," I mutter through suddenly numb lips. "Every monster, every story . . . maybe they're all true."

"Bubbe has these notes written down. Like, rules. 'Never drink from a cup or eat from a plate that's been sitting overnight. Garlic, onion, or eggs must be thrown away after peeling, and not left out. Never sleep under the shade of a many-branched or prickly tree, particularly the sorb tree.' There are pages of this stuff."

"So . . ." I sift through this sudden wealth of information. "We need the afterbirth of a black she-cat?" I sink down onto the mattress beside Ari.

She sighs. "Petco is probably sold out."

Gabe, still crouched on the floor, surprises us both with a wild bark of laughter.

Ari shows one deep dimple in return. "Anyway, I don't think that's a problem solver. It's just supposed to help you see a sheyd. Because, you know, they're invisible unless they w*ant* you to see them."

That's . . . unsettling.

"Iron is supposed to hurt them, but it doesn't get rid of

them. There's this story, wait . . . okay, back here." She finds the place with one long finger. "'Never sleep under the shade of a many-branched or prickly tree, particularly the sorb tree. It may harbor sixty demons, which can only be exorcised by a sixty-demon amulet, a great treasure.'" She lets out a nervous chuckle. "Lucky we just have the one, I guess."

"We found that box of amulets at the shop," I point out. "Couldn't we use one of them?"

"Not so much." Ari frowns. "I mean, there are a lot of amulets with a lot of uses. To cure insomnia, prevent disease, keep your baby safe, protect you from gossip or the evil eye, clear out your, uh, plumbing." She waves a hand around her general intestinal region. "You can't just pick one. They all have specific uses. If that's what your mom wanted from Bubbe, I don't know how we'd figure it out. None of it looked like 'a great treasure.'"

All this talk of treasures jogs my memory, and I scramble from the bed to find my own backpack in the corner. I throw it open, claw through the contents, and pull out the cardboard box—my heart stops when I open it to find it empty. Then I find the joggers I woke up in, the same pair I wore yesterday. The hamsa is still in the zippered pocket, where I tucked it away and forgot it.

With a deep breath of relief, I hold the pendant up to Ari. "What about this? Mom said she got it from a friend of her mother's. Someone who meant a lot to her when she was a kid."

"Bubbe?" Ari whispers, awed.

"Who else? Think it's one of hers, an amulet?"

With great care, she plucks it out of my palm and cradles it, examining the petal fingers, the turquoise stones roughly shaped into an eye, the tiny, engraved stars. "It *looks* like something Bubbe would've worn."

"There's something on the back. Writing I can't read. I thought it was a jeweler's mark."

Flipping the pendant over, she squints down at the dull silver, smoothing a thumb over the engravings. "It's Hebrew, some of it—there are some other symbols too. I don't know what it means, but it looks legit, for what that's worth. Bubbe could have told us."

"Could a rabbi?" I ask.

Ari raises her pierced eyebrow. "In theory. But I wouldn't get your hopes up—most modern rabbis don't believe in literal demons, and Kayla is the chillest rabbi Beth El's ever had; I doubt she's any sort of expert in Jewish demonology. She's all about myth and metaphor, not so much afterbirth and iron. If you want to debate the possible historical origin of the story of Noah's ark, she's your girl; if you want to ward off the evil eye, you go to Bubbe. Or, you would've."

"So I won't open with 'there's a sheyd in my yard,'" I say, "but she likely knows *something* about whatever we're dealing with, right? How would I find her today?"

"Probably she's in her office at Beth El. She does bar and bat mitzvah prep lessons on Monday afternoons. I can drive us over. Mom came in her own car, since she's gonna pick up Dad and leave right after. I just have to tell her I'm going."

"You two go," Gabe declares, startling us both—he's been so quiet, cradling his head in corner, I'd almost forgotten he was here. Now he stands, smooths his hair back into its blue swoop, and raises his chin. "I need to go get the golem anyway. Put them in the barn, or in the woods, somewhere close by."

I blink up at him. "What for?"

"Jitka made them to protect our family. Seems like this sheyd or whatever is what Mom was so scared of, right? She got mixed up with an actual literal fucking demon somehow, came back thirty years later to deal with it, and failed. Now it obviously knows we're here. It wanted you to see it. So who knows what else it wants? We should be ready when it comes after you, like it probably came for Mom."

He's only saying what we're all thinking, but I didn't expect him to put it so bluntly. "Okay." The word trembles out of me, and I clear my throat. "Yeah, that's smart. We can keep them out of sight, or at least somewhere nobody will look too closely. Just . . . be careful in the woods?"

He gives a tight nod, avoiding my gaze as he leaves us. My brother is doing this for me, but I don't think he's forgiven me for yesterday, and I don't have the words to fix it right now.

Back to work, then. "So. To the synagogue?"

"Sure."

I tug at my baggy jeans and button-up. "Should I take these off, though?"

Ari blinks at me.

"I mean, no," I stammer. "I have a dress, the one I wore the other day. I could put that on."

"You don't have to get fancy just to step inside a synagogue," she says lightly—but I see her eyes dart up and down my body.

"It's a tail," I say, my voice turning brittle. "If that's what you're thinking about, it's a tail today."

Ari meets my eyes. "You don't think much of me, do you?" she asks with unexpected passion.

"Huh?"

"Or maybe you just don't trust me to think much of you," she revises. "Like, you're standing here about to strip, and you catch me checking you out, and you just assume I'm thinking about today's transformation?"

"I—I don't—" But I stop speaking as she steps closer.

"What would you think," she asks, "if you saw a boy looking at your brother the way I'm looking at you?" Closer still, now her eyes—steel with a little bit of ocean in them—follow the same path down my body, then back up again. Eyes wide enough to fall into and sink, if only I were brave enough to let myself.

If only.

"That's Gabe," I protest. "People know him for five minutes and they're already in love with him. And that's fine. I don't need that, and I'm not looking for it."

"Who told you that you were any different?" Ari challenges.

"What? Nobody. No one ever . . . It just is what it is."

"Well, *somebody* is telling you, right now, that you're wrong."

I'm not sinking. I'm not.

Suddenly, Ari rubs her neck where the hair is shaved close and steps away, tossing me gasping back onto dry land. "Sorry, I'm sorry. I shouldn't be . . . Um, we should get going, if we want to catch Rabbi Kayla. Change if you want to, doesn't matter." Cheeks just a shade less pink than her space buns, she flees the bedroom as though it were on fire.

Maybe it is, judging by the flames that flash-heat my own skin and settle in my belly.

I never felt like I needed to be beautiful—which is good, because I've also never felt beautiful. Too freckled, too flat-chested. My hair, left to grow out, gets this not-quite curl that won't be tamed without getting up an hour early, so I would always keep it in a neat pixie cut. I would wear foundation to dull my dark freckles down to a pale olive. I would scour thrift stores, not for unique pieces that speak to my artistic soul the way Mom does, but for clothes that round out my body while vaguely resembling the $300 jeans my classmates wear on weekends out of uniform. I can't help what I wasn't born with, but with enough hard work, I *can* control it.

At least, I thought I could.

Now, my pixie cut is grown out, untamed hair flopping across my forehead and brushing my ears. I ran out of makeup last month and never bothered to restock. Who do I have to impress? The waitress who works nonrush hours at the Thai

Tiger? My brother? My teddy bear? I live in Gabe's unremarkable hand-me-downs to hide a body that I barely had control over, even before it started its nightly involuntary transformations. But in dreams, I still see myself the way I was: sun-warmed and loose on my old striped towel in Griggs Park. I remember those summer afternoons when I would close my eyes, listen to Gabe and his not-boyfriend of the moment snark and poke at one another. I would imagine someone—definitely not Atticus, but *somebody*—beside me, who wanted to be nowhere else in the world. Somebody who thought I was everything, and enough. Our fingers creeping across the prickling summer grass to touch. Soft, flushed skin that wasn't mine beneath my palm.

THAT NIGHT, SIMAN knocks lightly enough that anyone listening might mistake it for a breeze rattling the back door. But even this much isn't necessary—Malka has been waiting with her nose practically pressed to the window since her father started snoring at 10:12. Mama took her pills before climbing into bed (despite the lump of the fox tooth pouch still tucked beneath her nightgown), so she'll be asleep by now, and won't wake easily. Nobody's stirred in the last half hour, not even her sisters. They should be safe.

Still, her heart jumps. She tiptoes to the door and grasps the knob, opening it before he's had the chance to knock again.

"Shhhh," she hushes while giggling, and dares to pinch his T-shirt sleeve to draw him inside.

"You want to stay here?" he whispers nervously.

She nods. "There's a place. Follow me."

His smile is like an unexpected shaft of light in the dark.

Malka leads Siman down the front hall to the basement steps. With its dirt floor and damp stone walls, it isn't romantic— not that she knows much of anything about romance—but it *is* private. No sound will drift up to the second floor, and no light will leak out beneath the door to expose them, since the glow from the single stripped bulb dangling down from between the beams and loose wires doesn't touch the top of the staircase.

While Siman glances around the room, Malka spreads out the quilt from her bed, which she smuggled downstairs for the occasion. They settle onto a childish patchwork pattern in primary colors. She thinks briefly of the fact that Siman has probably sat with girls in the grass of the Champs de Mars under the shadow of the Eiffel Tower, and in the warm sand of a Moroccan shore, and beneath that glistening, glittering cave ceiling in New Zealand. How could an unfinished basement in Fox Hollow possibly compare? How could *she*?

But she shoves her insecurities aside while he fumbles inside the small nylon duffel bag he brought with him. If anything, he seems as nervous as she feels. He grins shyly as he pulls out a cardboard pie box from Bubbe's Kitchen, the kosher bakery down the street from Frager's, as well as a bottle of white wine, two plastic cups as kid-like as her quilt, and two forks. He lifts the flap and she catches a whiff of chocolate and cream and tart fruit—it's Bubbe's chocolate pomegranate pie, her second-favorite. Surely a sign!

They eat and they sip and they talk in soft voices, lowering them overcautiously to laugh. He tells her about his childhood home in Kennett Square, Pennsylvania. "The mushroom capitol of the world!" he fake-brags. "Some Quaker florists in, like, the 1800s went to Europe and brought back spores to plant under the carnation beds in their greenhouses. They hired some local laid-off Italians to do the labor, and those guys started their own farms and hired Mexican workers. Now there's hundreds of mushroom farmers in this tiny little corner of the state, all these ugly cinder-block buildings built into the hills for miles. And we didn't even grow up next to those! Our house was by the compost yard that supplies the farms. Just acres and acres of corn cobs, hay, cocoa shells from the Hershey factory, and poop, excuse my saying so. Smells as bad as it sounds. Near enough that every summer we'd get a plague of flies in our backyard. They were so thick, Mom had to go around with the vacuum and suck dozens of 'em up through the extension every time we opened the door. Between that and seven brothers and sisters sharing two bedrooms, you can guess why I got out as soon as I could."

Once again, Malka feels silly for complaining about her own childhood. "When you put it like that, growing up in a big house in a flower field doesn't seem so bad."

Siman shrugs. "There are lots of ways to feel stuck," he says generously, topping off his own plastic cup.

Malka's is still half full. She's never drunk more than the two-ounce plastic cups they use for kiddush at Beth El, filled with grape juice for the kids and weak Manischewitz for those past bar or bat mitzvah age. Her stomach feels warm and her head just a bit balloon-like, floating a little above her body. She drains her cup in three swallows to keep up, and holds it out for more. "I don't know. There were a bunch of us, but mostly that was okay. My oldest sisters were out of the house before I was a teenager, and it was nice to have Shosh and Geela so close when we were kids." She casts her eyes around the dimly lit basement walls. "We would come down here sometimes and play archaeologist, make believe we were looking for lost Egyptian treasure. Then Shosh cut her finger on the lock trying to break into the coal room—we were pretending it was a pharaoh's tomb—and Mama freaked out about tetanus and black lung from the leftover coal dust and all the ways we could've died. They wouldn't let us play in the basement anymore after that."

Siman laughs, looking toward the ugly steel door in the wall across from them. "Honestly, that thing's creepy as hell. There could definitely be a mummy in there."

"Or treasure," she counters. "Like Papa said, he had the house built on the old foundation. Maybe the previous owners kept their valuables in there and forgot them, or couldn't get to them after the flood. That's what Geela would say."

Carrying his cup with him, he drifts over to examine the door. He takes a long sip, then touches the padlock with fingertips she knows to be work-callused, having memorized each brief brush against her own skin. "It's newer than the door, but it still looks a couple decades old."

"My parents locked it when they moved in," Malka explains. "To keep their future kids from the coal dust and the tetanus and the death and the treasure. Mama wasn't wild about us being in the basement even before Shosh cut herself. She thought it'd cave in on us."

"Bet I could open it. I've done a few jobs clearing out old properties and sheds, so I'd have to break padlocks when no one could find the keys. You wouldn't be able to tell from a glance that it was broken, though. Think they'll find out?"

"Nobody comes down here except Papa to get some tools, or if the boiler breaks. I don't know why they would."

With freshly poured cups of wine, they huddle around Papa's toolbox on one of the metal shelves along the wall. Siman selects two wrenches from the tray. Then he kneels in the dirt by the padlock, Malka trailing after him, trying not to block what little light there is. He slips the heads around the padlock, each straddling one side of the shackle. Holding them side by side, he squeezes the handles together in one swift, expert motion. The old lock clicks. He brushes away a bit of rusted metal that's chipped off, and the shackle swings open.

"Ha ha!" he cries triumphantly, and Malka's too excited to remind him to whisper. Instead, fueled by cheap white wine and victory, she drops down beside Siman, lays a palm against his lightly stubbled cheek to turn it, and presses her lips to his.

Their knees shuffle for position in the dirt. Siman fumbles the full cup and the lock he's still holding. And then they're not just kneeling there with their mouths together but actually kissing, with purpose, with passion.

Malka's very first kiss tastes like tart wine and chocolate pomegranate pie. And it makes her feel like a woman in a way nothing ever has before. Not her period at twelve or her bat mitzvah at thirteen, or the time she'd nearly figured out how to masturbate at sixteen from her school copy of *The Bluest Eye*, but stopped because she was sure somebody—her sisters, her parents, God, a ghost—could hear the guilty quickening of her breath.

Everything about this moment belongs to her; *her* body, *her* choice, *her* secret, *her* boy.

Siman doesn't pull away so much as drift backward an inch, allowing space for her to stop the kiss she started. She does, and then they're both giggling as they help each other up. He takes her hand, squeezes, and swings the door open.

Honestly, Malka can see right away why her mother didn't want them in here: the room looks like the inside of a crypt. It's a tight space, maybe five feet by five feet. The same rough stone walls as the rest of the basement. The floor is a shallow, sloping pile of coal dust, as she might've expected, but otherwise, bare. "Poo," she says, disappointed. "Not even one mummy."

"Don't lose hope! We haven't checked the chute. There could be a very little mummy."

"A mini mummy!"

Laughing, he steps carefully inside the room, and Malka follows. Woman or not, she doubts she'd be brave enough to without Siman. The air in here is even danker, damper, older than Malka herself. Older than Esther, most likely. They move carefully toward the small rectangular door that swims into vision out of the dark, set halfway up the outside wall. Siman wraps a strong hand around the door's rusty bar-pull and, with another reassuring squeeze of her hand, tugs down.

An unearthly screech of metal on stone splits the silence.

In terror, Malka turns toward the door of the coal room, wondering whether it was loud enough to be heard two floors up. But Siman tugs her back when she starts toward the main basement.

"Malka, look . . ."

She does, and unbelievably, there's something inside the open chute. A dull glint, a softer shadow in the pitch-black, a little bigger than a shoebox. Did the last owners leave treasure here after all?

That's when Malka hears a creak overhead.

Her heart stops. She shushes Siman, even though he wasn't speaking, and stumbles from the coal room, a little clumsy and loose with wine, she realizes. At the top of the basement steps, she crouches to listen at the door. The hallway light hasn't flicked on, and there are no passing footsteps. Could be that creak was just the house settling, but now she's spooked, the half-serious treasure hunt forgotten. She's never even snuck a friend into the house—how did she think she could sneak in a boy, drink with him, kiss him right beneath her parents' feet, and get away with it?

On marshmallow knees, she forces herself to rise and walk back down the steps. "Siman, come on!" she hisses, bundling up her quilt with the plastic cups inside it. She stuffs the empty wine bottle back into his duffel bag, pressing it into his arms as he emerges from the coal room. "You should go. I think—I don't know if someone heard us."

They sneak upstairs together, pause to listen. Down the hall, pause to listen.

Easing open the back door, Malka instructs, "Head for the river and circle around, okay? My parents' window faces the front of the house, so stick to the woods until you can come out farther up the driveway."

He nods so seriously that she can't help kissing his barely suppressed smile.

Then he's gone, dashing out into the dark. She imagines the flowers parting for him and falling back, the way her life now seems to bend around Siman.

Behind her, a heavy creak.

Let it be the settling bones of the house, she prays, the blush draining from her cheeks. Let it be ghosts. Anything but—

Mama. She's standing in the kitchen doorway, staring at her in gray-faced terror, as though Malka were the ghost.

EIGHTEEN

THAT RABBI KAYLA didn't expect to see me so soon is clear when she opens the door to find Ari and me midknock. "Well, hello, girls. I didn't know you two knew each other?"

"I've been showing Hannah around town," Ari explains.

"Right," I say. "I had some questions, and she offered to drive me—is this an okay time?"

The rabbi glances at the wall clock behind her, then turns back with a genuine smile. "Of course. I invited you to talk, and I meant it. Come in."

We follow her into a small, brightly lit office. I'm glad I didn't change after all; Rabbi Kayla's dressed more casually than Ari in jeans and a long Green Day T-shirt, her natural hair scooped up into a pineapple bun. Out from behind the podium and dressed down, she looks younger than Mom—I don't know why I assumed they were the same age. We take a seat on the worn maroon couch as she pulls out the rolling chair from a desk stacked with books.

"My next lesson isn't for twenty minutes, so we've got some time to chat. What can I do for you, Hannah?"

No time to reconsider. I dig into my backpack, still stuffed with the clues I've gathered in Fox Hollow—the Loew family book, Jitka's letter, and the locket. For now, I just pull out the cardboard box with the hamsa in it. "My mom gave this to me a few weeks ago, before my grandmother died. She said it belonged to a friend of the family, and we think that was Ari's bubbe. But we don't know much about it beyond that. I was wondering if—being, like, a rabbi—you might?"

Rabbi Kayla blinks in surprise; I'm sure this wasn't what she had in mind when she offered to chat. But she takes the box when I pass it over, and lifts out the hamsa with careful fingers. "It's lovely."

"We thought maybe it was an amulet," Ari chimes in, "knowing Bubbe."

"And there's writing on the back," I add.

"In Hebrew," Ari confirms.

Rabbi Kayla smiles fondly. "Now, you know your bubbe and I loved our chats. I've been at Beth El for nearly a decade," she explains to me, "and Ida was always one of my favorite congregants, may her memory be a blessing. Of course, Maimonides himself denounced amulets, though he did admit—and I agree—that they might be useful for the kind of illnesses we now consider psychosomatic—"

"Hannah's just here to learn a little more about her mom," Ari interrupts, her smile growing brittle around the edges. "Promise, I'm not corrupting her."

"I'd never accuse you of that," Rabbi Kayla says, chuckling.

"Okay, let's have a look." Flipping over the hamsa, she frowns, then rolls herself back to the desk. She fishes through the top drawer to pull out a small pewter magnifying glass, then squints through the lens. "It looks like an incantation. Most written amulets of the past were scribed for a specific person, or to guard against a specific illness or disaster. So they might've held a verse from the Torah, or a blessing. This one—I think it's part of a verse from Deuteronomy, something a parent would say over their child's bed to protect them. Here: 'As an eagle that stirreth up her nest, hovereth over her young, spreadeth abroad her wings, taketh them, beareth them on her pinions—the Lord alone did lead him, and there was no strange god with Him.' See?" She beckons me to lean in, and hands me the magnifying glass.

I glance politely through the lens, though of course, I can't read the Hebrew. "To protect children from what?"

"From evil."

"Like, a demon?"

"For instance."

I think of last night in the woods, the stink of rot and corruption, and the claw prints piercing the ground where I woke up. If there was a sheyd out there, it didn't touch me, even as I was close enough to smell it. And I *did* have the hamsa on me, forgotten in my pocket.

"If you belong to Ida's school of thought, someone knowledgeable and powerful enough could make an amulet for just about anything. Warding off demons, curing a bad fever, finding a husband, anything. A few years ago, they even found a scroll belonging to an ancient gambler, meant to curse a chariot race in his favor." Rabbi Kayla's eyes gleam as she tells us this. It's as Ari guessed—she doesn't believe in any of it.

I'm not about to pull down my pants and whip out my temporary tail in a rabbi's office, but I wonder if it'd change her mind if I did.

"If you could ward off a demon with an amulet like this, could you trap one?" I scramble to remember the details from the story in Ida's journal, "The Underwater Palace." "There's this story we heard—a family story—about a rabbi who traps a demon in a chest with . . . secret words, I think? And a chain. It had something called the Seal of Solomon on the links. Could that have been an amulet like this?"

The rabbi scratches her head. "Not like this one, exactly, but an amulet, sure. You know the story of Solomon and Ashmedai?"

I shake my head, and this time, so does Ari.

"Solomon was a famously wise king of Israel, though wise men can do foolish things. He had a ring made of brass and iron, supposedly engraved by Adonai, by God himself, with which he could—again, supposedly—command both good and evil spirits. That ring was called the Seal of Solomon. In one story, Solomon captures Ashmedai himself, the king of the shedim, using the seal. And the demon king's name, of course. Names are a very powerful element in Judaism. When we name our children, we do it very carefully. The name of a deceased ancestor, given to a baby, carries with it the qualities of the ancestor, like a stamp on the new child. Some names are good luck—you don't want to accidentally give your kid a name with bad luck—and the meaning can influence the person the child grows into. Hannah, for instance, comes from the Hebrew 'Channah,' and means favor, or grace. The whole story of a man is contained in his name. And if you know it, then according to some—maybe according to Ida—you know his nature and history and soul, and that gives you a kind of control over him."

I'm reminded of what Ari said about the golem. *You're its master. It won't have a name unless you give it one.* Like you have the power to call a person your own once you know who they are.

What does it mean, then, that I never knew my mother's true name? That I barely knew mine?

If nobody knows or remembers your name, do you belong to yourself, or to nobody?

"Sorry, I'm off topic, aren't I?" Rabbi Kayla smiles. "It's all pretty fascinating to think about, at least for me. We were talking about Ashmedai, how knowing his name gave Solomon power. But you know, the story still doesn't end well for Solomon. Ashmedai tricked him into setting him loose and handing over the ring. Which you might guess was a big mistake. The demon king threw Solomon out of his own kingdom, took his form, and ruled Israel with Solomon's ring while Solomon was left to beg and wander for years before returning home. That's the trouble in dealing with demons—well, one of them. Assume you're in control, and you're in greater danger than ever. Even after Solomon reclaimed his throne, he lived in terror of the demon's return."

"Sucks for Solomon," Ari mutters.

"Seriously." Rabbi Kayla winks. "Anyway, stories aside, you girls want to know what this amulet means?" She hands the box back to me. "It means that somewhere, sometime, a parent loved their child and wanted to keep them safe from the world. It's an artifact of love. So treasure it, okay?"

I feel the weight of Ari's arm beside me, the heat of her skin pressed against mine even through thick fabric, and realize my own limbs are shaking.

We stand on the concrete stoop outside the synagogue because we're not sure where to go next. I hold the hamsa close to my face to study the writing that nobody ever taught me how to read. Just one of the many secrets Mom kept to herself—one of the many corners of her life she never let me inside, preferring to live there alone rather than with her own daughter. Speaking of . . . "Why would Ida have given this to my mom instead of yours, do you think?"

Ari undoes the top button of her collared jumpsuit, flapping it back and forth for a breeze. "I told you, Mom and Bubbe didn't get along."

"As grown-ups, sure, but when she was just a kid?"

"I don't know. Obviously it got worse as Bubbe got worse—Mom would say she was going downhill even when Rabbi

Kayla met her. But it's like, every memory I have of being in the same room with them, Bubbe was talking to me, and Mom was talking to me, but neither of them were talking to each other."

"Families are complicated." I repeat our line, the understatement of the century, and am rewarded with dimples. "But I don't get it. If I was Mom, and I had a magic demon-repelling amulet, I'd ask for it back before going off to face a demon, right? Why would she leave this behind?"

"Because of what the rabbi said," Ari says gently, tucking away a pink strand that's slipped from her space buns. "She wanted to keep you safe more than she wanted to be safe. She loves you."

"Hmm." I cough to clear the burr out of my throat at this simple statement, not so simple at all. "Okay, okay, let's recap. What do we know now?" I tick the items off on my fingers. "One: Mom and Siman Melkes tried to leave town together thirty-one years ago. Two: Something went wrong. Something Mom did . . . a mistake she made. Let's call that Unknown X. Three: Siman washed up dead in the Hudson less than two months later. Four: Mom never came back to Fox Hollow, never saw her family again, and quit talking to them completely after I was born. She moved us all around the country, until I made her stop so I could go to Winthrop. Five: I wake up on my seventeenth birthday with freaky eyes, which Mom is convinced is related to Unknown X. Six: She leaves us behind, supposedly for our own safety, and returns to Fox Hollow at last. She goes to your mom to find Ida, and something that might've been in

Ida's things—let's call that Unknown Y—but Ida is gone, and your mom shuts mine out, claiming she threw everything out when your bubbe died. Seven: Your mom lied." Ari nods; this is nothing but the truth. "Eight: Jitka made the golem to protect Mom from a literal fucking demon"—I repeat Gabe's words—"and nine: Jitka is dead, Mom is gone, and said sheyd seems to be here, in Fox Hollow. Uh . . . is that everything?"

"Also, according to Rabbi Kayla, it would be super convenient if we could find a Seal of Solomon. Also, the name of the sheyd." She blinks at me in the bright sun and tugs at the dagger in her earlobe, something I've noticed she does when she's anxious, the way Gabe teethes his lip stud. Maybe I need to pierce something, too. Lord knows I have the anxiety.

"We need to solve for X and Y. We don't know whether your mom knows anything about X, but Y—"

"So let's find out. Mom's back from Pennsylvania tomorrow. I think it's time we make her talk to us."

My lungs seize up inside my chest. I'm just beginning to get used to Ari looking at me. In fact, I'm starting to like it. But the idea of bringing somebody else in . . . "Tomorrow's the last day of shiva, and then we're out of reasons to stay around. If your mom can't help us . . . Or what if she doesn't want to? Or what if it's dangerous? I mean, this isn't just a story anymore. Jitka's gone, and my mom . . . we don't know where she is. It's bad enough that you could get hurt, and I get that you believe in tik-tikoon . . ."

"Tikkun olam?" she supplies.

"Yeah, that. You're a good person, I know that, and I'm grateful, but you don't have to—"

"Hey," Ari interrupts, reaching out so her fingers brush mine. She holds her palm open.

So I give her my hand.

"I—I actually wanted to see the amulet." She smiles shyly.

"Oh, oh my God, obviously." I slacken my fingers and try to slip free.

But Ari holds on tight. "How about I take both, okay?"

I will myself to breathe. Then I cup my free hand to hers to pass the pendant without dropping it, fighting a shiver even in the heat.

She lifts it to study, still holding tight to me. "It sounds like some deep bullshit to say I had, like, a crisis of faith when Bubbe died. I was thirteen, right? I'd just had my own bat mitzvah— Mom didn't think it was safe to take her mom out of the nursing home for that—and I was helping out in the Hebrew school kindergarten group, basically babysitting. When they're that little, you just teach them the basic Torah stories. Adam and Eve and Noah's ark and Joseph in Egypt, et cetera. I gave them paper and crayons so they could draw what they thought God looked like, and markers and empty toilet paper rolls to make their own mezuzot. Everything I'd learned and done when I was their age. I wasn't telling them about Ida Silver sorts of stuff, or anything—that was just for Bubbe and me. Plus, I don't think Mrs. Guralnick would've let me teach them about shedim. But I think I still believed. Then Bubbe died, and like I told you, it was really rough. Mom was so . . . It wasn't like we weren't expecting it, and I guess I thought . . . it's stupid, but I thought my mom was *fine*. Bubbe was *my* person, not Mom's. And she seemed like she was keeping it together. So I tried to talk to her before the funeral. I asked her about this story I was remembering, the one about the ibbur. About the woman who thought her husband was still with her? I asked Mom if she'd ever believed in stuff like that. And she looked down at me and said, 'None of it's real, Arielle. People just leave you. You love them, and they leave you, and they don't come back. Anybody who thinks different is just scared to admit they're alone.'"

"Fucking ouch," I murmur.

"Yeah. But I mean, we were about to bury her mom, so . . . she probably wasn't in a super healthy space to talk about death, and I don't know why I thought she would be. I don't think she was trying to plunge me into existential crisis or whatever. But I had to wonder, like, what if none of it *is* real? Not just the wild stuff, like the demons and the ibburim and the Bar Juchne. Not even Noah's ark and all that because, sure, I get that stories don't have to be true to mean something to the people who tell them. But everything I'd just accepted my whole life—God and tikkun olam and this community, this supposed family of chosen people that we belong to. What if none of it meant anything without her, and what if it never had?"

I find the courage to look at her, expecting to see something familiar: the reflection of every terrible feeling I had when the events of my seventeenth birthday wiped out years of planning, of work, of certainty that I actually had a say in my own life.

But I don't. I find something else entirely glittering in her eyes.

"Then I met you, and within two days, it turns out that every bad thing Bubbe believed in could be real. And you wouldn't think that would be comforting, but all I can think is that if all that stuff is true, then maybe every good thing she believed in is real, too. Anything is possible, you know? Like, even if this had nothing to do with me or my family—which it clearly does—I can't stop vibrating from this feeling of possibility. I thought . . . I thought I'd lost it."

"But you still went to synagogue? Even when you didn't believe?"

"I did. Because . . . I don't know. The people at Beth El loved Bubbe, and they love me. I meant what I said, about living in a small town. How you can try to change, but eventually, people just stop seeing *you* and only see the version of you that makes them happiest. But they're still my people. So at least I wasn't alone. Does that make sense?"

"Sort of," I say. "I don't have people like that. I mean, there's Gabe, and he loves me no matter what, but it's not like he has a choice." *Even when I hurt him for no reason.* "And there's my mom, and . . ."

And I don't know who Mom sees when she looks at me. I have no idea who she thinks I am. I never asked, because I was too afraid to find out—that I was a disappointment, an obligation. That I was another thing to bubble wrap and bundle from house to house, a memento of something she wished she could forget, but she couldn't bring herself to throw away.

Ari squeezes my hand tight, fingertips digging into my knuckles. "We're gonna find her."

"You don't know that, though," I insist. "You don't even know me."

"I know you're smart, and strong, and your freckles are bananas, and . . . look, I could go on, but please stop me if I'm making things weird. I, uh, don't have a ton of practical experience. So just, tell me if I'm totally imagining this?"

There's no part of me that isn't blushing, and when her fingers slacken around mine, I squeeze tight to trap them. "You're not."

We stand there in the sun for a long moment, watching cars pass and summer birds peck at the blazing green lawn, and my heart is not a stone but a flaming coal, the sparks rising, rising.

Curses are real, and monsters too.

But so is magic. So are weapons. So is *this*.

FOOLISHLY, MALKA HOPED that things would be better in the light of morning. But when her parents call her downstairs and tell her to sit at the dining room table, her father's voice is sour with disgust. And Mama . . . she looks as ragged as Malka feels.

"What's going on between you and this boy?" Mama demands.

"I . . . nothing. We haven't done anything wrong."

"And just what *have* you done?" Papa speaks up.

Now the blood rushes back, boiling her cheeks and the tips of her ears. "Gross, you can't ask me that!"

"Can't we? You sneak a boy into this house, after dark, with no thought for your parents or for your own safety, and now you want to act like an innocent child?"

"You treat me like a child!" Malka pounds a fist on the table-top, surprising her parents—surprising herself. But she won't be stopped now. "If I could go out with Siman like a normal person, I wouldn't have had to sneak him in. I've done everything you ever told me to, until now. I never broke the rules, no matter how much I hated them, and I didn't even get to ask why, because it would upset you. How is that fair?"

Though Malka stares them both down while she says this, they must know she's asking Mama. Yet it's Papa who replies. "You don't need to ask the purpose behind our rules when you know it already."

"Because you say so?"

"To keep you safe," Mama pleads. "Malkala, listen to your father."

"Why? Nobody ever listens to me."

"It's you we're thinking of, only you. Whatever is going on with this boy, whatever he's promised you, he won't be coming back here. Your father already let him go. He's told Gerald—"

"You *ratted us out to Mr. Frager*?" She feels her voice rising to a shriek.

"—told him what kind of character this boy has who stays above his business," Mama forges on. "He'll be out by the end of the month."

"So I'll leave with him."

Silence, for a long moment.

Then, "You will *not*." Her mother's quiet words are rimed with ice.

"Try and stop me," she challenges.

"Go to your room," Papa orders, before turning to soothe Mama. "Meyn lib, hush, don't let her upset you so . . ."

Frustrated beyond words, Malka screams her throat sore, stands, and bolts. From the parlor, down the hall, out the back door in the kitchen. Already sobbing for breath, she streaks through the wildflower field. With no better plan, she heads for the Hollow. She plunges downstream, stumbling through trees and tearing her skirt on thick river brush, half blinded by her own simmering rage by the time she veers into Rachael's yard.

When she hurtles up the familiar red porch and pounds on their back door, Mrs. Silver answers in a whirl of gauzy flowered scarves and a tinkle of necklaces and charms, her kind eyes bewildered. "Malka? Come in, come in, bubeleh."

It's a little cooler in the Silvers' kitchen, with a box fan in their wide-open window. Malka sits at the table with Rachael while Mrs. Silver scoops the sachets out of a pitcher of cold-brew lavender tea that's been chilling in their refrigerator.

"I know you don't see eye to eye with your parents," she says when Malka has finished spilling her sorrows, "but you know they love you, and you know they wish the best for you. You know your mother acts out of fear, always. She's faced so much in her life, and you're her baby girl. Of course she's terrified to lose you. You can honor that, even when you don't understand it."

Malka looks to Rachael for help. But her best friend is quiet, picking at a chip in the table with a midnight-blue fingernail.

Stung, she spits out, "So I have to do everything she says, forever?"

"No, not everything." She goes for the pitcher to pour refills for the three of them, then settles back down in a chair between the girls. "And as for forever, your parents won't be around that long," Mrs. Silver says wryly.

"You're just trying to make me feel guilty." Malka knows

she sounds just like the child she claimed not to be.

"I'm telling you how it is." Reaching for the cat-shaped porcelain sugar bowl on the table, Mrs. Silver lifts the lid and, to Malka's astonishment, pours half the contents onto the tabletop. Still, Rachael is silent as her mother smooths the pile with her palm, then carves Hebrew letters into the sugar with her fingertip:

אמת

Truth.

"You are yourself and belong to you. But you only have one mother, and one day she'll be gone, and you may in fact miss the parts of her that drive you crazy now." Mrs. Silver holds up a hand to halt Malka's protest. "I know that doesn't make her right. I know you feel for this boy. He means something to you, and that's yours to keep, even if he isn't. People come and go through our lives. They leave impressions on us, like letters in dust." Then she bends over and blows on the sugar, scattering the grains across the tabletop, onto the floor. "Impermanent things can still change us forever."

NINETEEN

"WE, UH, HAVEN'T been able to reach your mom." Aunt Esther tries to sound casual between bites of baked salmon. "Her voice mail's still full, and her phone's been off for days. That normal for her?"

I nudge an ugly green caper from my filet with my fork, remembering Mom's caper phase. Every night, pasta with garlic caper sauce, salad with caper dressing, brussels sprouts with caper butter. I thought it was an artistic choice, like her pastel chalk period, or her season of neon, but way more offensive. In actual fact, it had been because we'd just moved to this rental RV on Lake Jocassee in South Carolina, and she was between jobs for clients, so she was making the most of the jar of capers the previous tenants had left behind in the fridge.

I still hate capers, though.

"It happens sometimes." I answer Aunt Esther when Gabe doesn't. "She forgets to charge her phone, and she lets voice mails pile up. Her freelance clients know to email or text." None of this is a lie, not that Esther would have any better luck writing to Mom.

"But you've talked, and she knows when to expect you home?"

"She'll meet us at the station Wednesday night," my brother assures her. We'd needed some answer to the expected *How long will you be staying with us?* Since Jitka's shiva ends tomorrow evening, we have no excuse for lingering. Especially when nobody's been able to reach Mom. We have no plan beyond Wednesday morning, when we're allegedly catching the local bus to Hudson, then the train to Boston. Nothing besides packing up, pretending to board the train, then sneaking back to hide in Ida's abandoned place, relying on Ari for everything, and losing access to this house and all its secrets.

I try to meet Gabe's eyes, but he won't even look at me.

"Good, good," Bernie says. "All's well, then." He reaches over to squeeze our aunt's shoulder.

As far as Aunt Esther knows, her sister is out there instead of here with us—with her—by choice. They could hear each other's voices for the first time in seventeen years, if Mom would only turn on her phone. They could stand in the same room, tonight even, if Mom would hop in her car and drive here. Maybe it wouldn't fix everything, but as far as Esther knows, the only thing standing between them and a new start is Mom's indifference.

She rests her hand on top of Bernie's, squeezes back, then returns to her dinner.

Gabe and I clear the table and do the dishes, despite Esther's protests. It's the literal least we can do for her.

I glance over at his familiar profile as the last light drains from the sky beyond the kitchen window. He dries a plate, places it on the stack. Dries a handful of forks, tumbles them into the silverware drawer. He doesn't speak, doesn't look at me. And, shit. I'd hoped that what went wrong between us last night had been buried by the busyness of the day. Gabe walked miles this afternoon—he went to Ida's and back while Ari and I were with Rabbi Kayla, stashing the golem just beyond the tree line. There, they can sit in relative peace behind the massive spidery oak, hidden from view while keeping an eye on the river. I thought maybe he'd be too pooped from the trek to remember being mad at me.

But it was always going to rise back up in the first quiet moment.

I tell myself it'll be fine; we'll talk to Rachael Leydon tomorrow. We'll figure out what Mom so desperately needed. We'll find her. And whatever it takes, we'll fix me, we'll fix all of us—Gabe and me, us and Mom, Mom and Esther and the whole Eggers family. Everything will be better then.

But what if . . . well, what if? It's like Jitka said: *There is so much to be sorry for, and not enough time to say what needs saying.*

There would never be enough time to make up for what we've lost.

"Gabe," I start, blurting so suddenly and forcefully that he fumbles a cup, catching it just before it falls and shatters. "I'm sorry. About last night? I'm really, really sorry. You were thinking about me—you're *always* thinking of me—and I shouldn't have made you feel bad about California. You're allowed to want something for yourself, for once." My throat constricts like a fist, and my voice roughens. "You're a really good brother."

"Well, I'm supposed to take care of you." He clears his own throat. "And I'm supposed to say, 'I'm supposed to take care of you,' right? That's, like, my line." He waves dismissively when I open my mouth to answer, and the dish towel flaps through the air. "No, don't. It's not your fault. I'm not snarking." Turning, he sits on the bottom step to the attic bedroom, still twisting the dishrag.

Since the staircase is too narrow, I sit cross-legged on the tiled floor at his feet, careful not to settle my weight on my tail. The joint has grown sore by now, and I'm impatient to trade the damn thing in.

But enough about me.

"What do you mean, 'That's my line'?"

"I don't know," he mumbles, running a dishwater-damp hand through his purposely messy hair and sending it into an accidentally messy turquoise tumble. "Do you ever feel like you're in a play, and everything you're saying is some line in the script, and everything you're doing is part of the scene? And you don't even know who wrote the fucking play, but it *definitely* wasn't you. Plus you don't know what you'd do or say differently offstage, and it would take so much more energy to figure that out, so you just keep going?"

"I . . ."

"Okay, that was the *most* on-brand metaphor. I just mean that half the time . . . maybe most of the time . . . I have no idea whether I'm acting like myself, or capital-a Acting like myself.

You know? Even with Mom. Even, sometimes, with you. I can't help but be whoever I think somebody wants me to be."

Well, doesn't that sound familiar. "But . . . but everybody *loves* you, just being you. Literally everyone you meet. *I* love you. And you know you're Mom's favorite." I wish I could draw the words back in—we're supposed to be talking about him, not me—but hell, they were always going to come out. "You guys are, like, peanut butter and jelly, and I'm capers."

"Hannah—"

"She's gone to every performance of every play you've ever been in. She's been to two mock trial competitions since I joined the team freshman year, and I caught her reading *The Life-Changing Magic of Tidying Up* at the last one, while I was presenting my defense. And she never even fucking tidied after that! She just used the illustrations to decoupage." I want to stop, I do, but I just keep rolling along like the salty little caper I am. "Every time we move, she packs up every half-finished scrap of art you've ever made, ones *you* don't even remember making. But when we moved from Richmond to Maine, she threw away Vlad!"

"To be fair," he says, holding his hands out as though he could stop a speeding train, "you didn't need an inhaler any-more."

"But that's not the point. Vlad was important to me, and she should've known that, but she tossed him out like an old banana peel. She doesn't know anything about *anything* that matters to me. She doesn't know my PSAT scores or my class ranking. If I asked her my future college major, or what I want to do with my degree—"

"Health care administration, and medical and health services manager," he supplies matter-of-factly.

"Right, *you* know, but Mom doesn't. *You* know how hard I work to get what I want, all the time, and she doesn't have any clue."

"So why do you care so much?" Gabe asks, not unkindly. "I mean, if you're going for what you want, then that's, like, the ultimate goal, right? Why does it matter how much Mom sees?"

"I . . . I don't know." I sniff. It doesn't feel entirely true, but it still pains me to admit it. "I guess it shouldn't. Why are we like this?"

Gabe scoots off the bottom step to sit on the tiles next to me. "Who even knows? Let's spin a wheel and see where it lands. Mommy issues, Daddy issues, divorce issues, adopted kid issues, human issues—"

"Wait, are you having adopted kid issues? Like, currently?" I interrupt to ask. We don't often talk about this. My brother doesn't bring it up, and so I don't. It was Mom who sat me down to tell me when I was six, right after she sat down seven-year-old Gabe.

But I think of those strange, strained moments between us since we came to Fox Hollow. His comment to Rabbi Kayla about being adopted . . . and to me, about being "the lesser Williams."

It's occurring to me, for the first time, that this trip has been a different experience for Gabe than it has for me. The shame is a writhing animal behind my breast, trapped and frantic.

He sighs. "I don't know. Maybe? It's weird being here. These people are my family, because you and Mom are my family, and nobody's told me any different. It's not their fault. I just don't know what all of this is supposed to mean, or how I'm supposed to feel about it. Like, I spend my whole life waiting for someone to tell me who I am, the person I'm supposed to be, but I'm still scared of the answer. You know how Mom offered to tell me who my birth parents were, and I said no?"

I did know that. It's what's called a semi-open adoption— Mom and Dad were picked by the birth family, who I suppose liked the idea of an artist and an accountant raising their child. Mom has his medical history, and sends yearly update letters to his birth family through an attorney. If Gabe wanted to, we could also go through the attorney to learn about his heritage. But he's never asked. "What about now? Do you want to know?"

"I . . . I'm not sure. I've tried not to think about the fact that I might have this whole other family out there, brothers and sisters and a dad and whoever. I tried not to wonder what my birth parents look like, what they do, if they're alive, if they love each other or hate each other, if they're loud or scared or flaky or if they're just as shitty at math as I am. If they're anything like me, or exactly like me. Because if I knew what kind of people my birth parents were, and why they gave me up, then . . . maybe I would know something about myself, something that I couldn't take back, or change.

"And then there's you guys. Mom always said it would be okay, and it wouldn't change anything for our family, but . . . look, I never want you to think you're *not* enough. Like, being your brother isn't enough."

"Gabe," I choke out.

He shakes his head. "I know, I know what you're gonna say. I believe you. And I swear, you've always been enough."

My heart thrums pathetically at his reassurance.

"Then . . . then we come here, and we're getting all these answers about Mom. But it's also bringing all the old questions back: What parts of me are real, and what's me just faking it until something works or feels right? What parts come from my birth parents, or Mom, or just belong to me?"

I speak slowly, so my voice won't splinter. "I think it all belongs to you. But also, it's okay that you're not sure. And that being here brings up questions. Maybe this is a chance for both of us. We're off script in Fox Hollow," I say, borrowing his metaphor. "We get to figure out who we are," I continue, and then, with a deep breath, "like . . . if some of us are a little bit gay?"

His eyes round with surprise. "Go onnnn . . ."

"Maybe I'm a little gay. I think. A little bi? I haven't figured that out yet. Like, I don't think I ever felt it with Atticus, but he—"

"Had the sexual magnetism of a paper napkin?"

"Yes," I have to admit. "But . . .. he had nice qualities."

"Not as nice as Ari's, though?" Gabe guesses.

I refuse to blush when Gabe has been so historically unashamed of the random drama club cast members, baseball players, and skater boys whose qualities he's enjoyed, however briefly. Instead, I lift my chin. "You don't like her?"

"She's . . . bossy."

"You're bossy."

He waves away this undeniable truth. "I have a responsibility to share the nectar of my age and wisdom."

"Gross," I grumble, "nobody wants your nectar." But as Gabe gasps dramatically and slaps me with the dishrag like an invitation to duel, my whole body feels lighter, the emotional detritus of yesterday's fight cleaned and cleared away. Tomorrow terrifies me. There's still so much we don't know, and our only assets are a golem we know almost nothing about and an amulet that may or may not work. Before my seventeenth birthday, I spent each day planning every detail, anticipating every circumstance; now, we have no plan at all.

But we've got each other, and that's all we've ever needed before.

Later that night, I'm curled up in bed, my room washed bright and pale by the comforting light of a nearly full moon over the trees. I slip a hand into the pocket of my sweatpants to touch the hamsa I've tucked inside; I feel a little safer with it on me. Still, I can't sleep, and my thoughts drift toward Mom. And, against my will, to the moment I might have ruined everything.

I think about Spring Valley.

I received my Winthrop Academy welcome packet and scholarship info in the mail the summer before my freshman year. Having applied, gathered teacher recommendations, interviewed via Skype, and tested in all without telling Mom, I went about informing her of what would be happening in the most passive-aggressive way possible: I left the royal-purple folder with its embossed silver seal—a graceful hand plucking an apple from a branch—in the most conspicuous places possible, ripe for discovery.

All of this is to say that it would've been really hard for Mom to miss the packet. Yet somehow, she did. I put it on the countertop in front of the coffeepot, and she used it as a coaster, stamping it permanently with coffee rings. I left it on the couch, and she shifted it to the top of the TV to pull out her bed that night.

"Why don't you just talk to her?" Gabe asked as he shoved the folder over to make room on the porch floor for his cereal bowl.

By then it was a point of pride. But after a full week of waiting for Mom to open her eyes and realize this was important to me, I waylaid her in the bathroom before her dinner shift at the restaurant. I'd meant to present my case calmly; alas, the speech I'd outlined with bullet points and sub-bullets dissolved on my tongue when she said, barely thirty seconds in, "It's not that easy, Banana. And I've checked into the schools around here—the local public high school is great!" Mom meant the *only* high school in Spring Valley, public or otherwise. It looked fine, but wasn't an illustrious and hypercompetitive prep school that just so happened to have a small quota of low-income student admissions to fill, which also happened to be located in the heart of ivies country.

So I snapped.

"I've never asked for anything like this," I practically screamed, "and I've always done what you wanted, picked up and moved whenever you felt like it, not that I had any choice. Why can't you do this one thing, for me?"

Mom's reflection gaped at mine in the bathroom mirror. "You don't know what you're asking for. I'm sure this place, whatever it is—"

"Win-throp A-ca-de-my!" I enunciated loudly, each syllable a sharpened knife.

"I'm sure it's lovely, but to move the whole family across the country . . ."

Winthrop is a coed full boarding school, but my scholarship only covers tuition, so I couldn't have attended if we didn't move nearby. But we'd moved farther away for less important reasons than my entire future. Every time, I'd tuck my own ill feelings away to help wrap our few valuables in newspaper and plot a course for our next nonhome. Maybe I resented my role as luggage, but I still didn't want to become burdensome.

The only thing worse than being dragged along with my

little family was my constant fear of being shaken off and left behind.

Maybe she did have her reasons, and maybe she was trying to keep me safe; seems like she believed that. She was alone, and she was probably doing her best. I can admit that much, now. But in Spring Valley, I lost it. I threatened to leave and live with Poppy and Grammy if she wouldn't take us to Boston.

Mom didn't call my bluff. Which was good. Because I didn't really *want* to leave Mom.

Why do you care so much? Gabe had asked me. *Why does it matter how much Mom sees?*

Alone in the dark, I can finally admit the truth to myself. That I could spend forever wondering why I thought I needed the perfect grades, or the ivies, or a mathematically perfect career to force Mom to look directly at me, just once. Even if— even *when* I see her again and get the chance to ask her, maybe Jitka was right, and there will never be enough time to make up for everything that's gone wrong between us.

EVERYTHING FALLS APART that Saturday morning with the crash of crystal on porcelain.

Malka never *meant* to break the platter. Yes, she still burns with the fury of last week's fight. She's seethed through Papa's crisp commands and Mama's anguished glances—as though *she's* the one who's been unfairly treated, not Malka. What's worse, she hasn't seen Siman since that night. Geela says she saw Papa leaving Siman's tools and his last check by the roadside at the mouth of their driveway. And even if he is still in town, hasn't moved out from above Frager's yet, it's not like she can see him. She's grounded—probably until college. Possibly beyond. Maybe her parents won't even let her live with Papa's cousin while she attends Stern; maybe it's the nearest community college in Basin or nothing. Maybe they'll never let her out of their sight again.

Malka doesn't even have any number for Siman, and he hasn't called the house. Not that she knows of, anyway. Certainly Mama and Papa wouldn't have told her if he had, and they've taken the cordless phone into their bedroom, for which

Geela and Shosh have been glowering at Malka. She can't bring herself to care.

She's lost Siman before she ever had him.

So when Papa stops her on her way through the kitchen on Saturday and tells her to take the pastries out to the dining room table, while Mama eyes her in that freshly wounded way, maybe she jerks the platter, one of their good Sabbath dishes, more aggressively than necessary from the countertop.

Still, she does not fumble it on purpose when she then slips on a damp patch of kitchen tile. Nevertheless, as she swings her body to stay upright, the platter strikes the rim of the farmhouse sink and ricochets to the checkered floor, where it smashes to splinters amid two dozen of her mother's rugelach.

For a long moment, nobody moves.

Then Papa whisks Mama behind him, as though she'd thrown the dish directly at her mother. "Have you lost your mind, Malka?" he asks through clenched teeth.

"I didn't do it on—"

"Apologize to your mother," he cuts in. "Now."

"W-what?" she splutters. "For *what*?"

"All week long, you've been prowling around this house like a wild animal about to strike," Papa accuses. "Do you care so little about the pain you cause your mother?"

"I haven't done anything to her!" Malka's voice is an indignant shriek, painful to her own ears, but she won't be quieted, and she won't be stopped by her father's anger or her mother's cringing. "I *never* do anything, because she doesn't let me do anything! I'm not allowed to get my license, or take the bus, or take a train to the city. I wasn't allowed to go see Soundgarden at the New Ritz with Rachael, even though her freaking grandmother was going and it's, like, the only thing I've ever wanted! I wasn't allowed to go to Holli Down's birthday party just because her parents weren't there, even though we're almost adults and it's not even a mile and a half away, and only three boys showed up. I'm not allowed to have a boyfriend, anyway. I'm not allowed to have a life—*she* won't let me! So why do you always take her side instead of mine?"

"Because he knows that everything I do is to protect you!" Mama shouts.

Papa looks as though he's about to speak, but Malka's sure it won't be to defend her.

"I don't want you to protect me!" she cries.

"You say this, but you don't know what you want. You don't know anything about life, or what the world is like, or what it will do to you."

"That's your fault! I can't breathe in this stupid house, but you won't let me go anywhere else. I hate this place. I'm sick of it, and getting rid of Siman won't keep me here. I won't sleep in your attic forever, or come home from school every weekend just so you can try to convince me never to leave. I don't even want to go to college—"

"Poor Malka, so put upon," Mama scoffs. Scoffs! "Trapped in this big, beautiful house your father built for you, with your nice things and plenty of food and your big, beautiful family who love you. You've never known what it feels like to be hungry, or scared, or unsafe." By now, she's stepped around Papa, moved forward to stand in front of Malka. "And you want to throw all that away because a pretty boy comes along and tells you fairy tales about the world, and you believe them?"

"Well, if I have to stay here, I'll throw myself in the Hollow, and you'll lose me anyway."

The moment the words leave her mouth, Malka regrets them. But faster than she can take them back, her mother reaches out and slaps her across the face.

Stunned, Malka presses her palm to her cheek the way she's seen women do on TV—a role she never thought she'd play. Her skin is blood-stung, her left ear ringing lightly.

Her empty threat has unlocked something inside of Mama, let loose a fury that seems to possess her. "Are we not enough for you?" she screams, eyes wild, like a panicked horse. "Have we not given you enough? Have I not loved you enough? Do you *know* what I would give for another day, just one more, with my own mama? Do you know how lucky you are? My parents, gone. My sisters and brothers, gone. My nieces and nephews, my friends, my—everyone, gone. And you stand in front of your mother and speak of leaving, for what? For a *boy*?" Her eyes narrow, and she spits, "May you be blessed with so grateful a daughter."

Malka's blood boils with shame, but also, with rage. They never speak of Mama's ghosts so as not to hurt her, yet she summons them now to hurt Malka?

Her mother clutches at her blouse, claws at her breastbone, caving inward, and Papa, pale behind his thick beard, hurries to *her* side. He wraps his strong arms around *her* narrow shoulders and kisses the hair at *her* temple, as though she were the one struck.

Then Malka is up the stairs and bursting through her bedroom door, slamming it behind her so hard the whole house rattles down to its rotten roots.

She throws herself into bed and crawls under her summer blanket like the child she swears she isn't. She needn't have. Nobody comes to yell at her, or comfort her. Her sisters don't even come up to check on her, though they can't have missed the fight. Heaving for breath in the airless heat beneath her covers, she doesn't move again until she hears her family leave the house to walk to Shabbat services without her.

She flings off her blanket, scrapes the frazzled hair back from her sweaty, tearstained face, and gets to work.

Whipping off her dress for synagogue, she steps into a pair of cuffed jean shorts and a T-shirt. She grabs pajamas and extra T-shirts and underwear and pulls her school backpack out from beneath her bed, where it had been abandoned for the summer. She fishes her wallet out of the battered straw purse hanging from her bedpost, and sweeps in a few haphazard toiletries from atop her bureau. Whatever she doesn't have, Rachael will lend her. Malka certainly won't be coming back for a clean bra or a forgotten toothbrush. She won't come back until things change, until her mother stops clinging to her like a drowning woman does a piece of driftwood, while Papa only watches from shore.

She turns eighteen next month; maybe she won't come back at all.

She doubts her older sisters will take her side over Mama's, but surely Mrs. Silver will let Malka stay with them, through senior year if she needs. After that, she can find a place with Rachael—her best friend doesn't have college plans yet, and wants to get out of Fox Hollow as badly as she does. Down the stairs two at a time, she stops only long enough to tear a piece of paper from the pad by the wall phone, pin it to the fridge with a magnet, and scrawl in thick black marker from the junk drawer: *Don't come after me!!!*

The Silvers will be home; Rachael's mom sprained her ankle partying too hard at Tu B'Av (or so Rachael claims) and has been home with her leg elevated. She hasn't even been by this week to visit her mother. Mrs. Silver can call her parents after services, though they'll assume she's at Rachael's, anyway. Where else would she go? How far could she get?

Then it's out the back door, into the sun and the heat. Past the bare patch where only the stumps of the dead oaks remain, a single tree left to fell—Siman wouldn't have been around much longer, even if he hadn't been fired. Through the woods and straight to the Hollow, green and high with the week's heavy rainfall.

"Malka!" a voice calls.

She stops short and spins toward the water, spotting the

boy on the riverbank. She's not sure how she missed him as she marched past, but her heart expands to fill her whole body at the sight of him, at once beautifully new and familiar. She almost cries.

"Siman!"

TWENTY

WHEN THE DREAM comes this time, I know it, even in sleep: flashes of city, of river, of spires and woodlands. As the scenery settles, I'm still in Prague—I recognize it now—but not at the parade. I'm in a house.

My home, but not, in the way of places in dreams. Like it belongs to another me, from another life. Artwork covers most of the dark wood-paneled walls of a study; framed and unframed, in every style of oil and acrylic and watercolor. Clay and stone sculptures sit on end tables, in corners on the blue-and-red oriental carpet, atop a sturdy oak desk stacked with books. Dream-me is curled on a citrine-colored sofa, staring at a two-foot-tall bronze sculpture of a naked woman with golden hair on that desk. Her neck is encircled by a long snake that she cradles lovingly, though it appears to be choking her. I'm studying the sculpture so as *not* to think, not to feel, when a man with a long, neat beard, black sprinkled with silver, and denim-blue eyes walks into the room. My father.

Well, not *my* father.

"Jitkala," he says fondly, easing onto the sofa beside me.

"How are you?"

"Just . . . tired," I hear myself say.

"You should be resting. Tomorrow is . . ."

A big day? Is that what he was going to say? Such an understatement, it's laughable. Tomorrow is the day I leave him, my whole family, my world. After that train pulls out of Franz Josef Station, who knows whether another train will ever bring me back?

"Your trunk is packed?" he asks.

"Yes, Táta." My father's friend, the painter, has promised to buy me whatever I need when I get to England. So I'm bringing only a few changes of clothes, a handful of photographs, and my family's gifts. Nothing more.

"Good, that's good. But I hope you'll have room enough for one more thing." Táta stands with a sigh, crosses to the desk—his desk—and removes something from the bottom drawer. A small, thick, rectangular box, about the size of the pochade case Táta keeps for sunny days when he might paint in the park. As he returns to sit beside me on the couch, I see it clearly. The box is old, perhaps as old as the book he gave me earlier, which might have come from Judah Loew ben Bezalel himself. But it's better preserved, at least. The wood looks sound, though the leather wrapping flakes off in places. Thousands of tiny brass nail heads pounded into the boards draw an intricate design across it. It has no lock, just a tarnished silver chain wrapped several times around it and knotted in place.

"You remember Dědeček Loew's story? The one I told to

you the night I . . . I told you we had to let you go? 'The Underwater Palace'—our version, anyhow."

"Why? What has that to do with anything?"

"It's important, Jitka. So is this." He hefts the box. "I wish I could send you off with only our blessings. But just as we can't choose our blood, we can't always choose our burdens. I've kept this chest safe as my own táta asked of me, as his asked of him. It can't stay in the city, where it might fall into terrible hands. It can't be buried, where worms might eat through the wood, or thrown in the river, where the tide could shift the chain. It cannot be thrown away, where an unwary fool might find it. Take it with you, and protect it. *Never* open it—the box is no more divine than any other, but the chain must remain in place. Bring it home when . . . when things are settled. And if you have sons or daughters, warn them."

"But it doesn't mean anything," I insist, angry now. "It's just a bedtime tale. And this is just a box."

"It *isn't*. And even as every instinct you have might tell you to protect your children, to keep them in the dark, you must tell them, as I'm telling you. Pretending won't keep you safe. The past has teeth, Jitkala. It may catch you if you turn your back on it."

I wake to the patter of rain, like fingers drumming against my bedroom window. There's an ache in my chest, so sharp that at first I mistake it for a new transformation. I roll over and tug down the neckline of my tank top to examine myself, but even

284

as I do, I feel the tail underneath me. Nothing has changed. The pain must have been part of the dream—or the memory. It *felt* more like a memory, as yesterday's did. One that lives so deep inside of you for so long, it aches like an old injury. A snapped bone that knit crookedly and pains you in bad weather.

Still rubbing my breastbone, I sit upright. The clock reads 3:45. Just like last night, I woke earlier than the curse.

Just like last night . . .

I cross reluctantly to the water-stippled window. Thick rainclouds cover the full moon and blot out the stars, droplets pattering the roof. The woods should be an even blacker crater in the black night, but the pearly light between the trees—the light I knew in my bones would be there—shows the way to the Hollow beyond.

I pat down my sweatpants to find the amulet; still in my pocket, safe and sound. Then I ease open my bedroom door and pad down the hallway to my brother's room, where I slip inside without knocking.

"Gabe," I whisper urgently. "Gabe!"

But he isn't in his bed.

I pause a step from the footboard, unsure. Should I check the bathroom? The kitchen? After six weeks of living alone in our apartment, we're both known to forage well past midnight. I should find him, tell him. If Mom is out there again, if we could get to her . . .

Anxiously, I glance out Gabe's window, where the diaphanous light still swirls behind the tree trunks. How did I ever mistake it for a flashlight, or even a lantern? It's as bright as though the moon has crashed to earth and into the Hollow. And so I can clearly see the boy striding across the wildflower field, passing the barn, headed for the woods.

This time I don't stop to pull on shoes. I don't even try to be quiet as I pound down the stairs, through the hall, and out the kitchen door, calling for Gabe. But he's already in the trees.

I dash across the field, wet flowers and long grass tangling around my toes and ankles. Past the barn. Into the trees, half running, half perpetually stumbling forward over roots and rocks. My clothes catch on low branches, hold me back, but then I'm through. I hear the roar of the Hollow, swollen with rain, and see the riverbank. I smell damp earth and lingering spearmint.

Mom.

There: maybe thirty yards down the river, I see her. And I see Gabe, now with the golem, their lean bodies aglow, plastered with rain. They stop halfway between us when I scream into the unexpectedly cold wind, "Gabe!"

My brother half turns. He seems to waver between me and Mom.

And then I hear her call out, "Please, he's coming, go back . . ."

Gabe hesitates, then grabs for the golem's shoulder. He must give some command I can't hear, because they nod— reluctantly, it seems—and pivot toward me. But Gabe moves onward. He doesn't stop again when I shout for him, or when Mom holds her hands out to warn him the way she warned me.

So he doesn't see the shadow that rises from the river just behind him.

I open my mouth to scream again, but gag on the terrible stench that once again fills my nostrils and coats my tongue. I make to run toward Gabe, but the golem catches me around the waist with arms like unforgiving stone, and half the breath whooshes out of my body. They throw me over their shoulder, marching us back into the trees just as Gabe reaches Mom at the very edge of the riverbank.

He turns at last to see the shadow, shaped like . . . like a boy, not much bigger than Gabe.

"Stop," I wheeze at the golem, "go *back*!"

"He told me to take you home," their voice rumbles over the rain. "He told me to make sure you're safe."

"That's not his choice!" I insist breathlessly, but it is. Because Gabe can tell the golem what to do, and I can't. I can't stop them—there's no breaking free from their strength, though I bruise my fists pounding against their shoulders, and my knees, kicking at their unyielding chest. They whisk me into the trees just as my brother bellows, and Mom screams.

FOX HOLLOW, 1990

THEY LIE FOR what feels like an hour, listening to rushing water, to the chirp and croak of river frogs, to the shush of a hot summer breeze through the branches above them. No longer in a rush to get to Rachael's, Malka could stay here forever, nestled into the crook of Siman's arm. Her fingers dance across his lean stomach. It's not exactly comfortable, the hard muscle of his chest beneath her cheekbone, but she wouldn't wish herself anywhere else. She can't remember being so perfectly happy in her whole life, and wants to keep every part of this moment forever. She has a terrible sense of smell—she's accidentally cooked and served rotten eggs, and missed the telltale stench of a gas burner left unlit—but she buries her nose in his T-shirt and breathes deep, trying. He smells . . . like the river. Like rich earth and dead moss and things that thrive in water. Malka reaches up to run a hand through his dark curls and finds them damp. It's early still, but already a scorcher; he must've taken a dip in the Hollow to cool off before she found him.

"How long have you been out here?" Malka keeps her voice low so as not to break whatever spell has brought him to her just when she needed him most.

"I've been waiting for you for a very long time," he answers her, low and serious.

Malka curls even nearer to him, if possible. She can't get close enough. "I'm so sorry you got fired. I wanted to come and find you, but I'm grounded." Because that sounds ridiculous and childish—Siman has crossed the *world* by himself, and she can't find a ride downtown—she hurries to add, "Of course, I was gonna come anyway. As soon as I could. But I didn't even know if you were still in Fox Hollow. I thought . . . maybe you left already, and I'd never get to say goodbye."

"Shh, ahuvati," he soothes.

He sounds so formal that she giggles against his chest. He's Jewish, of course, but he'd mumbled his way through most of the blessings on Shabbat; she was watching him so closely, even then. Perhaps he picked it up from Papa . . . although Papa uses the Yiddish. "So you won't leave?"

His arm tightens around her shoulders, pressing her down. "I'll never leave you." His palm glides down her spine to the small of her back, skimming the waist of her shorts.

She shivers. "But what about traveling, and work? What will you do?"

"Take you with me."

It's an invitation she hardly dared to dream of, and so she doesn't trust it at first. "Really? Where would we go?"

"Into the world. A world wilder than you've ever imagined."

She feels like one of those Disney princesses Rachael hates. The Little Mermaid, bargaining for a life on land. But in the next moment, the sea reclaims her. "My parents won't let me. Mama won't even let me out of the house."

"You don't belong to them, Malka," he whispers into her hair. "Belong to *me*—choose me over the people who claim to love you, but would trap you—and I'll worship you forever."

Isn't this everything she's spent her whole summer wanting, her whole life? "I—yes, okay." She wills strength into her voice. "Forget them! I don't care if I never see them again."

"Promise me," he breathes.

"I promise. I want to go with you."

Siman lays her gently aside to stand, offering one strong hand. His eyes stare into hers, beautiful and dark. "Then let us go."

For just a moment, she wavers. There's Rachael to think of—they were supposed to leave town together. Rent an apartment in the city, any city, and eat bacon for the first time, and stay out until three a.m., and never ask anybody permission for anything. But Rachael has Ida, a mother who, in Malka's most secret heart, she's sometimes wished was hers. When Rachael's time comes to leave Fox Hollow, Ida Silver will let her daughter go.

Mama never will.

It isn't just that she'll ground Malka; her parents can keep her locked in the attic until her next birthday, but she turns eighteen in three weeks. Technically, she could walk out the door that midnight, free at last, and they could say nothing to stop her. But would Malka be strong enough to go? She understands, deep down, that it isn't only Papa's rules that keep her tied to Fox Hollow. There are the ghosts haunting 4 Woodland Lane; ghosts they almost never name, but feel constantly; ghosts Mama won't let go of, or who won't let go of her. If Malka doesn't take this chance, she might become one of them. You just can't fight a love like Mama's. Not forever.

Siman is gazing down at her, adoration in his eyes—why had she thought his eyes were blue when they're dark as a coal room in a cold basement?—as he asks, "Follow me?"

"Forever," she says. Letting him pull her to her feet, she trails close behind him, hand in hand, expecting him to turn for the meadow. He must be parked in front of her house—no, what *was* her house. But when he moves toward the river, she guesses he must have parked up the road somewhere instead, wary of her parents, and the quickest way to get there is to cut through the woods.

Then he strides to the steeply sloped bank and over the edge, toward the water.

When she stops, he turns to look over his shoulder. "Come, Malka."

She looks at the damp soil beneath his sneakers, which is how she sees footprints: as long as her father's when he doesn't wipe his boots properly after coming in from the yard, but narrow, three-pronged at the toes. They trail down the slope, right to Siman.

Without meaning to, she takes a full step back, slipping her hand from his.

"*Come*, ahuvati," he says, this time insistent. "You promised."

"I'm not supposed to swim in the river when it's this high. Mama says—"

"But you don't belong to your mother anymore," he explains patiently, coolly. "You belong to me. So come."

Malka takes another step back, just beyond his reach. "We should get to your car, Siman. My family will come back—"

"I've been waiting for so long," he repeats himself, dark eyes dancing. "You have no idea how long."

"I—I'm glad you came."

"How could I not? I knew it was you. I was alone for so long—grieving my bride, my daughter, my kingdom, hating the man who took everything from me, yimakh shemo." Siman spits twice into the dirt, the toes of his sneakers nearly touching the river—nothing inhuman about them. "All alone, I dreamt of the world outside. I dreamt of a revolution that almost was, men dragged from train cars and slaughtered on sight. Bodies on the tracks. I dreamt of a city ever-rising around my prison—synagogues and banks and theaters, cafés and concert halls, bridges over an empty river, spires and rooftops and clock towers—while I lay in darkness that never changed. I dreamt of war. Of boots on cobblestone streets, and bloodred flags against a gray winter sky. I dreamt of another train, then a ship, then a new city, high and loud and stinking of charred meat and salt and steam. Then there was only dark, only silence, awake or dreaming.

"And then there was you, Malka. You opened the door. The

boy might have unwrapped the chain that freed me, but *you* let in the light."

Her heart is no longer in her chest, but somewhere down in the reeds and bracken on the bank. This is a joke, or some cruel test she doesn't understand. Or there's something truly, deeply wrong with the boy she thought she knew—thought she might love, if not now, then someday soon.

Another step back. Desperately, she searches his face for some sign of suppressed laughter. "This isn't funny, Siman. You're scaring me."

But he doesn't apologize, and he doesn't stop. "The boy smelled of sweat and wine and sweets and pomegranates and *you*, ahuvati. I followed him into the woods that night and found the river, my new home. Our new home." He tips his head. "It isn't as grand as the Vltava, but water is water, and a kingdom is a kingdom, and a bride is a bride. Clumsy boy, he slipped on the mud and fell in—I suppose he'd claim he was grabbed, if he had breath to speak. No matter. He went into the river, and I came out. For you, Malka. The descendent of the ben zonah who stripped me of everything I was and everything I loved. This—you—are what's owed to me. Don't you see? My due. My love." A shadow, a strange ripple, seems to pass across his face, like a glimpse of something dark flickering just beneath the surface of water.

"I—I want to go home," Malka whimpers, wishing desperately that she sounded strong.

"The river is your home now, ahuvati. I am your home.

You've promised yourself to me, and surely you wouldn't break your vow. For I owe your family a great deal of suffering. Everything that was taken from me, I may be tempted to take back." Siman smiles broadly, as if this *is* a joke. His teeth are very white, sharp as fishhooks. "But I've no need of vengeance, if I have you."

Everything that strings her bones together is coming undone. Siman is insane. Dangerous. He wants to drown them both. And if she refuses, if she tries to fight, he could leave her small, soft body on the forest floor and then wait for Shosh and Geela and Papa and Mama to come walking down the road after services, completely unaware. Papa is in his sixties with an older man's belly and strong prescription glasses, no kind of match for a muscled nineteen-year-old boy who fells trees. And Mama has survived so much, more than Malka even knows, but against Siman . . .

"Okay," she manages, dry throated. "I'll . . . I'll go with you, but . . . just let me say goodbye to my family? And then I'll come back. I p-promise."

He considers this, then leaves the precipice of the river to reclaim her hand. And now, this near and in shadow, she can see that his eyes aren't just dark. They're black as the bottom of a very deep sea, she imagines.

She forces herself to smile, even as the world upends, willing him to believe her.

Satisfied, he nods. "You'll see that I am not cruel. You'll serve me, and I'll worship you, as *I* promised. So I give you an hour. Say your farewells to whomever you wish. I can wait that long in exchange for forever. If you do not return," he says simply, "then I'll come to claim you, and tear through anybody that stands between us."

"I . . . yes. Okay." An hour is plenty of time. She only needs to get to the house, lock the doors, and call the police. Fox Hollow's tiny station is only a little farther than Beth El.

Unbelievably, he steps away and lets her go.

On shaking legs, she turns, forcing herself to walk as long as she's in sight, waiting until she reaches the meadow to be safe.

As soon as the sunlight touches her, she runs.

TWENTY-ONE

THE GOLEM DUMPS me unceremoniously on Aunt Esther's kitchen floor, still struggling. "Who was that?" I shriek, heedless of whom I might be waking.

"You *know.*"

They're right, I realize. The three-pronged footprints we found on the riverbank, the stench of water-rot in the air, the terror in my mother's voice. *He's coming.*

"The sheyd," I answer myself. "Why would Gabe go out there?"

"He was waiting, watching to see the light from his window. He wanted to find your mother."

"He was *planning* to go out tonight? He—he didn't tell me."

The golem says nothing.

"Why didn't he tell me?" I demand.

They stare down at me with dark, unblinking eyes, perfect body tensed to stop me should I try to scramble past, but their voice is gentle when they answer at last, "He meant to protect you, and I . . . meant to protect him. I tried."

Shivering hard enough that my molars click together, I shout up at them, "Well, go back! You have to help them!"

Rain sluices down their skin and clothes to puddle on the slick tiles as they hesitate in the doorway. "I was told to—"

"He told you to get me somewhere safe, and look! I'm here, I'm safe." I twist my fingers in my short, soaking wet hair and tug to keep from shrieking my frustration into their sculpted face. "I won't go anywhere. Just please, please go back?" Without the ability to command them, I try reasoning with them, as though they're a person instead of a weapon. "I know I'm not your master. But he's my brother, and I need him, and you're strong enough to help him, if you can—" I can't even force out the rest.

Thank God, I don't have to. The golem nods once, turns, and strides back out into the dark just as the kitchen light flicks on overhead.

"Hannah? What . . . we thought somebody had broken in!"

In the sudden glare, I blink up at my aunt and uncle. Esther clutches the collar of an old robe tight around her throat, eyes wild with fear. Bernie stands behind her, wielding an iron fireplace poker from the parlor like a knightly sword. Together, they stare down at me: sprawled on their clean kitchen floor, barefoot and dirty, dripping with tears and snot and rainwater. They wait for an explanation, and I scramble to come up with something, anything.

I could tell them the truth—it's just behind my shivering lips. Every lie I've told, every secret I'm keeping. They're family, and they're grown-ups—it's their job to take care of this for me while I slink upstairs to hide under my covers, isn't it? But that's childish thinking. Even if they believed one word of my story, accepted that Gabe and my missing mother were standing on the riverbank, and then they weren't, they'd head straight for the Hollow. They'd call more people—the police, other family members and townsfolk, a search party—all parading through the woods and wading through the shallows. Not in a million years would they believe that some demon stalks the forest. Probably not even if I showed them my tail.

I scramble to my feet. "I—I'm s-sorry I woke you up. I just . . . I think I'm gonna . . ." I rush past their bewildered faces and throw myself into the bathroom off the kitchen. Locking the door, I peel off my soaked T-shirt and sweatpants, taking the hamsa from my pocket to set on the sink top before I drop my clothes on the floor. I'm shaking so hard I think I can hear my bones rattling. I run my icy hands over my goose-bumped flesh, feeling for the tail, but my spine is smooth. It ends exactly where it should. I stand on my toes and twist this way and that, contorting to check my whole body, and double-check it in the mirror. Have I changed while still awake?

There's nothing. And I mean *nothing*. As far as I can tell, I'm perfectly normal.

Esther knocks, and my heart skips a beat. "Hannah? Are you all right in there? Do, uh, do you need anything?"

"I'm . . . okay," I answer faintly. "Could you . . . Can I borrow a towel?"

As her footsteps fade across the creaking tiles, I stare at my face in the mirror—cheekbone-length hair plastered to my face, pale and purple-lipped with cold—and I want to cry with disgust.

The tail is gone. Nothing replaced it. Does this mean that the curse is gone? That my body is just my body again?

At this moment, I wish for anything else. It would be better for everyone if I was a golem. If I was stronger, faster, a weapon made of clay instead of this weak, scared, useless little girl, then I'd have my brother and my mother.

I think of those nightmares, the ones where my family would leave average, unextraordinary me behind in search of their next adventure. Now average, unextraordinary me is all that's left.

This time, Esther's knock doesn't move my heart. "I've got a towel and some dry clothes—I didn't want to go through your things, but my daughter left some clothes in the laundry when she cleared the family out, and she's not much bigger than you. Open up, honey?"

I crack the door wide enough to take the bath towel, wrapping it around me, then let Esther swing the door open to set some folded clothes on the counter. "Thanks," I mumble through numb lips.

"I think you need to tell me what's going on," Esther bosses me gently.

"We just . . . Gabe and me, we were fighting."

"What in the hell were you fighting about in the rain at four a.m.?"

"Mom." It's the first answer that comes to me, and fortunately, the closest thing to the truth that I could tell her. "We were arguing about her, and home. He wanted to go back to Boston, but I wanted to stay here longer." The lie tumbles out.

I'm quick under pressure; maybe I have debate club to thank for that. "We screamed at each other, and he walked out. He said he was going to Hudson and getting on a train by himself, if I wouldn't come."

As if Gabe would *ever* leave me behind like that in real life. But Esther doesn't really know us, so it isn't hard for her to believe. She fists her robe tighter. "At this hour? Is he hitch-hiking?" she asks, aghast.

"I think . . . maybe he's calling an Uber from the road?" I'm not even sure you can get an Uber out here. Gabe and I took a yellow cab from the bus station to the house, which Ari assured me was the only one of its kind in Fox Hollow. But I'm fairly certain Esther and Bernie wouldn't know, either way.

She sighs. "Better tell Bernie to get his car keys. He can drive up and down the road a ways, see if he can catch Gabe."

Good. Whatever sends him in the opposite direction from the river, and lets me slip off to my bedroom to fall apart completely.

In my guest bedroom, I keep my promise and wait for the golem to return—though I could probably bluff my way out of the house and into the woods, they'd only drag me back here if they found me, and I need them out there, patrolling the riverbank for my mom and brother on their tireless legs. So I perch on the edge of the bed in my cousin's yoga pants and "I ❤ Coffee" T-shirt, ankles bouncing with nerves. I'm too edgy even too change into my own clothes. Instead, I sit with Gabe's phone in hand, staring out the window toward the trees.

After I'd dried off and dressed, I kept my shit together just long enough to rush to his guest room, shove everything into his suitcase, and hide it under my own bed. I stole his phone, too, still plugged in on the nightstand.

I press the home button now to check the time, and have to stifle a sob when I see my brother's lock screen. Before we left Jamaica Plain, the wallpaper was of a gay K-pop idol with a mop of blond hair and cheekbones carved by the gods, throwing a peace sign. Now, it's a photo of Mom, Gabe, and me, taken in New Mexico when I was thirteen. We sit at the counter of the fifties-style burger joint where Mom was waitressing that spring—she briefly dated the line cook who took the picture. I'm an absolute preteen train wreck. Spaghetti-limbed, frizzy-haired, wearing a velveteen scrunchie and an oversize graphic tee with "Sorry I'm Not Listening" printed aggressively across my nonexistent chest. Gabe looks like . . . like my beautiful brother, grinning wildly, blindingly. Even before the biceps and four-inch growth spurt, before the outrageous fashion and the tattoo and the teal hair, he shone. A night-light in a dark room.

And there's Mom on the swivel stool between us: blond hair pinned up with a claw clip, eyes hooded after a long shift, arms hooked around our shoulders, holding us all together as best she could.

I swipe at my eyes, throat burning, and glance back out the window just in time to see the golem under a faintly lightening sky.

They walk out of the woods, unburdened and alone.

FOX HOLLOW, 1990

MALKA SPRINTS FOR her house. *Don't panic*, she tells herself. *Almost there. Almost safe.* She only has to keep it together for a few more minutes. Just long enough to lock Siman out and call the police. Then she can crawl under her covers, wait for help from grown-ups with badges and guns, and pretend this all away.

Throwing herself through the back door, she slams the latch. Then she sprints to the front door to do the same. She staggers from window to window, but they're all closed and locked on the ground floor to keep in the air-conditioning. Except, now that she's stopped in the hall to catch her breath, she realizes she can't hear the hum of the AC, which should be nearly constant by this time of day. Already it feels warmer in the house, damper than it should—like the air by the river, she tries not to think. When she turns the lights on in the parlor as a test, the bulbs in the chandelier stay dark.

How can the power have gone out in the last hour, on a perfectly cloudless day with only a soft breeze?

Dread pooling in her belly, Malka takes the steps two at a

time to reach her parents' bedroom. The phone cradle sits on Papa's chest of drawers. She nearly drops the cordless twice before calming enough to grasp it. Still breathless, she jabs the button and presses it to her ear.

No dial tone.

Hanging up, she tries again, but the buttons make no sound at all. Their only phone is dead.

Malka sinks onto her parents' bed to think, sneakers tapping nervously against the pale-green carpet.

Okay. Okay. She can just stay here. She's safe, isn't she? Maybe Siman cut the power somehow before he caught up with her by the river, or . . . or something else is happening, something she can't yet name. But he can't get inside, can he? Unless he breaks a window. Or kicks down a door. They're not made of steel, after all. Wood can splinter, bolts can give way. Besides, once services are over, her family will be walking home, completely unaware, unprepared . . .

It's a little less than three miles to the synagogue, and she balks at the thought of trekking along the wooded road where cars pass infrequently, even if she could make one stop.

But she has most of her hour left, and it's only a fraction of that distance to Rachael's. She can make it, even taking the long way around, keeping to the road instead of the river. Plus, if Siman changes his mind or changes the game before the hour is up, he'll expect her to run toward town, not away from it. If she can get to the Silvers' house, Mrs. Silver will call the police. She'll take care of everything, while Rachael whisks Malka to her bedroom and throws her thin but strong arms around her to keep her in one piece. Mrs. Silver can tell the cops to stop at Beth El to warn Malka's parents, since nobody in synagogue will pick up the office phone on Shabbat.

Before she gives into fear, she forces her tired, shaking body from the bed and down the stairs, heading for the front door this time. But her footsteps slow as she passes the basement door.

And then there was you, Malka. You opened the door. The boy might have unwrapped the chain that freed me, but you let in the light.

Malka watches herself turn the knob. Without thinking, she finds herself treading down the raw wood staircase into the basement. With the bulb dead, it's illuminated only by the small sliver of light through the high window.

She crosses to the coal room door, the broken lock still dangling from the hatch where they left it—Siman was fired before he could sneak her a replacement. She fumbles to unhook it, letting the lock slip from her trembling fingers to the dirt. Opening the door as wide as it can go to let as much of the weak light in as possible, she forces herself to step inside. Though it's day, the claustrophobic little room is even creepier than she remembers, and it's harder to be brave without the boy she thought she loved by her side, squeezing her hand. Not that she'd want him here now.

She spins in place, terrifying herself with the idea of his body slipping through the door behind her, his breath on the back of her neck. But she's alone in the coal room, and the basement beyond is silent.

Malka tells herself she's wasting time down here. She should go back.

Instead, she drifts forward to the chute, nearly invisible in the dark. Bracing her feet, she grabs the bar-pull and tugs with her full weight.

Just to be sure. Just to know, beyond a shadow of a doubt, that Siman is damaged in some deep, unfixable way. That his words are insanity. That there was never anything but an old box in here, and nothing followed him out of this basement and into the night.

The door falls open more easily than last time, if just as noisily. Malka peers into the black that no light can touch. Too panicked to wait for her eyes to adjust, she pats around inside the chute with one shaking hand, closes it around cold metal. She holds it in front of her face for inspection: a thick silver chain, just barely glinting in her palm.

Otherwise, the chute is empty. The box—along with whatever it contained—is gone.

TWENTY-TWO

IT'S NOT LONG after sunrise, and Ari listens to my frenzied retelling of events as she drives us to Forget-Me-Not, starting with my latest dream about the man who must have been my great-grandfather, and the girl who must have been my grandmother. "It was just like the dream with the soldiers. I wasn't watching Jitka's father give her the box and tell her about that story, 'The Underwater Palace.' I mean I was, but *as* Jitka. I don't know how . . . I don't know how any of this is possible. But I think he said it wasn't just a story, and it wasn't just a box. He believed it had really happened. I think . . . maybe it's still happening."

"I do too," Ari says, knuckles white on the steering wheel.

I let out a breath that sounds like a sob.

Sliding one hand from the wheel, she slips it into mine and holds on tight. "Where's the golem now?"

"Back in the barn."

They had run along the bank for miles and back, tireless as they are bloodless, but found nothing. Only the inhuman footprints leading into the water, and tracks in the mud, like something—someone—dragged down the bank.

Someone *alive*, I tell myself. Everybody the sheyd brought below the surface in the story was alive underwater. The alternative . . . No. The golem would know if Gabe was gone, surely. They would feel it.

"What did you tell Esther and Bernie?" Ari asks, interrupting my downward spiral.

I explain how I texted myself from Gabe's phone this morning, then ran to show a relieved Esther the message on my screen.

Gabe: Sorry, Banana. I shouldn't have left like that. I was just upset. On the train now. See you soon?

She still seemed bewildered, but didn't press. And she couldn't exactly say no when I told her Ari was stopping by to take me around town yet again—she isn't my mother.

You're not my mom.

My sharp words haunt me, no matter that Gabe and I made up. What a terrible thing to say to the brother who's never, ever put himself before me.

"I think my aunt and uncle are safe for now," I croak. "They won't go looking for Gabe."

"Are you okay, Hannah?" Ari asks delicately. "Sorry, I guess that's the most useless question of the millennium."

My nose begins to burn, tears prickling, and I squint out the side window at the streets of Fox Hollow, damp with last night's rainfall. "I am extremely un-okay," I admit in a wobbling voice.

We slow as we pull up to a stop sign, and Ari throws the truck into park. "Hey," she says, unbuckling her seat belt to face me, and the petal-softness of her low voice is enough to tip me over the edge. Reaching across the center console, she smudges away a tear caught on the corner of my wobbling lips with her thumb. "My mom's gonna help us, all right? We'll make her."

She slides her hand around to cup the back of my neck, ghosting her now-damp thumb across the soft skin behind my ear. I let my head fall back, cradled.

No other cars come upon us—this isn't Boston, just the historic neighborhood in tiny Fox Hollow—but eventually, Ari has to start the car again. She doesn't let go of my hand until she slows her behemoth of a truck outside the antique shop to turn down the alley, and we catch our first break of the day: her parents' car is parked in the lot, little trailer still attached. It's morning, and they're home from the estate sale in Pennsylvania as we hoped they might be by now, unloading boxes. I get my first look at Mr. Leydon, a middle-aged man in a denim baseball cap with Ari's plumlike cheeks and long limbs. Mrs. Leydon, I've seen before, of course. She's more at ease outside of the Eggerses' home, laughing with her husband, but as Ari kills the engine and I step out of her truck, Rachael Leydon's eyes go wide and her whole body tenses.

"Are you . . . Are you *her*?" She grasps for my name, finds it. "Hannah Eggers?"

"Williams," I correct, pointlessly. I don't know if she can even see Mom in my heavy freckles, light eyes, and narrow body. But then, she *is* Mom's childhood best friend; the woman who, despite the decades and the disappointment, might know her better than anybody in the world. Certainly better than me.

I nod, and she lifts a thin hand to scrabble unconsciously at her breastbone, as if feeling the ghost of a long-ago break.

"Hey, Mom." Ari greets her in a cooler voice than I've heard her use, joining me in the parking lot. "We, uh, need to talk. Now."

The three of us stand across from one another in the Leydons' living room. In other circumstances, I could better appreciate being inside Ari's house. I'd peek around to find embarrassing school pictures, pre-pink hair, and breathe deeply to confirm that their apartment has that sweet-dark antique book smell, like Ari promised. As it is, there's too much pain inside of me for my lungs to expand properly, and I wrap my arms around my body to hold it together.

"I don't see any of this as your business, Arielle," Mrs. Leydon dismisses us, glancing toward the closed living room door. "It's *nobody's* business but mine, in fact, and I'd prefer you stay out of it."

"Well, I'd *prefer* that whatever happened between you two when you were kids, you get over it. Act your age—isn't that what you tell me when I leave a cereal bowl in the sink? People are in trouble, Mom, and you can help. All you have to do is talk to me!" Her voice rises to a shout.

"Enough!" Mrs. Leydon's voice rises to match it. "You're

the child in this relationship, and you don't actually know what you're talking about, so lower your—"

"I know Malka came here, asking for help. Something she needed, to fix Hannah."

Mrs. Leydon eyes me briefly. "What does that mean?"

"I know you lied to Malka," Ari pushes onward. "You didn't throw Bubbe's stuff away—it's down in the shop storage. So why tell her you did?"

"I'm not discussing this with you," her mother snaps, then takes a slow, purposeful breath to calm herself and turns to me. "Hannah, I'm truly sorry that your mother left you alone in Boston. That's awful, and I hope your family in Fox Hollow can help you. They're good people, I can tell you that much. And if you have reason to think she and your brother are in real trouble, you need to reach out to the police, as I encouraged her to do weeks ago. But I don't owe anything more to Malka Eggers. Not my time, not my mother's belongings, not my . . ." A wave of pain crashes across her face. "Not anything. She's the one who walked out on me."

"I know, my aunts told me, but—"

Her laughter is as sharp as the rest of her. "They told me Malka was living her dream, traveling the world. At least they *heard* from her. She sent postcards from a new continent every few months. To them. I tried writing her a couple of times—I got her return addresses from Shoshanna—but they always came back undeliverable. Even when she settled down in Colorado, and Jitka shared your brother's baby picture with my mother, I never heard a word from my best friend, and I don't know *why*. I don't know why she forgot about me completely, unless . . . Maybe she knew how I felt about her, and she was disgusted. She was so disgusted, she ran away with the first boy she ever kissed, and never spoke to me again."

Ari takes a step away, bumping into a solid little end table with a record player on top. If music were playing, it would've been knocked off its groove. "You liked her," she says. "Like, *liked* her."

We watch the tip of her nose turn pink, and her eyes—more like Ari's eyes now, soft as the sky after rain.

"No . . . Mom wouldn't do that," I insist, needing to defend my mother from this much at least. "She's not that person. My brother, he's gay, and . . ." I meet Ari's eyes and flush. "And she didn't run away with Siman, anyway. He died, not long after my mom left. We found an obituary from October that year. So whatever you think happened that summer, it's not true."

"I . . . I didn't know that. I never heard . . ." Mrs. Leydon swipes viciously at her eyes. "Well, I'm sorry for that boy, then. I only met him once or twice. He seemed . . . But it doesn't matter anymore. That's not why I'm upset. Malka left town, and life went on. I grew up. I forgave her, even if she never knew. We were young. Kids do hurtful things, but they can change. She might have turned into a wonderful person, anything's possible. I would've let it all go a long time ago.

"But I'll never forgive Malka for what she did to my mother."

FOX HOLLOW, 1990

BY THE TIME she beats her palms against the Silvers' door, Malka's sobbing for breath and cursing her own body. It took much too long to get here by the road. And when Mrs. Silver finally makes her way to the door on her good leg, one heavily wrapped ankle hovering over the floor, it takes Malka too long to recover. Her hour is nearly up. Siman could be battering on the door of her house right now, smashing a side window, slipping one strong arm through to let himself inside. He could be walking her hallway. Climbing her attic stairs. Touching her things and fouling her air. Waiting for her family to return . . .

Or he could've followed her, keeping to the woods to let her think she was alone. Maybe he's watching them right now.

"We need to lock it!" She stumbles into the bright kitchen, where she throws the sliding door shut in front of the screen and thumbs up the latch. It doesn't seem like much—why had she always thought a shut door meant anything? All it would take to break this down is a solid kick. The truth, she's just realizing, is that very little stands between safety and chaos.

Mrs. Silver joins her, moving easier now with her crutches. "Malkala, sit! Breathe!"

She does, collapsing into a chair at the kitchen table. "Where's . . . Rachael?" she asks between ragged gulps of air, aching for the comfort of her best friend.

Mrs. Silver makes her way to the kitchen sink and fills a water glass, which she sets in front of Malka. "She's left a little bit ago to run errands for me. She'll be gone a while. Tell me what's happening, girl."

She eases into the chair beside Malka. It was only a week ago that Mrs. Silver sat her and Rachael down, tipped the sugar bowl, and counseled her that Mama wouldn't be around to love or rage against forever. It feels like years.

Malka rushes through the story—her fight with Mama and Papa, her plan to stay with the Silvers, how Siman had caught up with her in the meadow. What he'd said by the river, how he'd hardly been himself. Then there are the details she stumbles over, unable to explain them properly. Like his eyes, not the pale blue that shone in her dreams, but dark as a windowless room. His serrated smile, and the animal footprints, and the way his face flickered, a shadow moving beneath his skin. "He . . . his face *changed*," she insists, hardly believing herself.

But Mrs. Silver isn't looking at her like she's a stupid, hysterical girl. "Keep going," she says, and sounds as though she means it.

Malka plunges on. "When I was back at my house, the power was out and the phone was dead, and . . . See, something happened in our basement. I didn't tell you the last time I visited, because I didn't think it mattered, but Siman and I broke into the coal room, and we found . . . it was just a box," she pleads, with Mrs. Silver and with herself. "Like, something the last owners must have left behind. We didn't even open it. At least, I didn't open anything, I swear. But I left Siman alone for a minute—not even—and I think he might have. I looked in the coal room today, just to see, and the chute was empty, except for this."

She jams her hand into her shorts pocket and pulls out the chain, as though that's any kind of proof. "I know you won't believe me, but . . ." She trails off, with no end to the sentence that will reassure either of them.

Mrs. Silver only holds her hand out for the chain.

Malka passes it over. This is the first time she's stopped running long enough to look at it. Clearly it's old, an antique, the silver tarnished in spots. But it looks like it meant something to somebody once. Each link is as thick as her thumbnail, more like a hollow bead, carved with an ornamental design that looks like an elaborate Star of David. Maybe it'll be worth money when polished; she really doesn't care. And she isn't sure why Mrs. Silver cares, eyes combing across the chain as though the links are words in a language she alone can read.

"We need to call somebody," Malka speaks up, remembering her mission: get to safety, get a grown-up, get help. "Can you call 911? I think we should call 911, shouldn't we?"

"Tell me again," Mrs. Silver says, "exactly what happened at the river. I need to know every word that boy said to you, and everything you said to him."

She obeys, because one adult telling her what to do feels as good as another when she's on the verge of physical and emotional collapse. Until she finishes, and Mrs. Silver speaks, laying a steady palm against her cheek. "Malkala, listen to me. I don't believe this boy is playing a joke on you. I don't even believe that *is* Siman waiting for you in the woods."

"W-what?"

Her touch is still reassuring and motherly, but her voice is urgent. "I don't know why it chose you, or what it meant by everything it said to you. These creatures, they lie and they trick, but sometimes, they tell the truth. I think that *your* Siman opened this box and set something free that night. I believe that he went into the river, and this sheyd came out instead."

"A sheyd?" She knows Mrs. Silver is superstitious, even worshipful in her belief in Jewish mysticism and magic. Rachael has bemoaned the strange wisdom her mother imparts to them both over bowls of SpaghettiOs and between commercials during her soap operas. Bury an iron knife under a bush with the sufferer's hair tied around the handle to cure a deadly fever. Wear emeralds to inspire wisdom and open the heart. And never say hello to a stranger after dark. Not because they'll kidnap you and steal you across state lines, never to be heard from again, as her own mother insists—but because what you mistake for a man between the streetlights may be one of the shedim.

A demon, in non-Hebrew terms.

"Do you trust me, Malka?" Mrs. Silver leans in to ask, wincing as the movement puts pressure on her injured ankle.

In this moment, Malka desperately doesn't want to. She wants this to be as simple and awful as the boy she thought she loved turning cruel and possessive before her eyes. She wants . . .

She wants to go home.

But she thinks of everything she can't explain about the Siman she saw by the Hollow, and nods.

Mrs. Silver nods back. "Then listen. The police can't stop him. Even I can't stop him, not without the demon's name."

"But I told you, Siman—"

"No," Mrs. Silver cuts her off. "This thing? It isn't the boy you loved, Malkala. And the demon would never give its power away so freely as to use its true name."

"I don't understand any of this—what was it doing in our house? Did my parents know? Mama never wanted us going into the basement, but I thought it was just, you know, Mom worries. Tetanus and splinters and stuff. Did she know this thing was down there? Why didn't she tell us?"

Ida frowns. "People don't always keep secrets with ill intentions, Malka. Sometimes they do it because they're scared, or they're afraid to burden the people they love. But you and I, we'll talk to her. She'll help us to stop this thing. We just need to keep you safe until then. Here, go to my bedroom and bring back the box on top of my dresser."

Malka hurries to do so, and returns quickly, setting the

gold vinyl jewelry box on the table. Ida lifts the lid and sifts through the carefully arranged charms, selecting one and laying the silver chain among the others on the green satin lining in its place. It's a hamsa, one Malka's never seen her wear before, also antique-looking, with an eye made of tiny turquoise stones embedded in the palm, and a small Star of David etched into each fingertip.

"This was my mother's," Ida says, "and my grandmother's, and so on. The sheyd won't be able to lay a hand on you so long as you keep this with you. It will protect you."

Malka accepts the gift, holding it tight in her fist to feel the thin edges press into her flesh. As weapons go, it doesn't seem like much. "What about my family? He said he'd go through everyone I loved to get to me."

"Then you'll need to stay brave. Take the hamsa, and go back to meet him before he comes to claim you. Listen to me very carefully now, because lives depend upon what you do next."

Faintly, Malka asks, "What do I have to do?"

TWENTY-THREE

"WHAT DID MALKA ever do to Bubbe?" Ari demands of her mother.

I'm not so sure I want to know the answer.

Certainly, Mrs. Leydon looks like she regrets bringing it up. "Mom and Malka were close. Her parents were strict—maybe the strictest in Fox Hollow. Ours was the only house she was allowed over to freely, and of course, my mother loved her. Like a second daughter. She would fawn over those postcards Jitka got from every corner of the earth—honestly, she was more excited about them than Malka's own mother. But when Malka seemed to disappear for good, Mom developed this . . . fixation. I was going through my own hard time. I was in my last trimester with you then. It had taken me years to get pregnant, and a lot to stay that way—I never really told you, Arielle. I . . . I'd had two miscarriages before you. I was scared, and I needed my mom." Mrs. Leydon looks to the popcorn ceiling for help. "But this delusion was already taking root. She talked about some story Jitka had told her after Isaac died—"

"The Underwater Palace?"

Mrs. Leydon falters for a moment. "Yes," she murmurs. "She'd always been superstitious, but I thought it was just a part of her faith, no worse than any devout person. Religion never made much sense to me, anyhow. I didn't realize . . . By the time Mom had to be moved to the home—"

"To the nursing home," Ari clarifies for me, pointedly, and turns back to her mother. "Not to our home."

"She was sick, Arielle," Mrs. Leydon snaps back. "She was diagnosed with a nonspecific progressive dementia, she needed much more help than I could give her. Supervision at all hours, a professional psychiatric team . . ."

"She *needed* to be forty minutes away, where I hardly got to see her?"

Her mother shakes her head. "They had the best program, doctors who knew how to give her the highest quality of—"

"What about the story?" I interrupt them both. There must be a better time to rehash what's clearly a familiar fight. Ari falls silent, the angry set of her jaw like the blade of a knife.

Her mother takes a breath. "I looked it up once. Found it in a story collection I got online. I tried to understand what might've drawn her in, like there was any sense to be found in losing my mother to her own mind. And I guess I can see the appeal, wanting to believe your loved one isn't dead—or missing, or estranged, or senile—but living happily ever after in a castle under the water. That wasn't her only delusion, of course—she would talk about my dead father as though he'd just left the room, or a family trip from decades earlier like we'd just stepped off the Jersey shore boardwalk. She really wasn't well, Ari. But her obsession with Malka got worse and worse. She'd tell anybody who'd listen that a demon had taken Malka Eggers."

I exchange a glance with Ari; we never came across such a claim in her notebooks. "She said that?" Ari asks.

"Frequently. Even when I was standing right in front of her, trying to talk to her about you, show her your school pictures, or trying to shift the topic to happier memories like Dad's Saturday morning pancakes. She'd play along for a little while, but she'd always drift back to talking about Malka. Going on about the *river*, and the *chain*, and the *name* . . . well, it didn't make any sense. Of course it didn't."

"Do you know the last night I saw my mother?" Mrs. Leydon asks us both, absently rubbing at her collarbone again. "She gave me an envelope from her nightstand drawer and said to take it to Jitka, that it could save her daughter—who, I'll remind you, was definitely *not* at the bottom of some river but who, nevertheless, nobody had heard from for thirteen years at this point. And who wouldn't even show up to her own mother's funeral three years later."

I wince at that, and Ari starts to protest, but I put a hand on her tensed bicep to stop her.

Her mother does look sorry, anyhow. "I took it," she says more gently, "and then an aide wheeled her off to dinner, and I went home. And that was the last thing she said to me. Her last words, and they weren't for me, her own daughter."

I can't help but feel a pang for her, but if Ari feels the same, she doesn't show it. "And? Did you give it to Jitka?"

"Of course not," she says, as if the answer was obvious. "It was nonsense, that's what I've been telling you! It wasn't some sweet goodbye to her old friend. Wasn't even a letter from Mom, but some rabbi she'd written to about that damn story. That's all she left behind."

"But she *told* you to give it to Jitka," Ari insists. "She told you it was important, and you just threw it away? Do you get what you've done?"

Mrs. Leydon hesitates, and holds her hands out to Ari. "I . . . I didn't want to cause any more pain. Losing my mother day by day was painful enough, for Jitka as well, I'm sure. They'd been such good friends, and Jitka didn't know how bad your bubbe had gotten in the last months. It's not like she could have driven herself to see her in the home, and Esther was busy with her own grandkids. I didn't want . . . I wanted her to have better memories of Mom."

"That's the same bullshit reason you offered for why you kept me away," Ari snarls.

Wobbling toward the couch on tired legs, I sink onto the cushions and say nothing. I can't stop a storm that's been brewing for three years; all I can do is wait for it to pass, then steer us back on course.

"Arielle—"

"Don't call me that!" Her voice breaks. "You're the only one who does, and I've asked you not to, but you never listen!"

"I *want* to talk to you, Ari, I try . . ."

"Hah! You never even told me you were queer," she accuses. "Don't you know how much that would've meant to me? You never said anything, and you kept me away from the only woman I *could* talk to. And then she was gone, and I barely got to see her before she died. At least you had Bubbe's last words. At least you had that last day. You got time with her, good or bad, and you didn't give that to me because . . . because you wanted to protect her memory? Fucking fuck, Mom, if you took away all of our shitty memories, there'd be almost nothing left!"

Ari's words are arrows, and Mrs. Leydon rocks under the onslaught.

They're both crying now. I feel like crying too.

"All I can say—" Mrs. Leydon starts, pauses, tries to collect herself. "All I can say is, I was doing my best. Nobody tells you how to be the perfect parent when you still feel like a kid who desperately needs her mother. And there's this . . . endless list of everything I'm supposed to protect you from—uncut grapes, swing sets, rusty nails, the sun, the cold, strangers, relatives, boys and girls, too much to ever know . . . And when my mother was dying, I had to guess at what I was supposed to do, and . . . and maybe I failed, maybe I hurt you, maybe you hate me, but I did the best that I could." She collapses back against the wall behind her, picture frames pushed askew by her thin shoulder blades, tears bubbling up from deep inside of her.

Ari shoves her fists through her watermelon hair, loose and

still bed-rumpled—she basically rolled out of her sheets and into her truck at my first sunrise text—and I think she's about to scream. But then, she sags onto the sofa next to me and drops her head into her hands, mumbling through her fingers, "I don't hate you, Mom. I just . . ." She rakes her fingers back through her hair, tangling it further. "Sometimes I feel like I don't know anything about you."

Mrs. Leydon drags a palm across her damp cheeks, letting out one rough chuckle. "The feeling's mutual, kid."

My throat tightens for the millionth time today as I wonder: Will I ever get the chance to yell at Mom like this? And to cry with her afterward? What exactly was I so afraid of, that living in silence seemed preferable?

Ari's mom gives one long shudder of a sigh, then stands, smoothing down her lightweight cardigan. "Just . . . give me a moment, girls, all right?" Still sniffling, she strides out of the living room, leaving us alone.

"Ugh," Ari groans in her absence. "I'm sorry, Hannah. You didn't come here to watch us sling shit at each other."

I bump her shoulder with mine. "It's okay. This is something, right? The details all match up with our theories. 'The Underwater Palace,'" and the demon, and my dream—"

I cut myself off as a puzzle piece slots itself unexpectedly into place. It's like the rush I get solving proofs in math class when, after staring at the screen for ages, the pattern all of a sudden unspools for me. Prying Ari's hand free from her hair, I grip it tightly. "Ida told your mom about a chain. Just like in the story—the chain with the Seal of Solomon, right? And there was this chain around the box Jitka's father gave her in my dream." I hadn't been thinking like myself at the time, but as my grandmother, which I guess checks out with dream logic. I hadn't recognized the box *or* the chain.

But now, awake and in my own body, I realize I have. "Her stuff downstairs . . ."

"Her amulets?" Ari lifts her head to ask, eyes clearing.

"There *was* a silver chain." I'd thought it was a broken necklace at the time, missing its clasp and dulled with age. I hadn't even looked closely at the quality, or the design. Not that I'd have recognized a Seal of Solomon.

We rise together, but before we can rush down to the storeroom, Mrs. Leydon reappears in the living room archway. Her lips are pressed together in a firm line; faintly glistening tracks in her makeup are the only trace of her dried tears. In her outstretched hands, she holds an envelope, and a notebook—a match for the boxful in Ida's old house.

"That's Bubbe's," Ari identifies at once, but in a tone that says *that's mine.*

"I found it in her nightstand while we were clearing out her room, after. I hadn't even known she was still writing. And this, it's the letter she gave me for Jitka Eggers."

Ari accepts both, and hands the envelope to me without looking away from her mother. "Why did you keep these? I thought you didn't believe her."

"I loved my mother, Ari." Mrs. Leydon wipes a knuckle across her lower lashes, though they're dry. "I kept the things that mattered to her, whether I understood them or not. I started to read the journal once, a few days after she'd been gone—there's only a page or two—but it was more of the same, and it hurt too much. I didn't want anybody to see it, but I couldn't let go of it either. So I just . . . kept it. Like a secret."

Flipping eagerly to the beginning, Ari wastes no time in reading aloud:

Twenty years ago, my dearest friend told me a story.

Thirteen years ago, her daughter disappeared.

It unsettled something in me, a shipwreck revealed on the seafloor by shifting sands. I couldn't rid myself of the feeling that the two had everything to do with each other. I would lie awake at night, turning the details over in my head. I tried to talk to Jitka, but she'd say no more about Malkala, or the version of the story that belonged to her family alone. I dug up what I could about the original tale, which traces its roots to Prague and the Czech Republic in the mid-nineteenth century. Retellings vary a little, but I never found any that resembled Jitka's. So I wrote to historians, rabbis, publishers and editors of Jewish folklore collections. I kept searching, even when I was made to move to this home.

Maybe that's not fair to Rachael. She worries about me. I know she has reason to. The doctors talk to me and around me, so I know what they think. That I'm still too young to have memory troubles the way I do, that I get confused. Disoriented, they say. Visual hallucinations. I lose things, forget small details of my life, can't remember the residents after their introduction luncheons.

But I remember the important things. The people I've loved, and the people I've healed, and the people I've failed, and the people I've lost. Maybe not all at once, or all of the time, but I remember. And I remember every detail of this story, as though I heard it yesterday. I know it isn't just a mystery I need to unlock.

It's the key.

Here's what I remember about the day Malka Eggers left: I remember Isaac pulling into my driveway, pounding on my door, though the Eggerses never drove on the Sabbath. Showing me her note, pleading to know whether she'd come to me, if I knew where she was. I remember their power was out that day, though the weather was clear, and I couldn't drive with a sprained ankle, so I kept sending Rachael back and forth for any news. I remember trying to talk Jitka and Isaac into calling the police, but instead, Isaac went to Frager's and learned that the boy Malka was seeing in secret had disappeared, and after that, he wouldn't listen to me. I remember that night, finding that one of my amulets was missing from the box on my dresser top, which had belonged to my mother. In its place was a chain I'd never seen before. I recognized the symbols repeated on it—I have other charms with the Seal of Solomon, though no variation like this. When I asked Rachael whether she'd been in my bedroom, she denied it. I always wondered, but never learned anything about it until nearly a decade later. I'd been sending around a picture I took with the camera phone Rachael bought me, when at last, the Jewish Museum in Prague wrote back. Their archives turned up an illustration of the same version of the Seal, traced back to a rabbi who'd served at the Old-New Synagogue in the early 1800s, and who claimed the lineage of Judah Loew ben Bezalel himself. I wrote to the synagogue's leadership, but they could tell me nothing new. I've turned up nothing more, but I haven't given up.

I write this down to remind myself. I write it to remember when memory eludes me. And I write it so that, if I can't find the answer, the question may outlive me, and be solved by another.

The Malka I knew would never leave her family, leave my Rachael, leave me without reason. I cannot believe it. I won't accept that the girl I considered a daughter is gone forever, and I can't forget her, even if it would make everything easier. Even if my Rachael wishes I would.

"That's all," Ari says, thumbing through the rest of the notebook without much hope.

"Like I said." Her mother stands with her arms crossed over her narrow chest, shields back up.

I tear into the envelope, dumping out two sheets of paper, still crisply folded. It turns out to be a three-year-old printed email. Though the signature is in a foreign language—Czech, I guess from context clues—the body is typed in imperfect English. It's from a Rabbi Götz at the . . .

"What does this mean, the Alt-neu-schul?" I struggle through the pronunciation.

"That's what Bubbe was talking about, the Old-New Synagogue in Prague. It's, like, one of the most famous temples in Jewish history and folklore. The one where your great-great-however-many-greats-grandfather supposedly built and kept the golem?"

The synagogue I saw in my dreams. Touched it, even, dragging my fingers across the cold stones.

Returning to the email, I summarize as I scan ahead. "It's from the rabbi your bubbe wrote to, two years before she died. He didn't have any new information for her then, but they'd just been cataloging an older section of the library, and found notes and records from some of his predecessors. One belonged to Rabbi Loew. Not *the* Rabbi Loew," I clarify when Ari gasps, "unless he was immortal. One who served in the thirties and forties, and died in 1852. But his writings included the version of the story Ida had asked after. Which is why Rabbi Götz thought of her. He copied it out . . ." I read faster, through the beginning of the same "Underwater Palace" retelling passed down through Jitka's family—through *my* family. Only this one's more detailed than my grandmother's synopsis, particularly when I reach the part where the girl's aunt is summoned to the palace to act as midwife:

Her aunt thrilled to see her niece alive and well, in love and with child. "When I tell your father of your fate, his sorrows will turn to joy!" she exclaimed.

But the girl insisted, "You mustn't, Auntie! My father is not the sort to let lost things go. He may plunge into the river and drown himself searching for me, or stop at nothing to bring me home safe. It grieves me to think of his grief, but I belong to my husband now, not my father, and I am faithful to him alone."

Unconvinced, her aunt asked, "But niece, how can you possibly know your prince will remain faithful to you alone? He comes and goes as he pleases—I have seen it, during my stay—yet you remain below."

"Because." She gave a secret smile. "He belongs to me as well. See, Auntie?" The girl handed the babe to her maid and took up a rippled square of parchment, a quill, and an ink pot, and wrote a brief letter before her aunt's eyes. "He has given me his name, and every night before he leaves for the shore, I write it down with a command to return. He tucks it into his coat as a promise he must keep. Such were our vows: that I would ever remain below water, and he would ever come home to me."

Thus did the aunt learn the name of the prince of the palace underwater.

From there, it continues much the same as the story we read in Ida's notebook. Until the girl's father, his grief turned to fear and jealousy, presses her aunt for any information that will help him best the demon and reclaim his daughter. In this version, she gives her brother the name of the demon. And with that, the rabbi learns the secret words to trap the sheyd inside of a chest, sealing its fate. Sealing everyone's fate.

I read everything back aloud while Mrs. Leydon watches us, completely bewildered by our interest.

"Does it say what the name is?" Ari near-whispers.

I keep reading till the very end of Rabbi Götz's email, even flip the pages over, though I know I'll find nothing on the back. "The Rabbi Loew who kept the diary didn't include it, 'lest his children or his children's children be tempted to set loose the demon and use it for their own foolish purposes,'" I quote.

"So that's it," she sighs, defeated. "We can't trap a sheyd without its name, and we don't have it. We're fucked back to square one. Maybe square two."

Refolding the email very precisely, I take the moment to think. "Maybe . . ."

But I don't feel defeated.

I feel the first glimmer of a plan.

As I jostle back and forth in the jump seat, I let the silver chain slither between my fingers into one cupped palm, then the other. Ari rides shotgun in front of me, cradling a heavy but slim rosewood and brass box—a writing box, according to the hand-penciled price tag. We picked it out from the haul her parents brought back to Forget-Me-Not. It's lined with crackled leather, with straps for pencils and paper and things, but that shouldn't matter. If the dream-memories can be trusted, the magic that trapped the sheyd was in the chain and not the container, so anything sturdily made should serve.

In a turn of events I didn't see coming, Rachael Leydon is driving.

My mother's once best friend still doesn't believe in

demons. I'm sure she wouldn't have volunteered to take us to the river if she did. But, as she told Ari in the antique shop's storeroom, "I believe this is important to you. And whatever it is you girls think you're about to do, I really don't think you should be doing it alone."

What more can any kid ask for?

When we reach the farmhouse, Mrs. Leydon pulls into the empty driveway—the final day of Jitka's shiva hasn't started just yet. This is good and bad news. The fewer folks within range of the river, the better, but the busier Esther is, the less likely that she'd involve herself. Case in point: my aunt must've been keeping an eye out for us. A lacy curtain flutters and the lilac door swings open as we start to circle the house. And, just like the day we arrived, Aunt Esther comes out onto the porch, dressed all in black.

My déjà vu just contributes to this swelling sense that everywhere I go in Fox Hollow, I'm stepping into a footprint—my own, my mother's, my grandmother's—that was pressed into the earth days or years or decades or lifetimes ago.

"Hannah?" she says, eyes flickering between the Leydons and me. "What's this?"

Mrs. Leydon gives us one long, inscrutable look before she turns a reassuring Mom smile on my aunt. "Esther!" she calls. "I know I'm off hours, but I could help set up for today, if you like? Or I can come back—"

"Nonsense, Rachael," Esther says gruffly. "You're family, and we hardly got to catch up the other day. Come on in."

Hugging the writing box to her chest, Ari glances in surprise at her mother.

"Do what you need to do," she tells Ari in a low voice, "then come and find me here."

"Seriously?"

With a gentleness that makes me ache, she smooths back the bright flyaway hairs at Ari's temple. "You're a good girl. I'm choosing to trust you, even if I don't understand any of this. Just keep back from the river? It'll be high after the rain." Then she leaves our sides to join Esther and, already chatting, lead her back inside.

"What just happened?" Ari asks.

I shrug, winding the chain around my fist like a set of brass knuckles. "She thinks we're about to walk down to the Hollow, shout the name of a sheyd that doesn't exist, then give up and come back inside for coffee and cookies."

"Well . . . what a sweet, patronizing gesture."

"Yep! Let's not waste it."

We press on through the flowers, around the house, past the barn, and to the big oak where we found the locket—the tree where the golem and I agreed this morning to meet up. They've made themself a spot to sit vigil between the thick, mossy roots that crisscross the earth, among small ferns and underbrush. They look up with hope when they see us. "You have what you need to help Gabe?"

"I think so."

Washed by dappled forest light, they seem so human. Their

clothes, the ones my brother picked out, are rumpled, a mud-stained sweater and pants, and pulled askew by this morning's dash through the woods. Their close-shorn hair has grown in the last few days, a dark crop of it, and there's a shadow of a beard like smudged charcoal across their sharp jawline, the kind it takes Gabe days to grow. More than ever, they resemble the boy from the locket. Even the Hebrew lettering inked below their hairline looks like an old tattoo. Only their smell gives them away—they should stink of sweat after stewing in a hot barn for hours, but smell instead like petrichor, like the earth after rainfall following dry weather.

"Then what is the plan?" they ask.

"It's bullshit is what it is," Ari grumbles. As if she hasn't already made her objections clear.

"Can you, um, give us a second?" I ask, startling Ari by gesturing between me and the golem. When she stomps back toward the field, sniffing, I sink down into the dirt across from them to explain without interruption. "We can't trap the sheyd without a name, and even if we had that, we need my family back first. According to the story, if we don't find them, Mom and Gabe . . . they'll get lost below the water. I have to save them first, which means the sheyd can't know what we're planning. Which *also* means that you have to stay put."

"I'm supposed to keep you safe," the golem says stubbornly. "Gabe ordered me to keep you safe."

"Well, I have the hamsa." I don't really know the limits of an amulet—does purposefully seeking out a demon cancel out its demon-repellent properties? "Look, I know you think it's your job to protect me. Gabe thinks it's his job, too. But you can't keep somebody safe forever. That's just not how the world works. It's not fair, and it sucks, and I'm sorry, because it's not like you asked to be here. You didn't ask for any of this, and it's not your fault. That's just how it is. So you have to let me do this." Tentatively, I reach across with the hand that doesn't have the chain wrapped around it, and lay it over theirs. It's inhumanly cool, but I don't shudder the way I would've only days ago. "You have to let me go."

At last, though the words seem painful, they say, "You go. And I will wait."

With the final potential obstacle removed, I find Ari just beyond the woods, leaning against the back wall of the barn and squinting up at the sky, her hair a pink wildfire in the sunlight.

She's so pretty, I forget to breathe.

"You'll wait for me too, right?" I ask once my brain catches up with my lungs. "You won't leave?"

She carefully sets the box down inside the barn entrance. "You have the chain?"

I hold out my left hand, and she gently unwinds the links from my palm and knuckles, tucking it into the pocket of her high-waisted shorts. Then she steps closer. Close enough that my field of vision is filled by dark-lashed eyes, steel flecked with sea.

Oops, there goes my breath again.

"You *will* get the name, and you *will* get your family out, and I'll be here," she promises.

Impossibly, she moves even closer—

And kisses me.

I've been kissed before. By the previously mentioned Atticus, and once by Mike Rodriguez, my date to a seventh grade school dance. He later admitted that he *actually* had a crush on Gabe, and only asked me hoping to catch a glimpse of my brother when his dad dropped him off at our trailer. I didn't blame him. Neither time was unpleasant. They just . . . *weren't.* They weren't any more exciting than putting my mouth on a sandwich, or two of my own fingers pressed together, which I certainly never did for practice . . .

But Ari's lips are warm and generous, her flickering tongue an invitation rather than an invasion. Instead of drowning in self-doubt, wondering if the kiss is wrong or the other person is wrong or *I'm* wrong, her kiss makes me certain. And brave, enough to wrap my arms around her and bunch her cropped T-shirt in my fists, my knuckles brushing the soft skin at the small of her back. She cups one hand around the back of my neck, and I do the same, running my fingers across her shaved hair, scraping my nails through it until she shivers.

When she finally pulls back, she leaves a hand on me, keeping me close. "Just be careful, okay?" she says huskily, eyes warm and swimming. "Call for me the second you can, and yell really, *really* loudly."

"Yeah. Yes, I will."

I have no proof that kisses are magic, but as I walk into the woods alone, I believe it. Though the curse is gone, my body feels different—supernaturally strong, and yet more *mine* than it ever has been. The feeling carries me all the way to the riverbank. It gives me the courage I need to edge down the slope of the Hollow and stand with the toes of my sneakers in the water. With a deep breath as though I plan to plunge under, I call, "It's Hannah! Malka Williams's daughter? Or . . . Malka Eggers."

Nothing happens.

The mud by the river's edge is still slick from this morning's rain, and I adjust my stance before trying again.

"This is Hannah Williams! C-come out!"

Still nothing.

What next? Should I shout louder? Wade out into the water? Will the sheyd not come before nightfall, or at all? Oh God, what if the stories are wrong, or we've misread everything? What if, after all of this, Ari's mom was right, and we're about to trudge back to the house with empty hands and shattered hopes—

"Hannah," a boy's low voice drifts from downriver.

I spin, stupidly expecting Gabe, until the unfamiliarity of that voice registers.

My heartbeat stutters, because I do know the boy who straddles the bank and the water only a few yards away. I've seen him in pictures. I recognize him from his own obituary, and from the article about the Tu B'Av festival three decades ago.

The only difference between the boy that stands before me and the one who sat beside my mother is his clothing—he wears a moss-green suit that looks as though it's been moldering in a basement or decomposing in a steamer trunk at the bottom of the sea for centuries, the once-luxurious fabric nibbled through or worn shiny in spots, the gold buttons tarnished and hanging by a thread, or missing altogether. Otherwise, I could be looking at his ghost.

No. Not a ghost.

"I waited for you," Siman Melkes tells me, "for a long time. I had given up hope."

My mouth is dry as a sand dune. They found Siman's body in the Hudson, brought it home to his family. This may look like the boy my mother loved, but the only explanation is that the dark, gently curling hair and farm-boy-broad shoulders are nothing more than a mask worn by a monster. "Where are they?" I croak, clear my throat, and try again. "Where's my family?"

"You know where they are, Hannah, or you wouldn't have come."

"So give them back."

Siman—or not-Siman—tips his head. "I'm afraid I cannot oblige. Your mother made me a promise. A wife and a child I was owed, and a wife and a child I've collected."

There it is, at last: the solution to Unknown X. The mistake my mother made as a teenager that's haunted her for the rest of her life and cast its shadow on me.

I remember dreading the idea that Mom was somehow involved with—perhaps even caused—the death of the boy she loved. Maybe this is preferable. Maybe I should've guessed the truth before now. But knowing my mother bargained herself away, bargained *me* away before I even existed . . . it's like the confirmation of every secret, terrible thought I've ever had about both of us.

The sheyd may be a monster, but what kind of a person promises such a thing?

EVERY STEP SHE takes toward the Hollow feels like marching toward her own grave, but Malka tries her best to carry herself like a bride marching down the aisle, dignified and deserving, the way Mrs. Silver coached her to. Even though she feels more like a child than she has in years, and wishes childishly that Siman won't be waiting for her at the river's edge.

Of course, he is, leaning against the pale, papery trunk of a river birch with its roots in the water.

"Ahuvati!" he cheers. "You've said your farewells?"

"Some."

"Good, that's good." His pitch-dark eyes sparkle from the shade below the branches. "Of course, you must know that whomever you've spoken with won't remember—you would never betray me, I'm sure, but it's best for both of us if we aren't followed. I've learned my lesson."

Malka freezes. "H-how . . . ?"

"Magic, my love. Don't you believe by now? So." He shoves off from the tree trunk, reaching for her. "Shall we go?"

Malka licks the salt of sweat from her lips. The river-damp

August air is suffocating, and she holds on to the thin trunk of a young sycamore to steady herself while she runs through the script Ida gave her. Tipping her chin up, she stitches a smile across her cheeks as best she can. "First, I want to ask for something. A . . . a wedding gift?" If she doesn't deliver the line as confidently as she meant to, at least she holds Siman's gaze without flinching. "As proof that you're . . . committed to me."

"And will you give me a gift in return?" he asks slyly.

She nods, trying not to seem overeager. "Anything."

"Ask, then." He holds up one callused finger, so like the one Siman once used to trace a slow path across her jawline. "For anything but my name. As I say, I've learned my lesson."

"But . . ." Panic quickens her breathing. "Don't you love me?"

Not-Siman's face ripples once more, this time with what seems like genuine pain. "I loved my first wife, and it was the downfall of us. The end of everything. I gave her my name—I wanted her to have a part of me, you see. That was a mistake." His smile returns now, nearly gentle, his sharp teeth sheathed. "Now, I'll settle for obedience."

Malka can't move, can't think. Without a name, there's no plan, no hope, no way to protect the people she loves.

She thought she'd loved Siman, or was certain that she could. Maybe she only loved the world that came with him, the promise of something outside of Fox Hollow, something better . . .

Malka digs her fingers into the bark. "You say you want obedience. Faithfulness? But how do I know you'll be faithful?

You could find somebody you like better. Now that you're free to travel the world."

He chuckles fondly. "My previous wife asked the same, once."

"Well . . . she had a point, right? I'm stuck in your—your kingdom, forever, while you come and go? That doesn't seem fair. I want . . . I need . . . a commitment."

"Very well. I promise to take no other love, so long as you live. Will this satisfy you?"

"But you're a . . . you're so powerful, and I'm just a girl who barely knows anything." This is no less than the truth. "You could go anywhere, couldn't you? What if you get bored, and leave me for . . . I don't know, Paris, or Morocco, or the Glowworm Caves of New Zealand, and don't come back for decades? I'll be trapped, all alone, waiting for you. I'm a person. Time lasts a lot longer for me than you. I could die of a broken heart." Forcing strength into her limbs, she shoves off from the tree trunk to stand just out of arm's reach. She presses her trembling lips into a pout, like the one Shosh uses to get her way. "I want you to promise that you won't leave the water. Ever."

He grins with all of his sharp teeth. "My kingdom extends to whatever land the water touches. The bank is mine, too." He sweeps his eyes up and down the waterline. "This all belongs to me."

"Your kingdom, then," she amends.

"Well . . ." His black eyes burrow into hers. "I'll have my loyal bride, and my palace, and my vengeance. I need nothing more. And now your gift to me—let's call it your dowry, on your parents' behalf? I want a child. A daughter, in place of the girl that was stolen from me."

It might as well be winter, as cold as Malka feels.

After everything she and her mother have said and done to one another, the last thing she could ever want is a child, especially a daughter. What if she set out to raise one, determined never to smother her or abandon her or cause her pain, and found that motherhood turned her monstrous?

Besides, the thought of bearing a child for him, with him . . .

"Ahuvati?"

Ida warned her to promise nothing. But what else can she do? What's one more mistake?

"All right," she says. "A child. I promise."

Siman retreats deliberately toward the Hollow. Stepping backward down the shore until his heels touch water, he beckons her to join him. She follows—close enough for him to touch her, should he try it, but just shy of the highest waterline where the river swells after heavy rainfall.

"For so long as you live, I vow never to set foot outside my kingdom."

Their promises are exchanged, and according to Mrs. Silver, unbreakable.

He spreads his arms in welcome. "Now come, Malka."

She stays where she is. Terrified, hardly daring the breath it takes to speak, she replies lightly, "Come and make me."

Perhaps he thinks it a new game, because he bows cheekily

before lunging forward, too quick for her to get clear of him—

Then shrinks back, growling, as though repelled by force.

Malka stoops down and scrabbles in the mulch for any kind of weapon. The sheyd starts forward again just as she scrapes her fingers on the edge of a fist-sized rock, pries it from the earth, and scuttles back into the trees, her heart faltering for a beat.

But now she's made it up the bank, and he stops again, not three feet from the river.

"You can't." Her laughter is a wild thing. "You can't leave your kingdom. You made a promise."

He tilts his head, shadows swimming in whole schools beneath the skin of his face, his neck, his arms. "You think you're clever? I don't know what it is you carry, but I speak the truth when I tell you it would be better for you to cast it aside and join me now. You made promises too, don't forget."

"Maybe I did, but you can't collect. I wouldn't give you a quarter, never mind a kid."

Flashing his fishhook smile, Siman assures her, "Your daughter will belong to me—she belongs to me already—and she'll come to me, too. When she's no older than you are now, I think. I can see it now. But don't forget your first promise. The one you made to me today. You vowed to choose me over your family, did you not?"

She feels the thrill of victory slipping, slipping.

"You break yours, and I'll be free to break mine," Siman snarls. "The moment you set eyes on your loved ones—and we

343

spoke of family, not of blood—I will tear through them to get to you. You'll see. I won't be trapped like an animal, not again. Go home, Malka Eggers, and see what happens."

"So I'll—I'll leave. I'll figure out how to kill you. I'll stay gone until I find a way."

Now it's his turn to laugh. "Run, then! Run as far as you can, little girl. Your world is small, your life is short, and my kingdom is eternal. The vows you made today will lead you back to my river. So I can wait. What's a few decades more for me, when it means a wife and daughter to serve me till death?"

Malka runs.

For thirty-one long years, she will never stop running.

TWENTY-FOUR

THE CREATURE'S SMILE is half snarl as he watches me work through my mother's long-ago promise, his wide lips peeling back to show impossibly sharp white teeth. "I asked for a daughter," he says, "but it was a son who crossed my bank first. Boy, girl, yeled, yalda—these words mean nothing, certainly not to one such as me. A child is what I wanted, a child of Malka's, and a child I have forever. I am satisfied. And you? You're free, my spell lifted. Is that not what you wanted?"

"No!" I insist. "Not like this." I never wanted my life back in exchange for Gabe's. I only wanted . . .

What did I want? To be fixed, of course. To be normal. To return to the life I've clawed out for myself, my grades, my plans for the future. I thought Jamaica Plain was home, and just days ago, I would've given anything to go back there, curse-free, and forget that any of this had happened.

Almost anything.

But I don't want that anymore. I just want what I think my brother, at least, has always given me: to be loved, and to trust that that love is mine to keep, no matter how much of a mess or a monster I am.

When I thought Gabe was leaving us for California, leaving me, that love didn't feel like enough. Now, it's everything.

Siman takes a step toward me, and I slip a hand into the phone pocket of Esther's daughter's yoga pants to touch the hamsa. He stops, eyes flitting toward it. "Be glad your mother kept her promise," he advises, still watching my pocket, "as that's all that binds me to my kingdom. Without it, I'd be free to leave this bank and wander your world. And the vengeance I would take, the blood your people would forfeit . . . you should be thankful."

I don't understand, not all of it, but I hold on to this: if Mom and Gabe are the cost of my freedom, I don't accept. Jitka had no choice at all but to leave her family behind forever. She had no weapons to fight with. *What good is clay against tanks?*

But I have weapons. I have the hamsa, and the golem. I have Ari.

I have a choice, and a chance.

I can fight.

"Then I want you to take me to them."

I don't breathe while Siman considers this.

"Perhaps we can make a bargain of our own," he finally says. "You carry something of your mother's—do I guess right?" When I nod, gripping it tight inside my pocket, he says, "I recognize the cursed thing. I know I can't touch you while you hold it. Toss it into the river, and I will take you down."

For a long moment, I don't move. This isn't part of the plan. Ari would forbid me. Her bubbe would, too. So would Mom.

But Mom isn't here.

"Throw it aside," Siman insists, "or turn back."

I press my lips together until they ache. Then, slowly, I pull out the hamsa. It takes every bit of strength and every ounce of belief in myself—that I'll be brave enough and strong enough and smart enough to steal back my family—before I let it slip from my fingers and into the water. I watch it sink.

When I look up, Siman stands right in front of me.

"Hannnnnah." My name slithers eagerly out of him, and I smell mold and rot and death in the moment before he wraps callused fingers around my wrist. They end in a boy's blunt fingernails, but I feel claws.

Then we're falling.

When we break the surface of the river, it stings like a slap that leaves ice instead of fire in its wake. The current tugs at me, but the sheyd's grip on my wrist is so much stronger. Panicked now, I waste the last of the air in my lungs. Does he plan to drown me and drop my body at my family's feet? There's water in my nose, in my mouth, grainy and bitter. Far from shore now and deep enough down that distant daggers of sunlight barely pierce the darkness, my knees smack rocks. Buffeted by water, with little sense of direction and no breath left in my body, I'm shoved into some kind of sunken debris on the river bottom, at once rough and slick. And then, impossibly, we sink down . . .

Down . . .

Down.

TWENTY-FIVE

I NEVER PAID much attention to the volume of my own lungs until I'm on my hands and knees, coughing half of the Hollow out of them. River water scores my throat as it comes back up, but at least I'm heaving instead of drowning.

I've lost count of every impossibility that's happened to me since my seventeenth birthday. Among them, though, is certainly the small dinghy that brought us here. It sat at the bottom of the river, half buried in weeds and rocks and silt. Somehow, it delivered us *below* the river.

I curl over the splintered hull of the boat, water still trickling out of me to patter the ground below. Instead of slimy rocks and grit beneath us, we're docked on a path that is smooth and frosted and green, like beach glass. Beyond the path, sickly green seaweed as tall as the grass in the meadow writhes, as if stirred by a current I can't feel. It's only air down here, damp and cool enough to cause goose bumps, smelling of rotting vegetation and soggy earth.

Siman braces one worm-eaten black leather boot on the gunwale inches from my cheek. "I bid you welcome," he says grandly, "to my kingdom."

I shouldn't be surprised. The "palace" part of the story I chased to the bottom of the Hollow is right there in the title. But when I can stop coughing and spluttering long enough to lift my head, the structure in front of me is enormous in a way I couldn't have imagined. It is—and I stress this—an underwater fucking palace. One I've seen before, or a version of it: a castle on a hill overlooking the frozen river of Jitka's dream-memories, its ice-glazed spires piercing the winter sky. This could be a copy, with the same sprawling outer walls, the gothic spires and simpler peaked roofs rising beyond them. Except Siman's palace is made of the same beach glass as the path, in every shade of blue and green: cerulean and aqua and bottle and pine and sapphire. And like beach glass, the sharpest points of the steeples are dulled, the edges buffed down by water and time.

Beyond it all is a sky as dark as deep water. The only source of illumination is the glass of the palace itself, lit by the same wavering, pearlescent halo that shone from the surface of the river and through the trees the last couple of nights.

Stupidly, I rasp out, "How . . . ?"

Hooking sharp fingers into my bicep, he hauls me roughly over the side of the dinghy, and my sopping-wet sneakers squeak along the glass before I find my footing. "Magic, little girl," he hisses, near enough that his cold lips brush my earlobe. They feel nothing like Ari's, not even like Atticus's. More like touching a foul dead thing in the dark.

He half drags me up the path to a gate that from a distance looked like iron, but now it, too, appears to be glass; the thin, delicate bars stand like inverted icicles. "Apologies for the lack of a proper welcome," he says as he marches me through. "My last palace had attendants—the vodníci who haunt the Vltava. Perhaps you've heard of them? Some thought I was one of them. My story was known, if not my name. But have you met a vodník? Ridiculous. Gills and green skin and tangled beards. Drowning swimmers to collect their souls in porcelain teapots, smoking their pipes and scrabbling over pinches of tobacco dropped by sailors. A creature such as them might serve, but never rule. Unfortunate, then, that no such spirits dwell in this land."

Beyond the glass gates and through an even grander pair of gates set in the outer buildings, the palace unfolds; it's more like a walled medieval village than one large castle. We enter an abandoned courtyard, the kind that should be paved with cobblestones, but again, strands of seaweed wave in the motionless wet air. They tangle around my ankles, tripping me. Only Siman's clawed hold on my arm keeps me upright as we pass a tiered glass fountain filled with silt instead of water.

Though my senses are awash in the vibrations of my wild heartbeat, from my ears down to my fingertips, I take note of everything we pass along the way, bread crumbs I'll need to find my way back. A looming cathedral inside a second courtyard, with its steepled silhouette. A tiered garden with glass statues, empty fountains, and more sinuous seaweed in place of flowers or hedges. Multistoried halls, and narrow streets crowded with small, simple structures where nobody lives. Siman tows me down a lane with a single cylindrical tower rising at the end.

Its walls are perfectly smooth but for tiny, far-spaced windows that pierce a glass facade the palest possible shade of blue, like mist over a river.

Of course, the ominous tower is our destination.

He pulls me through a narrow doorway with no door, up a carved, clear spiral staircase that glows with the same light as the rest of the palace. The walls are just translucent enough that as he marches me down a cramped passageway, I can see two figures in a room on the other side of the thick, frosted pane—one seated, one sprawled.

"Gabe? Mom!" My scream reverberates around us.

As with the tower entrance, there is no door, no bars. When we reach a doorway, I wrestle against the sheyd's grip, but he releases me freely. My own force propels me into the ice-blue floor, my knee cracking against the glass. With an "umf" of pain, I struggle upright and limp the few paces to my family.

"Hannah?" Mom cries, clearly stunned and horrified to see me.

I feel the same. Her face, the one I know in the brightest and darkest corners of my heart, has changed. Her cheeks are hollowed, carved down as if by a sculptor's tools. Her skin is bluish pale and tight over sharpened bones that show beneath a wrinkled ivory dress, which looks . . . well, like it washed up on a riverbank, the same as Siman's suit. Lacy embellishments hang from the collar and cuffs, beading dangles on its threads, and the hem is torn or nibbled through in spots. Even Mom's wheat-blond hair has lost its shine, and is now long enough that the limp strands brush the floor from where she sits, partially curtaining my brother.

Gabe lies on his back, unconscious, unmoving, his head cradled in Mom's lap. I stoop over them both to examine the bruise that covers one of his cheekbones, as dark as a storm cloud. It seems unnecessary that an ugly iron chain rusted to powdery orange is knotted hopelessly around one wrist, the other end punched into an ugly, cracked wound in the glass floor. He's not going anywhere.

My heart quickening to hummingbird speed, I press light fingers to his forehead. Though his lips are purpled with cold like Mom's, his skin is hot. The teal wave of his hair shifts at my touch, revealing an inch-long gash, deep and bloody, just below his hairline, where the ink letters would be found on the golem.

Glaring over my shoulder at the demon pacing the tiny room—ten steps forward, turn, ten steps back—I snarl, "What did you do?"

"Gabriel has not been an obedient and loving child," Siman explains simply. "But I'm sure he'll learn, with your mother's good example."

"What does *that* mean?" I turn to Mom, but she only sits, silent and frozen, so the sheyd answers for her.

"My Malka walked right into the water to meet me, didn't you, ahuvati? She *wants* to be here, just as I told her she someday would. And here she stays."

"You're lying," I accuse when Mom still doesn't answer. "You took her. And you've been trying to take me. Mom found a way up to warn us, before Gabe—"

"May I have some time with my daughter?" Mom interrupts in a flat voice.

Siman doesn't hesitate for a moment before answering. "You may not. Hannah, you wished to see your family, and you have. Now, it's time to return."

Stubbornly, I plant myself on the chilled floor beside my mother and brother, wrapping an arm awkwardly around his knees. "I'm not leaving without them."

"I was promised a wife and a child."

"Then . . . maybe we can make another deal?"

At that, Mom shows some sign of life at last.

I look down at my brother—his swelling cheekbone and flickering eyelids and the pale skin that should be tanned golden by this time in the summer. Except that he's spent it all inside, hiding with me, taking care of me.

I'm supposed to take care of you. And I'm supposed to say, 'I'm supposed to take care of you,' right?

Gabe has always looked out for me, in every new state and school and not-quite-home. But it shouldn't have been his job. Isn't that what I told the golem?

This was his last summer before college, and he's given up friends and boyfriends, sunny days in Griggs Park and neon-lit nights at the harbor. I know he'd tell me he did it gladly. I know he'd give up California if I asked him to. But he has the right to go and figure out who he is without me, and without Mom. He deserves that chance. He deserves a life. I know my brother loves me, as much as I love him, but he doesn't owe me his freedom. And I won't take it from him.

"A trade," I tell Siman. "Me for him."

The demon stops pacing.

"Hannah, don't," my mother whispers. "You don't know what you're doing."

"But *you* did?" I shoot back. "You're the one who sold yourself and a *child* to a *demon*."

"Come now!" Siman says. "Is it so terrible here?"

"Gosh, no, I've always wanted to be trapped in an underwater prison forever."

"Not forever," he corrects, striding over to drag a possessive hand through Mom's lank hair. "Just until your mother dies. I'm confined to my kingdom only so long as she lives. Once we're freed, we'll roam lakes, and oceans, and rivers as long as continents. I'll show you corners of this earth you've never dreamed of. All of it would belong to you, Hannah. Have you never wished to be something more? By my side, your life would be extraordinary. *You* would be extraordinary. Stay, serve me, please me, and I will care for you. Isn't that love?"

"It's captivity," my mother snaps.

Siman raises an eyebrow at her. "Call it what you want," he returns, "it needn't be unpleasant."

Maybe the thought of it—of giving in and being swept along by some impossible fantasy instead of kicking against the current—should tempt me. No more spreadsheets, no more disguises. No more struggling or overthinking or trying as hard as I can, *all the damn time*. I could just . . . let go.

But that's not what I'm thinking about. I'm thinking that

if the sheyd will let me stay—and if I can get my brother out before he's hurt worse—it's a trade I'm more than willing to make.

"You can't do it, Hannah." Mom insists, reaching for me, maybe seeing what I'm about to say. Her dirty fingers dig into my shoulder.

I shrug free. "Sorry, but this isn't your choice. It's mine." And then that mean, feral feeling rears up in me again, gnashing its way out. "Anyway, you and I both know you'd choose to save Gabe too."

The shadows around her eyes grow deeper still, if that's possible. "Maybe you and I weren't as close growing up as—"

"You never even tried!" I snap. "You never *talked* to me. You didn't even tell me about my own family, like you didn't tell them about me. Would you ever have?"

"You don't understand," she pleads, "it was—"

"To keep me safe?" I guess. "Yeah, look where that's gotten us."

Mom falls silent. Good. I turn my back on her.

"Take Gabe back to land," I tell the sheyd, then add, "alive, and on the bank. Not in the water. I'll stay."

Siman bows, but the look on his handsome, phony face is victorious. "At once. Tonight, we begin our life together. As a family."

Even though it's what I asked for, I'm not ready when Siman wraps a hand around my brother's ankle and drags his limp body from Mom's lap, like he's a child's doll.

"Wait!" I cry as he hauls Gabe across the floor and out of the cell, into the hallway—their faint shapes recede beyond the glass. Instinctively, I scramble after them, but jerk painfully to a stop as I reach the end of the rusted chain—no longer tied to my brother, but wound in a knot around my left ankle, biting and bruising.

Then they're gone.

"Hannah, oh Hannah . . ." Mom sobs, crawling forward to tug at the links. Her hands are shaking so hard, she can't even lift the chain.

"I'll do it," I snap, jerking my leg away to work at the jumbled knot all by myself. "I don't want your apologies. The only thing I want from you is the truth, finally. You owe it to me. And to Gabe."

Nodding tearfully, my mother tells me a story.

It's a long story, and it isn't very happy. It's about a girl, almost exactly my age, who wanted to be free. She tells me about her childhood, her mother's fear and her father's acquiescence to it. About Siman—not the monster wearing his face and holding us prisoner now, but the boy she'd made up her mind to love. The night they snuck into Jitka's basement, and the thing that was set free. How she and her parents fought, and how Siman found her by the river that Shabbat. The promises she'd made without understanding until it was too late. Ida Silver's plan, how it spun sideways, and the only way she felt she could save herself, and the people she loved.

"I left," Mom confesses, staring down at the rust stains on her tattered dress. "Before my family came home from services.

I took what little money I had and walked to the bus station, stayed off the road, deep in the trees, so we wouldn't pass each other along the way. I was so scared, and I had nowhere to go. There was my family in Brooklyn, but I didn't know whether I'd be putting them in danger, too. Whether Siman would be set free the moment I saw them. Besides, they'd just call my parents to drive down and get me. And I couldn't go to Ida's, either, that would be the first place they'd come looking.

"So I picked the next bus leaving Fox Hollow, and then bought the farthest train ticket I could afford. It took me to Maine, where I slept in stations until I turned eighteen and got a job in a diner, and a cheap room I could rent by the week in . . . God, this little town called Saltville. I haven't thought of that place in decades. So many towns just like Fox Hollow, so many people living their lives, and I just passed through them all. I lived the way Siman had—the real Siman. Working until I had enough money to move on to the next place, renting the cheapest rooms. I got braver as I got older, and eventually, I traveled farther. I visited some of the places I'd always planned to, and some I'd never heard of." She looks up at me pleadingly. "Sometimes life is like that, you know? It costs you more than you ever imagined, and it takes you places you never dreamed of. And the longer I stayed gone, the easier it became to believe that wherever I was, it was where I was meant to be. That I could . . . that I *should* leave my past behind me for good. Better for the family I mostly talked to through postcards. Better for me, even. At least I was free.

"And then there was your dad. He was . . . a really good guy,

Hannah. And he was there for me when Papa died. Shosh called to tell me—I'd never stayed anywhere so long, but for once, I had an address and a landline. I couldn't risk going back for the funeral. I was grieving, and so, so lonely, and I missed my family so badly, I couldn't breathe through it. But Michael was there, and he was so sweet. I remembered what it was like, to be loved like that. When he asked me to marry him, I couldn't say no." She tugs on the hem of her dress so hard, she tears a strip up to one pale, bruised knee. "And when he asked me for children . . . I couldn't say no to that, either. He was even happy to adopt, and we managed to take your brother home a year later. I thought—I *hoped*—a boy would be safe."

"What if Gabe wasn't really a boy?" I find my voice to challenge her. "You can't just pick and choose your kids like that. He could've been trans—"

"*Yes*, Hannah." With her exasperated expression, she almost looks like herself again. "I know that now. It was almost twenty years ago, and I wasn't that woke. I considered it later, when your brother came out—not that he had to, he'd been using my laptop to browse Tumblr for years, and never even erased his searches—but back then, I thought I'd figured everything out. I thought my plan was perfect. We all got exactly what we wanted."

Swallowing hard, I dare to ask, "I guess I'm not included in that category?"

By the pain that crosses her face, I know I've guessed right. "We thought we were being careful. But then I was pregnant, and I was absolutely terrified. I felt like I was all alone on the edge of a cliff, and instead of rocks below me, it was everything I'd spent my whole adult life running from."

To avoid looking at her, I return to pulling at the chain, chafing my ankle with every failed attempt to free myself. I kick off my sneaker and try to slip the loop free over my soaking wet sock, but it won't budge. "So why did you have me?"

"Because." She slips her fingers over mine to stop me from tearing into my goose-bumped skin. "I did want you, Hannah. I couldn't help it. Another selfish choice—I never said that I wasn't selfish, and foolish—but I wanted you before I even knew you. Gabe is my son, and nothing about getting pregnant changed that. I never cared about carrying a child. So I was shocked by this feeling, this . . . hunger. And when I found out you were a girl—that you were assigned female," she corrects herself, "I knew I should run. But your dad, he was—well, he was happy in Colorado. I didn't know how to begin to convince him."

"But then, he died," I say, sounding harsher than I'd meant to.

Mom winces with her entire body.

Whether because of pity or guilt—or both—I feel the flame of my anger sputtering low. It would be so much simpler if I could hate my mother. We're here because of her. Gabe is hurt because of her. I've spent weeks trapped and terrified because of her. Because of a choice she made. Except now that I'm learning the truth, it doesn't seem like she had much choice in what happened to her, after all; little more than her mother did.

It's like Jitka's father told her in my dream-memory. We can't choose our burdens, any more than we can choose our blood. We don't get to pick the good out of the bad, like sorting the ripe strawberries from the rotten. We have to live with everything.

I move on. "So you left Colorado. You kept us moving. That's what you meant when you said you tried to keep me safe, right?"

"I . . . I tried. I never even spoke to my family again. Like, maybe if nobody in the world knew you or remembered me, the demon couldn't find us. But he did, somehow. When I saw you change on your birthday, I knew."

"*How?* I spent weeks researching, and I couldn't find anything like what was happening to me."

"It was something the sheyd said. That he'd make sure you came to him when you were my age. And about . . . being trapped. Like an animal. I just . . . that first day, I thought it could be something he'd cooked up. By the second day, I *knew*. He wasn't only trying to hurt you. He wanted my attention. So I came home. I was careful—rented a car, got a room at a motel out of town, and kept clear of my family. I told you about the specialist, the one I thought could heal you?"

"Ida Silver," I whisper.

Mom blinks at me, surprised. "I should've guessed you'd figured that out. My brilliant girl." She reaches for my hand.

I'm not quite ready for that, and so I duck my head, pretending to inspect the chain again. "But Ida wasn't in her house, so you went to see Rachael."

"Y-yes. I found out that she was gone. And that Rachael had thrown away . . . I guess it doesn't matter now. She couldn't help me. She wouldn't listen."

"You never called *her*," I can't stop myself from snapping. "Maybe you couldn't come back to Fox Hollow, but you couldn't drop a postcard in the mail for her, too? She was your best friend."

On the verge of tears for the hundredth time, Mom bites at her lip. "Rachael was the only person who wouldn't have let me go. Not unless she really believed I didn't care about her. And I couldn't think of a way to tell her what I'd done without pulling her down in my mess."

"You should have tried." I give up on the chains and slump back against the column, flinching at the cold glass on my skin. I'm still wearing my borrowed clothing, wrinkled and dripping. I sit in the small pool of water collecting beneath me, longing for the sunlit meadow above.

"Maybe," Mom admits. "I'm sorry, Hannah. If I could do things differently with her . . . With us—"

"I get that things were complicated. You never planned on me, and you felt all kinds of ways about having me. But why couldn't you have *tried*, just a little harder, to look at me the way you looked at Gabe?"

"I was *scared*," Mom shouts suddenly, her words ricocheting off the glass cathedral ceiling, startling me into opening my eyes. "And I saw who my own mother became, after she lost everything as a teenager. How she never could do more than survive, clutching at us like the edge of a cliff, as if the rock could give way any second. How it would have killed her to let go, and if we ever left her . . . Hannah, I didn't want to be that way with you. I didn't want to be terrified. And I didn't want you to feel the same way I had, smothered and trapped. Like my mother's love was a cage. So I tried not to get too close, in case . . ."

"You lost me?"

"More like, in case you didn't belong to me. But I was wrong, about so many things." Mom scoots closer, forcing me to meet her eyes or look away.

I don't look away.

"I've always loved you," she says, her voice raw with the force of it, and I feel the burn in my own throat. "Even if I could go back, if I could change it all, starting when I was your age . . . I don't think I would. Because then I wouldn't have Gabe, and I wouldn't have you. I can't say who we could've been without Siman hanging over my whole life, what kind of mom I could've been. I don't know who *you* could've been, with a better mother. We'll never know, Hannah. Pain changes you. It just does. So does grief, and heartbreak, and hatred so bright that you can't see anything around it. So does love . . . so does the world. But it doesn't have to destroy you. You have your whole life in front of you. You are all possible things. You *are* enough, whoever you are and whoever you'll become." Now she takes my face in her icy hands. "You can't stay down here, Hannah. You can't give up."

It's everything I've wanted to hear from her for so long. But . . .

"*You* gave up," I whisper so my voice won't break completely. "The sheyd said so."

"Maybe . . . maybe on myself, *not* on you. Without Ida, I had no choice. I couldn't fix what I'd done. I hoped if I came to the river and gave myself up, the sheyd would let you go. I called out to Siman, and when he came for me, I went with him. At least that way, I thought the rest of my family would be safe. That *you* would be safe. After all this time, it seemed like the only way."

"Except it wasn't enough for him."

"Not until he had a child." She dips her head, bedraggled hair falling across her face. "He doesn't understand mercy, or forgiveness, or acceptance. All he cares about is what was taken away from him, and what it would drive him mad to lose. I've been with him for weeks. I've tried to talk to him, tell him about my life, the people who love me. But he doesn't love anything. He only owns."

"He sounds like a dick," I mutter.

"Yes," she agrees. "Maybe you hate me for not saying good-bye, but I didn't want you two coming to stop me, or to save me. I didn't want you anywhere near the Hollow. How did you even find me here? Gabe never got the chance to say."

"Ari—Rachael's daughter." I shrug. "She found your rental car in Ida's driveway, after she heard you and her mom fighting.

It had our address on the paperwork. That's how she knew where to send the death notice."

Mom swipes a wrist across her nose. "What death notice?"

Oh, God. She doesn't know.

Whatever rage I have left inside of me cools to ash. "Mom . . . I'm really sorry. Jitka . . ."

"What?" It isn't a word, but a wound.

Now it's my turn to share the pieces of the story I've managed to collect, and everything that's happened since we came to Fox Hollow. Meeting the family. Finding Ari's name in the visitors book. The search that led us to the golem in the barn, along with her mother's letter. I don't have it memorized, but I recount as much of it as I can. Enough that Mom buries her face in her knees for a long moment before she can respond.

"I spoke to her. After I left Rachael's, and before I went to the river, I called Mama. I couldn't see her—it would have set the sheyd free. But I had to tell her the truth about that summer. I didn't . . . I didn't want her to think I never loved her. Maybe I shouldn't have. I didn't tell her I was leaving, but she knew I was scared. She could tell." That must be why Jitka decided to bring the golem to life. "I didn't want her to . . . to die without knowing her own daughter." Mom sounds so young right now; I can imagine exactly the girl she was that summer long ago. Hopeful and scared. Lonely and maybe a little bit in love.

Not so different from me.

I say the only thing I can think of. "May her memory be a blessing."

Tears track down Mom's cheeks, glittering like ice in the strange underwater light when she lifts her head. "Where did you learn that phrase?" She makes it sound as though I've picked up dirty language down by the docks.

I have to laugh, just a little. "Not from you, for sure."

Mom sighs, sniffling. "Judaism and me, it's . . . complicated. I told you on your birthday—we have a lot to talk about. But now, we have to get you out."

"How?"

"I couldn't get away from Siman for longer than a few moments a night to watch over the riverbank, just in case. And I couldn't stop him from taking Gabe—I wasn't strong enough—but I would have found a way to get him out. I *will* find a way to get you out." She bends over to work on the chains once more. "Just don't offer him a gift, and don't accept one in return. Don't make any more deals with him, okay? That's a trap, as dangerous as this palace. But somehow, we're going to get you free."

"Except I'm not leaving without you."

"Hannah—"

"Mom, Ari and Gabe and I, we found a way to beat him. You and I are going back tonight, together. *Nobody* is staying behind this time." Quickly, I catch her up on Ida Silver and her fixation with saving Mom, right up until the end of her life. "She found this new piece of the story. Every night before the demon went ashore, his first wife wrote his name on a scrap of paper and put it in his coat, commanding him to come back to her. Siman might have had the paper in his coat pocket when your great-great-something trapped him. He might still have it."

Mom ponders this. "You think he'd keep something like that, if it was so dangerous?"

"The parchment would be all he'd have of her," I point out. "I've been thinking . . . Jitka kept the chest. Maybe she didn't really believe, and she never passed on the story the way she should've, but she never got rid of it. It meant something to her father, and as much as she might've hated it, it meant something to her. We can't . . . we can't choose our burdens."

"That's true." Mom chews at her cracked bottom lip while she thinks, the same way Gabe teethes his piercing. "If he's carrying it on him, I can get it. I can try, at least. And if not, I can distract him while you search the palace."

"Distract him how?"

Her smile is as sharp as a knife's edge. "He wants an obedient wife? He'll get one for the evening. And that's the last thing he'll have from me before we take *everything* from him."

"If he's not keeping it with him, where would I even start to look? This place is huge. There's no way I can—"

"The cathedral," she cuts in, the glimmering of an idea in her hooded hazel eyes. "I haven't been in this tower the whole time—only since your brother's been here. Most everywhere you go here is like . . . like a movie set, or a copy of a castle he only saw from the outside. But there's a building in the second courtyard, a church or something. He keeps things inside. Precious things. Whatever's sunk in the waterways between the Hollow and the Hudson. He took me there once, tried to put this necklace on me—broken and tarnished, I don't know how long it must have sat in the muck. I threw it back at him. I would've thrown the crown jewels in his face. He . . . he never took me there again. But it's the only place I know of that isn't empty."

The story mentioned a treasure chamber inside of a cathedral, where the sheyd piled gold into the aunt's pocket as payment for delivering his daughter.

"Then I'll go there," I say. "And if one of us finds the letter?"

"We go to the surface." Mom lifts a section of the rusted links wound around my ankle. "It's not pleasant, but I can get us to shore. The boat tied up beyond the gate goes both ways. He doesn't need it to travel back and forth, but we do. He doesn't guard it. He knows we can't leave the bank—no farther than the water touches. That's as far as I could go, but I came every night to warn you off, just in case you followed me to Fox Hollow. I thought you might, somehow." She cups a thin, cold hand against my cheek and lets herself soften, eyes shining as she smiles at me. "My brave, brilliant girl."

The way my heart cracks open like a clamshell . . .

"Then we'll go," I squeeze out.

"He'll find us, though. He always does."

"It's okay. If you can get us above water, I don't need much time."

At last, we untangle the chains together, setting me free.

It's a start.

TWENTY-SIX

WITH NO LIGHT source underwater besides the palace itself, it's impossible to tell what time it is up above. At least, for me it is. But somehow Mom knows.

"He'll be here soon," she says, like we're characters in one of Gabe's horror movies. "Every sundown for the last ten days, he finds me and asks me to join him for supper. I tell him no, and he tosses me scraps—half-cooked fish, soggy plants, whatever grows along the water." That explains her thin frame, how her curves have turned to angles. "It's the fun dance we do."

My stomach gurgles against my will—I gulped down iced coffee at the Leydons' house and gnawed on a cold Pop-Tart while we waited for her mom to make some excuse to her dad. I haven't eaten since, and can imagine that by this time tomorrow night, limp water plants will look pretty good.

"When he comes this evening," Mom continues, "I'll say yes."

"What if you can't get away from him?" I like this plan less and less with each passing moment, and I hated it from the start.

Smoothing down her tattered dress and straggling hair with something like dignity, she scoffs. "I've faked food poisoning and period cramps to get out of bad dates and bad lays before. Both, once."

"Mom!" I shriek. "God, can you not?"

"Sorry to inform you that your mother is a person, Hannah," she says, than carries on calmly. "Worry about you. I'll make sure Siman isn't carrying a letter on him, and keep him busy long enough for you to get to the cathedral. When you find it, or if you're sure it isn't there—"

"I'll head for the boat," I finish, interrupting. It's my damn plan after all, thanks very much. "And you'll do the same."

"But Hannah, if something happens . . . If it's not as easy as we hope, then *you* can steer the boat by—"

"Nope, no thanks." I cut her off again. "We get out together, or we wait. We'll try again tomorrow." As if I'd leave my mother, embarrassing and infuriating though she may be, to drown in a doomed kingdom.

"You're sure your friend will still be waiting?"

My friend. The girl who's brave and badass and resourceful and determined, and luckily, has serious emotional currency with Rachael Leydon right now, and her house smells of old books, and her kiss is like the first full breath after almost drowning.

"She'll be there," is what I say. Maybe I don't know it absolutely, but I have faith. "Do you think . . ." I summon the courage to mention the unmentionable. "Do you think Gabe is okay?"

Mom pulls her knees up to her chest, pale arms banded around them. "Siman can't break a promise. Not when you kept yours."

"So Gabe was alive when he left him, but—"

"No," Mom interrupts fiercely. "He's okay, baby. He's a strong kid, right? Probably he's even made it back to Esther and Bernie, and they're taking care of him right now. He won't even remember all this—the boat below the water, the kingdom. Siman wouldn't let him. He'll be confused, but . . . but he's going to be fine, I promise."

It's a promise that shouldn't mean much—Mom can't possibly know, any more than I can—but Mom doesn't make promises she doesn't expect to keep.

I guess I finally understand why.

When Siman comes a short while later, we've loosely reknotted the chain around my ankle, and I'm sitting in the back of the cell, feigning a sulky refusal to look at either of them.

"Ahuvati," he says to Mom, then bows slightly in my direction. "Habat sheli. Will you join me to dine?"

"I . . ." Mom hesitates, looks desperately toward me, as we planned. "If I agree, will you give my . . . our daughter something to eat?"

"I don't want anything from *him.*" I bar my arms across my chest. "Both of you can fuck right off."

"Hannah, be reasonable," she begs. "You have to eat. We're here, we can't survive without him, and—"

"Have fun on your date, *Mom*." I snarl the word.

Siman offers her his hand, looking entirely too pleased. "Come, Malka. She will see in time."

With one last glance at me, Mom takes his hand—how she doesn't shudder, I don't know—and rises to follow Siman from our cell.

I count down the seconds until five minutes have passed, making sure I'm alone in the tower. Then I shimmy out of the chain and creep down the hallway to the stairs, pausing at a window so small I couldn't squeeze my shoulders through even if I did in fact want to fall four stories and break my bones against the glass ground below. I look up the narrow lane: empty.

At last, I hurry down the staircase to the street, sticking close to the small, squat buildings that border the lane. A glance through the square window on a one-story structure proves Mom right; there's nothing inside. I don't know who lived in these buildings in the version above water, but down below, they're meaningless props.

Carefully, I wind my way toward the front of the palace, retracing our path from the narrow streets to the grander halls and the tiered garden, with its dry fountains and glass statues like ice sculptures. Nothing moves beyond the weeds in their invisible current. I have no idea where Siman took Mom, so I stay low and keep far from the ground floor—the seafloor?— windows, to be safe.

Finally, I pass into the second courtyard and find the

cathedral. I steal a moment to stare up at it, astonished. Though the steepled towers have been buffed down, they would still scrape clouds, if there were clouds above us. Carved gargoyles, dragons, and angels overhang the roofs, any sharpness dulled from their features. The tall archways that would be set with stained glass windows in any other church are empty sockets, aglow with pearly ghost light.

I slip through the entryway and stand inside a long, soaring chamber that should be lined with pews and crowned with an altar, from what little I know of churches. But again, there's nothing, and I feel a burst of dread—what if this place is as hollow as the rest of the palace?

Well, the only way to find out is to move forward.

Narrow aisles run along either side of the main chamber, and I take the left one, peering through empty doorways into smaller rooms, like bubbles in blown glass. Empty, every one of them. Backtracking, dread building to panic with every step I take, I try the right corridor. Room after room of nothing, nothing, nothing.

Until I stick my head through a doorway halfway down the aisle and find it.

I don't know what I'd expected. Piles of rugged gold coins and fig-sized rubies, maybe. Which was hopelessly stupid, I'll own; I've never heard of pirate's booty washing ashore in Poughkeepsie. Some of what litters the pale-green glass floor might be valuable; there's a tangle of tarnished jewelry nearby, and several perfectly round, fist-sized rocks in the corner look suspiciously like the antique cannon balls I saw on a field trip to the American Revolution Museum when we lived in Virginia. Lying just inside the doorway is a three-foot-long bronze statue of a cherub-cheeked naked woman, holding a basketball-sized globe above her head; it might've broken off a ship's bow a long time ago. But the rest is definitely garbage. A whippy fishing rod snapped at the reel. A heap of ruined, mud-crusted clothing and boots with peeling soles—Siman probably dug Mom's dress out of this stash.

I shudder to think how he'd try to dress me up.

Though I wouldn't call this a treasure chamber so much as an indoor junkyard, I pick my way carefully through the debris, inspecting everything. I can't believe he'd leave something of actual personal worth lying among splintered timbers and rusted scrap metal. Just in case, I nudge a sneaker through the piles.

I'm so busy staring intently at the ground that it takes me longer than it should to notice the small door in the wall across from me, solid and wooden, like the kind you'd see on an old boat cabin. There's even a little porthole. It doesn't seem that secure, but then, it's the only door I've seen in this place. Even the prison tower was wide open. Crossing over to inspect it, I see that smooth blue glass kisses the very edges of the warped doorframe, as though the door existed here before the walls.

I tug on the handle. It's nothing fancy, corroded green in spots, but it won't budge. Locked from the inside? I try the porthole itself, but it must be rusted shut. Cupping my hands,

I try to peek through. The plain old window glass is cloudy and cracked, impossible to see past. I turn and dash back to the doorway, crunching Siman's "treasure" underfoot. Skidding to a stop beside the figurehead, I wrap one arm around her waist and palm a breast to keep her steady—she's heavy for a little naked lady—and carry her back to the door, struggling under her weight. I wobble a little as I lift her high enough to aim the solid bronze globe at the broken glass.

With a running start, I ram into the porthole. It gives a little, spidering at the crack through its center, but it takes another charge before the glass shatters altogether. Glittering shards cling to the circular plate, and I try my best to clear them away before I drop the figurehead to snake my arm through. Even so, I feel a vicious pinch as I swipe my hand around for the latch, a spike slicing the skin inside my elbow. "Nngf," I grunt, but shove my shoulder against the door to reach as far as possible, until I finally feel the bolt beneath my fingertips. I fumble with it until it squeaks slowly open.

Sliding free, I find a half-inch cut above a track of blood that runs from elbow to wrist. Not ideal, but when I rattle the latch this time, the door swings inward to reveal a chamber, about the size of the coal room in Jitka's basement.

Just as small, and just as empty.

"Fuck!" I scream, and then a second time, my ragged voice rebounding back to me. It doesn't help, and I sink to the floor of the chamber and clutch my arm, blood slowly pooling in the crook of my elbow to drip down and spatter my T-shirt. The sheyd could find me at any moment, I suppose . . . but where else is there to go?

The only difference between the coal room and this chamber is the light, pearly and rippling even in here. I watch it waver across the cold, blue walls, willing myself to stand up, to retreat, to try again tonight or tomorrow.

Jitka didn't give up.

Gabe wouldn't give up.

Mom won't give up.

And Ari is waiting for me.

I shove myself to my feet, then slip on the blood-slicked floor until I catch myself against the far wall of the little room . . . where I feel a crack in the glass below my left palm. Stooping down to inspect the hair-thin gap, I trace it around with one finger to find a roughly drawn rectangle, around the size of the coal chute. I press my nose to it to peer through, the frosted glass cleaner than the porthole and, it turns out, thinner than the rest of the palace walls. It's faint, but I see it.

There's something on the other side.

Back out into the treasure chamber, I heft my trusty bronze lady and swing her one-handed, shielding my eyes with my nonbloodied elbow. She leaves a chip in center of the rectangle on the first swing, a crack on the second. The third swing shatters it, the pieces tinkling to the floor to leave a hollowed-out pocket behind.

Unlike the coal chute, it isn't empty. A mildewed cushion sits in the little cavern, and set atop it, a single curl of parchment.

I don't even dare to breathe as I reach toward it. What if it turns to crumbs and dust beneath my fingertips? But slowly—like, excruciatingly slowly—I unroll the paper, wrinkled and brown and fragile with age, to read the single sentence inked across it.

Waiting for Mom in the little busted dinghy docked outside the gates, shivering and alone, I'm somehow more scared than ever. There's no way to gauge how long it's been besides the festering ache in my empty stomach and the quickening of my own breath. Even if I knew how to steer back to shore, I can't leave without my mother. But I can't wait here forever, out in the open where Siman will eventually find me.

Maybe Mom couldn't get away. Maybe he sensed she was lying to him, made her tell him our plan, and now he'll never, ever let us up to the surface. How long should I wait? Should I creep back through the palace grounds to the prison tower to try to find her? Should I—

"Hannah," Mom calls from the other side of the icicle-like gate.

It's like my heart restarts.

Her bare feet slap across the glass ground to get to me, and she almost falls over the gunwale, hugging me fiercely. In this moment, the only thing I feel is terrible, wonderful love. It isn't that everything's fixed or forgiven between us. *If* we manage to get to shore in one piece; *if* we can reach Ari before the demon realizes we're missing and catches up with us; *if* the

name works, and the chain holds, and we're both set free . . .
If everything goes right, we'll still have to find a way forward
with the strangers we've just met in each other.

All I know is that my mother loves me, and she's doing her
best. I can believe that she was always doing her best.

Pulling back, she asks, "Do you have it?"

I nod because I can't speak around the cannon-ball-sized
lump in my throat.

"Thank God." Mom takes a shuddering breath of her own,
then eyes the looming black not-sky above us and whispers,
"Okay, Banana. Up we go."

TWENTY-SEVEN

ONE MOMENT I'M squeezing my eyes shut against the sudden swoop of vertigo; the next, the dinghy breaks the surface of the river. Or more accurately, the bottom of the river, plunging us into the Hollow. The splintered prow lodges itself with the sudden grind of wood on rocks, tossing us against the hull. Even though we're right side up, it feels as if we've capsized, trapping us underwater. It's ice cold and night dark; I can't see a thing, even when I pry my eyes open. I reach out for Mom, flailing around the empty water where last she sat, until I feel her bony fingers cuff my wrist and pull me up, out of the boat. I kick toward the surface; at least, I hope we're moving that way. I have no choice but to trust her. Air bubbles leak from between my numb lips as we struggle upward.

When we emerge, gasping, we do it together. We've come up in a narrower stretch of the Hollow, the current faster than I remembered. I'm disoriented, unsure of where we are or which bank to swim for. The woods that should be vaguely familiar by now look strange in the eerie glow that our arrival seems to have cast on the surrounding trees. It's as though we've left a door open to the underwater realm, its light leaking through. I try to spin in place while holding tight to my mother.

But Mom knows. She shouts and paddles to the right, pulling me along. We reach the shore and haul each other up onto the riverbank, coughing and shivering.

"Where are we?" I ask between gasps, digging my fingers gratefully into damp earth.

She lifts her head to look around just as the clouds peel back to reveal the full moon, like a bared tooth. "Between the Silvers' and home," she answers. "We're lucky. Last night I first came up miles away. Come on, quickly. And remember to keep to the water. We haven't broken the spell yet, we can't leave the riverbank."

I scan the bank around us, for all that's worth. "Gabe . . ."

"We'll find him, Hannah, but we can't stay here," she says firmly.

Though I'm tired and terrified enough to lie curled up in my own rapidly expanding puddle until I freeze, I know she's right. I let her pull me up, and arm in arm, we help each other along the slope of the bank, sticking to the shallow water and the ground that squishes beneath my waterlogged sneakers. At this point, I doubt they'll ever dry.

I'm sure that Jitka's property is upriver from Ida's, so at least we're headed in the right direction. As long as Mom is right about where we surfaced, that is. Whenever her ragged, impractical dress catches on roots and reeds, I work to free it. Otherwise, I'm so busy watching out for my brother—and for the demon—that I forget to watch my feet. I trip over a root that snakes out of the earth, stumbling sideways to rebalance—

And veer beyond the edge of the bank without meaning to.

The moment I do, I feel like I'm back at the very bottom of the cold heart of the Hollow. No more moonlight or waterlight. No chirp of crickets or frogs, no cry from the creatures that live in the woods, unbothered by our passage. No air. No Mom. Just me, drowning on dry land, alone.

Again, my mother's hand finds me in the dark and tugs me back. "Unpleasant, isn't it?"

I keep my shoes safely in the shallow water after that.

At last, we reach a patch of woods that I recognize. There's the clump of ash trees I slipped through on my way back from Ida Silver's house. We're getting close. I'm wondering whether we're near enough to risk calling out to Ari when Mom digs her nails into my elbow, stopping me in my tracks.

I follow her gaze to the bank ahead of us, and to a long, dark shape haloed by river light. Not the sheyd. It's slumped on the ground, half buried in the reeds.

Pulling free, I splash ahead at full speed until I reach my brother and drop to my knees in the mud and crushed grass beside him. "Gabe?"

"H-h-hey, B-banana," he manages through clacking teeth.

I feel light-headed with relief. Sinking back onto my bottom, I allow myself one moment to breathe through the feeling before conducting my amateur examination.

Though the temperature's fallen since sunset, it can't be

much below seventy degrees. Even in damp clothes, hypothermia isn't a threat—so far as I'm aware, anyway. I'm no expert. I do know enough from Winthrop's optional CPR and first aid elective to worry that Gabe might have a concussion (I never imagined this precise situation while crafting my study flash cards, but I'm grateful for them). The bruise that blooms across his cheekbone is wicked looking, and if he's been out for the hours since Siman returned him, the danger is real. "Do you feel nauseated?" I ask, trying to peer down into his slivered eyes to check for unequal pupils, like I've been taught. Impossible in the near dark. "Or, um, does your head hurt? Or your neck, or back?" I cautiously pat his hair, which has dried wildly.

"Nothing doesn't hurt," he groans, then swallows hard. "My face feels like it ran into a train. Wh-what's happening?"

"What do you remember?"

"Uhh . . ." He grits his chattering teeth.

"Never mind. It's gonna be okay. I've got Mom, she's—" I glance downriver to find where I left her. It hits me again how much she's changed, her once enviably curved body whittled into unrecognizability these past weeks. Like she's a kid again. The sight of her is so jarring, it takes me a moment to see the full picture: her back to us, bare feet planted in the muck, standing between us and the tall, broad shadow of a boy.

But of course, it's not a boy.

I don't know whether we're close enough to the barn, but as soon as I find my voice I scream "Ari, NOW!" Then I tug on Gabe's T-shirt and slip an arm behind his neck to awkwardly peel him out of the dirt, hoping that nothing is broken inside of my brother. I hook my arms beneath his to tow him down the bank, and he moves with me as best he can, kicking weakly to propel us backward. It's probably a waste of both our energy; I know I don't have the strength to get us both to safety. But what else can I do?

When I hear the cracking branches behind us, it's like the sound of an answered prayer.

"Hannah!" Ari shouts. She's sprinting toward us through the woods, the slim, sturdy writing box tucked under one arm. She skids to a stop behind us, setting the box on the trampled earth just as Gabe shouts for Mom.

I turn back in time to watch her crumple to the ground.

In a moment, the sheyd stands before us, so suddenly I drop Gabe and fall to the mud with him. Curly-haired and strong-shouldered and easy-smiling, he's the boy who sat beside my mother on the synagogue lawn, who snuck down to her basement with a bottle of wine, who unknowingly set loose this doom because of my mother and grandmother and the things they never said to one another.

In the next moment, though, he spots the box at our feet. And he changes.

The boy vanishes in a blink, leaving behind a horrific creature. Long, sharp limbs and clawed feet. Jagged wings unfolding from its back, two sets of them, blotting out the woods behind him. Horns rising up to stab the sky. It is hard angles and ragged edges and hot, stinking breath.

I open my mouth to speak its name, to stop it. But before I can, a razor-clawed foot connects with my rib cage, scoring my flesh and knocking the breath from my body. I roll down the bank toward the deeper water, gasping like a beached fish, working just to muscle my head above the surface. My brother cries out for me, but can only drag himself a foot or so toward me before he has to stop and squeeze his eyes shut.

Helplessly, I watch the demon step over his body to grab Ari around her slim throat. As the monster lifts her, she pedals her sneakers uselessly against his bulbous, heaving torso until, slowly but inevitably, her kicks weaken. Her hands stop scrabbling at his arms and drop, twitching, to her sides.

I can't do anything. I can't stand, can't even breathe, as the demon tosses Ari into the trees, sending her crashing through branches and tumbling through brush.

That's when something else comes streaking past, barreling straight into the sheyd.

The golem.

The two meet with a sound like boulders falling and stone splitting—I swear, the collision strikes sparks. The sheyd and the golem wrestle right on the edge of the bank, in and out of the shallows, plowing through reeds and kicking up great plumes of water, turning over and over each other until it's impossible to tell who has the upper hand.

Struggling upright, I wheeze out, "Ari . . ." Then louder, with my lungs at least half functioning, "Ari?"

"Mmf, I'm here!" she calls back, voice wavering. "I think . . .

I think something's broken. I landed wrong . . ."

I let out a breath of relief. I can see her now, just inside the woods, propping her back against one of the ash trees. "Where's the chain, Ari? I can't—" Cradling my ribs with one arm, I force myself to stand. "I can't come to you!"

"I have it!"

Gabe rolls slowly and rises to his hands and knees, head hanging. "I can get it," he says, but his voice is thick and distorted—the nausea kicking in.

Before he can drag himself toward the woods, a flash of silver arcs out of the night, skipping across the dirt and landing in the river with a quiet plop.

My whole heart sinks beneath the water with it.

"Fuck!" Ari calls. "I'm sorry!"

Down the river, the golem bellows the way they did in the barn that first day, when they woke in terror and pain. But then there's another thunderous crash, and the enraged scream of the sheyd, and I know they're still fighting.

I drop to all fours to look for any sign of the chain beneath the surface, but the water is all movement, rippling and glimmering. Crawling forward, I sift with outstretched fingers through the rocks and silt along the sharply sloping bottom. I think I pray. Not to any god in particular, but to the river. To the land where my mother was born. I feel for something I'm not altogether certain is still there, but I believe, I have to . . .

My fingertips touch metal.

Scooping up the chain along with a fistful of earth, I tell my brother in a trembling voice, "Open the chest."

Hauling himself the short distance back to the writing box, he does. And it is at that moment that the demon rears up out of the water beside us.

For everybody touched and damaged by this story; for my mother and my grandmother, her lost family and our dead ancestors; for Ida Silver and her daughter and her granddaughter; even for the human wife and baby girl who drowned at the bottom of the Vltava for love of the prince who would become a monster, I scream: "Jabez ben Ashmedai! I order you to get in the *fucking chest*!"

The sound he makes is of whining dogs and roaring beasts, of gnashing teeth and claws scissoring through flesh, a wail of despair and fury all at once. It rises to a pitch that vibrates in my bones, sizzling my blood like a live wire dropped in water. Gabe claps his hands over his ears as we watch the sheyd disintegrate. His skin crackles and flakes. Fragments of his wings fall to the ground like dead, dried leaves, and his body shreds down to black bone, then withers to dust. At that moment, a sudden wind whips down the river, lifting the insect-like swarm that had been Jabez ben Ashmedai into the air, then into the yawning mouth of the box. My brother slams it closed, and I fall onto it, winding the filthy chain around and around and around until I run out of links.

In an instant, the wavering light over the river dims, surges, and then winks out for good.

TWENTY-EIGHT

MY FIRST STEP beyond the boundary of Jabez's realm is tentative; I edge up the bank, preparing myself for the blinding, breathless cold. But it doesn't come. There's only the river sounds, and the settled breeze, and free air I swear didn't smell so sweet this morning. The thing that killed Siman, tormented my mother, and tore apart my family and Ari's three decades ago is beaten. His kingdom is gone. The fight is over.

I take only a moment to feel . . . what? Victory? Relief? Grief for every moment lost and every broken heart between then and now? Then I turn back to help Gabe to his feet. He wavers a little, still woozy—we need to get him to a doctor. And Ari . . .

"Can you walk?" I ask him.

He winces, knuckling his forehead. "Let's find out."

Downriver, Mom is just picking herself up. Gabe goes to her, while I head into the trees. Ari waits for me with her back against a paper birch, her left leg outstretched, and even with the moon as our only light, I can see that it's fractured or broken. Already, it's swelling around the ankle. But it could be worse.

First aid lessons didn't teach me how to splint a leg with a tree branch, unfortunately. "How does it feel?" I ask, my hands hovering above the swollen skin.

"Pretty not great." She starts to flex her ankle, then hisses through her teeth, but forces a trembling smirk. "Guess you're gonna have to carry me."

I brush the tangled pink strands of loose hair back from her face to rest my sweaty forehead against hers, almost giggling with relief. "What a damsel."

We make our way to Mom and Gabe with Ari's arm slung across my shoulder, clutching a fistful of my T-shirt, and my arm around her waist to help bear her weight. Mom has to wrap her thin arms around both of us to hug me, tugging Gabe in as well.

"My babies," she breathes between us.

We stand like this for a long while before my brother pulls back to search the bank. "Where's the golem?"

We find them a few dozen yards upriver, in a patch of trampled reeds. They lie like a shattered statue—right arm smashed up to the shoulder, right side of their chest caved in. The pieces shift beneath their mud-stained, claw-slashed sweater when they turn their head to gaze up at Gabe.

"Did you . . . win?"

For a being who doesn't need it, they seem to be struggling for air. Breath of life or no, they sound like . . . like they're dying.

Ari's grip on me tightens, and mine around her, while Mom stands speechless. To hear about the golem is one thing,

I suppose, but to actually see them in the flesh, so to speak, is another. Gabe doesn't sit so much as fall down beside them, still unsteady on his feet.

"We did," he croaks unsteadily. "Listen, what do I do? What—what can I do for you?"

The golem is watching us all, and though I feel my lips wobble, I try to smile reassuringly.

"I . . . serve. You . . . command," they remind Gabe.

He chokes on a laugh.

"Gabe . . ." I clear my own throat and try again. "You need a doctor. Ari too, and Mom—"

"We *need* to help them," he insists. "They're, like, my responsibility, right? You don't just . . . I can't abandon them."

"Of course not. But . . . we don't know how to fix them."

"I know," Ari whispers. "I mean, I know what to do. The aleph, the first letter on the right? Erase it, and the word goes from 'emet' to 'met,' which means . . . That's, um, how the rabbis do it in stories."

"Do what?" my brother demands, though he must realize.

Mom sinks down beside my brother. "Gabey . . . ," she says gently, using the baby name that fell into disuse around the time he went to kindergarten, while "Banana" shadows me still. "I can—"

"I got it," he growls, swiping a wrist beneath his nose. He asks the golem, "Can you . . . um, can you close your eyes?"

Trustingly, they let their dark eyes fall shut.

An unexpected tear traces a hot path down my cheek.

I know from the hitch in Gabe's voice that he's swallowing down his own tears. "Thank you." He reaches up, then pauses, gulps in a breath. "Do you—would you like a name?"

Without opening their eyes, the golem smiles. "I think . . . I had one, once. Another . . . time. Another . . . me. I remember now. That is . . . enough." Their words whistle out like a gust through a broken window.

Gabe nods once, sniffs, then smooths his thumb over the golem's forehead, rubbing away a letter. Truth becomes death.

Nothing changes outwardly—the golem doesn't struggle or groan in pain—but it's obvious, even by moonlight, that they're gone. Whatever divine spark or breath of life was inside of them, it's winked out as surely as the light over the Hollow.

Struggling under their weight, Gabe carries what's left of them through the trees while I help Ari. Mom looks on the verge of collapse, but she holds the chest, grimly determined.

When we make it through, my brother nods for us to go on ahead and veers toward the barn to lay the golem down. I want to follow, but if I know him at all, he needs time to himself. So we forge ahead, across the meadow, approaching the house, where every window on the ground floor is alight.

"Mom's in there," Ari tells us. "She hustled for an invite to the Eggers family dinner after shiva. She must be on her eighth cup of coffee by now. Or wine."

"I can't believe she let you stay."

Threading her fingers through mine where my hand rests at her waist, she says, "She kind of had to. I'm not going anywhere."

When we're near enough to count the silhouettes moving past the windows, something catches my eye on the upper floors. Movement in Mom's childhood bedroom. The dormer window that faces the backyard isn't lit, of course—nobody's been sleeping in there since Gabe and I moved downstairs. Which is why I'm surprised to see a face pressed close to the panes.

"Mom?" I reach out with my free hand to grab her elbow, pulling her to a stop.

She follows my gaze, squinting into the dark, then lets out the faintest ghost of a gasp.

I remember yesterday morning, the photo album with its stern, sad pictures of Jitka. The woman in the window doesn't look sad—not at this distance in the dark, anyway. But Ari, who actually knew my grandmother near the end, clutches my hand so hard that my fingertips go numb.

"Are we taking a moment, or what?" Gabe asks, suddenly among us.

I startle, and Ari groans in protest as the weight falls on her injured leg.

"Sorry, sorry!" I cry.

By the time I turn back to the attic window, it's empty.

"Are you okay?" I ask Mom, silent beside me, knowing that it really is the most useless question of the millennium.

She takes a shaky breath. "I don't know. I . . . I just miss her. And there are so many people in there who I haven't seen since I was a kid . . . Oh God, they must hate me."

"Well, maybe," I admit. "But they'll forgive you when they know the whole story."

She hugs the rosewood box with its dully glinting chain to her ribs as if to shield herself, forgetting that the real danger is inside. "They won't believe it."

"We'll tell them," I promise her. "We can tell it together."

SEPTEMBER, FOX HOLLOW

ACCORDING TO MOM, Rosh Hashanah at Beth El is much the same as Tu B'Av used to be. Watery punch, music crackling from the latest in a line of ancient boom boxes, and a series of congregants approaching every five minutes to ask how we're settling in, and whether we're looking for a hairdresser in town, because their cousin Sonja happens to run a studio out of her kitchenette.

I love every bit of it. And as I sit on the front steps while Ari refills our communal plate from a card table on the lawn, I wish Gabe were here to make fun of me for that. But my brother left for California last week, just in time for freshman orientation at CCA.

The night before, we sat on the tiny back balcony of the apartment Mom rented for us above the downtown shops of Fox Hollow, just a few blocks from the Leydons'. Ours is over a place called Tunes, which Mom says sold music cassette tapes and vinyl records when she was my age. Now the cassettes are gone, but the vinyl remains, along with secondhand video games, collectibles, and action figures. Gabe picked up a little Babadook doll, the nerd.

"You're all packed, right?" I asked him.

He ran a hand through his hair, faded to seafoam—he plans to cut it off and go back to natural in California—and I remarked again how much he'd changed in the last weeks. Gone were the guyliner and obnoxious-couture clothing; he'd reverted to chinos and tees now that I was hornless, clawless, wingless. He'd bagged up his patterned Bermudas, neon tops, and this, like, summer-green men's short suit printed all over with halved avocados when we went back to Jamaica Plain to box up the apartment, then dropped them off at a Goodwill en route (except for the button-up with the drunk flamingos. That I kept, and am wearing today, French tucked into my khaki shorts. Sue me, I like it.).

Gabe chuckled theatrically. "Sweet Banana, you know that I am not. But, um . . . there *was* something I wanted to take with me, if it's cool with you. The golem book?"

"It's not mine, Gabe," I reminded him. The leather-bound diary Jitka left in the barn for Mom sat in a place of honor in our new apartment, tucked inside the slim drawer of our grandmother's gorgeous wood drafting table, which replaced my mother's own battered one at last (the only artist among her newly reconciled sisters, everyone agreed it should belong to her). "But why? We can't read it. Are you majoring in Hebrew?"

I meant it as a joke, and he smiled, cheek dimpling and labret stud winking in the sun—he kept that much from the last two months. But then he surprised me. "I was thinking I'd take lessons? They teach adult Hebrew classes at a synagogue by the college, you know."

And then I got it. "You want to figure out how to fix them."

"If I can. I've been looking through the book, you know. With gloves—I'm not trying to get taco-sauce stains on a priceless Jewish artifact. Obviously, I can't read ninety-nine percent of it, but did you know Jitka wrote her own notes? She added them while she was building the golem, I guess. Her dad had this theory that golems go rogue because—"

"They don't have a past," I filled in, remembering her story in Ida's notebook. "No memories, no roots, no humanity."

"Yeah. Well, Jitka didn't agree. She had her own theory that you can't treat golems like property. Just because you create them doesn't mean you own them—whatever you want from the golem, you owe back to them."

"Like, you're responsible for them," I said, remembering my brother's words.

"Right. So she made our golem to look human, instead of like a pile of mud on legs. And she picked somebody she'd once loved, hoping whoever brought them to life would see them that way. As a person instead of a monster."

"Why didn't she do it? Years ago, I mean, when she built them? Why didn't she bring them to life?"

"Scared that she was wrong, maybe? But I don't think she was."

"No," I murmured, "of course not." The golem might have

believed they were made to be controlled, but when I begged them for help, they gave it. They helped a girl with no power over them, which is more than you can say for some of my species. "So what, you've been looking up synagogues in Oakland? Is that just about the golem, or . . ."

"*Or*, I guess? I don't know. There's all these rules for adopted kids converting, and it depends on the synagogue."

"Plus there's the whole God thing."

"Yeah, but I've always kind of believed in the God thing."

"Seriously? You never told me that."

Gabe scratched his jaw and squinted up into the cloudless, cornflower depths of the early evening sky. "I never thought too much about it, except that I could've ended up anywhere, with any mom and sister, and I didn't. I know we're not perfect, but us being a family always felt kind of . . ."

"Miraculous?" I guessed around the boulder lodged in my throat.

"Aww, Banana," he cooed, slinging an arm over my neck in something between a hug and a headlock. Pursing his lips, he blew a very unnecessary fart noise into my hair, then went inside to try and sneak a beer from the fridge.

When we came back from dropping him off at the airport the next morning, I slipped back into bed, planning to spend a few hours feeling sorry for myself below the covers . . . only to find the Babadook doll grinning up at me from my pillow.

Fucking nerd.

Now, Ari eases down on the steps beside me with fresh

punch and a plate of cookies, still favoring her left ankle though it's mostly healed. Both she and my brother were lucky. Relatively, I mean. Gabe was diagnosed with a grade three concussion—that's the deep-red zone of all those colorized charts you see when you google "grade 3 concussion," as I did the moment the doctor left the exam room. He *was* out for half a day, waking up on the bank of the Hollow just before sunset, too dizzy and disoriented to drag himself to the house for help. The fact that he couldn't remember anything that had happened since the night before only solidified the diagnosis. But after some headaches and sleepiness, and a few nights of Mom and me taking turns to wake him every two hours, he was declared recovered.

Ari had what was called a lateral malleolus fracture, a break in her fibula at her ankle. She wore a brace, iced it, and used crutches for a few weeks after, trading them in for her purple high-tops just a little while ago. Today, she's paired them with a tie-dyed T-shirt dress for the Jewish New Year, and is, in my opinion, an absolute smokeshow.

"So, how does it feel, skipping school on a Tuesday?"

Ah, yes. Rosalyn Yalow High School, a half-mile walk from our apartment (or a half-mile ride in Ari's salmon behemoth) doesn't have off for Rosh Hashanah the way Winthrop did, not that I was spending the time doing anything but studying. Honestly, it was easier than I thought it'd be, making the choice to transfer to Fox Hollow. I'll miss seeing my Winthrop friends every day, but I won't miss the ping of panic every time one of them aces a test or a report I fell slightly short on. I won't miss lying awake at night, mentally calculating who among us has pulled ahead academically, like we're jockeys whipping our prized racehorse brains for the approval of the roaring audience (which is pretty much just our parents). And I get to see Ari even more often than I did this summer, as she's a frequent visitor to our apartment. Maybe my room is all of eight paces by ten, but it belongs to me, and Mom lets me close the door when Ari comes around, so long as we don't lock it . . .

Blushing at the thought, I take a long sip of sticky-sweet punch. "I'm coping," I answer her at last.

As we pick through the cookies, holding them out to each other to take bites, I tell her about St. Helena, and Richmond, and South Portland, and El Trampero, and all of the temporary nonhomes I can remember. In exchange, she tells me more about Fox Hollow: the farmers markets in the school parking lot each summer, the pancakes-in-the-park event the local church hosts every spring, and how the whole downtown turns out for Halloween as only New Englanders can. I eat it up, knowing I'll be here to see all of it at least once before it's my turn to leave for college. And then I'll have a home to come back to on holidays, and stranger yet, a massive family to spend my school breaks with.

Once Gabe and Mom were up to it, the whole lot of us went to visit Jitka's grave—eleven cars full. We added rocks to the pile atop my grandmother's granite headstone, the family wandering and chatting to give us time. For my brother and me, it was both an introduction and a farewell. For Mom, it was a chance to forgive and ask forgiveness, trusting that somewhere, her mother heard her. If golems and shedim and dream-memories are possible, why not this?

I haven't dreamed of Prague once in the weeks since my grandmother's ghost (her ibbur, Ari says) vanished from the attic window. I think about her a lot, though. And, as much as I wish I could forget him, I think about the sheyd.

I wonder what might have happened had my great-great-et-cetera-grandfather never trapped the sheyd in the first place, dooming Jabez's wife and daughter. Two hundred years with nothing but rage and grief to keep you company would make a monster out of anybody. And if Jabez ben Ashmedai ever got free again, after another imprisonment . . .

But he won't.

In the freshly locked coal room in Jitka's basement, there sits the best fire safe money could buy from the Home Depot in Warborough. The morning after we pulled Mom from the underwater palace, we tipped it over and set the writing box inside, the silver chain duct taped around it. Then Mom, Gabe, and I filled the cavity with drymix cement—also purchased by the bucket from the Depot, prepared in a wheelbarrow out in the meadow. Mom's sisters watched us, indulging our strange ritual. We'd told them our story, as I'd promised we would, and I can't be certain they believed every bit of it. But they swore not to disturb the safe. They couldn't deny that *something* had happened to us. We had the shattered golem as a kind of evidence—it proved Jitka's part in the tale, if nothing else—and the two teenagers who'd walked down to the river, then limped home hours later. They've taken our word, just like they've taken us in.

I'm still figuring out just what it means to be a part of this family; maybe even without knowing them (and how could a name ever tell you everything you need to know about another person, even when you share it?), they still belong to me, and I belong to them. Or maybe Jitka was right, and we don't belong to the people we love at all; we're just a part of the same story that started before we were born, and will go on after us.

Either way, it's nice to be a part of something I didn't plan or study for or build all by myself.

Ari presses a kiss to the wrinkle between my pinched eyebrows. "What are you worrying about?" she asks, and I realize I've fallen silent for too long.

"Now? Not a thing." I am actually thinking that *she's* miraculous. So of course, I'm also worried. Once the newness of us and the wildness of our story wears thin, will I hold her attention? And beyond that, when we graduate and she leaves Fox Hollow to discover a deeper dating pool than one insufferable lesbian and one . . . whatever I am (I haven't settled on an answer just yet; there's enough to sort out without putting pressure on myself to pick a letter), will I still be enough for her?

I don't know.

But that's faith, right? Trusting in what you can't know for sure. Accepting what can't be planned impeccably. Believing in what can't be verified. Okay, faith means different things to different people, but this feels like the beginning of it, at least. True, some things have ended, like Gabe's summer with us; I'm coping by compiling a detailed spreadsheet of places to go the first time I visit him in Oakland, because I'm still me.

And yet, somehow, today still feels like the start of everything.

ACKNOWLEDGMENTS

Thank you to the inimitable Eric Smith for pep-talking me through this monster of a fantasy novel every step of the way. And to Jordan Brown, the best editor and publishing partner I could have hoped for; thank you for seven years of making magic and millennial angst together.

Thank you to the wonderful team at HarperCollins! To Sarah Kaufman, my long-time cover designer and the best in the biz, and to artist Lisa Sheehan, who blessed us with this utterly badass cover. To Alessandra Balzer and Donna Bray, Tiara Kittrell, Alison Donalty, Jenna Stempel-Lobell, Laura Harshberger, Lisa Calcasola, Audrey Diestelkamp, and Lauren Levite—thank you all.

To Katie Locke, Elana K. Arnold, and Kalyn Josephson for blurbing; I'm a super fan of every one of you, and to have you reading my first officially Jewish book means the entire world to me. And thanks to phenomenal writer Kristian Macaron for the use of her poem in the epigraph (everyone pick up her poetry collection, *Storm*, because it's stunning).

Thank you to my family, for everything.